THE BER...
CAND...

SHATTERPROOF BOND #6

Isobel Starling

www.decentfellowspress.com

CONTENTS

THE REBEL CANDIDATE

By

Isobel Starling

Inigo Montoya: "Can you guess what I'm doing?"
Count Rugen: "Cutting my heart out?"
Inigo Montoya: "You took mine when I was ten; I want yours now. We are lovers of justice, you and I — what could be more just than that?"

'The Princess Bride' by William Goldman

PROLOGUE

Agent Sam Aiken and his husband Declan Ramsay both believed it was pure madness to keep an assassin locked in a cell at the A.L.L. subterranean London facility, no matter how high the security measures were.

On the steps outside the compromised headquarters, their eyes met. There was something visceral in the knowledge the men shared—the wordless understanding—they knew that what they'd feared had finally come to pass. James's enemies, whoever they were, had made their move. Knowing how the prisoner in the basement operated, neither would enter the house at Holland Park without a firearm.

Sam felt somehow detached as he viewed the surreal events that had taken place at his father's home. What struck Sam first was that there was *so much blood* in a human body, and seeing the rivers of bright crimson spilt over the once pristine polished marble floors of his father's hall was anathema, foreign, and horrifying. He couldn't allow himself to think deeply about Mr Steele, the dead man he found at his feet when he eased the front door open.

Having donned Kevlar vests and with loaded guns at low ready, Sam and Declan had stepped into the hallway and began to investigate what had gone so tragically wrong at Sir James Aiken's London mansion.

They'd discovered Sam's sister, Annabelle in a downstairs bathroom about to give birth to her first child.

1

Between violently painful contractions she'd told of the arranged lunch date with James and that when she'd parked outside the house there was a woman at the front door—a woman in black leather with long silky black hair—and when the butler, Mr Steele had opened the door she'd shot him in the head. From Annabelle's witness statement, they knew Erik Madsson had received assistance to break out of his cell and so they proceeded with extra caution.

Declan alerted the Unit facility near Heathrow that their HQ was compromised and they needed an ambulance. Then reluctantly, the agents had left Annabelle and gone down into Sir James Aiken's basement complex.

Following fresh blood, they were led by drag marks from their boss's office to the body of Agent Ranier Strauss. But the blood trails did not end with their fallen colleague. The blood continued into the subterranean garage and across the mottled grey concrete with its scuffs and oil leak stains, past the lines of luxury cars, SUVs, and motorbikes used by those who worked at the headquarters of the security agency. The blood trails led to the innocuous metal door painted in poppy red gloss on the opposite side of the echoic basement garage.

The mansion house was located beside the fifty-four-acre Holland Park and was once owned by a member of the British Government. Like the lost rivers buried beneath the London streets, the underground tunnels rumbled deep below and wove themselves into the history of the metropolis. The London Underground tunnels had famously sheltered sixty-three million Londoners from bombing raids during World War II. The first tunnel from the Holland Park house was constructed in September 1939 at the outbreak of the war. A door at the back of the then-wine cellar led to a tunnel and to the red metal door that signified a staff-only entrance to the underground system which the government minister used as a bomb shelter. On purchasing the property Sir James Aiken expanded on the idea and over many years he designed and built a vast super-basement complex beneath the house and garden, some of which ran beneath Holland Park itself. The usage of the complex and true size wasn't even known to Sam.

A passing Tube train rumbled under foot bringing Sam to a stark awareness. The train sounded louder than usual. This was because whoever assisted Madsson had forced the red door open and they'd made their escape with an injured or even dead captive into the London Tube tunnels.

Sam and Declan ground to a halt and stared at the gaping darkness beyond the red door.

"Ye do know there are around two-hundred-and-fifty miles of Tube tunnels underneath London," Declan said ominously.

Sam realized in the blink of an eye that not only was his father now missing, but his and Declan's dreams of freedom lay in tatters. They could not leave A.L.L.—not while Erik Madsson was free, and James was missing. Sam stared at the cavernous darkness leading to the London Underground and in a disconnected voice said,

"My God. They could be anywhere!" He inhaled a despairing breath of foul air, his firearm still aimed towards the darkness in case something malevolent lurched from it.

"Turn around slowly. Lower your weapons... Desert Fox, Lucky Boy."

Sam was surprised that he hadn't heard anyone approaching from behind and secretly admired the woman's light footedness. The voice was American, steely, and determined. It was the kind of voice that came with a raised gun attached.

"Identify yerself," Declan said coolly, his gun still raised as he turned aiming his weapon at the woman while Sam's remained trained on the open doorway. Declan took a step to the left so he and Sam were back to back.

"Codename, Luna Willow," she replied.

Declan hadn't been with the agency for long when compared to Sam and didn't know every agent James employed. He turned his head a little and asked, "Safe?"

"Yes, she's one of us," Sam replied. He addressed the agent in a louder tone. "Are you alone Lopez?"

"I have seven agents with me and the cavalry's en-route from the facility."

Sam turned away from the gaping door to face the A.L.L. agent. Both he and Declan lowered their weapons, but the other agent wasn't so trusting. She kept her revolver aimed at them. Agent Lopez was Latino, her dark black hair cropped in a masculine style and oiled to her scalp. She wore the uniform black suit and white shirt combo with a tactical vest.

James had instructed that if by a rare occurrence, the HQ was ever breached; the police were not to be informed. He deemed that his own people were sufficiently experienced to investigate. The protocol was that if the basement was breached the silent alarm would be triggered, with the lighting in the complex turning blue. All employees were to remain in their rooms until the backup arrived from the Unit and cleared the basement in a room-by-room sweep. The initial team led by Agent Lopez must have arrived not long after Sam and Declan began their descent into the basement. However, from the determined glare on the agent's face, the first team was not clued-in on the truth of what had occurred.

"On your knees," Lopez said with a dangerous tone to her voice. Did this agent think Sam and Declan had gone on a killing spree?

Declan sent her a scalding look. "Are you fuckin' shittin' me? I was the one who sent the distress call. Madsson's escaped. He's been on the rampage. An' he's not alone. They've abducted Viper and the fuckers got away through that door behind us that leads to the Tube network!"

Sam was in a daze. He came back to himself at hearing his husband's roars of frustration ringing around the underground car park. Agent Angelica Lopez stood erect and gave him an unreadable look. Sam recognized the agent's face. He'd never worked with her but recalled James chose Lopez for several of the U.S. assignments, including a mission to clone the laptop of Dr Tobias Hunter. The agent lowered her weapon, turned her head, and spoke into a comms device.

"Luna Willow to Control, over."

"What's your 20?"

"Viper Code Red, repeat, Viper Code Red, Over." Then addressing them both she said, "Sorry guys, the intranet was attacked and automatically shut down. We came in blind."

Four armed agents entered the car park and began checking beneath vehicles to secure the area.

"Report," Lopez barked at the three men and one woman.

"Two fatalities on the first floor, both male staff members. We found Viper's daughter in labour in a bathroom. The rest of the staff was locked in the pantry." The female agent relayed. Sam let out a sigh of relief at hearing the rest of the staff weren't harmed.

"We'll need to do a room-by-room sweep of the complex, but secure the perimeter first. Lockdown all entrances and exits." Lopez ordered.

One of the agents closed the red door. Sam couldn't deny his relief. He strode across the garage towards Agent Lopez.

"Where is Mrs K? Who's on Control?"

"Agent Nighthawk is Control Leader today. We can't locate Agent 47."

That was…unusual. Where the hell was Akiko Kimura? Sam felt a shift in his brain, like a machine coming online, and with his adrenaline pumping; he knew what he had to do. If Mrs K wasn't around to deal with this he had to step up and take charge.

"Tell them to activate protocols to boost Viper's intramural tracker and send the loaded tracking app to my phone. Declan and I are going into the tunnels."

"Shouldn't we wait for Agent 47?" Lopez enquired suspiciously. Mrs K was technically second-in-command, and with James out of the picture, *she* was supposed to give the orders.

"He's my father," Sam snapped with the kind of haughty venom he'd heard from James many a time. He regretted the tone immediately, and in a less abrasive voice said,

"Instruct Control to continue attempts to locate 47, but we don't have time to wait. I need to find my father. They've got maybe a ten-minute head start. Please…relay the information." Chastened, Lopez nodded.

Declan couldn't hide his concern. He took Sam aside as agents continued their search of the car park, ensuring there were no other incumbents or devices left to give them a nasty surprise. Since Declan had saved Sam from a dark, lonely death in a sinkhole in the Scottish Highlands Sam's physical scars had healed, but the psychological scars were never far from the surface. Sam had once enjoyed the submission of restraint in their love making, but he couldn't bare it any more. Ropes and cuffs were a trigger, as was pitch darkness. The thought of Sam going into the tunnels and having a panic attack was a possibility Declan could not ignore.

"Are ye sure you're up to this? It's okay if ye want to step aside and let other agents search the tunnels. No one will think any less of ye!" Declan suggested as he laid a comforting hand on Sam's shoulder and squeezed. Sam's expression was pained as he fought against the fear that threatened to overwhelm him.

7

"He's my dad," Sam said softly. "This is what he's trained me for…I'm a tool…a weapon…and his only son. I can't back out of this. I have to go into the tunnels," he said, resigned to his fate.

"Very well, I'll no' argue. I'll be with ye every step. What do ye need?"

"We'll need two armed agents to take point. Find comms devices and high beam torches for us." Declan gave Sam another squeeze, nodded and moved away towards the newly arrived agents from the facility who were filing into the car park with cases of tech equipment.

Sam turned back to Lopez who was still relaying information to Control. When she was done he said, "As 47 isn't here, I'm ordering you to take the scene of event lead and to activate emergency protocols". She nodded and barked orders to several agents.

Declan returned clasping two comms devices and torches. When Agent Lopez had finished dealing with her team, Declan moved to her side and in a low voice said, "Can ye find out what's happening with Annabelle? The ambulance will need to take her to the Portland Hospital."

"She's doing okay. She has a medic looking after her while we wait for the ambulance."

Sam joined them and added, "Please ensure Mr Steel's body is removed from the hallway and the blood is cleaned up. The ambulance crew cannot know that anything is going on here, apart from a woman in labour."

"On it!" Lopez said, and then she turned and called to an idle agent and tasked him with moving the butler's body.

Sam was distracted from his train of thought when his phone pinged in his pocket. Retrieving the device he found a link for the tracking app and then logged on using his thumbprint. The app displayed their location on a grid map.

Declan was soon joined by two burly agents with body cams clipped to the front of their vests, both were armed. Sam inserted his earpiece and Declan clipped the mic to Sam's Kevlar vest. He caught Sam's gaze and held his steely pale green stare. Declan knew that look; Sam was terrified, for himself, his father, and his sister.

"Good te go?" Declan queried unable to hide the concern in his voice. Sam grimaced and nodded. Declan reached out and pulled his husband into a hug, not caring that they were surrounded by agents setting up a base in the garage.

"I'm with ye all the way, love. We'll do what we've got te do."

Sam sank into his husband's bulk, and even though he wanted to stay there and let the world go to hell around him he sighed, pulled away, and gave his husband a wan smile. He turned to the additional agents who introduced themselves as codenames: Phoenix and Lightening. Phoenix was built like a rugby player and his accent was Northern English. Lightening was a tall wiry German. They were both in full tactical gear and appeared keen to get going.

Sam pivoted to Declan and shared a look of despair mixed with determination. They needed a resolution here to be able to move on with their lives. They had to find James and throw a spanner in this grand plan once and for all.

"Phoenix, Lightening you're on point, Lucky Boy, I need

you at the rear with your eyes on the geo-locator," Sam relayed, passing his phone to Declan as Declan swapped it for a high-beam torch.

"Desert Fox to Control," Sam said to the mic on his vest.

"Ten-four, Desert Fox,"

"We're good to go."

"Copy, over, and out."

Agents Phoenix and Lightning clicked their body cams on, then lit up their head torches and finally the tactical torches on their rifles. Sam and Declan readied themselves, standing to the left of the closed red door.

"Okay everyone, silence," Lopez called to the other agents and techs setting up workstations around the garage. Sam looked to Lopez who nodded.

"Go!" Sam ordered and Phoenix dragged the red door open so that his partner could enter first with his assault rifle at a high ready position. A gush of warm air rushed out—a revolting mix of dampness, engine fumes, and decay.

"Clear" Phoenix called from the entrance and stepped onto the metal stair landing, the dull clang of his boots echoing. Lightening went next, then Sam, and then Declan. Beams of torchlight sliced through the darkness from the head and tactical torches. With weapons raised, Phoenix and Lightning turned left taking stairs down into the cavernous maw of the tunnel.

Sam used his high-beam torch in wide arcs to illuminate the ornate Victorian brickwork above in a bid to anchor himself in reality. *This isn't a cave, and there's no sinkhole here!*

"Blood!" Phoenix's deep northern voice drew Sam back

10

to himself.

"Where?"

"All over t' stairs…a trail of droplets leads into the tunnel ahead."

Sam looked down, and yes, on the stair treads, there were dots of glistening red liquid. Sam wondered what kind of wound had been inflicted to make James bleed like this. Was it a broken nose or something worse? Head wounds always bled profusely. His father's blood had led them in drag tracks from his office, like the trail of breadcrumbs left by Hansel and Gretel. Now the blood was in droplets that fell left and right on the stair treads. Sam recognized this was caused by a hoisted swaying body. At the top of the stairway, Madsson had stopped dragging James and instead lifted his victim. Nausea came on quickly and Sam lurched and tripped over his feet, grabbing the railing to steady himself. He remembered the feeling in his drugged state, of being hoisted onto Madsson's shoulder during his abduction in the Highlands. The memory of the man's physical strength, the musky scent of his sweat and his long regular loping strides were like a body blow. Declan reached out and placed his firm hand on Sam's shoulder to steady him.

"Y'alright?" he asked at Sam's back.

"Yes, yes. I'm okay, sorry." Sam inhaled deeply through his nose to try and calm himself and then at once regretted it as he breathed in the funk from the bowels of London. "I'll be okay," he reassured, his voice sounding too loud to his ears. Declan let go and Sam moved on.

"Madsson wasn't as weak and injured as James believed

11

him to be," Sam stated. "He lifted dad from here and carried him," Sam said grimly as they reached the foot of the stairs. Torchlight dissevered the inky blackness ahead and displayed the arched opening of a brick tunnel with a sloping concrete floor that would take them downward…deeper underground. Sam steeled himself and strode on behind Lightening and Phoenix into a waking nightmare.

****

The phone in Declan's hand let out a sharp pinging sound that echoed off the curved walls. The agents on point ceased their advance.

"The Geo-locator's just updated," Declan informed. "I've got the map of the tunnels." "This tunnel leads to another stairway around five meters ahead, and at the bottom of the stairs there's a service tunnel for Holland Park station."

"For now, we'll follow the blood," Sam directed.

"Copy that," Phoenix replied as he and his colleague moved off, their tactical torches illuminating the gloom. The four men moved to the end of the tunnel and then made their way down concrete stairs following the blood trail that appeared stark against the rough, gunmetal grey surface. At the bottom of the stairs was a short tunnel constructed from red Victorian brick. The darkness was met by the first beam of a head torch.

"Have you picked up Viper's tracker signal yet?" Sam asked warily.

"Nope, not a sausie,'" Declan replied resignedly.

Phoenix and Lightning stepped carefully forward, broken

glass crunched underfoot. One of the agents sent their torch beam to the ceiling. Sam saw that the strip lights in this service tunnel had all been smashed.

"We're on the level for the station now. Can ye feel that?" Declan commented. The ground beneath their feet rumbled violently. The air quality changed swiftly as a rush of warm displaced foul smelling air washed over them and an underground train sped past in one of the adjacent tunnels. The lead agents moved on, their booted feet shattering glass with each step. A few meters ahead, Phoenix's deep northern drawl echoed, "Here, the blood stains lead to the right," He turned into an offshoot tunnel.

"I've got a signal fer Viper," Declan announced as soon as he turned into the tiled tunnel.

"How far ahead?" Sam asked.

"They're on the move—" Declan pinched the screen, the gesture enlarging the map, "—in the tunnel heading to Sloane Square Station".

Sam opened Comms. "Desert Fox to Control. Over."

"Go Desert Fox, over."

"The target is on the move. Get the Swift Response team to Sloane Square, that's the closest exit at ground level. Over."

"On it. Over."

Sam then asked, "Was Agent 47 located? Over."

The response was immediate. "Agent 47 took the private jet three hours ago. It just landed in Copenhagen. I'll inform you when she checks in. Over, and out."

Sam turned and shared a querulous look with Declan.

He'd received the same information on his Comms and Declan's ash-grey eyes had narrowed, saying exactly what Sam was thinking. How suspicious that Akiko was scarce when a deadly attack occurred on the HQ? Did Mrs K know an attack was imminent, or did someone make sure James' most loyal and feared agent was out of the country?

Sam followed down yet another tunnel his mind a whirl. Several minutes later his thoughts were interrupted by a voice in his ear.

"Control to Desert Fox, over."

"Copy Control."

"I've got your location on my screen. You're walking the route of the *River Westbourne*," she informed as all of the agents listened in on their devices.

"The *River Westbourne* is one of the three lost rivers. It was redirected underground into culverts to aid the redevelopment of Kensington and Chelsea. The river now runs through man-made tunnels and it's used to direct sewer runoff and flood water into the Thames. A combined sewer and pipe storm drain run through a conduit above the platform of Sloane Square tube station. Over".

"They must be heading fer the underground river to find an exit," Declan said excitedly. Sam didn't share Declan's enthusiasm. He hated being underground and was trying very hard not to think of the state they'd find James in—if they found him at all!

"Egress at three o'clock," Lightning called out. Sam sent his torch beam to the right. Further down the tunnel on the wall, a rusty metal door hung open and the malodorous scent of filth hit Sam's nose. A swipe of the torch along the walkway showed the trail of blood terminated at the rusty door.

"Where are we?"

"Street level is Sloane Terrace. The underground river conduit surfaces at Sloane Square then goes back underground," Declan explained as he showed Sam their location on the map overlaid with James' geo-location tracker.

"Got it," Sam said decisively. "Phoenix, Lightening, clear the doorway." The agents pressed their backs to the damp fetid tunnel wall. Phoenix opened the door wider and Lightning pushed his rifle around the door jamb and then moved it around to illuminate whatever was on the other side.

"Clear. We've got a ladder into the waterway," Phoenix relayed, then without a fuss, both agents entered the river tunnel. Sam heard the eerie echo of boots clanking on metal and then splashdown into the river.

"Rats pish an' jobbies, oh my!" Declan exclaimed. "Fuck! I'm so not dressed fer this!" he complained. The other agents kitted out in full waterproof tactical gear had vanished into the river tunnel.

Sam turned and offered his husband a weak smile. "The glamorous life of working in counter-intelligence, ay!"

Declan pushed the phone into his tactical vest pouch and then took Sam's torch so his husband had both hands free to climb down the slippery ladder. When Sam splashed down into ankle-deep water he said brightly,

"It's not so bad, it's quite shallow. It would be a different story if it had rained this week!"

Declan stared down at the murky stream of the River Westbourne and grimaced. "My brogues are gonna be ruined, aren't they!"

"Not just your brogues. I think we're going to have to strip and burn everything when we get out of here."

Declan passed the torch back and Sam used it to give Declan a clear view of the ladder. He climbed down and cursed as his feet sank into slippery sludge to his ankles. Water wasn't the problem, it was the mud. He lifted a foot and fought with the suction to keep his shoe. He wiggled his foot, pulled it free, and moved into the stream of water flowing down the centre of the tunnel. "Gods, I never thought I'd be wading through shite fer James!" he grumbled.

Things had become real very quickly and Sam hadn't even begun to process the ramifications of what occurred at the HQ and why. He knew Declan owned a whole rack of expensive footwear in his walk-in closet at home, and the shoes he was wearing were, in fact, the cheap brogues from his Tobias Hunter disguise. Declan was fussing about his shoes and behaving like a grumbly bear to distract him. Sam was grateful for it.

The agents ahead sent their torches to light up and down the brick tunnel created by the Victorians to redirect the river underground so they could build on top of it. There wasn't much to see as the darkness met the light. Red brick, pea-green algae staining the walls and sticky mud silted either side of the limpid stream. The smell was revolting and there was no alternative but to breathe in the fetid air. Tide marks half way up on the tunnel walls showed how high the water became when the backwash from the Thames filled the tunnel, or when the sewers overflowed during rain storms. Sam recalled being stranded when several stations on the inner London Tube network flooded during a rainstorm because the old Victorian drainage system could not cope with the demands of the modern city. Even though their present circumstances were unpleasant, during a storm trying to navigate the underground river Westbourne would be the stuff of nightmares.

The phone lodged in Declan's Kevlar vest pinged. He retrieved it and checked the Geo-location map.

"I've still got Viper's signal. They're at the Sloane Square culvert and still on the move. We're around a kilometre from the Thames."

Sam felt like he'd been underground forever, and had walked for miles when in reality, they'd been down there for less than an hour. The team began wading along the river in earnest, the incessant drip-drip-drip of water, and the splash and squelch of booted feet in the sticky mud echoing eerily in the enclosed space. The materials used in each of the sections of the river tunnel changed as they progressed, from stone to brick, then to more durable concrete and steel as the river tunnel was reinforced.

Minutes later they trudged from slippery brick beneath their feet to walking on a slimy metallic surface that clanged like cowbells with each booted step. Torchlight bounced off the sheet steel walls and the ceiling displayed uniform lines of welded rivets.

"We're in the river culvert above the rail tracks at Sloane Square Station," Declan told the team as he watched Sam trudge on ahead. Declan had seen the culvert from the train platform but never guessed that a river ran through it. The steel shaft was six meters wide and three meters high and from the station platform Declan recalled that it appeared like an innocuous piece of railway architecture painted with thick dark green gloss paint.

"Shite! Viper's tracker's still moving. The target didnae take the exit, they've gone back below ground."

"Damn it," Sam exclaimed. "Desert Fox to Control, Over," he said into his Comms device.

"Copy Desert Fox, what's your 20, over?"

"We're in the Westbourne culvert above Sloane Square. The target didn't go for the exit. He's still moving underground. Mobilize the team and tell them to stand by. Over."

"On it. Over and out."

Once they'd passed through the wide culvert the agents came to sluice gates with a metal stairway on either side. Water continued to dribble around gaps in the closed gates, trickling along a steel sheet slope and back into a Victorian brick arched tunnel. A passing glance of torchlight revealed blood droplets on the grey metal runners of the staircase to the left of the gates.

"Look, here, and here. We've still got the blood trail, but the drops...they're becoming less frequent," Phoenix noted.

Sam hurried to the agent's side to see the evidence. He was right. Was the wound closing up, or did Madsson change his carrying position to stop the trail of blood?

When the agents splashed down into the river bed at the bottom of the staircase they discovered that the mud and water here were past their knees.

"Guys. Stop fer a minute an' listen," Declan called. They all paused.

"From here it's approximately a kilometre of straight tunnel," Declan explained. The four men stood, waited, and listened. The incessant drip-drip of water was the only sound until a distant splashing sound rushed up the tunnel. The sound was repetitive.

"Did you hear that? Someone's running in the river channel. He's not far ahead!" Sam pressed the button for his mic.

"Control, we can hear him ahead of us. We're in the stretch of tunnel past Sloane Square heading to the river. Mobilize the team and send them to the Embankment. Over."

"Copy, over and out."

To agents, Phoenix and Lightning Sam said, "Jog on ahead, and see if you can catch up with him." The men nodded and set off. Sam and Declan were not shod for running in a silted tunnel and so they waded on behind in determined silence. Minutes later the scent in the air changed. Phoenix and Lightning were out of sight by then, their torches no longer visible.

"We must be close to the Thames by now," Sam

19

suggested. He saw a bend in the tunnel and after taking the turn found the two agents.

"Shite. Lads. The signal stopped moving." The team crowded Declan to look at the map on the screen.

"Where?"

Declan pointed to where the signal remained stationary. "I'd guess they're around six hundred meters ahead."

"Control. We're beneath Ranelagh Gardens, close to Chelsea Bridge. Over." Sam relayed.

"Got it. The team are on their way! Over."

James could be lying in the rancid mud, dead or dying. Time was of the essence.

Phoenix and Lightning jogged on ahead with confident steps. Sam and Declan weren't far behind. They caught up with the point agents at the end of the tunnel where the River Westbourne met the River Thames taking sewage and floodwater out to sea. Sam noticed that a huge grill made of steel rebar covered the exit for the tunnel, preventing any human from entering, or exiting. Staring through the bars Sam could see that around twenty meters beyond the grill were overcast daylight and the Chelsea—Thames foreshore at low tide.

"Where's the tracker signal?" Sam asked urgently.

"It's here!" Declan replied staring at the map.

"It can't be here." Sam snapped. "Where the fuck are they?"

"I'm just telling you what the app says." Declan snapped back.

"Boss. Someone was in here before the assault on HQ.

They prepared the route. The bars have been cut through here, and here. The only way to do it is with an angle grinder. The hole's big enough to allow a person to slide through." Phoenix informed dourly.

"But the tracker's still here! I don't understand it!" Declan's frustrated exclamation echoed.

Sam didn't understand either. The tracker said James was there in the tunnel with them. What was going on?

"Desert Fox, come and look at this," Lightning focused his torch light on an area at the opposite side of the tunnel. Sam, Declan and the other agent joined. They saw that there were fresh footprints and an impression in the mud. The impression looked like a bum print, and beside it, there was a small button device and a puddle of something darker in the silt. Blood. Declan hunkered down and ran the phone over the blood, the phone pinged an alert. He thrust his fingers into the muddy blood and fished around. Amid the scarlet pool, he found the tiny white, rice-sized intramural tracker that had once been in Sir James Aiken's left arm.

"Madsson cut the tracker out!" Declan revealed.

Phoenix picked up the small device. "I've seen this used before. Does Viper have trackers elsewhere...somewhere that cannot be accessed by impromptu surgery?"

"He has a second tracker in his kneecap,"

"Not any more. This device sends a high-frequency signal to burn up an embedded tracker."

"Fuuhk!" Sam spat. Madsson was toying with him. They'd waded through this hell for nothing. This was exactly what Madsson had wanted. Sam turned in frustration and desperation then trudged to the hole in the rebar. He needed to get out of here. Sam sank to his knees in the mud and slid through the gap.

Declan grumbled unintelligible curses as he placed Sam's phone in his vest pocket, gritted his teeth, and followed.

Sam was smeared in mud from head to foot as he trudged across the foreshore to where the Thames lapped at his feet. He'd followed two sets of booted footprints to the waterline. *Two sets.* He did not believe for one moment James had walked to the waiting boat. Whoever had helped Madsson escape his cell was with him all the way and prepared his route beforehand. Sam turned to his left to see the imposing granite and steel of Chelsea Bridge just twenty meters away, and searching beneath the bridge, on the horizon a white speedboat was barely visible and then in the blink of an eye, was gone.

When Declan reached his partner's side Sam was speaking into his Comms device.

"Control. We've just missed them. They left by speed boat heading east. Over and out."

Sam experienced a confusing mixture of feelings, anger, frustration, and guilt. Wasn't this what he'd been trained for from childhood, to be the best, most efficient tool in his father's arsenal? He'd failed. Numbness overtook and Sam looked down at his body noticing for the first time that he was smeared in foul, shitty mud.

"Fuck! We're gonna have to get to the Swift Response team van, strip and bag everything," he said distractedly.

"Aye, mebe we should just burn the lot of it an' bathe in

bleach!" An equally muddy Declan replied morosely.

****

CHAPTER 1
UNRAVEL

There was something surreal about arriving at the Mayfair apartment after months away. While Sam and Declan had carried out their Vienna mission thwarting a cabal of Eco-terrorists, their home remained in stasis, as if an omnipotent being had pressed pause on their real lives while they were off doing other things. Now, life was on fast-forward.

Sam walked into the living room and let his gaze wander. He spied the fantasy book on the coffee table he'd been reading months before. The couple's wedding bands remained hooked over the swords of the Dread Pirate Roberts and Inigo Montoya statues on the mantle. Declan's rock collection on the bookcase was covered in a fine layer of dust–the cleaner having missed them when she gave the place a quick once-over. Everything appeared the same, mundane, ordinary. Everything *was* the same, apart from Sam Aiken-Ramsay.

Wearing a Tyvek paper overall and blue plastic shoe covers on his feet, Sam stood straight-backed and inhaled the scents of home. The smell was at once familiar but somehow stagnant and out of place—or maybe it was Sam who was out of place? Sam had experienced this dissociated headspace before in the aftermath of life-threatening situations. The sensation of overwhelm had been growing since they'd entered the Holland Park house and found death and destruction everywhere they looked. Sam recognized the emotional dissonance—in this instance, the belief that he should be feeling something particular, maybe he should be grieving or worried for his father. But now, Sam was home. *Yes, I'm home.* He focused on the sheer relief of being back here again, in his safe space and finally alone with Declan.

"Westley, you hit the shower first," Declan ordered as he entered the apartment, dragging both of their wheeled suitcases through the front door and toward the bedroom. Seconds of silence passed and Sam stared into space.

"Hey, love, did ye hear me?" Declan hollered as he passed by the living room on his way to the kitchen. Sam was startled to awareness at hearing his husband's rough Scots brogue the second time. He moved like an automaton, walking toward the bay window. Sam stepped up and parted the blinds with two fingers. He stared outside across to the Connaught Hotel. The silhouettes of guests and staff members in the rooms opposite seemed so normal. People were going about their daily business and there was no imminent threat. Sam then looked left and right to take in the view up and down Mount Street. Mayfair was buzzing with shoppers, business people and tourists—again, an ordinary day with no imminent threat. The need for constant vigilance was exhausting. Sam wished he could let go, switch off, and forget everything, but the stark reality was that his family was in grave danger. Sam's father was missing and Belle with her newborn daughter added to the weight of Sam's new responsibilities. With James no longer around and Mrs K seemingly AWOL, it was all on Sam's shoulders.

His attention was stolen by the familiar sound of a drawer opening and then sliding closed in the kitchen. He heard the tread of heavy footsteps and as Declan passed down the hall again,

"Ye know," Declan grumbled conversationally, "it boils mah pish that we were so close to extracting ourselves, so fuckin' close, an' now we're back te square one!" He paused in the doorway to the living room and stilled. Sam turned away from the window and met Declan's endearing silver-grey gaze.

"C'mon love," Declan said in a softer brogue, "I've put the shower on te heat. The sooner we're cleaned up the better!"

Sam's shoulders sagged, that small surrender allowing his twisted tight muscles to relax a little. He sighed and subserviently followed his husband back to their bedroom.

Declan had retrieved a black refuse sack from the kitchen and he stripped hurriedly from the Tyvek CSI suit and shoe covers he'd been given to change into so he didn't bring the foulness of the sewers into the A.L.L. Rapid Response van. Now naked, Declan displayed his battered and bruised physique for Sam to see. Less than a day ago, Declan had been disguised as Batman and tied to a St Andrews Cross in a BDSM dungeon while his captors, an Eco-terrorist group who used prostitution, drugs and blackmail to fund their activities, had threatened to slice him up for fun. Sam's

26

raked his husband's body. He'd forgotten for a moment that Declan had been injured during their fight to take down Mads Hendrik. Sam reached out and let his fingers lightly caress a rainbow bruise on Declan's furry chest. Then he followed the scabbed scratches of the BDSM *Wartenberg pinwheel* device that Hendrik had used to torture Declan with.

"Poor baby," Sam sighed in a dreamy voice.

"Och, ama big boy, I'll live. It's just a few wee scratches. C'mon, get that off!" Declan encouraged nodding towards the white paper suit Sam wore. He shook the trash bag impatiently waiting for Sam to strip.

Sam toed off the foot covers, dragged the zip down, and slid out of the paper overall. The adrenaline boost that had kept him moving during the chase through the tunnels had worn off. And now, standing in his bedroom, naked, Sam was hit by a wave of vulnerability. He looked down at his hands and saw how his fingers trembled, and then he suddenly became hyperaware of tight lungs. Sam was on the bow of a ship in a mighty storm and he couldn't catch his breath.

"Hey, hey, easy now," Declan gentled, his voice an anchor. "It's been a shite old day!"

Sam gave a wan smile at the understatement as Declan stepped forward to offer an embrace. Sam held his hands up defensively and stepped back, "I'll be okay, I just need a minute," he insisted.

"Fine, I'll get rid of this." Declan scooped the Tyvek suit and shoe covers from the floor and pushed them into the

27

refuse sack. He gave Sam a concerned once over as he tied the bag, seemingly not convinced that Sam was on the level, and then left the bedroom to place the bag by the front door.

Sam stumbled to the warm steamy bathroom and inhaled familiar, comforting smells of his husband's expensive aftershave and their mingled personal scents. The shower was ready, the pulsing hot water fogging up the mirrors. Sam stepped under the stream. His skin was numb, the same as his insides.

Declan's concerned face peered around the open shower a second later. "Jesus, Sam!" He exclaimed, "That water's fuckin' roasting, what are ye trying te do, cook yersel?" His hand snuck in and turned the lever to a cooler setting.

"D'ye need anything?" he asked, concerned by Sam's distanced behaviour.

Sam had no idea what he needed at that moment but replied in a very British, "No, no, I'll be fine". So Declan turned to get on with his personal grooming routine. Sam stepped out of the water stream and wiped condensation from the mirrored tiles. He doused his face and rubbed at his stinging eyes, fighting to hold back tears. From the reflection in the mirror tiles, Sam could see Declan had moved to stand at the basin and was lathering foam along his jaw line to shave the raspy stubble that had quickly grown in since he didn't have to wear the fake moustache and goatee for Tobias Hunter's disguise anymore.

Sam leaned his head out of the shower "Don't!" he said in a plea. Declan turned and gave him a quizzical look.

"Don't what?"

28

"Shave. Please don't shave."

Declan nodded, gave a lopsided grin and turned on the tap to wash the foam from his face. Sam stepped back under the shower jets and blindly grabbed for shower gel. He squirted a dollop into his hand, and then rubbed it all over his glistening chest suddenly desperate to be clean and wash away all traces of stench and filth of the underground tunnels. It was then that Sam realized he'd picked up Declan's shower gel and not his own brand. The woodsy smell surrounded him like a hug, reminding Sam that, yes, *he was home,* and just like the scent of Declan's aftershave, it had a grounding effect. It was these mingled scents of familiarity that pushed Sam over the edge. This was a safe space. He could finally, *finally* let go. Sam's knees buckled. He folded to the floor of the shower with a wet thud.

"Sam—?"

For a few minutes after they'd touched down at Heathrow airport, Sam was happy to be back in London and to know that, at last, he had bested his father. He was prepared to take his power back, and then he and Declan would release James's grip on their lives. Sam had longed to come home to the apartment, for them both to peel off their disguises and become their true selves again. This was not the sort of homecoming Sam had envisaged. He couldn't get the faces of the dead out of his mind. He was consumed by guilt for his failure in catching Erik Madsson in the tunnels, and for being healthy, secure and loved while members of James's household staff had died solely because they'd worked for the Aiken family. Sam's father was missing, and yet, when it came to thoughts of James, Sam didn't feel the 'right' emotions that a loving son *should* feel. Sam was consumed with disgust and hatred for all James had done to make the events at his underground compound come to pass. Some part of his brain was *relieved* that James was missing. It was a selfish kind of relief, one less burden for him to deal with, one less thorn in his side. But then Sam's thoughts strayed to Annabelle and the relief morphed into a wave of gut-wrenching sadness that was expressed in a near vomit of tears wracking his whole body. By now, it was likely that James had become a grandfather. Sam wondered if he would ever know.

"Hey... Hey?" Declan's warmth surrounded Sam as he joined him on the floor of the shower, dragging his slippery wet husband into his arms.

"Jesus, don't." Sam tried ineffectually to push Declan away. "I'm... a...fucking... mess," he said between sobs.

"Christ! Yer not a robot, Sam, you *are* allowed to have feelings! C'mere." Declan dragged Sam onto his lap and cradled Sam's head against his shoulder. Sam submitted and sank into the solidity of Declan's bulk. The shower rained down on them both as Sam cried.

"They...they didn't deserve that – Strauss... Mr Steele, Piotr the gardener..." Appalled, Sam paused for a hiccupping breath, "Jesus, I don't even know the man's full name."

Declan rubbed Sam's back, kissed his sodden bleached blond hair, and listened while Sam worked through his grief.

"We fucking told him!" Sam spat, "We told dad that Madsson was dangerous. We knew he had a plan and would act, but nooo, James thought better, and now—how many, how many did Madsson kill to get to him?" Sam shot angrily.

"Yes, you were right all along, love, an' I'm so, so sorry."

"I don't care if they find him," Sam gave a slightly hysterical laugh, "Isn't that awful? I'm his son and I'm not that fussed about finding the scheming bastard. Y'know, for a split-second back in his office, when I saw he was gone I was... relieved to see he wasn't there. It was like... *thank God he's gone*," Sam admitted.

"Aye, I know what ye mean. Yer da's a... complicated man, an' he's been due a reckoning fer a while now. But, love, he's still yer da... an' whoever's abducted him took the lives of innocent people te get to him. We cannae let that stand. Those people need justice. You know as well as I that their deaths will get swept under the rug as if they never existed. They're not going te get justice via the regular channels!"

Sam looked up and met Declan's concern. He threaded his fingers into Declan's dyed salt and pepper hair, pushing the sodden strands back from his brow, letting out a deep sigh.

"Yes, I know...I know," he said softly. "They're the reason we have to see this through to the end."

Declan reached to grip onto a rail and pull himself up from the floor of the shower, bringing Sam with him to their feet.

31

"I know it's still the afternoon, but let's get washed up an' go te bed," Declan suggested, kissing Sam and then reaching for his shower gel,

"We're both fucking exhausted."

The spark of familiar heat igniting between them was comforting, like settling in front of an open fire in the winter. Watching his lover, Declan squeezed a generous dollop of gel onto his hand and began to soap up his hairy chest; his love-drunk eyes trained on Sam while Sam watched him right back.

Sam's gaze followed the lazy trail of fingers as Declan rubbed his hand over bruised ribs and down to caress the defined ridges of his abdomen, then moved to soaping up his hardening shaft and then dipping to wash his balls. After several moments hypnotized by Declan's distracting hands mapping the planes and contours of his hard muscles, Sam whispered,

"Let me do that."

Taking a step forward he picked up the shower gel from the shelf. "Turn around." Sam poured streams of the silky viscous gel over Declan's back and watched it dribble hypnotically down and over the globes of his firm, muscular arse. Sam put the shower gel back on the shelf, grabbed a pair of exfoliating gloves, and proceeded to knead and caress Declan's skin using the rough gloves to elicit deep moans of pleasure from his lover.

Sam bent down and caressed Declan's calves, then his thighs knowing full well that Declan was watching his bent-over reflection in the mirror tiles that covered one of the shower walls.

'Turn around', Declan turned on command and pulled Sam's slippery form to fit snugly against his own. Sam laced his hands around Declan's hips and rubbed the rough gloves over Declan's backside, eliciting a growl.

"Gods, I've fuckin' missed these simple pleasures," Declan gasped with arousal. He kissed along Sam's neck and threaded his fingers into Sam's wet hair. Sam's left hand moved to the front, and the sensation of the rough weave of the exfoliating glove on Declan's cock made him buck and curse.

"Fuck! Too much!" He took hold of Sam's wrists. "I'll bust a nut if you keep doing that!" he complained.

"Fine," Sam pouted, a little disappointed. Declan stepped back into the stream and washed the suds from his skin and then turned the water off. He stepped out of the shower, reaching for a couple of towels and tossing one to Sam which he snatched from the air. They dried one another's skin. Declan then rubbed Sam's hair and grinned with affection when he drew the towel back and saw Sam pink-cheeked, his forest green eyes sparkling. Sam kept his gaze locked on Declan and leaned in.

"Thank you… for being my rock. I love you."

Declan pulled Sam into a tight embrace "Thank you for being *mine!*"

"I…I need you," Sam exhaled in a vulnerable whisper to his lover's lips. Declan nodded, knowing exactly what Sam meant.

"Let's go to bed, aye?" Declan turned, scrubbing his hair

with the towel, then tossing it into the laundry basket as he strode into the bedroom.

****

CHAPTER 2
HOME COMFORTS

The sheets were cold when Sam slipped into bed. He lay there with his arms above his head looking at the ceiling in the muted light, his hair was still a little damp, but he didn't care. This is what he needed. Familiarity, routine, and home comforts. Declan was navigating the bedroom and then rifling in a suitcase.

"What the hell are you doing? Come and warm the bed up, its bloody freezing!" Declan strode to Sam's nightstand and placed his phone on it. Sam wished he hadn't. The phone was joined by a bottle of lubricant. Sam was glad he'd remembered that!

Declan slid under the covers and yelped, "Christ! It's fuckin' arctic. We'll have te do something about that!" He scooted over to Sam's side, threw an arm over Sam's chest, the other under his back, and a leg over Sam's thighs pulling him into a full-body hug, their bodies snuggling together.

"Ahhh, that's better," Sam sighed with pleasure as he wriggled to find the sweet spot. Nestled perfectly, they lay entwined for several minutes, not needing to do anything.

Breaking the silence with a whisper Sam admitted, "I don't have the words to say how much I've missed you, Buttercup."

"I've missed ye too. I'm glad it's over. Let's never do

that again! Agreed?" Declan squeezed Sam and planted a kiss on his lips.

"Agreed,"

"It's like, ever since we met we've had obstacles thrown in our path te try an' stop us from being together."

"But we survived, and here we are," Sam said sagely.

"Aye, true. But ye know we're done, right? No matter what happens when we find Jamesy we're full steam ahead wi our plans. This is our time now."

Sam was quiet for a second before admitting, "I made some calls and accelerated everything before we left Vienna. Obviously, I didn't know we would come back to *this*… but we can be off-grid as soon as dad is located alive." Sam assured.

"Good—we won't be short o' cash either, not with all of the dead drops we've done over the past year. It's reassuring to know we have cash an' passports stashed in every European city we've visited."

"That's true, in our business, you never know if we'll need to move on quickly. We'll not starve!"

"I'll call Campbell in the morning Te see how things are progressing WI' the build. I want te know if they at least got the new foundation down. The weather's been brutal since they broke ground three weeks ago",

"In the circumstances, tell him to go ahead with having my shipping containers moved from storage to the location too. It's sensible to have temporary accommodation ready so we can go to ground quickly."

"Aye, good idea." Declan kissed Sam on the brow and

ran his palm across Sam's chest to rest over his heart. "Ye know. I cannae wait to wake up on cold winter mornings and it just be us, all snugly wi' that stunning view."

"I know, it sounds idyllic, like a dream."

Declan bit his bottom lip, his dove grey eyes flickering, trained on Sam as his hand caressed, exploring Sam's chest, and ribs, and moved down over his hip. Thick fingers trailed, teasing the ridges and valleys of Sam's defined abdomen, then up, brushing over a nipple to make Sam shudder and gasp.

Sam was entranced as Declan read his skin like it was his favourite novel, his fingertip skirting each line. Declan leaned in, the tip of his nose sensually tracing the soft peach fuzz stubble that lined Sam's jaw. Sam whimpered and wriggled against Declan's bulk. The intense clutch of emotion in Sam's chest stole his words. Declan was everything, his lover, his best friend and the bravest man knew. He'd helped Sam cheat death twice, and he'd never wavered, never thought to walk away from Sam even though Sam's father was a cold-hearted tyrant and a royal pain in his arse. Declan was Sam's family, the one he *chose*. Sam's sparkling eyes raked Declan's mouth and his tongue darted out and licked a small circle on his plump lower lip. Declan watched, mesmerized, and grinned in consideration. Framed by whiskers, Declan's mouth intoxicated Sam just like it had done the very first time Sam slammed Declan against the wall of the Laird's bedroom in Dunloch Castle. Sam needed to show Declan just how loved he was.

Overcome by a wave of love Sam was crying again.

Declan kissed Sam, again and again, their tongues tangling and jousting. Sam moaned and writhed at the rasping scrape of Declan's beard against his skin. Their kisses deepened, and as if reacting to a silent cue, wordlessly, Declan rolled to lie on his back and Sam moved to straddle Declan's hips. They knew this dance well. More kisses made up for lost time, and when they came up for air Sam reached out, snagged the bottle of lube and prepped himself. Their cocks were rigid between their bellies as Declan's hands slid down Sam's back and gripped Sam's backside. He massaged the pale globes, rocking Sam against his hardness. "Such a fine, fine arse," he praised. Declan's finger slid into the crease, moving up and down around Sam's slick prepped pucker before easing inside. Sam gasped and groaned, working himself on Declan's thick blunt finger.

"Yesss, yess, do it," he hissed, so Declan's finger breached deeper.

Sam pushed his bottom backwards onto the intrusion.

"That's it, take what ye need, babe!" Declan groaned as he pushed a second finger inside. Sam was a demon of a bed partner, wanton, needy, and desperate. Declan loved to watch the show as his lover unravelled.

"Fuck me Buttercup, I need it. Make me forget who I am," Sam mewled as he shuddered. Declan stopped the stretching and probing. His free hand moved to cup the back of Sam's neck, pull him down, and direct his gaze.

"No, no, that won't do," Declan said softly.

"Why would I wantea make ye forget who ye are,

38

Westley?   I   love   who   ye   are.   You're
everything...everything."   Declan's mouth covered Sam's
and Sam's broken sob was muffled as he melted into the
kiss. When they came up for air, Sam insisted, "I'm ready,
God, please, just stick it in already."

Sam rose and Declan positioned his bare cock to line up
with Sam's entrance. Sam sank down, the slippery gel
easing the way. He placed his hands on Declan's chest and
then began to bounce, forcing Declan to penetrate deeper
and deeper with each downward stroke until his lover was
in him to the hilt. The slap-slap of thighs and colliding balls
resonated. Sam cried out, unabashed, as he frantically
writhed and pumped up and down on Declan's lap. It was
quick filthy fuck and exactly what both men needed. Sam
found the right angle to force Declan's cockhead to glide
against his prostate, he screamed with the lightening shock
and pleasure, and then they both laughed. It had been a
long time since they could let go like this. Sam's legs turned
to jelly and he tipped forward to bury his face into Declan's
nape, kissing and nipping him behind his ear and across his
shoulder.

Regaining his sea legs, Sam began riding Declan with a
fierce pounding rhythm until his whole body was alive with
sensation and he couldn't take anymore. He cried out
wordlessly and climaxed, white stringy ropes marking
Declan's hairy chest. Sam's convulsing body clamped
around Declan's hardness and squeezed, the grip pushing
his husband over the edge, this afternoon's delight
cementing their commitment in a way that always felt

perfect.

****

Sam's phone sprang to life on the nightstand, the jaunty ringtone making Declan shudder to alertness.

"Hmmm...you get it, babe," Sam mumbled sleepily. "I'm having such a nice dream."

"Babe?" Declan snickered quizzically, that was a new one! He reached blindly until his hand met the vibrating phone. He pulled it closer, opened his bleary eyes, and stared at the screen, trying to focus. The name *Ginger Tosser* was displayed. Declan understood then that Sam had never really forgiven Oliver for the way he'd treated them when they'd first revealed their relationship. Declan put the call on speaker.

"Sam—" Oliver was crying.

"Christ, Oli, what's goin' on?"

"Jesus, Dec! Why's yer phone off?" Oliver snuffled. Declan realized then that he'd turned it off after notifying HQ that they needed an ambulance for Annabelle and had forgotten to switch it back on.

"Mah wee Rosa's been born. I'm a daddy!" Oliver announced joyfully.

"Aww man! Congrats. We're so happy for ye both."

"How's Annabelle?" Sam interrupted, now very much awake and sitting up in bed.

"She's exhausted, but she's doing well."

"D'ye need us te do anythin'?" Declan asked.

"I've called Ma, Da, and Freya. I cannae get hold of James though. Could ye let him know he's a granddaddy?"

Sam and Declan shared a look. Oliver had no idea what had happened. How could he? A.L.L. protocols meant that all information would remain in-house, and neither Annabelle nor Oliver knew the true nature of James's business.

"Can we visit?" Sam asked hurriedly.

"Let me ask the nurse what's-what and I'll shoot ye a text."

"Okay, chat soon brother, give the girls our love."

****

CHAPTER 3
OLIVER

Where the hell was Mrs K?

Sam mulled this mystery over as he and Declan dressed. As second-in-command, it was Akiko Kimura's job to take the reins in James' absence. But, not this time. Mrs K had vanished at the very instant the HQ was compromised.

Sex, a little comfort, and a good night's sleep in his own bed had put a halt to Sam losing the plot. This was a new day and Sam was sure that fate was not done with them yet.

Text message updates told him that the forensics team began processing the crime scenes at the house overnight, and so Sam awoke with new, unwanted responsibilities. He'd never expected to be the temporary head of A.L.L. *ever*, and he resented it. Sam donned stonewashed black jeans and a long-sleeved navy t-shirt. His bleached blond hair from his previous job made him look younger than his twenty-five years, and he wanted it gone as soon as possible. Sam chose Declan's smart casual outfit of matching black jeans, a lavender button-down shirt with a dark navy sports coat. Declan dressed as Sam fumbled with his phone, more text messages making the device dance.

"This is all such a pain in the arse," Sam grumbled as he checked the messages, "I'll have to make some phone calls en-route," he explained. "One of the perks of the job for us is that we have kidnap and abduction insurance as part of our employment package. The first call needs to be to dad's lawyer, I'm sure dad has something even better in place for himself."

Declan raised a brow as he zipped up, "We have abduction insurance? That's news to me!" When Sam was abducted by Erik Madsson for the second time, James was decidedly lax about sending a ground team into the Scottish highlands to find his son. If it wasn't for Declan being on the ground already, his decisiveness and his knowledge of the terrain, Sam would have died.

Dressed, they paused in the living room to retrieve their wedding bands from the swords of Inigo Montoya and the Dread Pirate Roberts before heading out of the apartment. Declan drove the SUV, taking the ten-minute journey through the back roads of Mayfair and Marylebone in rush hour traffic while Sam made his calls.

"You're coming with me when I meet dad's lawyer, Dominic Soames, right?" Sam asked when he ended the call to the lawyer's office.

"If ye want me, ye got me!" Declan replied as he put his foot on the break at a zebra crossing and watched the gaggle of tourists cross the road. "Who's next on the call list?"

"I have to find Akiko. In all my years working with her I've never *not* been able to make contact. If she doesn't communicate within twenty-four hours I'll need to access her intramural tracker." Sam scrolled through his phone book, pressed his finger on her name, and then put the phone on speaker mode. The call didn't connect. The number was dead. Sam turned and Declan took his eyes off the road for a second to share a wary look. Could James' closest ally and friend have turned the tables and betrayed him? Had she sold him out?

It was eleven a.m. when they parked in the Devonshire Row Mews car park and strode around to Great Portland Street. The Portland Hospital was a private maternity facility and the birthplace of many a royal and aristocratic baby.

Sam reached for Declan's hand as they entered the maternity unit. He'd never spent much time with kids and so this whole baby business was new territory. The reception area of the unit had a bright, contemporary design and looked more like a high-end hotel than a hospital. A frosted glass-topped reception counter was dressed with a couple of floral arrangements and arty black and white images of newborns were displayed on the pale walls. The scent in the air wasn't the expected disinfectant smell of other hospitals; it was pleasant, calming lavender. The nurse in reception looked up from typing on a desktop computer and smiled a greeting as the two men, hand-in-hand approached. Looking around Sam immediately spotted Oliver so he gestured to let her know they'd found the daddy they were looking for!

Oliver Ramsay was seated on an armchair in a lounge area, his fingers moving rapidly over his phone screen as he typed a text message.

"Golden Balls!" Declan greeted his brother and then winced at the volume of his voice as if only then remembering where he was. Oliver looked up from his phone and his face glowed with joy.

"Numpty! Thank fuck!" Oliver exclaimed as he stood and enveloped his brother in a fierce bear hug. When they let go, Oliver hugged Sam.

"Jeez! I'm so glad you guys are here," he said wiping a hand across his brow. "Ma's been on the phone non-stop since she heard Belle was in labour. She says she's heading fer Waverly Station an' getting the next train down."

"Uh Ohhhh," Declan snickered.

Oliver's shoulders slumped in resignation.

"I was tryin' te get Da to delay her fer a day or two so we can get some rest, but she's no' havin' it!" He pushed his phone into the back pocket of his jeans and cupped his face, broad hands rubbing the tiredness away. "And did ye hear the other news?"

Sam and Declan shared a concerned glance. Did Annabelle tell Oliver about the horrors at James's house?

"Freya and Dom are expecting!" Oliver announced. Their little sister Freya was in a relationship with Declan's school and ex-army buddy Dominic Hennessey and as luck would have it, the couple had also hooked up at Oliver and Annabelle's Dunloch Castle wedding.

"Oh mah god, would you believe it? Two wee Ramsay bairns, like buses!" Declan rubbed a hand over his stubble beard. "Ma's gonna be in her element!"

"Aye, an' ye know two won't be enough, she'll be badgering you guys te get the baby-making machine going next!"

Declan shared a look with Sam. Sam couldn't hold in a nervous laugh that didn't disguise his alarm at the thought. Their current lifestyle and plans did not include adding to their family, but in trying to keep the family they already had safe. To shut that conversation down, Sam asked,

"Are they gettin' hitched? Will I need to buy a new hat?"

"Ehh, no and I'm sure Ma will have a few things te say about that too!" Oliver countered.

"But, anyway, it'll be lovely for Belle to have Eileen here to help her for a while... won't it?"

"Ye say that now—" Declan offered ominously.

Oliver winced, "Sam, ye don't get it. Ma's wanted grankids like...forever; she'll just take over an' organize everything."

"So, let her! She's a granny. I don't see the problem. I know Belle can be demanding, but our mum isn't around to support her, and I'm sure Belle's feeling conflicted about that and will be happy for Eileen's help."

"Gods, sorry, yer right. It's just...she's our first and I know Belle wants to do everything *her* way. She's read all the books, listened to parenting podcasts, joined inane online yummy-mummy chat rooms, and she follows all these social media accounts about perfect parenting. Te be honest, she's been kinda obsessed with doing things right, so I left her to it." Oliver admitted. "The way I see it, life is trial and error. We can work things out as we go. No matter what any o' these parenting gurus say, my wee-gurl is perfect," he beamed proudly.

"Tell us about her," Sam encouraged.

"Well..." Oliver started to tear up, "Rosalind Aiken-Ramsay was born at four-thirty three p.m. yesterday and weighed in at a mighty seven pounds and three ounces. A good healthy weight, apparently."

Sam felt a lump rise and stick in his throat and tears leapt to his eyes. "You're naming her after our mum? God, that's... that's lovely. Dad will be chuffed to bits." Sam realised what he'd just said. He wiped the tears that fell and hoped that James would get the chance to meet baby Rosalind.

"It was agreed that if we had a wee gurl she would be Rosalind and if we had a boy we'd choose a good fierce Scottish name, like Rurai, Lachlan, or Cailean,"

"Rosalind's a beautiful name. Congratulations bro!" Declan pulled his brother into another hug, and Sam joined in the crush.

When they pulled out of the hug Oli said, "Sam, I have te say, your sister's a goddess. I swear I don't know how women do *that*. It was incredible. Just you wait te see my baby. She's got Belle's eyes and a big shock o' red hair."

"Ahh! The ginger gene is strong wi' us, brother!" Declan joked and rubbed a hand on Oliver's head mussing up his bright orange hair.

"Can we go in and see them?" Sam was desperate to see proof that one single thing had gone right this week.

"Belle's wiped out. She's having a nap. The nurse said she'd come and get me when Belle wakes up."

"Did she tell you what happened at Dad's?" Sam enquired.

"No, not really, I know her waters broke when she was at the house fer lunch wi' James. Come to think of it, where is James? Belle was asking fer him and she was upset. She said something bad happened. I wasn't sure if it was the emotions of giving birth or the pain relief drugs talkin'."

Sam and Declan shared another telling glance. Their siblings were in the dark about the true nature of the A.L.L. organization, that it was, in fact, a front for James's private intelligence agency. Both were under the illusion that Sam was an interpreter, and Declan was a real estate manager for James. How would they broach the horror that had occurred at James' home? The revelations about what happened at the house would need to be worded carefully.

Sam took a breath, laid a hand on Oliver's shoulder, and concerned said,

"Look, Oliver, you might want to sit down."

"Why, what's going on?" Oliver sent a suspicious look between Sam and Declan and then shrugged away from Sam's touch.

"James was targeted by a criminal gang. Annabelle arrived at the house while a home invasion was taking place.
"

"What? Gods, no! Is James alright?"

Sam was silent for a beat too long. He hated to be the bearer of bad news, but they couldn't keep Oliver or Annabelle out of this.

"James was abducted. We have no idea if he's alive or dead," Sam admitted.

Oliver slumped back down into the armchair and held

his face in his hands. "Oh God, no! What am I gonna say to Belle? What are we gonna do? Have ye notified the police and the press?"

Declan hunkered down in front of Oliver's chair and rested his palms on his brother's knees.

"Look. Oli, I know we've just pissed on yer chips, but we couldnae not tell ye," he said.

"But, and I cannot stress this enough…this is a delicate situation. We need ye te keep schtum about the fact Jamesy's missing. His life may depend upon our silence."

"What?" Oliver looked up his face twisted with confusion. "Did the police say that?"

"The Metropolitan Police aren't involved," Declan replied flatly.

"Ye've got te be shittin' me," Oliver exclaimed in outrage. Declan stood, held his hands up in a placating gesture and stepped away.

Sam took Declan's place, "This is not something the Met can cope with. We've got a private company dealing with the situation—one that specializes in this kind of high-value abduction. We need to sit tight and wait for a ransom demand." Sam felt terrible about fabricating a story to tell his brother-in-law. It wasn't exactly all lies, but it wasn't the whole truth either. However, it was necessary to contain the situation and the flow of information. The fewer people who knew James had been outfoxed, the better.

Oliver looked up from his hands, all of the colour and joy now drained from his face.

"But… but… James has just become a grandfather!" he

49

stuttered, sounding childlike. "What do I tell Annabelle? She's gonna be devastated. Don't tell her, please, not yet!" he pleaded. "Keep the news back a while so we can enjoy the first few days wi' our daughter."

The look in Oliver's eyes squeezed Sam's heart. He could understand why Oliver wanted to shield Belle from such horrific news just after she'd given birth.

"We've got a suite here for three more days," Oliver said urgently, "I'm staying over. Please, don't say a word while we're here."

Behind Sam, Declan let out a deep sign of resignation. He took a hold of Sam's hand and drew Sam with him to the other end of the reception area lounge. Sam knew what Declan was going to say before Declan opened his mouth, and he was having none of it.

"A few days is all." Declan pleaded, trying the puppy dog eyes, "Please," he implored.

"I can't, I hate lying to her. There are too many secrets and lies in our family, Dec. It has to stop. Belle deserves to know the truth."

Oliver rose from his chair and strode over to the couple. "Please, Sam. We've waited so long for Rosa to arrive. The circumstances of her birth were traumatic enough. Please don't put Belle through this news too."

Sam knew Oliver and Declan were right. Annabelle had gone through so much and it was cruel to burden her with bad news. Reluctantly he caved, "Fine, I won't tell her, but if she asks me directly I won't lie to her either."

"Mr Ramsay?" They all turned in unison.

"Sorry to interrupt Mr Ramsay, your wife and daughter are ready for you now," the nurse beamed. A smile bloomed over Oliver's face again.

"Thank you, Sylvia. I'll be in shortly." Oliver turned back to Declan and Sam. "Can ye give us ten minutes?"

"Nae worries. Make it twenty. I'm famished. We'll go and get a quick bite."

****

CHAPTER 4
ROSALIND

"What do you fancy for lunch?" Sam enquired as they made their way past a gaggle of Japanese tourists heading toward the Tube station at Warren Street. There was a vast choice of cafes and fashionable eateries within a short walk of the hospital.

Declan inhaled the smell of fried food mixed with the exhaust fumes of passing black cabs. Then he spied the golden arches sign at the end of the street. He rubbed a hand over his stubbled jaw,

"Y'know, I'm gagging fer a dirty burger—mebe a quarter pounder with cheese?" he admitted, absently licking his lips.

Sam harrumphed disdainfully and gave him the side eye. He and Declan usually had discerning tastes when they ate takeout, and *clown food* was never on the menu.

"What? It's not as if I'm watching my figure," Declan declared, a hand on his flat abdomen. "Can ye not see I have the physique of a superhero?"

Sam pouted and didn't respond.

"Remember? *I'm Batman!*" Declan said in a gravely voice as he gave Sam a playful poke in the rib.

Sam poked him back and laughed, enjoying this rare moment of playful banter—something that had been sorely lacking in their lives. Sam perused his husband as Declan strode a few steps ahead and he decided that Declan needed to wear jeans more often. His thick muscled thighs and meaty arse looked fantastic. Sam bit his lip.

"You did look incredibly hot in that figure-hugging costume," Sam mused, "and the way you dealt with Hendrik was *so* macho. I swear you gave me wood!" he offered camply.

Declan snickered, "Macho, ye say?"

"Very." Sam reached out as he caught up with his husband and squeezed Declan's bottom,

"I think we'll need to buy Batman and Robin costumes for playtime!"

Declan stopped in his tracks and reached for Sam's arm. He looked quizzically at Sam as passers-by tutted at them for blocking the flow of traffic on the path. Declan was thoughtful for a beat before admitting.

"I do like it when we play silly buggers in public. Just like the old days. We haven't had much te joke about recently, have we love?" Declan slid his hand to cup Sam's cheek and laid a quick kiss on his lips, then moved off. Sam remained standing, although it was a hard task. Public displays of affection from Declan were as rare as comets and the simple gesture made Sam breathless. Walking away, Declan turned, "And as fer the costumes...I'm well up fer that!"

Sam grinned and jogged to catch up. They walked hand-in-hand not caring who saw, and as it happened, no one batted an eyelid.

After re-fuelling with greasy cheeseburgers, fries, and

coffee, they returned to the hospital.

"Mr Ramsay told me to send you both in when you came back," Nurse Sylvia, announced when she saw them. "Please use the anti-bacterial gel in the dispenser. Mrs Ramsay is in suite number 6."

On the way back they'd purchased gifts at a florist. They put them onto the glass-topped counter and then gelled up. Once they'd rubbed it in they collected the gifts and passed through the double doors. They walked down a corridor with no natural light, just artificial mood lighting alerting them that they were entering a space of calmness and peace. Arty monochrome images of newborns adorned the walls and the scent of baby and lavender hung in the air. A high-pitched wail made both men look at one another in alarm.

"Jesus, that's quite a pair of lungs!" Declan whispered.

Sam carried the bouquet and Declan held the soft teddy bear and 'New baby!' balloon on a stick. Sam paused at the door to room 6 and knocked.

"Come in unkie Sam and unkie Dec!" Sam gave Declan a querulous look, their brows arching at hearing the baby talk. Sam had wondered what kind of mother his sister would become and so he was amused. Annabelle had never been the kind of woman who used baby words before, but from what Oliver said about her obsession with perfect parenting social media accounts it sounded like she'd gone full throttle.

The private maternity suite was stylishly designed to be a home-from-home. The couple entered to have their senses assaulted by sights and smells that were alien to two men with zero experience with babies. Oliver sat on the wide double bed beside his wife. Baby Rosalind was in her mother's arms swaddled up in a blanket like a Fajita. Annabelle was gazing adoringly at the bundle. She looked up briefly to see the two handsome men bearing gifts.

"Put them with the others, will you, darlings!" she said absently, her love-drunk eyes back on her daughter.

From the mountain of unopened gifts and elaborate bouquets, news of the new arrival had travelled fast. Annabelle's friends had sent an array of gifts, from designer toiletries to flowers and soft toys. There was also a baby hamper from Fortnum and Mason. Declan placed the teddy bear on top of the hamper and glanced at the gift card.

Congratulations my darling, I'm so proud of you. Much love, Dad x

Declan turned to Sam and directed him with a nudge of his head. Sam placed the vase of flowers on a side table and looked at the hamper card that Declan held open for him to read. His jaw stiffened. Sam shared a knowing look with Declan then schooled his features and turned back to Annabelle.

Sam was practised at creating a mask of normality but inside a strange, unwelcome pang of jealousy burned. His father had never told Sam that he was proud of him, never, yet he was blatant in his adoration of his daughter. Sam pushed the unwanted feelings down. They seemed ridiculous and immature in the circumstances but his emotions were all over the place these days. He stepped up to the bed and Belle offered her cheek for a kiss.

"Congratulations sis," he said as he leaned in and gave his sister a peck on the cheek. Her complexion was flawless; her dark wavy hair was tied up with a colourful ethnic print silk scarf and she appeared to be tired but serene.

"Thank you unkie Sam," Annabelle replied playfully. Sam observed the face of the tiny baby in his sister's arms. He didn't know anything about kids, but for some reason, he hadn't thought newborn babies had hair. Baby Rosalind was graced with a full head of orange ginger hair and long strawberry blond eyelashes over huge blue-grey eyes. The ginger gene really was strong with the Ramsay clan!

"Look at those tiny fingers!" Sam couldn't help but lean in and unfold her little hand. He placed his index finger on her palm and was shocked with delight to see the tiny pink digits wrap around it.

"Well, would you look at that!" he exclaimed fondly.

"She's got ye! There's no help fer ye now," Oliver warned, a smile in his voice. He was right. Sam tried to pull his finger away but Rosalind had a bloody good grip for someone less than a day old, and it was a grip that went straight to Sam's heart. Her huge wide eyes seemed to fix on him and she cooed and gurgled.

"Hello little one," he said in response. The wave of love that washed through Sam made his eyes water. This new tiny person was his family, and Gods, what a clusterfuck of a world she'd been born into. He vowed secretly to do whatever he could to ensure she remained safe and that the sins of her grandfather did not affect her future.

"Dec, come and meet your niece?" Sam encouraged,

glancing up to find his husband standing pressed to the wall like he was in a hostage situation.

"No, no, yer grand, let her rest up."

"D'ye want te hold her?" Oliver asked as he turned to his wife and an unsaid question passed between them. Belle gave a nod of consent. Oliver leaned in and carefully lifted the baby from his wife's arms. Rosa let out a mewling cry.

"What's all that racket for, eh, darlin'? Daddy's just takin' ye te meet uncle Declan," Oliver said in a soft voice, rocking his daughter as he walked toward his brother. Rosalind stopped crying and stared up at the blurry face of her father.

"Show him the right way to hold her," Annabelle advised looking a little nervous now that Rosalind was out of her arms. Declan's pewter eyes widened in alarm as his brother approached carrying the precious bundle.

"I… eh, are ye sure? I don't want te drop her!" Declan said as he put his hands out.

"Jesus, Declan! A little tact!" Sam snickered.

"Och, you'll be fine, numpty! Just cradle her body with yer left arm, an' hold her head wi yer right hand like this." Oliver explained. "Apparently, her head'll be wobbly fer a few months."

Warily, Declan did as he was told taking the tiny baby into his arms. "She's so light!" Declan marvelled, and his smile widened as Oliver moved away and he held his niece on his own. Declan stared down into enormous orbs staring back at him with what seemed like endless wonder. A lump rose to his throat and he gently said,

"Hello there gorgeous, I'm your uncle Dec," and then he heard the click of a camera. He looked up to see Sam holding his phone and smiling triumphantly.

"Now, before you get too attached, let Sam have a cuddle and then give me back my daughter." Annabelle beamed.

Declan walked over to the bed, a little reluctant now to let the baby go, but after sharing a dazed glance with Sam he passed the baby into his husbands' arms. Oliver took a photo of Declan and Sam with Rosalind. Then the baby began to cry and Sam handed her back to Belle. As soon as she was back in her mother's arms, the baby settled. Oliver returned to the bed and snuggled up beside his wife and child. Sam and Declan pulled chairs closer and sat beside the bed.

"Right, now we're all sitting comfortably. Where's dad?" Annabelle demanded as haughtily as a queen holding court.

All three men exchanged awkward eye contact. "Ah, love, its no' the time for that—" Oliver stuttered.

"Don't you dare patronize me, Oliver Ramsay!" Belle chastised. "I've just pushed seven pounds of human out of my vagina. I'm not a fragile flower. One of you had better tell me what happened at the house and why my father isn't here to meet his granddaughter!"

Declan shot a glance to his brother and Oliver's shoulders slumped in resignation. There was no way he'd have his three days of peace with his wife and new baby.

"Sam," Oliver gestured with a flourish of his hand and then dejectedly slumped back against the pillows.

Sam moved his chair a little closer and took his sister's

58

hand. He met her watchful stare and said, "What do you remember about arriving at the house?"

"Honestly? My brain's still a bit fuzzy; they gave me *really* strong meds for the birth."

"Think about it, please. It will help."

Annabelle closed her eyes for a few seconds as if searching her memory.

"I was meeting dad at the house for lunch. When I pulled up Akiko was striding up the path to the front door. I thought maybe she'd lost her key—it was a bit odd that she rang the doorbell. But then Mr Steele opened the door and—" her expression twisted and her bravado vanished.

"Look, just tell me... is Dad okay?"

"Are you sure it was Akiko?" Declan pressed. "Did you see her face?"

Belle's expression twisted, "I don't know! I saw a woman with long black hair wearing black leather trousers, boots, and jacket...the clothes Akiko wears when she's using her motorbike to get around town."

"But you never saw her face?" Declan clarified.

"No... look, Sam, what's all this about? Where's dad?" Annabelle sounded scared now.

"Belle, I'm so sorry, but you witnessed the first move of a home invasion by a criminal gang. Mr Steele is dead, and they've abducted dad."

"Ye didnae tell me anyone got shot!" Oliver sounded stunned.

Annabelle's hand covered her mouth and as if Rosalind could sense her mother's change in mood, she let out an ear-splitting wail.

"Here, let me take her." Annabelle didn't protest as Oliver collected the screaming bundle into his arms and slid off the bed. He rocked her as he paced to the window of the suite overlooking a courtyard garden.

Annabelle brought her knees up and hid her face in her hands.

"Wh… what did the police say?" Belle whispered brokenly when she drew her hands down. Her eyes were red-rimmed and glistening.

"We can't tell the police," Sam admitted apologetically.

Belle was aghast. "What do you mean we can't tell the police?"

"Dad's a high-value target. We're working with a specialist company. They deal with the abduction of elite targets all over the world. When Declan and I are done here we'll be trawling through the CCTV at the house to see if we can get any clues to help, other than that, all we can do is wait for the kidnapper to make contact."

"There'll be some kind of ransom demand? Whoever took James will need to send ye proof of life, yes?" Oliver pitched in as he turned away from the window, the baby now content.

"Aye. It's gonna be a waiting game."

"What can I do to help? I can organize press interviews; maybe get a social media campaign going?" Annabelle's eyes were glistening with unshed tears and she looked stricken.

"Belle, I know you want te help but please understand,"

Declan interjected. "We can't let the media get hold o' this. Don't tell a soul that James is missing. It could put his life in danger. If anyone asks why he's no' here to meet his grandchild, tell them Rosa came early and James is stuck in the US."

"But...but I have to DO something. I can't do nothing, he's my father, for god's sake!" Annabelle complained.

"I know you don't want to hear this sis, but all you can do is focus on yourself, Rosa, and Oliver. Let us and the lawyers deal with finding dad. If there's a ransom demand we can pay whatever it takes to bring him home safely."

"Okay, okay," and as if hit by a wave of exhaustion Belle slumped resignedly to the pillow. She bit her lip and added sheepishly. "I've um... already announced Rosalind's birth on Twitter, Facebook, Tik Tok and Instagram."

"Already? She's less than a day old!" Sam exclaimed.

"I know, but everyone loves babies and good news. Parenting hash tags are a gold mine! This is a perfect opportunity for me to hit ten thousand followers." Annabelle pouted. Sam and Declan exchanged a withering look.

"Won't people think it's strange if Dad doesn't announce the birth of his first grandchild?" Annabelle asked.

"Don't worry, we'll get on it. One of dad's tech guys can access his social media and I'll post an announcement in The Times. We need everything to look as normal as possible." Sam reassured.

"Fine. Do whatever you have to do. But keep me informed and please... bring him back."

CHAPTER 5
THE MESSAGE

It was one thirty p.m. when they left the hospital. As they walked back to Devonshire Mews Declan rubbed his hands over his face to dispel the wave of tiredness that had hit him while sitting in the calm, pastel bubble of the maternity suite.

"Argh. That place was so relaxing I was ready te curl up an' taken a nap beside the bairn," he snickered.

"I must admit, seeing you with a baby in your arms did funny things to my insides."

"It did funny things to my inside too. I nearly shat meself wi' the fear of dropping the wee thing!" Declan replied flatly. Sam laughed out loud.

"Don't give me that. You loved it. You're a natural." After a few seconds of companionable silence, Sam asked,

"Can you see a kid in our future?"

Declan was a little taken aback. "Um. I dunno. Can *you*?"

"You'd make a wonderful father."

"So would you…"

"D'ye no think we should… ye know… mebe try a dog first—just to see if we can cope wi the responsibility?"

"That sounds reasonable. We'll have to think about what breed of dog would suit us. You know they say that dogs should look like their owners."

Declan clicked his key fob to unlock the vehicle. They eased into the leather upholstery and closed the doors. Declan was in the driving seat. He started the SUV, reversed, and drove out of the car park.

"If you were a dog, what breed would you be?" Sam quizzed.

"I dunno what I'd choose. But you'd be a cross between a greyhound an' a Labradoodle." Declan joked.

"Hey," Sam slapped Declan's forearm. "Then you'd be a cross between a St Bernard and a —" Sam didn't get the chance to complete his jibe because his phone vibrated again. They'd kept the devices on silent mode in the hospital and neither had responded to the vibrations as messages arrived. Sam palmed his phone to see ten text messages from an unknown number marked URGENT.

Declan paused at the traffic lights, checked his phone and flashed his screen to Sam. They matched. Each message demanded that they check-in immediately. Sam clicked the last text and then the secure link that was attached. He was connected with a voice message to: "Rendezvous at HQ immediately."

****

Declan drove through lunchtime traffic to Holland Park and pulled the Range Rover to the curb at the next available parking space. At the door to the house they were met by A.L.L. Forensic Scientist, and long-time friend of James, Dr Jonah Goldblume. The South African scientist appeared drained and dishevelled, his tanned skin now grey, and his bright, intelligent eyes missing their twinkle.

"Sam, Dicklan," Goldblume greeted on opening the door to permit entrance. The façade of normality vanished as soon as they stepped inside the house. Declan sent his gaze up and down the hall. The evidence of Mr Steele's murder had been washed away as if it had never happened. Forensic scene technicians wearing white Tyvek suits, gloves, and blue shoe covers were processing the scene in the kitchen and at the damaged stairway access to the basement.

"I'm so sorry, Sam. This is terrible…terrible." Jonah opened his arms and Sam stepped forward accepting comfort from a man he'd known since his childhood. Sam drew back from the embrace and gravely Goldblume said,

"You must remember, your father is a snake… a talented and resourceful bastard. You don't get to have your own spy agency by winging it!" he gave a mirthless laugh. "I'm sure James will find a way back to us if you don't find him first and set him free." He paused and his gaze raked the men.

"I'm glad you're both here. There are some things I need to show you. I won't beat around the bush, it is not pretty. You'll have to suit up first." Dr Goldblume directed them to step to the left into the small office that had been the domain of Mr Steele. When they were both dressed in CSI suits and shoe covers, Dr Goldblume led them down to the basement using the emergency staircase. He pulled Nitrile gloves onto his hands, as he walked and talked.

"Where are we going?" Sam enquired.

"The Active Operations Laboratory—we found something very disturbing," Dr Goldblume explained ominously.

"This has been a total disaster and I won't rest until we get to the bottom of what happened here. You know what a secretive bugger Viper is and there are so many rooms in this facility. We haven't been able to work all of the individual crime scenes yet. The unit is scrambling and I'm shorthanded, waiting for assistance." Goldblume grumbled as Sam and Declan walked silently beside him.

"We've had problems gaining access to rooms that have a keypad or handprint technology," Goldblume explained as they strode down the hall with the glass lap lane above. Declan had appreciated the play of light from the pool against the white walls and so habitually, he looked up. He was relieved to see the body of the gardener had been removed and that the pool was now drained of water... and blood. The lack of water changed the atmosphere of the hallway completely. The watery reflection once gave Declan a momentary sense of ease, a reprieve before he dealt with his overbearing boss, but now James was gone, the pool was empty and discomfort lingered.

"When the silent alarm sounded the IT technicians at A.S.S severed the intranet– if we are compromised this is the agreed protocol. The network here was designed to be separate from the main servers at the other complex. We're being cautious about restarting the system. CCTV is still down, so we're yet to find out what the blazes happened," Goldblume explained. "It's a mess!"

"When will the servers be back online?" Declan asked.

"Within the next thirty minutes, I hope." Jonah paused to pull open the hallway door that led to James' office. Yellow plastic marker tabs lined the hall where blood had trailed and the men all pressed to the wall as they moved past the evidence.

"How people many have we lost?" Sam asked in an emotionless clinical tone.

"I don't have a number yet. Currently, it appears that the initial losses were on ingress–two members of the domestic staff who were in the wrong place at the wrong time. Madsson's targets were in the Active Operations lab and of course, Viper," Goldblume stated.

This news was grim indeed.

"Go to *Bright Nail's* cell when we're done here," Dr Goldblume suggested. "I hope that the servers are up and running by then."

They passed by James's office; the door still open. Declan glanced in and noted yellow marker tabs on the carpet, the desk, and the wall. There was a yellow tag by a pen injector that Declan hadn't noticed before, and from the mess of the office and the amount of blood splatter, there'd been a fierce fight before it had been used. The men turned left at the end of the hall.

A sense of unease crept under Declan's skin as they approached the Active Ops lab. Dr Goldblume paused outside a door that on the outside looked no different from any of the others lining the hall, except that a keypad destroyed by a gunshot was hanging precariously.

Goldblume turned to meet their wary gazes.

"A word of warning gentlemen, this scene has not yet been processed. I doubt either of you has witnessed anything like this before, you'll need strong stomachs." He retrieved two pairs of Nitrile gloves from a pocket in his protective suit and handed them to Sam and Declan. Dr Goldblume then pressed his shoulder to the door and pushed it open.

It was the scent that hit Declan first as they stepped into the Active Ops laboratory, the coppery tang of blood, and then the lower note of wrongness—faeces, urine and corruption.

"Oh mah god!" Declan exclaimed. His stomach churned and he immediately regretted his choice of McDonald's for lunch!

"Jesus!" Sam exhaled in a barely audible whisper. His knees folded. Declan's hand shot out and he threaded an arm around Sam's waist to keep him on his feet. "I've got ye."

Sam appeared as pale as a ghost. "I'm fine, I'm fine, I..." Sam insisted, but Declan was sure Sam was not fine at all, in fact, Declan was very worried about Sam's mental health. He'd already broken down yesterday and the shock of this on top of everything else was too much.

Workstations lined the walls, each with a huge paper-thin monitor; a wireless keyboard, a mouse, and a chair in which an operations technician sat slumped. Declan counted ten people, six men, and four women, each with a bullet hole in the back of their head. The white walls of the

AO lab were defiled with blood splatter of the deepest crimson like some kind of macabre art project. As far as they knew, including these victims, thirteen members of James's staff were murdered after Erik Madsson was set free.

Sam found his feet and stepped out of Declan's side hug. A huge black server bank stood in the centre of the vast white room, lights blinking on and off intermittently. A young woman sat on the floor cross-legged facing away from them, clicking on a laptop. The laptop was plugged into the server bank.

"Gentlemen, this is Roksana Marketta, one of our Certified Ethical Hackers from the Unit." The woman appeared to be in her early twenties, was waif-thin, and had bleached buzz-cut hair and a line of ring piercings around her left ear. The tip tap of nails echoed on the keyboard.

"Roksana, I'd like to introduce you to—"

She turned around, gave Sam, and Declan a quick withering glance and as if Goldblume was patronizing her, she said "I *know* who they are." Her accent was abrasively Polish.

Goldblume paused for an instant before he tentatively asked, "How are you getting on?"

"Slow. There is a USB Rubber Ducky of undetermined origin in the server bank. I haven't removed it yet."

"What does that mean... in layman's terms?" Declan asked.

"A USB Rubber Ducky is a Human Interface Device designed to look like a USB. It injects commands, what we call payloads, into a network written in Ducky Script. This little bastard injected a multilayered virus which is buried in the network. This created a critical failure. That failure led to a domino effect which impacted every device connected to the network. Nothing is fucking working. Is that clear enough?" Roksana pouted. "The virus code is deeply encrypted. Once I stabilize the network, security analysts at the Unit can take over the decrypt."

"Will it take long to get things up and running?" Declan enquired. He was keen to get
access to the security camera footage.

"This operation cannot be rushed. I have billions of lines of complex code to search through to find and fix the points of failure. Then I have to find out what information was accessed and stolen. I've been at this for ten hours. So, what do you think?" Roksana replied petulantly. "The virus has split and multiplied, it may have activated an automatic transfer of protected files, or it could have tendrils that lay dormant in the network until whoever did this decides to activate remotely."

"Can we get access at all?" Declan asked in frustration.

"I'll put the server back up in safe mode, but we cannot risk an internet connection. CCTV will be accessible, as will security pass admittance data," she informed flatly.

Sam paced carefully around the scene, pausing at each workstation, looking at the destruction of life, searching for clues as to why these people had to die.

"I know it must be very difficult to see this," Goldblume said to Sam. "Each victim was a highly respected expert in their field."

"They were more than that, more than their fucking jobs, they were my friends and colleagues," Roksana snapped, "They didn't fucking deserve this."

"What were they working on?" Sam asked his voice deceptively calm.

"We have around twenty ongoing operations, but six techs were asked to focus on a cyber security project for your bastard father," Roksana sneered. Sam didn't take offence, he could understand her anger. Roksana turned and met Sam's fern-green eyes, "Sorry," she said, "I know you're a minion just like us. I was part of the original team but I moved to another team at the Unit six months ago. It could have been me."

"I'm sorry for your loss." The words sounded hollow and insufficient as they left Sam's mouth, but they were all he could offer her.

The three men stood in silence for several minutes as the enormity of what happened in the AO lab hit home.

"Okay. I'm restarting the server in safe mode now, we can access the security camera and biometric pass data," Roksana announced. The monitor screens that had been black mirrors a moment before flashed on. Letters of the alphabet rained down the screens in a mixture of fonts, the display taunting, and menacing.

"Did you do that?" Declan accused.

"Of course not!" Roksana spat affronted. "What you see is what he left behind."

"He's fucking with us," Sam stated.

Roksana removed the lead connecting her laptop to the

server bank, closed her laptop, and pushed herself up from the floor. She turned and addressed Sam.

"I'm can't stay in here any longer. I'm going to the security room to join Agent Riley, I can work from there. I'll let you know when we've retrieved footage from the cameras."

Sam nodded. "Thank you."

Dr Goldblume pulled out his phone and called for a team to begin processing the murder scene.

Sam and Declan made their way through the complex to the cell that had been Erik Madsson's home for twelve months. They'd seen it before, all-be-it via a monitor screen. Viper's guest accommodations were luxurious when compared with that of state-run prison cells. The cell door was fitted with an electromagnetic lock that, if touched when live would give a person a jolt of ten thousand volts– not enough to kill, but enough to put Madsson down until guards arrived to restrain him.

"Who was on security duty in the control room? Why did Madsson think it was safe to touch the door? Where did he access his weapon?" Sam reeled off questions as they viewed the room.

Declan paused with his hands on his hips at the foot of the single bed and noted the neatly folded clothes the prisoner had worn, his slippers placed on top of the bundle. It was a habitually military act–ritually folding the uniform as if Madsson believed he was still a soldier and would be inspected and scrutinized by his superiors.

Sam paced the small room, paused, and then looked up

at the security camera. "You know what I don't get. Why now? What happened for him to make his move now?"

"It was an inside job, no doubt. The electricity for the door was disabled. To me, it looks like he met his accomplice, and they kitted him out with guns and sent him on his killing spree like a wind-up toy. It's like he's some kind of super soldier experiment. He was triggered into action."

"Gods, we need to get hold of the security footage and fit the timeline together," Sam sighed and rubbed a hand across tired eyes.

They next went to the control room where a technician was busy scanning for fingerprints on the computer keyboard using a handheld device that Declan had seen Mrs K use when she processed the scene of a drugged abduction in Munich.

"Have you found anything significant?"

"Ah, hello Agent Ramsay. Yes, there are multiple prints on the keyboard and a disposable syringe behind the door. The agent on duty was found unconscious, he'd been drugged. There is something strange though," the agent said,

"A non-standard issue purple USB was lodged in a port."

"Can we see what's on that USB?" Sam asked. The technician pressed a button on the keyboard and sound filled the room—crackling, as if the recording was old and of poor quality. A light innocent child's voice spoke in what Sam recognized as Swedish:

"Pappa, kommer du att sjunga alfabetet med mig?"

(Papa will you sing the alphabet with me?)

Then a male voice replied:

"*Självklart min älskling*"

(Of course, my sweetheart)

The child began to sing off-key.

"Jesus, that's creepy. Does Madsson have a daughter?" Declan shivered and sent a side glance to Sam who appeared frozen to the spot, his gaze a million miles away.

"Turn it off," Declan barked and immediately the technician did. He picked up one of the baggies from his box and placed the purple USB inside.

****

CHAPTER 6

MRS K

"What is the meaning of this?" Akiko Kimura roared. "Unlock these handcuffs. Where is James?" she shouted furiously as Sam stepped into the interrogation room and paused to hold the door for Declan. Declan entered and gave a curt nod as he strode past his husband. He carried a tablet computer that contained the cleaned-up footage of the assault on the HQ that the techs had spent the night collating. Declan hadn't yet had time to watch it all, but he'd found some pertinent snippets to use for the interrogation.

Both men had slept fitfully, and when they were awoken by a seven a.m text message informing them that *'the package has been collected from the airport'* they decided to take their time and indulge in a morning tumble, and then enjoy pampering at the Connaught Hotel across the road from their apartment. An hour in the spa swimming pool, breakfast, and then some manscaping at the salon had worked wonders. All the while Mrs. K had been left to stew in the interrogation room.

Now, entering the room at midday Declan wore a navy *McQueen* suit with a soft cream shirt and Ramsay Tartan tie. His hair was trimmed and dyed so that all of the salt and pepper of his disguise as Dr Tobias Hunter was gone. A beard trim and a cloud of spicy aftershave later he felt more like himself than he had done in months.

Sam's peroxide for the previous mission was gone and his hair was now a more natural honey blond. He wore a petrol-blue *Tom Ford* suit, pastel pink shirt, and rainbow tie. The agents took seats across the table from Mrs K. Behind them a camera and tripod stood, the ominous red light blinking as it recorded the interview. Two agents had been drafted from the facility to observe in a room next door and assist if things got ugly. Field technician, Claudia Feurig, codename Storm Song, and Field Medic, Lena Weber, codename Deep Clean.

Both Declan and Sam had experienced interrogation at the hands of Akiko Kimura—as had every single agent drafted into James's covert agency. Akiko was a brutal interrogator who enjoyed medical intervention to get to the truth, but Sam and Declan would not be using the same strategy on her. There would be no injections, no Psychoactive B, or any other serums, but they did plan to play with her a little.

"Unlock these damn handcuffs!" Akiko demanded again. She was nearly frothing at the mouth with rage, her cuffed wrists attached to the table through a steel loop, and learning their lesson from Declan's interview, the table was now bolted to the floor. Akiko's silky black hair had partly fallen out of a chignon that once sat high on her head, artfully held together by a pair of small chopsticks. Her eyes were dark and fierce, her olive skin pinking at her cheeks.

"Unlock the cuffs, NOW. If you don't, *I will*," she warned in a low dangerous tone.

75

Sam and Declan remained silent and stared at her. It was clear Akiko did not enjoy the loss of control or restraint, and yet she had taken much satisfaction in giving this discomfiture to her colleagues. Everyone who worked for A.L.L. was terrified of Akiko Kimura, possibly even more than they were terrified of Sir James Aiken.

"Not very nice on the other side is it?" Sam said smugly as he sat back and folded his arms.

"Desert Fox. What the hell is going on? I am your superior. Viper will hear about this and you will pay for this outrage."

Sam was unsure if mentioning James was the play of a liar or if Mrs K was oblivious as to why she'd been picked up by agents and bundled into a van as soon as she stepped off the private jet.

Before they'd entered the room Sam briefed Declan and the two agents. They'd agreed to err on the side of caution. Akiko Kimura was highly skilled and dangerous and she knew many of Sir James Aiken's secrets. Everyone needed to remain alert.

"You touched down at Heathrow Airport six hours ago after using the private jet. Where did you go?" Sam asked conversationally.

Akiko's steely, unemotional gaze fixed on Sam. "Who sanctioned this interrogation? It's a joke right?"

"Where did you go?" Sam repeated.

"It was private business. James knows exactly where I was. If you want to know, why don't you ask him?" Akiko sneered with satisfaction.

76

Declan opened the cover of his tablet and turned it so that Akiko could view the screen. Her wary gaze flicked to stab a glare at Sam and then Declan and then it landed on the screen.

"Two days ago this woman arrived on our doorstep." Declan clicked the play button and the full-colour security camera footage began. It was filmed from the side, so both parties at the door could be viewed.

The woman was tall and slim, clad in black leather. She appeared in the frame with a motorcycle helmet threaded on one arm, and a black backpack over her shoulders. She stepped up to the wrought-iron awning-covered porch, her face shrouded by a curtain of dark hair and angled just so, therefore the camera didn't pick up her facial features. She rang the doorbell. Less than a minute later Mr Steele answered the door, his usual amiable smile for visitors etched on his face. He looked at the woman on the porch. His face twisted with confusion but he didn't get a chance to say a word. The woman drew a handgun from the motorcycle helmet and shot the butler at point-blank range. Mr Steele fell backwards, blood and brain matter spraying in a violent arc across the shiny marble hall. The woman placed the firearm back into the helmet, then stepped over Mr Steele's body, kicked his leg out of the way, and closed the door behind her.

The footage was stark and shocking, showing the ease with which this woman took a life. There was a mundane, clinical aspect to this murder that chilled Sam to the bone. Who had ordered this assassin to embark on a killing spree in broad daylight in a quiet suburb of central London?

Declan placed his fingertip on the tablet screen and the

footage sped, on fast-forward, displaying the passing of five minutes where nothing happened at the door to the Aiken house. He recognized the moment new action began and pressed play.

Clutching her belly and grimacing in pain, Annabelle staggered into the frame of the video camera at the front door. Her summer dress was stained with amniotic fluid and blood. She shakily pushed her key into the keyhole and slowly, warily opened the door to the house. Annabelle then stood for a moment in the doorway, her face stricken with horror at viewing Mr Steele's body on the marble hall floor. Her face twisted in pain, she sobbed and clutched the doorjamb, then bit on her forearm to keep her cry silent. When the contractions had passed she staggered further into the house, leaving the front door ajar.

Again, Declan fast-forwarded the footage, until he and Sam could be seen arriving, leaving, and returning armed and wearing Kevlar vests. They then entered the house.

Throughout the viewing, Akiko Kimura's face was blank and unreadable. Sam wasn't surprised by her lack of reaction. He'd known her for many years as a colleague and was familiar with her air of clinical detachment. She was a cleaner, after all, tasked with cleaning up after her agent's deadly mistakes. In her profession, it didn't pay to have a weak stomach or to display any tells.

"That woman is not me!" Akiko said in such a soft, measured way she could have been asking for the time. "Why would I ring the bell when I have a key?"

Sam and Declan remained silent, their narrowed eyes burning into Akiko until she broke the impasse.

"What happened here while I was out of the country? Why is James not taking my calls?"

Sam and Declan shared a look. Did Mrs K really not know?

Sam spoke up, relaying the information in a flat, unemotional tone.

"Two days ago at thirteen hundred hours, a woman resembling your description began a violent assault on A.L.L HQ. During the assault, Erik Madsson was released, and a total of thirteen staff members were murdered, including Agent Strauss." Sam waited for a beat and then said, "My father was abducted. So, you'll understand now why we must know where you went in the private jet and why."

Akiko's mask of detachment slipped, and her voice was no longer placid. "Has James been located? Is he injured?" The emotional reaction was uncharacteristic for such a buttoned-up personality but proved she was, after all, human. She made her hands into fists and bashed her cuffed hands on the tabletop.

"Tell me god damn it!" Akiko stood abruptly and kicked the chair backwards. It skidded away to hit the wall. Using the table as leverage Akiko propelled her legs up in an attempt to scissor Sam's neck between her thighs. Luckily, both men saw it coming and pushed themselves back from the table, their chairs screeching on the polished concrete floor. As he slid backwards Declan's chair hit the tripod and the video camera crashed to the ground.

Mrs K crouched on the tabletop. Her silky black hair flowed wild. A chopstick had fallen to the table. She gripped the bar that her cuffs were linked through and bent her sinuous body until the errant chopstick was in her mouth. To Sam's dismay, the small chopstick wasn't made of wood, but metal. Mrs K. folded forward until she held the chopstick between her restrained fingers and with her teeth she drew a fine tip from the end of the chopstick. Then she turned it around, placed the broad side between her teeth, and then used the pin to open the cuffs.

They let it happen, looking on in awe at her ingenuity, expecting nothing less. She wasn't James's right hand because she was beautiful and acerbic. James knew exactly what Akiko Kimura was capable of.

Once she'd unclasped the cuffs from her wrists, Akiko rubbed the bruised skin and shot Sam and Declan a withering look. Declan shuddered, comparing it to his mother Eileen's disdain when he'd stamped muddy boots over her clean kitchen floor.

Akiko turned and jumped gracefully from the table to the floor. Again, she glared at Sam and Declan as she re-set her chignon, pushing the chopsticks through the twist of dark, silken hair. She righted her clothing and then collected her chair from where it lay on the floor. Akiko dragged the chair to the table, sat down, and faced the agents.

"It appears I need to make it clear to you both that I would never betray James. Whoever the woman in that video is, you know she isn't me." Both men remained silent. Mrs K pursed her lips and shook her head once more like a disappointed mother.

"She's dressed to look like me for this exact reason. She

wants to distract you from the truth. Play that video again," Mrs K demanded.

Declan pulled his chair close to the table and turned the tablet screen on. He cued up the video and played it again from the start.

Sam watched with curious eyes. What was it that Akiko saw after one viewing that they had not noticed after multiple gruesome viewings?

The murder scene played out, and at the second the gun was pulled from the motorcycle helmet Mrs K snapped, "Here. Pause, and zoom in."

Declan did as directed. "Now, tell me, what can you see?"

Both men stared at the image on the screen of the woman in black gripping a handgun pointed at Mr Steele's temple. Sam had a gut feeling that something wasn't right from the first time he'd viewed the footage but he couldn't put his finger on it.

"Well, she's not wearing gloves an' she's left-handed," Declan observed.

"She's using an HK45 Tactical handgun with a suppressor," Sam said, "That weapon's used primarily by US Military, Law enforcement and security services."

"Very observant, Desert Fox, Lucky Boy. But look closer—"

Declan's brows knitted in concentration as he tried to comprehend what Mrs K was leading them to. It was like staring at a page from 'Where's Wally' and Declan always hated that bobble-hatted little shite!

Sam studied the image on the screen, the gun...he focused on the gun, and then what he was seeing hit him, and he felt stupid for not noticing it before.

"Jesus Christ!" he exclaimed. "The hand!"

"Wha' about the hand?" Declan asked in confusion. His gaze flashed between Akiko's slender, long-fingered hands resting on the tabletop, and the hand on the screen.

"Aye...it's bigger," Declan noted.

"Correct. That woman isn't me."

"Oh, my God! This is Amanda, Amanda Jamison!" Sam was horrified.

Both men sat back in their seats, the enormity of that revelation hitting home like a physical blow to the stomach.

Amanda Jamison assured that she only knew Erik Madsson–or as she'd called him 'Lars Pietersen' from when he was employed by her at the *G'wan Adventures* resort in the Scottish Highlands. She'd given quite the performance as the Hotel Manager who had no idea about Madsson's true identity or his nefarious reason for hiding out in Scotland. After the bloody events at *G'wan Adventures* James purchased the hotel and used his wealth to silence Amanda. He planned to use the Scottish resort as a high-altitude cold-weather training facility which he would rent out to the security services. Amanda was invited to London at James' behest to arrange the redesign and furnishings for the hotel renovation. James gave her an apartment where he could keep an eye on her and in turn, Amanda used her Scottish charms to worm her way into Sir James' social circle. Sam was sent in disguised as Kitty Franklin to befriend Amanda.

The pair became fast friends, but Sam never lost the gut feeling Amanda was up to something. He wasn't sure if she was trying to bag a Billionaire or if there was another agenda at play. Now it was clear Amanda Jamieson had fooled him….fooled them all!

"This makes sense now. There's something else yez need te see," Declan frowned as he pulled the tablet closer and swiped to a new video file.

"I havenae had a chance te view all of the footage or pin down the timeline, but I did notice this." He propped the tablet up so the other two could see, and then tapped the screen to press play. In this second video, the lighting was blue.

"This occurred after the silent alarm was tripped,"

The footage showed a view of the hallway with the watery reflections of the lap lane visible on the walls, the silhouette of a body floating in the pool adding to the macabre effect. At 13:40 Amanda Jamieson strutted confidently down the hall towards the doorway that led to James's office, her long hair still curtaining her features so the camera couldn't get a clear view of her face. She held a handgun with a suppressor and wore a black rucksack on her back, but she'd discarded the motorcycle helmet. She removed the rucksack and let it slump against the wall.

At 13:43 Erik Madsson exited through the door across the hallway from Amanda. He'd come from the other side of the complex, the side that housed the emergency medical facility, interrogation rooms, and cells.

This was the first footage that Sam had seen of Madsson from during the attack and he let out a shocked reflexive

83

gasp at seeing the serial killer free. "Why didn't you show this to me before?" Sam turned and glared at Declan, and Declan glared straight back as if to say, *you know damn well why!* Sam pinched his lips and pushed down his anger. Seeing Erik Madsson roaming free in these very halls chilled Sam to the bone. Logically he understood that Declan was trying to protect him. By the time they'd returned home all they were fit for inhaling a pizza slice, then bed. What could Sam have done about it anyway? Sam let his neurotic feelings ebb away in an exhaled breath and then he focused on the screen. Madsson was dressed in brand-new black garments. Sam wondered how he'd gotten access to the change of clothing. Madsson appeared fit and healthy, his damaged hand still wrapped in a brace. From his time with Erik Madsson in Norway and Scotland Sam believed that Madsson was a left-handed sniper. He'd hoped that the injury he'd inflicted with a cake knife during their tempestuous interrogation meant the bastard wouldn't be able to hold a gun again.

The assassin strode across the hall and met Amanda Jamison. He grinned widely and pulled her into an embrace. They kissed ravenously. When they parted Amanda bent down and scooped up the rucksack, which she helped Erik thread onto his shoulders, and then she passed him the handgun and several clips of ammunition. He reloaded as they talked, the weapon held between his injured hand and his belly. He then gripped the 45 with his right hand and tested the weight and sight. He spun the weapon like an old-time western gunfighter, and Amanda giggled coquettishly. Madsson pushed the gun into his waistband and after one final near-violent kiss, Madsson, and Jamison parted. Madsson travelled down the hall towards James' office and the Active Operations Lab, and Amanda Jamieson moved through the hidden door towards the subterranean garage.

"Christ! They're lovers!" Sam was stunned.

"And *Bright Nail* is ambidextrous," Mrs K observed. "Well, fuck! That fact is *not* in his file."

Declan ran his hands over his tired eyes as if to rub away what they'd just seen. "They've been in this together all along, even at *G'wan Adventures*." Declan was disgusted. He'd kept this from Sam because he'd known that he'd be devastated to realize that Amanda was part of planning his death.

In a faraway voice, Sam said, "I always wondered how Madsson set up the bodies in the Bothy on his own—how he'd set up everything in the cave without help."

Declan reached out and laid his hand on Sam's and gave a squeeze of reassurance. He hadn't wanted to bring the terrifying memories back to the front of Sam's mind, but there was no choice.

Sam mulled over all he'd known about Amanda Jamieson. The fiction Amanda told made Sam believe she was money-hungry and James was at the top of her wish list. In a way, that was true. Amanda had her own mission and James was her mark. She'd played the long game and set her sights on worming her way into James' life, not for sex or money, but to free her lover and to assist Madsson in completing his mission. Sam wondered why they had gone to so much effort and not just killed James. What information did James have that made assassinating him untenable?

The layers of lies and betrayals astonished Sam. Bile roiled in his belly and he felt like he was going to be sick. He stood abruptly.

"I...I need some air," he said, his voice reedy and thin, and then he bolted for the door.

Declan had anticipated a bad reaction to seeing the video footage and moved to get up and follow, but Akiko reached out and put her long-fingered hand on Declan's forearm, the grip light, but insistent.

"Leave him," she said sternly.

"But—"

"Sam needs to work through this himself. Give him some space." Mrs K advised. "Now, we are wasting time. Tell me what happened. Every. Last. Detail."

****

CHAPTER 7
HER SECRET

It was a pleasant spring day as Sam stepped into his father's garden. But despite the warm sun in a cloudless sky, and birds singing joyfully, Sam felt detached from it all. He took repetitive tidal breaths in an attempt to calm his heart, which was thrumming in his chest like he'd just come back from a run. Two agents were still fingertip searching through the manicured border planting that Piotr had so lovingly tended. The view above the garden wall was of the tree line in Holland Park. A gentle breeze made the boughs sway hypnotically to and fro. Sam focused on the movement for a minute, allowing it to distract him from the internal meltdown he was experiencing. If he hadn't seen the carnage for himself he wouldn't have believed that thirteen people died in this house the day before. Thirteen lives were cut short, and their passing would be swept under another carpet of lies, but still, the sun shone and birds sang as if nothing unusual had happened.

Watching the moment Madsson and Jamieson kissed had blown Sam's mind. He was conflicted and confused about the sight of the pair mauling one another on screen. Sam harboured a burning hated for Erik Madsson, and yet from her actions, Amanda seemed to be in love with him — in love with a monster. Amanda appeared to be so in love that she'd mounted her own secret mission to free her lover. Sam began to pace, walking the garden path, nodding to the agents who were gloved up and finger-deep in the flowerbeds. Sam attempted to look at Amanda's situation from other angles. He understood all-encompassing, blinding love—the kind of love where you would fight the whole god-damn world with your bare hands to get your loved one back. He knew that if the tables were turned he would have moved mountains to find Declan and free him — just as Declan had trekked through the highlands to find Sam. And so, Sam found himself empathizing a little with Amanda...but only a little. That was as far as his empathy toward her went, because, taking into consideration all Amanda had done, all she'd enabled, Amanda had crossed too many lines in the sand to be redeemed. From what Sam knew of Amanda, she was an intelligent woman who played on her Scots accent and glamour to manipulate men into giving her what she wanted. She liked to play the clueless coquette but Sam knew that beneath her *'Oh, dearie me, I'm so silly'* act she was far from stupid. What had Erik told Amanda to make her join him in taking down Sir James Aiken? What had James done to Madsson's employer to deserve this murderous attention?

Sam mulled things over as he paced the outline of the garden. His emotions swayed back and forth like the tree boughs in the park. He was fuelled by anger at her betrayal and then felt sorry for Amanda. Then Sam's thoughts swung the other way and he felt guilty for wasting a second of sympathy on her. She had murdered Mr Steele in cold blood, murdered their gardener, and imprisoned the house staff against their will. Amanda didn't care about anything other than setting a psychopath free to continue his killing spree and complete whatever mission he'd been programmed to do. What future did she think they had? The villain and villanelle had a romantic ring, but it was a doomed affair. Madsson had abducted one of Britain's richest men—a man who ran a covert spy agency and had connections in spy agencies all over the world. Amanda must have known that A.L.L. would leave no stone unturned to find James. She'd thrown away her future, of that Sam had no doubt. There could be no redemption for Amanda Jamieson.

****

"Are you feeling better? Mrs K asked as Sam took his seat and placed his palms flat on the icy metal table.

"A little, yes. The past few days have been... difficult," Sam offered in explanation. "I see Declan's gotten you up to speed," Sam noted observing the map of the underground River Westbourne on the tablet screen. Mrs K nodded. Sam felt a little guilty for leaving Declan in the lurch but he couldn't deny how relieved he was at seeing that Declan had gotten to the part in the story where they'd exited the tunnel at the Thames shoreline. Trailing his father's blood through the underbelly of London was something that would give Sam nightmares.

"I'm taking command of the investigation from now on," Mrs K announced, "Neither of you can be involved. Agents Feurig and Weber will assist me personally. And the analyst team at the Unit will get to work finding leads."

"But—" Declan began in outrage. He didn't get to finish his sentence.

"You've both been in the field for seven months and successfully completed your mission. So, you've earned some downtime. Both of you know that you're far too close to this. I'm relieving you of all duties for four weeks."

"Four weeks!" Declan protested. He appeared to be more put out by the forced R&R than Sam.

"Yes, four weeks. I am confident we will have Viper back by then." Mrs K said sternly.

Mrs K was correct, Sam surmised. He *was* too close to the investigation, and both he and Declan were mentally and emotionally drained after seven months of pretending to be other people. The downtime would be beneficial. Alexander had shared a lot of troubling information about James' secret past, and now Sam and Declan had the time to work out what the hell the Alphabet Club was, and what it had to do with James' disappearance.

Sam sat back in his chair and addressed Mrs K, "Very well. We'll take a step back, but I'd still like to know—we've been forthcoming and agreeable, so will you return the favour and tell us where you were?" Sam prodded.

Akiko pinned a considering gaze on Sam. "You may think you're special Samuel Aiken, but you can be just as nosey and infuriating as your father." She paused appearing deep in thought, and then asked,

"Do you know how I met your father, Samuel?"

"No. I've never been made a party to that information.

You know how James loves his secrets—nearly as much as he loves money."

"It is quite the story. Maybe I tell you sometime," she offered with a sly, cat-like smile.

"What does it have to do with why ye took the company jet to Copenhagen?" Declan interjected.

Akiko leaned in conspiratorially, "I will tell this to both of you and it will not leave this room."

They nodded.

"Storm Song, turn off the audio recording equipment," Akiko called to the agent she knew
was in another room monitoring the conversation.

"Switching off now," a disembodied German-accented voice replied.

Mrs K waited for a beat. "Very well," she began. Akiko appeared nervous, something Sam had not expected to see, her sharp, well-manicured nails drumming on the tabletop as she spoke.

"I have not returned to Japan or seen my mother for more than ten years. My father is a... complicated man." Sam understood how problematic a 'complicated' father could be!

"I discovered that my mother, *Kirika*, is not well. She is attending a hospital in Copenhagen for treatment. My father remains in Japan. James is...intimately familiar with my family situation. He understood how important it was for me to make peace with my mother. He permitted me to take the private jet. And so, I sat with my mother for several hours. That is why my phone was off and why I could not be contacted."

Sam spoke first. "Thank you for sharing that information," then Declan added, "I'm sorry to hear your mother's unwell."

Sam supposed it would be easy to verify if a Japanese citizen named *Kirika* had passed through Danish customs, but he decided then that he would trust Akiko until she gave him cause not to. "If there is anything we can do to help—"

Akiko batted the suggestion away, "Mother is receiving the best of care. That is all we can ask for."

"Indeed." Sam agreed.

"Right. Now we are on the same page," Mrs K said as she rose from her chair, "I have work to do."

Sam also rose from his chair, "You do. We have a meeting with my father's lawyer at three p.m. today. Declan will accompany us."

****

CHAPTER 8
THE LAWYER

Chance Bailey was one of the so-called 'magic circle' London law firms—firms whose reputations and connections were intricately entwined with the legal dealings of the global moneyed elite. Their offices were in a flashy glass skyscraper in the heart of the Canary Wharf financial business district. Sam and Declan arrived outside the building on Upper Bank Street at 2:45 p.m. and made their way through sliding glass doors to the foyer and then to the reception desk directly opposite.

"Sam Aiken and Declan Ramsay to see Dominic Soames," Sam announced, addressing the sharp-suited young man in reception. The receptionist checked his tablet screen.

"Yes. I have you for a three o'clock. Take the elevator on your right to the sixth floor, gentlemen. Rachel will meet you and bring you to Mr Soames' office."

Sam and Declan headed to the elevator and rode it to the sixth floor. There had been no word about James' whereabouts for nearly forty-eight hours. Sam was well aware the first seventy-two hours of a missing person's investigation were vital. After that, evidence degraded, memories faded, and the breadcrumbs of investigation became fewer without digging deeper. Sam knew for certain that James was drugged, had been injured, and then been forcibly removed from his office. He was extracted via the tunnels of the River Westbourne, and then loaded onto a speed boat. Each day more than five hundred vessels crossed the English Channel. James could be somewhere in the UK, in Europe, or he could be anywhere in the world. The not knowing was a maggot eating Sam from the inside out. James was hiding a nasty secret—and as if he'd been reading Sam's mind Declan severed the silence in the elevator,

"You know everythin' that happened is connected te James's past. There's something bad under a bloody great boulder, it's something yer da has done, stolen, or witnessed."

Sam gave his husband a speculative glance.

"What?"

"Simpatico" Sam smiled and reached to thread his fingers into Declan's. "You say things sometimes and it's like you're plucking thoughts from my head."

"Aye, we are simpatico!" Declan leaned in to brush his lips against Sam's. The elevator was a smooth and silent ride, and as Declan cupped Sam's face and deepened the kiss, the doors slid open.

"Uh hmmm!"

Sam and Declan parted, a little embarrassed to be caught snogging in a public elevator. They awkwardly met the gaze of the startled young woman waiting for them. She was small in stature with cropped dark hair and wore a charcoal tweed skirt suit, blouse, and black brogues. The woman couldn't retain eye contact after seeing the men sucking faces, so she turned away and began to walk back down the hall. In an indecently posh sing-song accent, she called,

"Mr Aiken, Mr Ramsay? Hello, I'm Rachel, PA to Mr Soames. If you'd like to follow me I'll take you to his office."

The men followed Rachel down wide hallways, their cheeks pink and mouths trying to hold in mischievous boyish grins at being caught out. Declan knew that Sam had always enjoyed illicit activity at inappropriate locations—it added an element of danger to the thrill of their relationship. But now, Sam appeared to become watchful of his surroundings, remembering where he was and why they were there.

Declan's businesslike mask was securely affixed now too. The offices on either side of the hall were partitioned with floor-to-ceiling glass. Declan hated office spaces like this where you couldn't scratch your arse without someone seeing. The other lawyers and their assistants were at their desks or dealing with legal files and several people passed them in the hall pushing trolleys containing boxes of documents. It appeared to be a huge law firm, and with all of the pies Sir James Aiken's fingers were securely wedged in Declan was sure that his lawyer was a very busy man, and party to many of James' secrets!

"Would you care for refreshments, gentlemen?" Rachel asked as she approached the honeyed oak
office door of the only office without glass walls.

"Water's fine, thank you," Sam said distractedly.

"I'll have a coffee, thanks, white, two sugars. If ye have a wee bickie or two it would be appreciated!" Declan added with a charming, hopeful grin.

"I'll see what I can do," Rachel returned Declan's smile and then knocked on the timber door of Dominic Soames's office.

"Come,"

Rachel opened the office door, "Mr Aiken and Mr Ramsay for your three o'clock, Sir."

Dominic Soames was nearly as round as he was tall, not at all the hot young lawyer Declan expected after all he'd seen of the men, and women in the glass box offices they'd just passed. Soames was in his late sixties; his brown hair was thinning, displaying a freckled ruddy pate. He had small piggy eyes, and his cheeks showed patches of *Rosacea*. His frame was generous, and as he eased up from his chair and reached his pudgy hand across the desk to shake Sam's hand, Declan understood that from the comfortable cut of his suit, the man had a fine personal tailor!

"My husband, Declan Ramsay," Sam introduced. Soames hand then moved to grip Declan's. Dominic Soames had a powerful, solid grip. Declan decided that he was a dependable, straightforward man.

"Good to meet you. Mr Aiken, Mr Ramsay. Can I call you Sam and Declan?" Both men nodded.

"This is a dreadful, dreadful situation", Dominic blustered. Declan knew from the timbre of the man's voice that he was an old Etonian. It was particularly haughty RP English with class-related inflexions that had the effect of making some feel inferior. The privileged used that accent as a calling card, and occasionally as a weapon. In Sir James

Aiken's world, an accent opened doors, or ensured that a door was slammed firmly in your face.

"Please, take a seat gentlemen, Mrs Kimura arrived a few minutes ago. She just popped to the loo." Soames explained as he squeezed himself back into his leather chair and shuffled his bottom like a bird resting on an egg.

There was an air of orderly chaos about Dominic Soames. On his desk a laptop sat to his right, a mountain of document files sat to his left, and in the centre, a legal pad, and a selection of fountain pens. A small double-sided digital clock ensured both he and the client knew how long the meeting had lasted—and Declan thought cynically, how much the client would be billed. A smartphone and a tablet computer were laid in a line in front of the legal pad. Soames was a collector of vintage fountain pens, and an array of very expensive fountain pens was displayed in Perspex boxes on a black timber shelf behind him.

"Forgive me," he said as his laptop pinged with an email. He reached to the right and tapped a few keys.

Rachel knocked on the door and entered with a tray containing their drinks.

"Thank you, Rachel," Soames said absently, still focused on his laptop. The PA placed the drinks on the desk in front of each visitor. Declan's shoulders slumped dejectedly at the lack of biscuits. As she left the office Rachel stood aside to allow Mrs Kimura to enter. Mrs K took the third chair in front of Soames' desk.

Dominic Soames closed the laptop and decisively placed his palms flat on the desk.

"Righty-oh. Now we're all here. It's my deepest regret to meet you under such desperate circumstances. Please be assured that what's said here will not leave the room." Soames took a sip from the glass of iced lime water that Rachel had placed on his desk.

He clasped his hands in front of himself and sat up straighter. "First let me say, I've known James since university, and it's my honour to call him a friend, as well as acting as his lawyer."

Sam was quite taken aback to hear this. He didn't think his father had many friends. There were hundreds of acquaintances—sycophants who would turn up for one of James' parties, but Sam could only think of a few people James would consider a friend.

Morosely, Soames continued. "While I have the greatest faith that with the resources available, you will do what you can to locate James alive and unharmed, we prepared legal contingencies for a range of eventualities." All three agents silently listened as Dominic Soames talked.

"James is considered to be a *high net worth individual* and therefore he has kidnap and ransom insurance with Hawker. The company has worked with kidnap and ransom extraction for more than thirty years. They are the best in the business. Once they're alerted to James's kidnap they will begin their own process to locate him and cover a ransom of up to fifty million dollars."

"Have they been alerted?" Mrs K asked icily. Sam could understand that this revelation had just stepped on her toes. It was a matter of honour for Akiko. She wanted to be the one to save James.

Soames appeared to notice the prickly demeanour of Akiko Kimura and he held his hands up in a placating gesture.

"No, I have not yet notified them. I understand the nature of A.L.L. to its foundations. Using Hawker to locate James is our backup plan, if you would. James expressed that he is confident his people can locate and extract him under any circumstances."

Mollified, Mrs K nodded and then relaxed back into her chair.

"Plans are detailed in a document drawn up by James and myself. The document lays out the process he wishes to be followed in the event of his abduction. As I've said, James is a high-profile individual and knew abduction was a possibility. I never thought it would happen on British soil. But I was wrong, and I'm sorry to learn he was right to be cautious." Soames paused and reached to the left. He collected three Manila document folders.

Soames slid two files across the table, one for Sam, and the other for Akiko.

"Declan, you may read Sam's copy," Soames informed.

Sam picked up the file and opened it, leaning closer to his husband so Declan could also see the contents. They glanced at the first page which they saw contained a list of orders to carry out in the event of James' abduction.

"The document states that, in the event of abduction you, Mrs Kimura, are to continue the daily running of A.L.L." Akiko nodded. This wasn't news to any of them.

"Sir James understood that he would be a prized asset to any dangerous individual or terrorist group trying to make a name for themselves. He's made a list of possible enemies and groups to be investigated in the event of his disappearance."

Sam let his gaze flit over the first page of the document, "So my father has begun the investigation into his own kidnapping!" he observed as he speed-read the first page and handed it to Declan.

"I will, of course, action investigations into these names and organizations when I return to the office." Mrs Kimura said. "What about a ransom?" she added, "We're working on the premise that the kidnapper will seek money to release James. Has he made funds available for a ransom? Mrs K asked her tone matter-of-fact and clinical.

"If you turn to page two, you'll see the paragraph titled *Proof of life.*" They all looked at the paragraph, and Soames read it aloud.

"In the event of abduction:

1. A media blackout must remain in place for at least a month. Media speculation will endanger my life and the lives of operatives in the field assisting in my release.

2. The Metropolitan Police and security services are not to be informed.

3. If a ransom demand is made it can be paid, no matter how high the price. If required, any investment can be liquidated to secure funds for my release. All financial dealings will be arranged by Dominic Soames and signed off by Samuel Aiken.

4. A video must be sent to either A.L.L. or Chance Bailey within two weeks of my abduction. If this does not occur, see clause 5.

5. Chance Bailey has been provided with a hard drive containing compromising material about the activities of my enemies. In the event of my death, they are authorized to upload the to the Anonymous Hacker website for worldwide sharing via news organizations. The result of the revelations contained within the files will be world-changing, and should not be underestimated.

"What is this? What information?" Sam sounded flabbergasted by the revelations. He shot an accusatory glare at Akiko Kimura.

"Did you know about this?"

"I'm not at liberty to say what I know, or do not know," she replied coyly.

"Jesus!" Sam threw his hands in the air infuriated by the non-answer. Could the contents of that hard drive be why there had been two attempts made on Sam's life, and why James had been kidnapped?

"What the hell does my father have in those files? Have you seen them?" Sam fired the question at Dominic Soames,

"No, I haven't viewed the drive. I don't know what information it contains, and if I knew, I wouldn't be at liberty to say – client privilege and all that!"

"If my father dies he'll bring his enemies to their knees as a parting shot!" Sam's fury was burning, choking heat at his sternum. His hands trembled and the folder slipped from his lap.

Soames spoke on by Sam didn't hear a word. Declan slid from his chair and knelt on the floor to collect the documents. Sam's blazing green eyes snapped down to

101

meet Declan's cool silver grey. Declan eased his hand onto Sam's thigh and gave him a reassuring squeeze. The result of the touch was immediate, like the completion of a circuit.

"Thanks," Sam said softly as he took hold of the reassembled documents.

Sam tuned back into the conversation. He tried and failed to suppress his anger as he listened, processed, and then addressed his father's lawyer,

"So, what this all boils down to is that A.L.L has twelve more days to find my father alive, twelve

God-damn days or he'll unleash hell by proxy!"

"Well, when you put it like that, yes," Soames said gravely.

Akiko Kimura closed the Manila file on her lap, clasped it, and stood. "There is no time to sit around and chit-chat, gentlemen. If you need to tell me anything else you know how to contact me, Mr Soames." She bowed her head, then turned and aimed for the door.

Sam and Declan were no longer a part of the investigation, and so now that James's wishes had been shared with those who needed to know there was nothing left to say. If A.L.L didn't find James, the other organization *Hawker* would be notified and take over his extraction, alive or dead. If James died, the world burned. This wasn't only a race against time, it was a competition. How very like James to make his rescue into a game! Sam and Declan shared a troubled glance, and in wordless agreement, they stood to leave.

"Thank you fer the help, Mr Soames, we'll see ourselves

out," Declan said as the awkward meeting ended.

"Sam, could I have a private word?" Dominic Soames asked with a wince in his tone as if he had something delicate to discuss.

"Very well", Sam passed the document folder to Declan.

"I'll wait for ye by the elevator," Declan informed and Sam nodded. When both Declan and Akiko were out of the office Soames eased himself up from his chair and made his way to the other side of the desk. He leaned his hefty frame against the table and said,

"Your father left two letters in my keeping that were only to be given in the event of abduction. One is to be handed to you Sam and the other to your sister Annabelle. I have no idea of the contents. He directed that they are to be read in private." The lawyer opened his suit jacket and drew out two ivory envelopes. He passed them to Sam.

Sam looked at the top envelope and saw his name scrawled in the confident black-inked penmanship of his father's hand.

"Can you please pass the other to your sister?"

"Yes, of course. Belle had her baby yesterday. We're visiting the hospital after we're done here."

"Good gracious! That puts a greater weight on proceedings, doesn't it?"

"It does indeed." Sam slid the letters into his jacket's inner pocket.

"I can see that you have your father's intelligence and tenacity. Please know you can call on me in any capacity. As a lawyer or even for private counsel if that's what you require. I hope that the next time we meet is under better circumstances." Soames gave Sam a paternal pat on the back. Sam nodded his thanks and left the office.

As he strode down the hall towards Declan, waiting by the elevator, Sam decided, no, he would not be fool enough to seek the counsel of any of his father's old friends. As far as he could see, they were all cut from the same duplicitous cloth!

****

CHAPTER 9
THE NOTE

The ominous iron grey clouds that Sam and Declan had observed as they rode the glass elevator down to the ground floor burst the moment they made it to their SUV.

"Christ! That was close!" Declan commented as both men caught their breath and stared ahead at the windscreen, the biblical downpour pummelling the vehicle so violently it shook. Declan couldn't see the road, cars, buildings or people. He turned to Sam and noted that he was sitting with his seatbelt securely fastened, his head rested on the back of the seat, and his eyes closed.

"You okay?"

Sam removed an ivory envelope from his jacket pocket and clutched it. "I will be."

"Visibility's gone to shite. We'll wait a few minutes and listen to the rain. Traffic's at a standstill anyways," Declan decided. He mirrored his husband, laid his head back, and closed his eyes, tuning in to the rhythmic sound of the downpour as it turned from rain into hailstones battering the car. There was a comfort to be found sitting silently with Sam. Declan was sure Sam's cogs were whirring at nine hundred miles an hour, Declan's certainly were! The meeting had been brief, but brutal, and even though Sir James Aiken wasn't present in body, he'd made his requirements perfectly clear. If his people failed to locate him—*failed him*, another organization would step in to take their place. To Mrs K, letting James down would be disrespectful and dishonourable. Declan was sure that the fact she had competition would inspire Akiko to move mountains, just to be the one to return James to his rightful place. But it was the other clause that worried Declan the most. Whatever information James had acquired could do major damage to political regimes, financial sectors, and to particularly dangerous high–value individuals. Having a plan ready to bring down those who'd betrayed him was quite the theatrical farewell in the event of his assassination.

The drumming hailstones soon became a pebble-like pitter-patter as the storm eased off. Without a word, Declan turned the engine on and started the windscreen wipers. The world outside glistened as if the storm had washed away the filth of London's financial district. Declan fastened his seatbelt, checked the mirrors, indicated, and when he had space, pulled out into the flow of traffic. All the while Sam sat in silence, his breaths measured as he clutched at the mysterious envelope.

Declan drove them toward central London. The sudden storm meant that traffic was bumper to bumper through the Docklands back towards the city. He switched on the radio hoping for a traffic report but instead, it was the 80s and 90s hour on his favourite station, Bowie's *Heroes* got Declan tapping on the steering wheel. They stopped for what Declan guessed would be a prolonged wait on the A1203 at Tower Hill.

Sam turned the ivory envelope over and over between his fingers.

"Are ye gonna open that?" Declan enquired breaking the silence between them. The vehicle behind frustratedly beeped its horn. Declan clenched his jaw. The traffic lights had reeled through the cycle three times and not one car moved an inch.

"What does that arsehole behind expect me te do, levitate the fuckin' car?" Declan grumbled.

Sam let out an unconvincing laugh and then revealed, "Soames gave me this envelope...from my father," he let out a despondent breath.

"It feels loaded, like it's weighted with buckshot, and could explode at any moment."

"Well, whatever's in that letter, James didnae want Akiko to know about it, therefore, he doesnae trust her as implicitly as we originally thought."

"True," Sam said taking up Declan's thread, "James wrote letters to be given to me and Belle if he was abducted. Therefore, he had an idea that abduction was a strong possibility, and —" Sam paused and took on a thousand-yard stare,

"Hey," Declan waved a hand in front of Sam's face, "Are ye with me, Westley?"

"He knows," Sam said in a soft, detached tone.

"Who knows?"

"James knows who abducted him. He's been waiting for it, expecting it, planning for it. He expected them to come for him years ago, but for some reason, they targeted me

107

instead," Sam relayed his thoughts with precise cut-glass diction. It was chilling.

"My father has information that he believes makes him untouchable. He's wrong. If he lives the information stays under lock and key, if he dies by their hand, the information is released. But, the thing is, James doesn't have to die... not straight away. He's crossed someone who wants to make him suffer—has made him suffer over many years. This isn't someone who necessarily wants James to die, they want to *best* him, make him feel subservient, make him feel like he's a failure." Sam said. "It's a personal war."

"What about the letter?"

"I don't know." Sam turned and gave Declan a nervous smile, but the green fire that usually burned in his eyes was absent.

"It feels...pertinent... final, you know what I mean?"

"Sam!" Declan let out an exasperated breath. "That is not his final letter. James has a contingency for everything. Christ, he's probably already done a deal wi' God *and* Satan so he can hedge his bets!" he snickered, hoping to lighten the atmosphere.

"Look, I'd wager a hundred quid that this isnae a goodbye letter. Mebe he's givin' ye special orders, or a clue. Gods, it could be a fuckin' winning lottery ticket for all we know!"

Sam smiled at hearing that.

Declan continued in a softer tone, appealing to the playful part of Sam's nature.

"How's about a deal? A hundred quid and a blow job,

108

whoever's right, that's what they'll get." The last bit of the proposed deal made Sam's mouth hitch unwillingly to a filthy grin.

"So, what-de-ye say? Do we have a deal?"

Sam's shoulders slumped in resignation. "Fine," he pouted.

"Good" Declan smiled triumphantly. They were still stuck at the traffic lights so Sam unclicked his seatbelt and leaned to the side and sealed the deal with a kiss. The kiss was a taste of treats to come, and as the sweeping orchestration of *Bittersweet Symphony* played on the radio they lingered...until a horn blared from the car behind again. The couple broke apart.

"Better buckle up, we're finally away!" Declan grinned as the traffic ahead began to move.

Sam fastened his seatbelt, and then without hesitation, he prized the envelope open. He drew out a folded sheet of fine ivory paper and opened it to see a handwritten letter,

Samuel.

Burn after reading.

Text the phrase: Green Grass *to* 545878

"Oh?" It was impossible to not hear the disappointment in that sigh. The letter was most definitely his father's handwriting, but James hadn't even signed his god-damn name. There was no goodbye, no 'lots of love', nothing. Sam was thunderstruck by how devastatingly impersonal the note was. It could well be the final note James ever sent his son and it was absent of even a hint of feeling.

"Well?" Declan prodded.

"When do you want to schedule the blow job?" Sam drawled, unimpressed.

"Ha! I knew it!" Declan slapped the steering wheel triumphantly. "What does it say?"

"Nothing, well, nothing of import! I'm to text a word to the number in the letter. Do you recognize it?" Declan took his eyes off the road for a second and scanned the pitifully short note.

"I dinna have a Scooby what tha' means! Why the hell is nothin' straightforward wi' yer father?" Declan impatiently tapped out a beat on the steering wheel as he waited at the next traffic lights on Southampton Row.

Sam drew out his phone and sent the word *Green Grass* in a text message to the number James had provided. The traffic lights changed from red to amber, then green, the wait feeling like hours when, in reality, it had only been minutes. Sam's knee jiggled nervously as he waited for a response. Declan reached out and laid his hand on Sam's thigh to cease the nervous twitch and offer a little comfort. Then the traffic lights changed and they moved off again. They were close to Regents Park when Sam read out the reply.

Saturday 23:30, Lion, Trafalgar Square.

"Well?" Declan was confused and curious in equal measure. "We've got a date!"

****

110

When Sam and Declan visited the maternity unit for the second time Annabelle was out of bed and dressed in loose-fitting sweatpants and a strappy tee. Baby Rosalind was awake in her cot, her huge wide eyes staring in wonder at the ceiling as her little arms and legs flailed in an uncoordinated dance. Sam delivered Annabelle's letter. When opened it revealed James's wish for Annabelle to go into hiding, and as expected, she was not happy about it.

"We can't just drop everything and leave London. Oliver has to work, and I have a life, and friends, everyone wants to meet Rosa." Annabelle exclaimed in anxious outrage.

"I know. I understand. Look Belle, you know that dad's not an easy man to do business with. He's made some...enemies, and one of those enemies abducted him. Whoever did this, they're not playing games. Dad's worried for your safety, and you know he wouldn't have arranged this if he didn't believe you would be in danger." Sam explained softly. Annabelle looked up fearfully from the page of handwritten text, her tear-filled gaze flitting to Sam and then Oliver.

"I've got six weeks off work," Oliver stated calmly. "I don't care where we are just as long as we're together. I'll do anythin' te keep you an' Rosa safe."

Tears rolled down Annabelle's face. Her shoulders slumped dejectedly and she said.

"But there are things we need...Rosa's things...clothes for ourselves. What do I tell my friends?" she complained, absently handing the letter to Sam to read. He browsed over his father's words and couldn't deny the stabbing pain in his

111

heart. This letter was the antithesis of his letter. Annabelle's note was longer, far more intimate and caring than the cold order in Sam's letter…and it was signed,

Love Dad x

Sam acknowledged a stab of jealousy but schooled his features. He looked up from the page and met his sister's tear-stained gaze.

"So, you'll do as Dad asked?"

"Daddy says we're to go into hiding separately. He said you have a place—"

Sam nodded, complicit in yet another lie. Sam had not been ordered to go into hiding. James had other uses for him.

Declan stepped in after seeing Sam struggling for words. "Look. I'll go te yer house wi' Oliver an' we'll pack a few bags, aye?"

"What about Eileen? She's staying at ours. She just popped home for a nap."

"Shite!" Declan turned an accusatory glare on Oliver, his eyes wide with disbelief.

"What? You knew, I told ye yesterday!" Oliver insisted, sending his brother's steely glare right back. Declan ran his hands through his hair and sighed. Sam met Declan's troubled look. They had both forgotten Eileen was in London.

"In the circumstances, there's no other option. She'll have to go with Belle, Rosa, and Oli." Sam said, "I'll leave it to you and Oliver to break the news." Declan grimaced but didn't argue.

Sam addressed Oliver and Annabelle, "An SUV will arrive outside the hospital at 5 p.m. You'll have a bodyguard who will drive you to the coordinates in the letter."

"This is... *a nightmare!*" Annabelle let out an anguished sob and hid her face in her hands. Oliver crouched beside his wife and pulled her into his arms. This was supposed to be a happy time for the couple, they were meant to be celebrating the birth of their first child, but there was nothing Sam or Declan could do. The safety of all family members was the priority.

****

CHAPTER 10
THE UNIT

Travelling after rush hour didn't mean much in London. Traffic was always bumper to bumper, stop-start, no matter what time you set off. This morning Sam had taken the wheel. It took an hour to reach Heathrow and Sam slowed the vehicle as they approached the storage unit. Immediately he could see something wasn't right. A knot twisted in his belly as he pulled up into the drive to see that, unusually, the gates were closed. Sam turned the engine off and stared at the sign that had once been for *Aiken Self Storage*. It was now covered up by a huge TO LET sign, seeking a tenant for the whole 20,000sq ft warehouse. The key card device had been removed. The only evidence it had been there at all was the shadow where the housing unit had once stood, the bolt holes and taped wires sticking up from the hole in the ground. The blue-painted gates were chained shut and sealed with a heavy, industrial padlock.

"What the hell's goin' on? Did you know about this?" Declan accused stormily and then regretted his tone as he turned to see Sam was as pale as a ghost, shell-shocked by the discovery.

"I'm sorry, I didnae mean—" Declan began, but Sam silently shook his head. Whether that meant the apology was unnecessary or Sam didn't know what was going on,

114

Declan was unsure. Bono was crooning, telling them it was a beautiful day. His gut told him this would not be a beautiful day! The song grated on Declan's nerves now. He reached to switch off the radio.

The men sat listening to the ticking of the cooling engine, both glaring at the storage facility. The car park outside the warehouse was always full of the cars of agents and analysts, and yet now there was only one vehicle remaining. Kitty's sporty red *Fiat*.

"That padlock should be a doddle," Declan said with false cheeriness as he opened the car door.

"I'll do a quick recce of the perimeter," Sam replied flatly. He exited the driver's side of the car and set off running.

At the gate, Declan paused and looked up. The security cameras were gone so no one cared whether the warehouse was broken into. He removed a key ring from his pocket and sorted through the set of keys to find the bump key he wanted. With the padlock swiftly picked up and the chain removed he tossed the heavy metal to the side of the entrance driveway. Declan slid his hand through the bar and pulled the gate locking bolt up, and then he pushed the gates open. As he turned toward the car he saw Sam running back to him.

"The whole place looks deserted, and the security cameras are all gone," Sam revealed, out of breath. Sliding back into the driving seat he drove the vehicle forward into the car park. Declan strode warily across the tarmac towards the entrance door while Sam parked the black SUV beside Kitty's Fiat. Sam then joined Declan at the front door of the storage unit. Declan cupped his hands on the filthy window to peer inside.

"There's not a soul around, it looks like they left in a rush. Forgive me if I'm getting a wee bit freaked out," Sam admitted.

"You're not the only one! Let's err on the side of caution, aye!" After what had happened at HQ there was every reason to be suspicious of this unexpected move. And so, for the second time in a week, they returned to the SUV to avail of the hidden weapons and Kevlar vests from the gun locker under the floor in the boot.

When both were kitted out they headed for the entrance door. Declan stood to Sam's right while Sam tugged at the door. To their dismay, the door flew open. Sam shared a concerned look with Declan before they entered.

The foyer was unlit; the fake leaflets that had once fanned on a small table in the seating area were strewn around on the floor. Again, the security camera that had been housed in the front office was gone, torn off by the look of the tentacle-like live wires that sprouted from the wall. Sam got his torch out and turned it on, letting the light beam arc around behind the counter where the attendant's desktop computer and the signing-in tablet had been removed. The white *Staff Only* door that led to a corridor into the secret storage area was ajar. Sam and Declan exchanged nervous looks. Declan opened the door while Sam sent the beam of torchlight ahead into the corridor. There had been a sensor light here, but no automatic light illuminated the shadows.

"What the hell is going on?" Sam whispered, his gut

116

churning with fear and apprehension. Surely they would have been informed if the unit was to be relocated, Sam didn't understand it. When they arrived at the other end of the hall Declan stepped out into the storage area first. Here, the automatic lights did blink to life, and both men gasped.

"What the ever-loving fuck?" Declan exclaimed, his voice echoing in the cavernous space. The last time they'd visited the unit was just before their last mission. The storage area had contained hundreds of steel cargo containers. But now the storage area echoed with each footstep as they moved forward.

"They're all gone? When, why?" Declan was confused and horrified by this turn of events.

"Not quite *all* gone," Sam added as they turned the corner into the vast main warehouse. He was right. Three shipping containers remained—the two containers that created Sam's secret apartment and Declan's container. The three steel storage containers now stood exposed in the middle of the huge empty space.

"Why didn't anyone tell us?" Sam asked unable to deny feelings of betrayal and abandonment.

"C'mon, mebe someone's around upstairs to tell us what the fuck is going on!" Declan suggested. They sprinted across the warehouse floor to the door to where A.L.L. analysts, tech developers, and Dr Jonah Goldblume worked.

Again, all that remained of the key card terminal was a shadow on the wall. Declan pushed the heavy door open and entered walking across what had once been a vibrant bustling office filled with tables, banks of computer screens

117

and listening stations for collating intelligence. The office was stripped. A worn navy carpet and ghostly sun-bleached stains showed where desks once stood.

"Akiko wouldn't do this without telling me," Sam insisted as he ran towards the stairs. Declan followed noticing how the place had been broken down, and stripped back, removing everything that was associated with the secret agency.

Declan found Sam sitting on the floor outside what had been Goldblume's Forensics lab clutching at his phone, his firearm on the floor beside him.

"I just...don't understand it...why they didn't tell me?" Sam sounded like a bewildered and hurt little boy. "I tried to call Akiko. Her number's dead."

Declan didn't know what to do for Sam. The rug had been pulled from under him, and it was unnecessarily cruel. Declan retrieved his phone and pressed the screen to call Mrs K. An automated voice said: *We're sorry this number has been disconnected goodbye.*

"Fuck" Declan spat. He tried Dr Goldblume and reeled through other agents' numbers getting the same response. Every number associated with A.L.L. had been disconnected.

"They've hung us out te dry! What the hell are we supposed to do now?"

"I guess it's true what they say," Sam offered in a low dreamy voice.

"And what's that?"

"Be careful what you wish for! I've wanted to walk away

for so long. I never considered for a moment that A.L.L. would walk away from me."

"This is Mrs K's doing. Seems she couldnae wait to get hold of the reins. C'mon, let's get what we need from our containers and get out of here."

Declan offered his hand to Sam who took it and Declan pulled him to stand.

****

It was so very strange to step into the musty warehouse and see just three solitary shipping containers. The sensor lights above clicked and buzzed to life as they walked towards their units. Sam was lost in his thoughts, in shock, the sting of abandonment stabbing at his core.

"What's that?" Declan's voice echoed. Sam came back to awareness and he focused on his storage containers. There was something on the front door. He sprinted over, tugged the white envelope from the door, and tore it open to remove a note. A list of numbers had been scrawled across it. Sam knew immediately it was an alphanumeric cypher and he worked it out at a glance. Declan reached Sam's side and looked over his shoulder at the note.

"What is it?"

"It's a simple cypher. It says *Compromised, gone dark. Avoid HQ* "

"No shit Sherlock, nice to let us know." Declan fumed and ran his hands through his hair. He let out a frustrated roar that reverberated off the walls and ceiling. They'd been warned off going back to James's Holland Park residence and now they had no access to tech, no back up, and they couldn't call in favours because that would mean involving the likes of Alexander, who was MI6. No one in the intelligence community could know A.L.L had been compromised. Everyone they worked with had gone to ground and who knew when Mrs K would be back in touch.

"Fuck!" Sam yelled in alarm as the note he clutched in his fingers started to smoke. He tossed it up into the air and watched it cartwheel, once, twice before it erupted into a ball of flame and floated to the cement floor.

"I'm such an idiot, I should have known," Sam said self-depreciatingly as he tossed the envelope into the flames and watched, entranced as they burned. Declan stamped the fire out until a small stain of black ash was all that remained. Then he stepped to Sam and pulled open the Velcro ties of his Kevlar vest, removing it before he removed his own. Sam stood like a mannequin and let it happen. Declan tossed the vests onto the floor, followed by the surplus to requirements holsters and guns. Then he stepped into Sam's personal space and pulled him into an embrace. Sam stood stiffly in Declan's arms at first, before surrendering and melting against his body. After a couple of minutes of holding one another, Sam whispered against Declan's nape.

"She really does want us to take R&R. Looks like we're on our own now, Buttercup," he let out a fragile sigh. "I'm sorry, I should have seen this coming a mile off."

"Ye've got nothin' to be sorry about. I understand why she did it, but, it's fuckin' harsh to pull the rug like this. She coulda given us the heads up and not bailed on us."

"I suppose she thinks she's protecting us in her own

strange way. Now we have no links to A.L.L and I wouldn't know how to get in touch even if we were held at gunpoint."

They had a lot to do now. Sam pulled away and asked,

"Did you call Campbell yesterday? We need to get my containers shipped out sooner than we planned."

"I did, I thought we'd have a few weeks te move stuff out, but I'll call him now and move the arrangements forward." Sam nodded and then turned away as Declan made the call.

Sam unlocked the front door to his unit and stepped inside, the lights blinked on. He bent down to collect the stack of mail for his aliases. *What a pain in the arse.* But, it hit him then that the aliases wouldn't be required for much longer! Sam tossed the mail on the coffee table and then headed through the lounge straight for the bedroom. He had so many clothes, too many for the suitcases he stored there. He would need to choose the best outfits and props for disguises and have the moving company deal with the rest. The two containers would have to be separated and then reassembled at their new location. It was lucky that easy separation had been part of the original design. On hearing the tinny echo of Declan's voice as he ended the call, Sam hollered,

"Buttercup, can you help me pack? We're not coming back here!"

"Aye, the shipping company will load up in two days. Pack up what we can fit into the two cars," Declan informed. He jogged away and hunted around the creepy warehouse offices until he found a supply of flat-pack brown file boxes in one of the stock rooms along with all tape and bubble wrap they could wish for.

Three hours later suitcases were jammed with Sam's clothes and boxes were filled with private paperwork, books, and knick-knacks. Declan hadn't stored many personal belongings at the storage facility. His two boxes contained work-related research, maps, protective clothing, and an array of 'just in case' small weapons, and surveillance devices he'd purchased.

As the hours wore on, it felt eerier and eerier to be in the cold warehouse just the two of them alone. They loaded cases and boxes onto a couple of stolen Heathrow airport luggage trolleys and in four trips had filled the rear seat and boot of the SUV and Kitty's car.

Sam wrote a note for the haulage company explaining the mechanism for separating the containers, and how to disconnect the electrical supply. He closed his unit for the final time, hoping he hadn't left anything compromising in there.

Following Sam in Kitty's *Fiat*, Declan drove the SUV out of the car park, then he got out of the vehicle and reset the chains and padlock. The dull thud of steel clattering against the gates did so with portentous finality.

****

CHAPTER 11

FLOWER OF SCOTLAND

They had a date, but not of the romantic kind. Sam parked in the multi-storey car park closest to Trafalgar Square, and then he and Declan took separate exits.

Sam arrived at the large open plaza of Trafalgar Square first. He was to wait by the lions on the left side of the square facing the National Gallery. Declan would observe from a distance and step in if Sam needed him.

Sam pulled up the zip on his parka to fend off the strong icy breeze that swirled around the plaza and spoke into the tiny Comms device.

"Heading over now," he said with Declan responding,

"Copy, I'm in position."

Trafalgar Square's most famous resident, Lord Nelson, stood in ever-vigilant watch atop a fifty-two-meter tall Corinthian pillar in the centre of the square, guarded at the base by four huge bronze lions. Several fountains with sculpted mermaids, dolphins, and fish-tailed sea gods spewing water decorated the plaza. Busts or life-sized sculptures of the 'historically significant' were dotted at the perimeter.

As one of the most popular tourist locations in London, the plaza was thronged with people even though it was a chilly night. The pedestrianized north terrace was linked to the National Gallery via a wide set of marble steps that was used as a gathering place for groups of young Spanish and Italian tourists. Crowds of noisy teenagers and twenty-something's sat on the steps or around the fountains, laughing, flirting, and drinking from bottles or cans. Native Londoners generally didn't hang around in Trafalgar Square after dark unless they were looking to experience some of the seedier offerings of the city at night.

Sam looked up at Nelson's Column, surprised to see there were a few pigeons around at this late hour. He strode in a circle pretending to view the bronze relief sculptures at the base explaining the historical details of *The Battle of Trafalgar*, and then he paused by the huge bronze lion on the left facing the National Gallery and leaned back against the giant Portland stone plinth.

It was noisy here tonight, with the distracting loud, drunken singing of 'OH FLOWWAHHR OF SCOOTLAND' by a mass of men in Rugby shirts and swathes of tartan. Sam chided himself for not checking the newspaper. It was clear now that there'd been a rugby match that day and from the tribal dregs of fans assembled in the square, one side in white and red, and the other in blue and white, it had been a five-nation's match, England vs. Scotland. From the songs and good humour, the Scots won this game! A few burly bearded men in kilts attempted to chat up Italian and Spanish girls on the steps while Sam stood watchful for whomever he was meeting. High-pitched female laughter made him turn to see the lifting of a kilt and a hairy bare arse wiggling playfully. Sam grinned, memories flooding back of when he and Declan were kilted for Belle and Oliver's wedding. He understood all too well what a temptation it was to see under a Scotsman's kilt!

The meeting was due to occur at 11:30 p.m. and it was now 11:45 pm. No one had approached Sam to talk or give him anything. He was cold and bored. He clutched his phone and occasionally looked at the screen in case the person he was meeting sent further instructions, but it was also a useful tool to avoid eye contact with any of the drunks who paused to sit at the base of the column. Sam didn't have eyes on Declan but he knew he was somewhere close.

"How long should I wait, thirty minutes, an hour?" he said into his collar.

"Decide at midnight, aye?" Declan replied.

"Fine. I'm so bored," Sam whined.

The gathering of Scotsmen increased as the pubs on the streets surrounding the square closed and the clubs denied entrance to those who were too drunk. They all came to the plaza like a siren call and soon enough had begun a rousing rendition of The Proclaimer's song *'(I'm Gonna Be) 500 Miles'*. The only people who had approached him during the time he'd been there were sex workers, beggars and a wiry young man who looked stoned off his gourd.

"You got a light darlin'?" the kid had asked provocatively. Sam suspected he was a rent boy, a pick-pocket, or maybe both.

"Sorry mate, I don't smoke." The youth's dead eyes raked over Sam in consideration, wondering if he was worth a bit more work, but then his gaze flicked to another man who sat on the wall of a fountain, and so he moved off to stalk his prey.

Sam was at a loss. His father had given him the message for a reason—in the event of his abduction; he wanted Sam to get hold of particular information. Leaving and missing the exchange was letting James down... again. But then again, Sam didn't want to hang around all night as there would surely be trouble as the night drew in; there always was when a football or rugby crowd was in town. Eventually, Sam decided he would send a text message to the number again in the morning and set up another rendezvous.

"Abort. Return to zero," Sam said into his collar, then he pulled up the hood of his parka and headed through the centre of the square towards the road that was the quickest route back to the multi-storey car park. A group of Scots fans in kilts of various colours of tartan crowded the exit. Warily, Sam inched through the crowd just as another man came the opposite way. The man collided with Sam sending him barrelling backwards. The crowd of Scotsmen gave a loud cheer of "Wahey" as one of them caught Sam and steadied him. The pedestrian who had knocked Sam over held his hands up in surrender,

"Sorry, bud, my fault, no offence," he said in a raspy, whisky and cigarette-laden Glaswegian accent. Sam didn't want to start anything, so smiled, said "No worries mate," and continued on his way.

By the time Sam arrived back at the car park, Declan was sitting in the SUV driving seat. Sam dragged the passenger door open and got in, slamming the door with fury.

"What a fucking waste of time that was," he spat in agitation. "Did you see anyone approach me and chicken out?"

"Nope, apart from the rent boy and the drunks no one attempted to make contact."

Sam doubted himself for an instant then. Was the rent boy the one who was supposed to pass the information to him? Had he turned away his contact? Shit! Reaching into his pocket to retrieve his phone Sam paused and turned to face Declan his eyes narrowed in confusion.

"What?"

From his pocket, Sam drew out his phone with a small gift card envelope.

"How did this get here?" Sam held up the envelope. There was no name on the front just the words EYES ONLY written in his father's hand.

"I thought you said—" Declan turned in his seat, equally confused.

"I *didn't* meet anyone."

"You musta met someone if that was put in yer pocket without you knowing!"

Sam sat back in his seat and his shoulders slumped as he scrolled through memories of the time he'd spent waiting in Trafalgar Square. He'd spoken to the rent boy and a drunk. "No one touched me," Sam insisted. "Not one of the people who approached me at the lion statue got close enough to put something in my pocket."

"Somebody musta touched ye. Unless spies are using

127

magic these days!" Declan suggested unhelpfully.

"Did you see anything?" Sam quizzed.

"Nope. I was watching ye from the north terrace. I saw a few people chat with you for a few moments but nothing was exchanged and no one got close enough to touch you," he agreed.

Then it hit Sam. "The Jammy bastard! He was hiding in plain sight…among a group of Scottish Rugby fans."

"What?"

"After I messaged you to abort I was trying to get through a crowd of them and a Glaswegian guy barrelled into me. I bet it was him, or the bloke who stopped me from landing on my arse. It could have been either of them, or they could have set it up together."

Declan grinned. "Well, ye do have form for bumping inte Scotsmen!" he joked. "Now let's get home and see what the hell's in that envelope."

****

At home, Sam used a nail to prize up a corner of the envelope seal. He removed two items: a typed Fortnum and Mason gift card message and a security pass card with a Ministry of Defence logo on one side and a QR code on the other. The gift card message was three printed words: *Dare.Bonds.Runs* and beneath it, a thirteen-digit number that Sam recognized as a barcode. So, James had supplied them with a security pass, three random words, and a bar code, but what did they mean? What were they for?

Sam stared at the words and code, his mind reeling. Declan picked up the security pass card. He turned it over in his fingers.

"Why's there no name, photo ID or signature required fer this? Its access for a M.O.D site, but where?"

"I have an idea!" Sam reached for his laptop. He pulled up the web page of a location app. The app mapped the whole world in one-meter squares and each square was given three words to identify the exact location. He typed in the three words James had supplied: *Dare.Bonds.Runs.* The location for these three words appeared on a map of the UK. Sam zoomed in to see the one-meter square linked to those three words was the side entrance door for what appeared to be a recycling facility in Hampshire. Sam's sea-green eyes sparkled as he looked up from the screen and met Declan's curious gaze.

"James gave us the key to Pandora's box!"

****

CHAPTER 12

ARCHIVE

Three days later, Declan was driving alone in a rented gunmetal grey Land Rover, a big bag of Maltesers and a bottle of water was on the passenger seat, and his phone was connected to the in-vehicle system.

Declan took the M4 and then the M25 motorway out of London. At the Thorpe Green roundabout, he followed the sign for the M3 to continue travelling west toward Hampshire. A red *Fiat* was in front of Declan all the way.

His phone rang and he accepted the call.

"Hello lover," Sam said with a smile in his voice. "Isn't this the life of glamour you signed up for!"

"Aye, we're livin' the dream. Whatcha eating?"

"I forgot I had a bag of Munchies in the glove compartment, it was a nice surprise."

Declan's belly grumbled.

"I know what you're thinking, but there are no rest stops on this stretch of motorway, so suck it up Buttercup!"

"Fine, but save me some. I'll try an' survive on my last three Maltesers. The traffic's not too bad though. We'll make it in good time."

"Okay, keep an eye-out for anyone trailing us! If you see anything suspicious in the rear view, tell me. We'll spilt up and meet at the location."

After just an hour on the road, Declan followed the Fiat and pulled off the M3 motorway following the A331 to Aldershot.

Known as the *'Home of the British Army'*, the garrison town of Aldershot had a long history of military and intelligence connections. Aldershot had the same supermarkets, coffee shops, bookies, fast food restaurants, and DIY stores as any other English provincial town. But while the car sped past pedestrians going about their daily business, there were uniformed soldiers in the mix, and road names like Government Road and Ordinance Road reflected the military history.

Declan trailed the red car along Ordinance Road and then turned onto North Lane. The car took a right on Alpha Road into the Spring Lakes Industrial estate. The estate was a mundane area of low-rise warehousing made of red brick and corrugated steel roof panels. Housing and offices were intertwined with manufacturing businesses that ranged from glazing, auto gears, plastics, and packaging products, plus the ubiquitous builder's merchant and recycling centre.

Declan overtook Sam and parked up at the curb close to their destination, the *Blackwater Recycling Center*, while Sam did another circuit of the side roads before returning to the location. The recycling centre was a huge warehouse with blue metal sheet walls and a grey corrugated steel roof. Declan noted that the property was gated and surrounded by grey steel palisade fencing with sharpened tips that would rip a new arsehole for anyone who tried to climb over. Security cameras were secreted beneath the sodium lamps on either side of the entrance to the facility. Declan called up Google Maps on his phone to remind himself of the terrain and what they'd discovered before setting out on their journey.

This recycling centre was just another banal warehouse in an industrial estate that mirrored thousands of such estates all over the country. But inside this building, there was information that James needed them to see.

The birds-eye view of the warehouse on the map app showed that, what conventionally would have been a car park for thousands of warehouse workers, was overtaken by huge recycling skips lined up to receive plastics, old household goods, wood, metal and electrics. There were loading bays along the back wall of the warehouse facing the skips. Traditionally these would be used for the delivery and collection of products by heavy goods vehicles. From their research, they discovered that members of the public were required to book a timeslot to get access to drop-off recyclables. No one was given access to the warehouse itself. Both Declan and Sam believed that the warehouse was a Ministry of Defence archive facility hiding in plain sight. If you didn't need to know the address of a Secret Service document store, then you didn't know!

A sentry stood at the gate barrier, and there was an area along the left side of the warehouse where cars specifically accessing the warehouse could park. Recycling Supervisors wearing high visibility vests ensured whoever was on site was supposed to be there, and that no one lingered once they'd dumped their recycling. It appeared to be a very efficient operation.

****

Kitty's car pulled up to the imposing front gates of the Blackwater Recycling centre. A security man wearing a hi-vis jacket stepped forward, a scanning device in his hand. Kitty smiled at him and flashed her lashes. She retracted the driver-side window and held out the laminated card with the QR code. The sentry didn't say a word, just scanned the code, and when his device beeped the guard nodded to Kitty and held a thumb up to a security camera positioned above the gate. The automated lock clicked and the steel and barbed wire gate slowly opened. Kitty drove into the recycling centre, parking in the car park closest to the entrance that was marked by the three words on the gift message card.

Kitty grabbed her handbag from the passenger-side footwell and then stepped out of the car. She was wearing slingback kitten heels, black stockings, and a grey marl knee-length skirt suit. Her blond tresses fell over her shoulders. All business, she sauntered away from the vehicle and as she did so, pressed the key fob to lock the car.

The three words that James had left for Sam were the location of the doorway ahead. Kitty did a primping hair flick and used it as a cover to check out the security camera situation. There were security cameras everywhere, on each telegraph pole, the exterior floodlights, and attached to the lamps beneath the roof guttering. Sam couldn't break wind without being watched.

Kitty tip-tapped up the steps to stand at the yellow door.

133

She found a QR code reader and above the door, a tiny camera. Kitty pressed the code card to the reader and looked up at the camera giving her best nonchalant, zero-fucks stare. The door clicked, she pushed it open and stepped into an anteroom.

The anteroom was bare. A door with a picture window opposite looked out onto a vast storage system. Sam stepped forward and took a closer look. The facility appeared to be automated and unmanned. It was rather magnificent. Instructions beside the door read:

1. Viewers must present their QR code to access the main facility.

2. Access to the stacks and facility floor is strictly prohibited.

3. Please go to the computer terminal situated on the other side of this door. Key in the code of the bin you require.

4. To your left and right are private viewing rooms. Go to your allotted viewing room and await delivery of your document bin.

5. The Official Secrets Act 1911 criminalizes espionage by prohibiting certain conduct carried out with a purpose prejudicial to the safety of interests of the UK, including obtaining or disclosing information which would be 'useful to an enemy'.

No documents are to be removed from this facility.

Sam considered the instructions and then he pressed the QR code card to the scanner. He opened the door and stepped out onto a metal mezzanine that wrapped around the interior of the warehouse. The scent of paper and dry air reminded Sam of the temperature-controlled conservation unit at the Imperial College archive—and a flash of the filthy things he and Declan had done in there! He smiled privately at the memory. The scent and lack of humidity were where comparisons with the Imperial College archive ended. Sam let his watchful eyes roam as he took in the enormity of the facility. He'd never seen anything like this place. A state-of-the-art automated storage and retrieval system had been installed in this bog-standard warehouse shell. The facility was filled from floor to ceiling with shelves containing aluminium store and retrieve document bins. The rows and rows of shelves held thousands of bins. The shelves were connected by a network of steel cables giving them stability and enabling tracking devices to travel up and down the cables. Each bin location had a barcode and robot cranes whizzed up and down the lines of shelving, depositing new files, or retrieving rectangular aluminium bins for viewing.

Sam looked left and right along the mezzanine and saw ten doorways on either side, each with a light above. One light, for the sixth room on the left, was green, the rest were red. Sam had no idea if the other rooms were occupied or not. He removed the Fortnum and Mason message card from Kitty's handbag and typed in the code shown at the bottom. When he pressed ENTER the result was returned as correct, and the instructions on the screen told him to go to viewing room six.

Kitty strode to the left and opened the door for room six then stepped in. It locked automatically on closing. Inside the windowless room, there was a chair and table, and opposite, a hatch. Sam placed Kitty's handbag on the table, drew out the chair, and sat. He removed his phone from the handbag and saw the time was 11:30 a.m. He also noticed that there was no phone signal, and no WIFI; therefore the facility had a signal jammer. This meant that if something went wrong he couldn't communicate with Declan.

Sam waited, anxiously drumming his fingernails on the table. He found a packet of Polo mints at the bottom of the handbag and ate one, and then he sat staring at the hatch. He glanced around at the camera affixed above the door. The unmanned facility was creeping him out. He did not feel comfortable knowing some anonymous person was sitting in a room somewhere watching him, noting his every move. How long would he be made to wait? Glancing at his phone Sam saw that only ten minutes had passed even though it felt like thirty. A clunking, whooshing sound stole his attention, and then the light on the hatch blinked green. Sam stood, strode around the table, and opened the hatch. He lifted the aluminium document bin out and carried it to the table. He sat and perused the metal container. There was a keypad on the front of the closed box and a label that instructed the viewer to input the code. He typed in the same code and the lid clicked open.

A file sat on the top of a small mountain of weathered foolscap notepads and several leather-bound diaries. The file was of Ministry of Defence origin, stamped EYES ONLY, and the name on the front of the file was:

Alfred Oscar Moxley.

A shiver ran down Sam's spine. "Christ!" he exclaimed in a stunned whisper. This was what his father had wanted him to see! Sam had known the late Professor Moxley well, or so he'd thought, and he'd considered the man to be a kind of father figure. He recalled that when his university tutor and mentor suddenly died all of Moxley's papers were impounded and taken away. Sam remembered that he and his fellow students were confused as to why the contents of Moxley's room appeared to be some kind of security risk. The dashing Alexander Deveraux had arrived on the scene as Moxley's temporary replacement, and it was then that young Sam had fallen in love for the first time. Alexander's placement was, in hindsight, convenient, and Sam now knew that Alex had been installed by MI5 as Moxley's replacement not only to deal with his Linguistics students but also to do Moxley's other job—protect Sam. Alexander had insisted that James was not recruited by Moxley, but Sam wasn't so sure. What else had Professor Moxley been up to that made his papers end up in a Ministry of Defence secret archive?

Aware of time limitations for his task, Sam removed everything from the bin and laid the items side-by-side on the table, trying to work out what pertinent information his father wanted him to find. The full contents of this particular document bin amounted to a pile of thirty-three manila folders, the first of which was Moxley's personal MoD file, ten foolscap pads of notes in the professor's recognisable pigeon scratch, eight journals, three scrapbooks with newspaper cuttings and one small address book. This haul was not the sum of Moxley's papers. Sam recalled the man's rooms were filled floor to ceiling with books and paperwork. The Secret Service had scanned through

Moxley's academic trove and put these items into a separate pile for a reason.

Sam placed the first manila file in front of him on the table and then opened it. Over several minutes using a notepad on his phone Sam catalogued the new information about his erstwhile tutor. No warning alarm sounded as Sam transferred the notes to his phone. It was curious, but Sam vowed to continue until he was told he couldn't!

From the photo affixed on the first page of the file, Alfred Moxley had been a good-looking young man, but to Sam's utter surprise, he wasn't Irish. Alfred Oscar Moxley was born in 1947 in Surrey to English parents and studied Linguistics at Trinity College, Dublin, in 1965. He then moved on to a Master's degree at Kings College, Oxford in 1970. It was there he was recruited by the Secret Service Principal Scientific Officer Charles Wright. After graduation, Alfred worked 'officially' as a crypto-linguistic translator at the Foreign Office for eight years before returning to Oxford to become an academic and a clandestine recruiter for the Secret Service. Over his years with the SIS, he was a spymaster. Between 1978 and 2010 he vetted and recruited 164 students to be fast-tracked into the agency after they graduated. The file held a list of the names of those Moxley recruited. Some of the names were redacted, and many were marked as deceased. Sam's finger trailed down the page of dates and names as he searched for the year 1981 when his father was a fresher at *Magdalen College*. There in black type were the names of the four students Moxley had recruited that year. Among the names

138

was James Samuel Aiken.

"Shit!" he said taking a shaky breath. Here was proof that Alexander was wrong. Alfred was James's recruiter. Sam hurriedly grabbed a leather-bound journal. This journal was filled with notes made in shorthand. He read, driven on by curiosity and a background tremor of fear as he feverishly consumed the contents of the first few pages. Sam paused and his jaw slackened with horror when he comprehended what he was reading. Bile churned in his gut. He squeezed his eyes shut and shook his head as if the action could dislodge what he'd read from his brain. This journal held the Faux-Irishman's clinical observations of students. It appeared that Moxley watched those students he wished to consider for recruitment to the SIS. There was something distinctly creepy about the details he went into that made Sam reconsider all of his interactions with a man he'd believed was an intelligent, gentle giant behaving in a fatherly manner toward him. Moxley observed which university clubs the students joined, who their friends were, which pubs they favoured, and particulars about their personalities. From notes in the margin on the first and second pages of the journal he saw the letters *MKY e/o LS,* and *BG e/o TY,* he deciphered that e-backslash-o meant 'eyes on'. Therefore, it appeared that Alfred had manipulated and coerced other students to spy on his targets in classes, in pubs, in their halls, and at student parties. He even listed the sexual liaisons he received Intel about. To have this kind of personal access, he must have gotten friends of the targets to spy on them. Nowadays such invasive behaviour would

139

be seen as grooming and stalking.

Next, Sam moved onto a scrapbook. It was full of precisely organized notes and yellowing newspaper clippings from the 1970s, the sticky tape decaying and losing adhesion on some clippings. The reports focused on the cold war, which, from the care and consideration Moxley took in organizing the clippings, was something he was obsessed about. He'd added notes in English beside the news stories, giving his impression of international events, and the way he believed the world would change once the USSR eventually fell. He believed that Oxford University, with its long history and wealthy connections, was THE place to build the cogs and wheels of the future. He believed the world was at the cusp of huge societal change and in looking to the future, he wrote passionately about his responsibility to choose the men who would be the future leaders. This, said by any other educator would sound like they took their responsibility to teach seriously. However, when juxtaposed with the notes, newspaper clippings and the stalker's diary entries it came together to form a more sinister picture in Sam's mind.

Turning the page of the scrapbook a clipping fell out and fluttered onto the floor. Sam leaned down to retrieve it. The news report was about a bombing at Canon Street Railway Station in the late 70s. Mr Irvine Aiken, a civil servant working at the Foreign Office was injured and later died in hospital. Sam's blood ran cold. He knew next to nothing about his extended family, apart from the fact they were dead. Sam's mother, Rosalind was a De Monfort. Her side

140

of the family had been wealthy, not his father's, and her inheritance, which passed to James on her death, was the seed from which James' empire grew. Sam had known the name Irvine Aiken was his grandfather and his grandmother had been named Agnes. Both sets of grandparents were gone before he was born. It now made a little sense to Sam why James had difficulty connecting with his son—because he'd spent some of his youth without a father.

Amid the swirl of emotions whipped up by his discoveries, Sam began to grow anxious. There was so much information in these files. He couldn't remove the documents and if he was gone for the hours required to read everything, Declan would become concerned and probably try to break in! Sam stared at the archive laid on the table before him and considered the contents again. He picked up another journal that had gilt embossed text on the cover. *Diary 1981.* He flicked through pages that contained notation markings in shorthand. Sam didn't have the time to read it all, but at the back of the A5 diary, he noticed that the endpaper looked like it had been tampered with. Sam threaded a very handy false nail beneath the paper and the yellowed adhesive gave way easily. Hidden behind the endpaper was a photograph. The photo featured twenty-six young men dressed in tailcoat suits, and one older man in the centre wearing a professor's cap and gown. All of the men looked fresh-faced, in their late teens or early twenties, apart from the bearded rotund, ruddy-faced professor who stood proudly with his boys. Sam was quick to notice young James Aiken. It struck Sam immediately what the photo

141

reminded him of—the photo of the Bullingdon Club from 1983 that the media printed every time one of the reprehensible, privileged Tories was involved in some kind of sordid scandal. If the members of that secret club had become elites, business moguls and prime ministers, what had the men from the Alphabet Club been groomed to become? Sam shuddered with the enormity of this discovery. He stared at the faces in the photograph, at Alfred, a man he'd trusted, and at his father, who Sam was loathed to admit, was his reflection! It hit Sam then, the realization that he'd seen the photograph before, but he couldn't recall where. Sam surreptitiously took a photograph of it on his phone, still waiting for an alarm to go off, or for someone to barge in and confiscate the device, but nothing happened. It was all very strange.

Had James directed Sam to the archive to see the diaries and photographs to understand Alfred's true nature or was there something else? What did this have to do with his abduction?

Sam closed his eyes and took a few deep calming breaths. When he opened them and perused the contents on the table a small address book caught Sam's attention. He picked up the brown leather-bound book, opened it, and turned to the first page. It was, as expected, a pre-printed page with spaces for the owner to fill in their personal details, but on this page, none of the details had been added. There was just one ink-scrawled word made up of four letters.

S-I-F-R.

Sam's heart skipped a beat. The word *Sifr* sounded like

the English word 'cypher' when read, but Sam was fluent in Arabic, and he knew that when translated this word meant *ZERO*. Sam licked his lips, and his heart drummed with excitement. Moxley had loved wordplay and the title alone was drenched in significance. Sam turned the page and saw the book contained alphabet tabs for each page. He flicked through the book to the end. Each page contained lines of Arabic script, but it wasn't as straightforward as that! This book, this tiny book was Sam's heroin. He knew in an instant that the alphabetized book titled *ZERO* was in fact a book of cyphers. He wasn't sure what kind, but he wouldn't stop until he cracked the code. Twenty-six cyphers for twenty-six names. Sam didn't need to see any more.

Kitty feigned indifference, closed the address book, and sighed deeply. Then she tossed the address book onto the table among the detritus of paperwork. She pushed back on her chair and stood, shoulders slumped, appearing dejected. Kitty then collected the journals, diaries, foolscap pads, scrapbooks, and manila files and placed them all back into the aluminium storage bin. She closed the container and carried it back to the open hatch. She loaded it in, closed the hatch, and pressed the button, hearing the whoosh of the automated crane returning the bin to the main archive. Kitty then picked up her phone and dropped it into the handbag. She threaded the bag onto her shoulder and made her way to the door. Kitty looked up at the camera above the door and arranged her long blonde hair over her shoulders. The door lock buzzed and released.

Sam readied for something—an alarm, a security officer,

something, but he met no resistance. Was everyone on their lunch break?

Kitty kept her straight, aloof posture as she strode along the metal mezzanine, her heels making a sharp clinking sound as they struck the surface. She opened the main door, stepped into the anteroom, and then within seconds stepped out into blinding daylight and a soft, welcome breeze whipping her blond tresses. She met no security agents, and heard no alarms—but, Sam reminded himself, it didn't mean an alarm hadn't been raised. Paranoid, Sam wasn't slowing down until he was in the car and past the security gate!

****

Declan had been getting nervous and was relieved to see the red Fiat leave the archive facility. He followed Kitty to the Tesco Superstore on the outskirts of Aldershot Town and watched as Kitty parked up. He took a parking space. Observing in his rear view mirror, Declan saw Kitty exit the car with her handbag and a small rucksack. Declan couldn't deny that Sam in drag gave him ball ache. He smiled lecherously, watching those delectable long legs and that sexy wiggle of her arse as she strode into the store. Declan remained vigilant in case they'd been followed. He tapped on the steering wheel and sang to Hall & Oates, "Kiss On My List" which was playing on the Everything 80s radio station.

Minutes later Sam sauntered out of the supermarket, wearing blue jeans, a long sleeve white tee and trainers, the disguise of Kitty Franklin now abandoned. Declan smiled as his husband strutted across the tarmac to the soundtrack of Bowie's 'Let's Dance' moving in time to the rhythm of the

144

song as if they'd choreographed this exit perfectly. Declan pressed the horn to get Sam's attention. Sam waved and grinned. He strutted to the SUV with an unhurried swagger, opened the passenger door, and got in with the rucksack, handbag, and a supermarket bag filled with food and drinks for the journey home.

"I'm dumping Kitty's car, let's go! I've been a naughty, naughty boy. We'll need to take an alternate route back to London," Sam announced abruptly as he dragged the seatbelt over his chest and fastened it. Declan checked his mirrors then reversed out of the parking space and drove toward the junction that led onto the motorway.

"And why's that? What did ye do? Did ye see someone following?"

"No. I um...stole something from the Ministry of Defence archive—not sure if they've noticed yet!" he announced matter-of-factly.

Declan didn't blink at hearing that. He grinned. "Good… we'll take the pretty route. I hope ye've got some sandwiches in that bag, I'm famished."

****

CHAPTER 13
DISTRACTION

The pretty route home consisted of a two-hour detour taking country roads, passing through small villages and hamlets as Declan drove north toward Ascot before taking the M3 east back into London. Sam made no attempt to fill Declan in on what had happened inside the archive before he fell asleep. They were both comfortable with shared silence, so Declan focused on the road and tapped his fingers to the tunes on the radio. Declan reassured himself that they were both safe, no one was following, and Sam would talk when he was good and ready.

Good and ready just so happened to be when the SUV ground to a halt, stuck in traffic on the Hammersmith flyover. It was 3.30 p.m and Sam had spent the last two hours with his eyes closed and head resting on the passenger door window. He righted himself, extended his arms above his head, and wriggled to stretch his spine in the tight confines of the car. He reached into the supermarket carrier bag for a bottle, unscrewed the cap, and took a long glug of water. When he was done Sam sagged back into his seat.

Declan reached out, an affectionate lopsided grin on his face as he finger-combed Sam's hair. Sam pushed into the simple, intimate gesture.

"Yer lookin' like a hedgehog on one side," Declan

informed, "You okay love, ye conked out?"

"Sorry babe. I haven't been sleeping well and I guess the road trip knocked me for six," Sam explained, letting out an irrepressible yawn.

"Aye, I can see that." Declan gripped the wheel as the cars in the traffic jam moved on a little.

"I've waited so patiently for you to read me in on what you discovered, so spill, what was inside that warehouse?"

"An automated Ministry Of Defence archive, just like we thought. Apart from the guard on the gate, I didn't see another human."

"Wow! That's pretty fucked up. And?"

"My father wanted me to see papers belonging to the late Professor Alfred Moxley."

"The guy who recruited Alexander to the SIS?"

"Yep. The Professor with a side job as a spymaster. He recruited dad too, and some of the notes in his files made my skin crawl."

"Fuck! Were there any clues to tell us where James could have been taken?"

"I wish. Let's just say I now have more questions than answers about this whole affair."

Declan's shoulders slumped dejectedly, and he let out a sigh. "I swear te God, it's like we're stuck in a spider's web an' every time one of us get a limb free something else sticks," he grumbled.

"I know...I know," Sam laid a hand on Declan's firm thigh and gave a reassuring squeeze. The silence that fell between them developed a fragile quality as Sam's whirring mind decided what to reveal first.

"Have you ever discovered that someone you believed you knew well wasn't who you thought they were?"

"Of course, we work in covert affairs, it's pretty much rule one in the Spy 101 handbook!" Declan chuckled. "Ye don't seem yerself love. What was in the archive that's rattled ye so much?"

Sam then proceeded to share the details of all he's learned from the spymaster's archive, of how the man Sam had believed to be a mentor had stalked students, used his position of power to coerce students to watch their friends and report back to him about their personal activities. Sam unloaded the whole disturbing weight of Moxley's duplicity as the traffic on the Hammersmith flyover moved at a snail's pace. Declan listened, silent and stony-faced at hearing a story that had developed over four decades.

"I think it was Moxley's death that made the Alphabet Club unravel."

"So what do you think Mox was really up to? What was the remit of the club? They certainly weren't the regular drinking and debauchery society that the posh boys flock to," Declan observed.

"He selected a group of young men who he planned to mould to his design to be the next generation of leaders in politics, industry, finance."

"We need te find out who they are," Declan asserted.

"Yes. I agree, finding their identities should be our next imperative."

Declan gave Sam a side glance to see he was frustratedly

148

biting his bottom lip. "But not today. Love, I'm serious, you're frazzled. Frankly, the last few weeks have been a bag o' shite and neither of us has stopped for a breather."

"But we don't have time to stop. If we don't find out what my father was involved in, I just—"

Declan reached out and with the back of his fingers, caressed Sam's cheek and then cupped it.

"If we keep going when we're wrecked we'll miss something. Let's say we put this fuckery to bed and deal with it tomorrow. We are, after all, supposed te be on R&R."

"Fine," Sam sighed resignedly, "You're right. I'm coiled up like a spring. I'll need something to take my mind off this clusterfuck. Something physical. A run or some yoga. Maybe, a swim at the Connaught Spa pool?"

"I could do wi' a swim," Declan agreed. "And then think I can manage to find a way to distract ye!" Declan took his eyes off the road for a second and met Sam's curious gaze. The look that passed between them was full of naughty possibilities.

****

Living across the road from a five-star hotel meant that not only could they avail of the restaurant, bar, gym, salon and spa, but with a little monetary sweetener their garments would be added to the hotel dry cleaning service. After a swim, and then dinner, Sam collected their bagged suits and shirts but he knew better than to hang them up. The walk-in closet was the domain of a control freak!

Declan busied himself with his lines of expensive suits, shirts and ties, all colour coded of course. When the

149

garments were organized and hung in the appropriate places Declan opened the wardrobe where they stored their luggage, and pushed his hand into one of the suitcase pockets. He grinned mischievously and pulled out a surprise for Sam that, in the drama and angst of their return home, he'd not gotten around to sharing.

While on the previous mission in Vienna, Declan had gone shopping! Sam was an emotional mess and he needed to be distracted. This was Declan's mission now. He strode down the hall and paused in the double doorway to the living room. He groaned, scratched his bare hairy chest, and reached up to grip the door jamb, displaying his toned physique while wearing small ass-less shorts and a leather chest harness with rings that framed the nubs of his taut dark nipples. Declan's stance in the doorway went unnoticed for several seconds—Sam was staring at the TV screen, not even blinking.

"Uh hmmm," Declan prodded, and Sam startled. He turned to face Declan "Sorry, I don't know where I—Oh!" and then he exploded with laughter.

"Hey!" Declan exclaimed sounding affronted and a little emasculated. This was not the reaction he'd expected, but Sam was distracted so he supposed it would do.

Sam turned off the TV, tossed the remote control onto the couch, and stood. "Well hello handsome," he drawled playfully as he prowled towards Declan taking his fill of the straining cock stuffed into shorts bearing the branded name *Bum Chum*. The taut musculature of Declan's shoulders and chest framed by the leather harness seemed to delight him.

Sam stood in front of his husband and pouted with faux outrage.

"You went sex-shop shopping without me?"

"Aye, yer damn right I did! I got these in Vienna. You'd have bought the whole fuckin' shop!" Declan laughed, his skin prickling with the thrill of Sam's intense gaze raking over him.

"I bought ye a little something too. Come and try it on!" Declan invited. Sam leaned in and claimed a kiss.

"What is it? Did you buy me *Bum Chums*?" Sam asked with the delight of a kid on their birthday. Sam had a fetish for underwear and so Declan's plan to help Sam forget for a little while would work just fine. Sam hooked a finger under the leather chest harness, turned, and Declan was led by his lover to their bedroom where three items waited on the bed. A shiny steel butt plug with holes in the flared end, a steel cock ring, and several lengths of thin gauge black Shibari cord. Sam strode ahead to inspect the presents.

"You didn't buy me underwear?"

"I most certainly did, but you won't need them quite yet!" Declan paused behind Sam and threaded his arms around his husband's trim waist. He sprinkled soft kisses over the nape of Sam's neck, and Sam moaned and wriggled appreciatively.

"So… uh….what's… uh all this then?" He groaned with the pleasure of Declan's talented mouth nipping and grazing at the places on his throat that made his knees weaken.

"D'ye trust me?"

"Of course, darling!"

151

"Let's get ye undressed then. This is gonna be fun!"

****

Sam lay silent and pliant while Declan prepared him, his eyes sparkling with excitement. Minutes later he was wearing a shaft ring harness against his gorgeous pale skin. Four lengths of the Shibari cord were looped around the steel cock ring at equidistant intervals. Declan had then threaded the cold metal ring onto Sam's half-hard dick, easing it to the base. Two strands of Shibari cord fell between Sam's balls. The two other strands were pulled across Sam's hips and beneath his pert arse cheeks. Declan collected each of the four cords and threaded them into the holes at the flared end of the steel butt plug. After prepping Sam with a slick lube-covered finger, Declan slid the plug into Sam's hole, enjoying the sharp gasp from Sam as the cold steel housed itself inside his heated passage. With burning eye contact and a wicked smile, Declan adjusted and tied the cords. When Sam flexed his hips even a tiny amount the cords pulled the cock ring flush to his body.

The vision of Sam laid out on their bed with the dark strands of Shibari cord running over his pale skin, defined hips, and between his balls was so much more than Declan expected from three such innocuous items. But put them together and BAM!

"How does it feel, love?" Declan asked as he sat back on his haunches and ran a light finger up Sam's thigh.

"Oh, God!" Sam whimpered as Declan's delicate touch made his body move which resulted in friction in all the right places.

152

"To say I'm stunned would be an understatement! You are…uhh… full of surprises Buttercup! How did you find out how to do this? The pressure… ahhh….the ring pressing on the base of my dick… on the ligaments," he lightly wriggled his hips and groaned, "It's nearly the same feeling as being balls deep inside you!"

"Aye. That's what the guy in the Sex Shop told me would happen. The ring presses on yer kegel muscles and forces yer cock to stand straight. As ye get more aroused it stops the blood flowing back. If you move, even a tiny bit the cords tug and make the ring push down and the plug push up."

Sam experimented, wiggling his hips and then he thrust up. "Uggghhh, fuck… yes, God's Buttercup. This is… delicious torture!" he gasped. "Get your phone, take a picture, I want to see what you see," Sam encouraged.

Declan was as hard as an iron girder watching how aroused Sam became wearing the shaft ring harness. He left the bed, reached for his phone and took a few shots of Sam helpless and hard, his pupils blown wide with desire. He returned to the bed and showed Sam the image.

"Wow. This is smokin'!"

"I know. My balls are fit te burst wi' how much I want you."

"So take me. I'm all yours," Sam said, cupping Declan's bearded jaw and drawing him down for a kiss.

"Hmmm. Not so fast! I'm gonna take my sweet time with you, love. Keep yer hands above yer head. I want te see yer fingers touching the headboard!" Declan instructed.

He understood that Sam had deep trauma concerning restraint, so Declan never restrained him when they made love. The only binding they both needed was the invisible, unbreakable, bond of love that held them together.

Declan leaned closer and before he kissed Sam, he whispered, "Don't let go!" The words and their significance made Sam's body shudder as Declan plundered his mouth. When Declan drew back tears of emotion had leaked from Sam's eyes. This was perfect.

Declan fixed on Sam's cock as if it was a science experiment then stroked the length slowly and gently with one finger. He loved how responsive Sam was. As if knowing its master, Sam's cock twitched and jumped, seeking sensation. Sam writhed, desperate for more friction, but Declan wouldn't allow it. Declan began the teasing torture, he took his time, letting one single finger explore Sam's body, making his lover twitch and moan. Muscles tensed and released with each pass of Declan's fingertip over nipples, pecs, abs, and hips. Long slow gentle strokes over Sam's abdomen and hips built up the anticipation of Declan's finger finally reaching Sam's cockhead again.

Sam was an instrument and one finger was playing him, making him sing. "Please, baby, please!" he begged, but Declan didn't go any further, not yet, he returned to the base of Sam's cock and re-started the slow, tickling journey from the base to just below the sensitive frenulum. Again Sam's flat abdomen tensed in anticipation and he bucked, the movement of muscle making the continued pressure of the steel ring sweeter, and with that, Sam couldn't prevent his

154

ass from clenching around the hardness of the steel butt plug. He cried out as it pressed against his prostate giving a rush of delicious pleasure.

Declan observed Sam's every move, pleased to see how lost his lover was. Sam's eyes were closed now, and he was biting at his bottom lip, moaning, and whimpering in ecstasy. There was no denying that seeing Sam so helplessly turned on put Declan on the edge. He intermittently squeezed the base of his own dick and tugged on his balls to ease the pressure a little. This session was all about Sam, so Declan would put his own pleasure on pause until Sam was so wrung out he forgot what day it was.

Declan waited for Sam to settle again—over stimulation would make this end far too soon, and that would not do. The *anticipation* of the next dainty touch would make the pleasure of the eventual touch so much better.

Declan traced the pattern of the veins standing out on Sam's prick, the engorgement of blood making it a deep rosy pink hue. When his finger reached the head of Sam's cock Declan lifted his finger up and away just a centimetre. Sam thrust up involuntarily seeking to meet Declan's fingertip with his cockhead. Sam did it again and again, mewling, so needy, so desperately searching for the tiniest touch. It was delicious to watch. Sam cried out as the ring pressed on his ligaments, and the cords tugged and squeezed at his balls giving darts of pleasure. Precum was now pearling on the tip.

"Please Buttercup, please lick it off," Sam begged but Declan didn't. Still using just one finger he gathered the clear viscous liquid and slowly spread it over Sam's head, making it glisten like a ripe, polished plum.

"Fuuuck! I've never had anyone give my dick such decadent attention," Sam admitted with an aroused laugh.

"Good, an' no one else ever will, cos yer mine." Knowing this fact pleased Declan, and pride purred in his chest.

"Yes, I'm yours Buttercup," Sam agreed.

By the time they'd been at this slow tease and denial for an hour Sam was overwhelmed with the pleasure of Declan's maddeningly light touches.

It was the perfect distraction. "Tell me what you're feeling, love," he asked in a bid to ease the pressure, directing Sam's thoughts away from his balls, which had drawn up readying to unload. He couldn't let that happen quite yet.

"Your...your finger feels like a fucking lightning rod. I anticipate each touch and when you do touch me, the pleasure intensifies. I've... I've never felt anything like it." Sam was delirious and this was exactly where Declan wanted Sam to be, letting go, forgetting the stress and angst of real life. He was ready now.

Declan eased up onto his knees and reached for the scissors he'd left on the nightstand. He cut the cords that were attached to the butt plug and Sam mewled as he slowly eased the now-hot metal out of Sam's body. Then Declan stepped off the bed and slid his Bum Chums down to expose his pumped and ready-to-roll erection. He stood for another moment and enjoyed Sam's lust-blown eyes on him as he slicked up his bare cock. Then Declan crawled onto the bed and pushed Sam's legs back so they met his chest.

"Yes, fuck, yes, do it...do it!" Sam begged and Declan did as he was asked this time. He drove his thick cock into Sam's relaxed, sensitive entrance and began pounding. The world vanished then and all that existed was the man beneath him, the love, and desire in his eyes, the fact that Sam had forgotten his words—it was perfection.

Declan let Sam's legs down to flatten his feet on the mattress. Sam removed his fingers from the headboard at that moment. He reached out and hooked the leather chest harness dragging Declan to him. With steely determination in his cum-drunk eyes, as if they were engaged in a competition, Sam joined the ride, canting his hips, meeting the pistoning thrusts. Sam begged for release, and all it took was a glancing brush of Declan's hairy abdomen on Sam's cockhead to send him over the edge. Sam let go of the chest harness and Declan rose, gripping Sam's arse cheeks, driving into him mercilessly as Sam's muscles squeezed Declan's cock. The climax was so powerful Sam cried out and his hips arched up from the mattress as he shot his hot release over his belly. Sam's face slackened and Declan felt him go limp as if all of the anxiety of the last few days had flowed out of his lover in the fountaining jets of milky semen. Knowing that he had done this for Sam filled Declan with warm, purring satisfaction.

Sam's hands claimed Declan's firm muscled arse, pulling him closer, deeper as if he wanted his man to crawl inside him. Declan came with a shout of triumph spilling inside Sam, and then collapsed, Sam, accepting him into his arms.

Sam mumbled something that could have been "Thank you". Then, they lay in the silence of their home, in their bed, the couple, a sweaty, satisfied heap of tangled limbs.

****

CHAPTER 14
PHOTOGRAPH

Declan brought a loaded breakfast tray into the bedroom. "Did ye sleep well?" he asked on finding Sam awake.

"Best sleep evah! Last night was exactly what I needed." Sam rolled over, yawned, and stretched. "This is nice!" he said when he sat up and saw what his ever-so-thoughtful husband had brought in on the tray.

"Ye know when I show a guy a good time he gets the full service."

"Is that right? I think I might need another oil change then," Sam smirked, feeling more relaxed and mellow than he had done in days. Sam took a hold of the tray so that Declan could climb back into bed and when he was settled, placed it in the middle of the bed.

"Fruit salad, porridge, Sausages, toast, and tea, the brekkie of champions!" Declan announced the menu and passed Sam a mug of tea. Sam took the mug and sipped at the tea. He looked over the rim and a shimmering dart of lust flashed between them. Sam put the mug on the nightstand and Declan followed the move, leaning in and kissing Sam tenderly on the lips.

"Are you determined to keep distracting me?" Sam returned the smiling kiss.

"Don't you think it would be a great way te spend the

159

day, fucking each other into the mattress? We've got the time. We don't have to deal wi' anything troubling today," Declan insisted.

A long pause from Sam and Declan drew back.

"Um, I wish, but we can't take the time. Not yet. I've got something to show you!" Sam stated, bursting the love bubble.

Declan's shoulder's sagged with disappointment. "Good or bad?" he asked dejectedly as he reached to the tray, snagged a sausage, and sat back.

"Both,"

Sam collected his phone, used his thumbprint to open it, swiped and clicked on the screen and then passed the device to Declan.

He glanced at the screen. "What's this?" The sausage was already consumed. Automatically, Declan made a pincer movement to enlarge the image. He scrolled left and right over the black-and-white image of a group of young men, his eyes widening as he recognized Sam. His brows knitted...no, not Sam, it was a young James Aiken.

"He wanted you to find this?"

Declan counted the young men, and one older man and his eyes widened in understanding. He turned to Sam unable to repress his amazement.

"Is this what I think it is?"

"Yup,"

"This is the Alphabet Club... we have a fuckin' photo of the Alphabet Club!"

"It was secreted behind the end paper of one of Professor

160

Alfred Moxley's diaries from 1981," Sam informed,

"Why didn't ye say so yesterday?"

"Because, wisely, you told me to put it all to bed. And you were right. My head was wrecked, I couldn't think straight and I needed to sleep. There was something about that photo I couldn't put my finger on and it bugged the hell out of me."

"Mebe it's that you're the spit of yer da?" Declan suggested with a wicked grin.

Sam gave him the hairy eyeball, "We look nothing alike," he insisted flatly,

"You keep tellin' yersel that love!" Declan snickered.

"No, listen, I'm serious. I realised what bugged me about that photo is that I've seen it before."

"Where?"

"It jumped into my brain this morning. It was framed, hanging on the wall of my dad's home office when I was a kid. I used to sneak up to his office when he was away for work because he had one of those Newton's Cradle metal ball toys on his desk and I was obsessed with watching the balls swing." Sam and Declan shared a wicked childish smirk. "I know, no change there! Anyway, I recall seeing that photo on the wall and staring at it cos my dad looked young and handsome, so smart in his tailcoat. We lived in Bayswater at the time."

"Bayswater! I think I remember that place. A big, white Georgian house on Princes Square?"

"Yes, that's the one!" Sam brightened. "How do you know about the house?"

161

"It's still part of his property portfolio. James personally gave me instructions to have a gardener spruce up the back and front garden once a month. Yer da was adamant I wasnae to go inside and most definitely not to rent it out, but always to keep an eye on it. I had hundreds of properties to manage. I didn't think anything of it," Declan revealed. "Did he not consider selling after yer mother passed?"

"Annabelle would have killed him. She loves that house. She was attempting to convince Dad to let her and Oliver move in because it was such a wonderful home for a family and it's been left empty for the past fourteen years. He's very reluctant to do anything with it at all. He refused to even give Belle the keys. Talking about the place made him angry, and he rarely raised his voice at Annabelle." Sam paused and was thoughtful for a beat. He lay back into the pillows, and as he spoke his voice took on a distant quality.

"I don't even remember moving out. Mum was sick but I didn't understand how sick she was. Dad shipped me and Annabelle off to private boarding school, and when we came back to London he told us mum had died and we were living at another house—the one in Holland Park. Our new bedrooms were filled with new belongings, new TVs, game consuls, books, and clothes. I remember losing my shit because all of my magic gear was missing, all of my props and tricks. Dad told me I was too old for such childish things and I needed to start playing computer games like the other boys. It was a very distressing, confusing time," Sam reminisced.

Declan handed the phone with the photograph back to Sam and reached for his own phone. He paused for a second to view the scorching photo of Sam he'd taken the night before, his cock chubbing up at the sight of Sam laying there, tied, hard and wanton, his eyes green pools of lust. Declan grinned and swiftly moved the images into his secure archive.

"Who are you calling?" Sam queried as he reached for a bowl of fruit salad. Declan clicked on a contact then on the speaker icon,

"Raj, hi, it's Declan,"

"Hello mate, how are things? I ain't seen you in ages, the boss is keeping you busy, yeah?" Raj Chandra said with the familiarity of an old friend. Raj had once been Declan's assistant and was now the current property manager of Aiken Luxury Lettings.

"Aye, ye know what he's like! No rest..."

"Do I ever!" Raj scoffed. "What can I do for you?"

"We need a favour?"

"Sure, name it."

"Do you have keys for a property on Princes Square in Bayswater?"

"Hang on a sec," Raj said sounding like he was walking, nasal breathing mingling with the noise of the busy workspace. "We upped security big-time after you left—got a fingerprint access cabinet for the keys and door fobs," Raj explained, "It's in my office". After a moment and a few clicking noises Raj said, "Dec, you there?"

"Aye,"

"Yes, the keys for the property at number one Princes Square are here, but you do know it's a non-rental, right?"

"Aye. I know. My father-in-law wants us to check something out. I'm gonna drop by with Sam and pick up the keys."

"You guys looking for a little more space? I'm sure Sir James could spare a mansion or two!"

"Aye I'm sure he could," Declan agreed. "We can be over in thirty minutes, does that suit you?"

"Yeah, that's fine. I won't be here cos I've got a meeting with *Azzmar Bin Faisal Al Saud*, but Jasminda, my new assistant will give you the keys."

"Prince Azzmar! Gods, he's a blast from the past. Is he still at the Bishops Avenue house?"

"Yeah, and he's pushing to get the rent reduced. Even Saudi Princes are tightening their belts these days."

"Don't you let him twist yer arm, if he cannae afford the place anymore, tell him he needs te downsize!"

"That's exactly what I was planning to do!"

"We'll have to meet up fer a pint soon, good to chat," Declan said before ending the call. He looked to his left and saw that Sam was gnawing on a cuticle.

"Are you alright with going to have a look at the house? I should have asked first."

"Yes, it's fine," Sam said, but from the anxious edge in his voice, Declan knew it wasn't fine at all.

"Tell me…" he asked softly.

Sam puffed out a long sigh. "I can't quite believe I never went back. What do you think we'll find there?"

164

"I don't know. But it's strange that yer da never did anything with the place. It's where you remember seeing the photo of the Alphabet Club members so I think we should go and take a look and see if there's anything that jogs yer memory."

****

CHAPTER 15
TOO MANY GHOSTS

The Westminster suburb of Bayswater attracted the affluent like bees to honey with its gorgeous Georgian and Victorian architecture, garden squares and a plethora of high-end shops, restaurants, and cafes. Declan turned the SUV into Princes Square. Long rows of white stucco mid-nineteenth-century, four-storey townhouses stood on all four sides, facing the verdant shared park in the centre. Each house was designed with a grand projecting Doric porch, above which black wrought iron balustrades were displayed for the master bedroom balcony giving the resident a wonderful view over the park and the elegant architecture of the area.

After taking a turn around the square to search for a parking space, Sam spotted a woman loading her toddler into the car parked outside number 15. Declan took another turn around the square to give the woman time to fasten her seat belt, and by the time they'd returned the hybrid car had pulled out and Declan slid into the vacant space.

With the keys gripped in a sweaty hand, Sam anxiously exited the vehicle and strode hurriedly back down the road to stand outside the first house on the row, a corner house. Immediately on seeing the house, the white steps leading up to a grand covered porch Sam felt like he'd stepped back in time. Sam noticed Declan's warmth at his back and his husband placed a broad firm hand on Sam's shoulder and gave a reassuring squeeze.

"Christ. Standing here I feel like a little boy again. It seems like yesterday that I was jumping up and down those steps playing games with Belle," Sam said with an emotional wobble in his voice.

"We don't have te do this," Declan reminded.

"No, it's okay. It's just that, when I left this place my childhood died, as well as my mum. I think I need to do this to get some closure."

"Okay. G'wan, up ye go then," Declan encouraged, patting Sam on the bottom.

Sam's feet unglued and he took the steps two at a time. He stood at the door and looked up into the stone porch ceiling, again, memories came swimming in his blood as he recalled sitting with his mum on a blanket and cushions under the shade of the porch on a hot summers day, Sam and Belle drawing on the stone with brightly coloured chalks while Rosalind, too weak to do much, watched the world go by. He hadn't understood how sick his mother was, that she wouldn't always be there, and so it was a bittersweet memory.

Sam unlocked the large front door and stepped onto the black and white checkerboard tiled hall. He went immediately to the burglar alarm panel and turned it off using the code on the key fob. Declan closed the door behind them.

With the sounds of the busy city now absent, they stood in the silent home. The absences made Sam's chest ache and his throat burn as he tried to hold in the emotions that returning to his childhood home dragged to the surface. He remembered that this was always a noisy, busy home, whether from him tearing up and down the stairs, Belle singing, the radio, television, or the laughter of children who had come over to play. There was always something cooking, the scent of garlic and herbs, of sourdough bread. He remembered the time his mum became obsessed with making cupcakes to compete with the other mums at Sam's nursery school fair and he'd loved it because he got to lick the spoon. There was a faint scent of lavender air freshener and the hallway was dust free, clean and looked exactly as it had done when Sam lived there, with one exception. The effect of the low light coming through the stained glass fanlight over the front door was startling. The furniture, the coat and shoe racks, the umbrella stand, wall sconces and paintings were all draped with white plastic covers like ghosts crawling up the walls. Sam pulled a cover off one of the decorative wall sconces and pressed the dimmer switch below illuminating the hallway.

"You okay?" Declan asked as he stepped up behind Sam and pulled him back into a hug. Sam's taut frame sagged a little and submitted to the tender care before he said,

"Come along Buttercup. I'll give you a tour." He threaded his fingers into Declan's and moved on to open the first door to the left.

In the lounge, Sam switched the chandelier light on. The curtains were closed. They discovered that the large square room was, again, clean, and plastic sheeting covered the furniture and art on the walls. Declan followed behind Sam but he didn't touch anything, letting Sam take the lead. The Laura Ashley brand was popular with yummy mummies twenty-five years ago when Sam was born, and it appeared Rosalind Aiken was a huge fan. Floral designs leapt from the wallpaper, the drapes, and the couch fabric. Sam pulled the cover from one of the two three-seater couches.

"It's like dad vacuum-packed the house," Sam observed unable to disguise how appalled he felt looking at the mummification of his childhood home. He lifted the plastic cover from the coffee table and his breath hitched as he saw his mother's Vogue, Elle, and Tatler magazines dated from fourteen years ago, and beside them, a scene young Sam must have set up, because there were his Star Wars action figures ready to do battle. Seeing them was what pushed Sam over the edge. Tears leapt to his eyes. He bit his lip, shook his head, and turned to leave the room.

Declan remained, giving Sam the space to compose himself. He moved further into the room, gravitating as always, toward the mantle. He carefully unhooked the plastic sheeting that covered the framed photographs sitting in a line upon its grand marble surface. Declan had always wondered why Sir James' house in Holland Park contained no photographs or mementoes of his wife or his children. There was nothing intimate in that house, nothing that spoke of love, of relationships, of family. Now Declan understood why. Holland Park *wasn't* James's family home; the Bayswater house was the place James associated with love and family. Declan was moved to gain insights into the

169

idyllic childhood Sam had known. It appeared that Sam had been a lucky little boy to live in such a grand home with a big sister and two parents who'd loved them. Declan picked up a silver frame containing a montage of images of a small blond toddler with mischievous sparkling green eyes sitting in a *Little Tikes* plastic car with an older child pushing the car, her dark curls billowing like an uncontrollable cloud around her head, both children wore beaming grins.

"Sam. C'mere!" Declan called out.

Sam returned to pause in the doorway. "What did you find?" he asked warily. "Oh my god!" he sighed at seeing the line of uncovered family photographs on the mantle, and what Declan held. His eyes fixed on a photograph of handsome, long-haired blond James kissing beautiful Rosalind on their wedding day, his mother's cloud of brunette curls woven with a crown of colourful wildflowers. And then platinum-haired Sam in his first school uniform, and Annabelle dressed up as a daffodil for her school play.

"I...I thought he must have gutted the house, I thought it was all gone." Sam admitted a stunned tremble in his voice. He took the photo from Declan and gazed at his toddler self.

"Aww, man, I loved that car," Sam said affectionately. "I used to pretend I'd broken down and Dad was the mechanic," he reminisced. "Back then I thought that my dad could fix everything," he sighed regretfully. "But I found out later that he couldn't."

Declan stepped to Sam's back and threaded his hands around Sam's hips, pulling him back into an embrace again. Sam laid his head on Declan's shoulder grateful for the comfort.

"Ye were a cutie!" Declan commented, a smile in his voice as they both looked at the photo in Sam's hand.

"Wasn't I! I wonder what happened?" Sam said drolly.

"You grew up to be...perfection. My perfect partner."

Sam kissed Declan on the cheek, "Gosh. You are surprisingly sentimental at the most inopportune moments Mr Ramsay," he said, "It quite takes my breath!"

Sam turned in Declan's arms and they remained in the embrace for several minutes before Sam said, "Dad left everything as it was for a reason. Let's leave it as we found it." Declan nodded in agreement.

Sam placed the photo back on the mantle and then covered the images with the plastic sheeting. They then re-covered the coffee table and couch.

Declan entered the dining room across the hall first and was floored by an overwhelming and eerie feeling of love and loss. He peeked under the plastic sheets covering artwork and found children's potato paintings had been lovingly framed like they were by an old master and put up on the wall. A large rustic pine table dominated the room where, when they pulled back the plastic sheet Sam showed Declan the colourful crayon marks running up the legs that he'd made. In this room, there was tangible evidence that this had been a busy space, full of activity, creativity, and love.

"Did you have a nanny?"

"Oh no, mum was with us until we were both at school. She'd worked for the *Saatchi and Saatchi* advertising agency

171

before she had me, and so when I was in day nursery she went back part-time. When I went to primary school she worked full-time. My mum was like a whirlwind, always on the go...when she wasn't having a bad day. She didn't have to work, but I guess she enjoyed it."

Declan could see the evidence of Rosalind's busy creative mind in the dining room, and again as they strode down a short flight of stairs into the original Victorian kitchen. It was a large square space with built-in glass-fronted cabinets that had been given a coat of cream paint. In the white ceramic butler's sink, a mug sat, the desiccated remnants of coffee tattooed in a ring at the bottom of the mug.

"Someone was here a while back!" Declan informed.

Sam pulled open cupboard doors, and drawers to find them empty of food, but the cutlery, plates, and cookware were exactly where they had been when Sam was a kid. There was not one spider web and relatively little dust.

Declan opened the fridge to find it empty except for a bottle of *Cristal* Champagne, 2002 vintage, unopened. Sam checked the kitchen backdoor, it was triply dead-bolted, and there was no sign of entry. He then opened one of the shutters and looked out onto a deck that led to a pristine manicured walled garden; the grass was cut, and flowerbeds well-tended.

"It's kinda sad, isn't it," Declan said as he joined Sam. "I didnae think James had this much love in him."

"Me too. I forgot what he used to be like." Coming back to this house reminded Sam that James had once been a loving father. He was moved by the way home was

172

preserved. It was a testament to love and the deep grief of having the perfect family and then losing it. Cancer doesn't care if you're rich or poor. It had taken Sam's mother, and after his wife's death, James had closed his heart and turned into a cold, ruthless, cruel man.

They left the kitchen and made their way to the stairs and up to the first floor to James and Rosalind's bedroom. They entered, Declan feeling a little as if he was invading a sacred, private space. The faint scent of roses lingered in the room. Again, the décor was floral Laura Ashley, and white plastic hung in ghostly shapes over wall sconces, artwork, and Rosalind's dressing table.

This room wasn't as Sam remembered. His mother required nursing care at home and there had been medical equipment on his mum's side of the king-sized bed, but all traces of that were gone.

Declan strode to the bookcase and perused the line of books, shelves of political memoirs, books on advertising and design, and a few Jilly Cooper and Jackie Collins novels, mixed with Robert Ludlum and Lee Child. He ran a finger along the edge of the shelf. Again, no dust. Declan moved off toward the French doors, pulling back the voile and taking in the view from the balcony over Princes Square park where small children and their parents were playing on the lawn.

"It would be wonderful if Belle and Oliver could raise wee Rosa here," Declan observed, turning back to Sam, who stood at the side of the plastic-covered bed. "There's a lot of love in this house," and Declan would know. He'd dealt

173

with countless properties for James over his years as a letting agent and had developed a sixth sense for whether a house was happy or not.

Sam drew back the sheeting covering the bed to see a single dried red rose on Rosalind's pillow, and beside it, there was evidence of a head impression on James' pillow. Sam's tear-glazed eyes met Declan's.

"I thought I smelled roses when we came in," Declan said,

"Mum's favourite flower,"

Declan had noticed a small bin beneath the dressing table and after investigation turned to Sam. "There are 13 dried red roses in here."

"Christ! He must have come back with a rose every year on their anniversary and lay beside her," Sam choked a sob and hid his face in his palms.

"He loved yer mother a great deal."

"I guess. I didn't understand the change in him after mum passed. I thought it was my fault in some way, and that he hated me."

"But you were only a bairn!" Declan stepped to his husband and pulled him into his arms, a little guilty for dragging the sad memories to the surface by coming here.

"All I had left was Belle."

Understanding Sam's story broke Declan's heart. Sam had gone from being a child with everything to one dealing with life-changing tragedy. No wonder he grew up to be a lonely, emotionally starved young man. James had let his son down in the most unimaginable ways and was the

174

catalyst for everything that had gone wrong in Sam's life.

"I can see how losing the love of yer life could break a man so completely. I get it. I think at that heart of it, that mebe James was just... broken," Declan suggested softly, "Even so, it doesnae excuse the way he's treated ye, or that he turned into such a heartless bastard."

"Come on," Sam said, drawing the plastic covering back over the bed. "I can't stand wallowing in this room anymore. We'll go to the office, it's in the loft.

Declan had assumed that the door in the corner of the hallway was for an airing cupboard, but Sam turned the key that was waiting in the keyhole and pulled the door open to show it hid the staircase to the loft room.

"Put the light on, the stairs are quite steep," Sam suggested standing aside so Declan could go first. The initial thing Declan noticed when the stairway was lit was that there were no cobwebs, and again, no dust in the stairway. He climbed the carpeted steps and reached the top to find a second locked door with the key in the keyhole. Declan unlocked it and stepped into James's man cave with Sam at his back. Sam switched the light on. It was clear then why there were no cobwebs.

The loft was a large space covering the whole footprint of the grand house with skylights along the far side of the gable roof. The room had been fitted out to a high standard and zoned into an open plan lounge area with a TV, coffee table and couch, a bedroom, bathroom, and office space. The office space was in use, and recently, if the newspaper's on the desk were anything to go by. Sam picked up a copy of

The Times where it appeared his father had been working on the crossword.

"It's dated from a month ago," he said.

"So, this was James's wee hidey hole. Hiding in plain sight, just ten minutes walk from his Holland Park lair. Wow!"

"No wonder he refused to let Belle have the keys. He couldn't let this place or the memories go."

"Can ye remember anything about being up here as a kid? Where did you see the photo?"

"It hasn't really changed that much, new flat screen TV and desktop. The Newton's Cradle toy is still in the same place. Dad used to have a few framed pictures on the wall from his student days, here," Sam directed Declan to a wall that now held a large framed antique map of London.

"They were what you'd expect, photos of mum and dad's graduation, the photo of the Alphabet Club members suited and booted, but they're gone."

"Your parents met at Uni?"

"Mum got a first in English, and dad got a first in Politics, Philosophy, and Economics. They had it all at one point."

"What's behind here? Declan asked abruptly as he strode towards the far wall where a floor-length red velvet curtain hung across the width of the wall. Declan fingered the centre of the two curtains aside expecting to see a window overlooking the street but he cursed, "Holy fuck, Sam," and then moved to the side to find a drawstring. He pulled the drawstring and in a near theatrical gesture, the curtains parted the second Sam turned to see what Declan had found.

Sam's jaw slackened in disbelief as Declan revealed the full extent of what could only be called... a murder wall.

For a moment Sam couldn't move. He was trying to comprehend what the hell he was looking at. The wall was covered in photographs, newspaper cuttings, and the ubiquitous pins and red string zig-zagging between them, making connections. And in the centre of it all, there was the black and white photograph that Sam had recognized. The photograph was taken by an unknown photographer, labelled beneath with the year 1981. It should have shown twenty-six beaming young men in tails and their corpulent bearded benefactor. Yet as he walked forward to stand beside Declan and take in the enormity of the murder wall, Sam noticed that on this copy of the photograph, sixteen of the twenty-six were now defaced by a thick red X mark. With eerie certainty, Sam turned to Declan and said,

"Good God. They're dead."

****

"What do we do now?" Declan asked.

They sat side by side on the floor of the Bayswater loft room staring at James's murder wall. Neither could begin to fathom exactly what they were looking at. The only names and faces they recognized were that of James, and his friend Sir Peter Maythorpe, whose supposed suicide had led Sam and Declan to the G'wan Adventures resort, and a near-death experience.

Declan stood and pulled his phone from his jacket pocket. "I'm gonna document the crazy," he informed holding up his device and taking the first shot, then moving and taking the next, continuing in a grid pattern.

"I'll focus on Book Zero then."

"What the hell's Book Zero?" Declan asked his eyes narrowed in confusion as he turned back to Sam

"I didn't get round to telling you earlier about what I stole. No, don't look at me like that, it's *your fault* for distracting me!" Sam scolded. "And then it wasn't the right time because we were coming here and well—looks like this is the right time to tell you." Sam rose gracefully to his feet, reached around and drew the small address book from the back pocket of his jeans and held it up.

"This little beauty was hidden among Moxley's papers," he explained, walking toward Declan. "It's an address book. I didn't think it was important until I saw this," Sam opened the small book and showed Declan the first page.

"Cypher?"

"No, not quite." Sam spelt the word out.

"S-I-F-R. Sifr. Moxley used wordplay. In pre-Islamic texts *sifr* had the meaning *empty* or was used as a placeholder, notifying to 'leave a space' in a manuscript. It's evolved since the 14th century to mean Zero," Sam enthused.

Declan's brows rose in astonishment. "And so? C'mon, don't hold me in suspense, what's in it? Please say it's got the names and addresses of this crowd of numpty reprobates… it would make life so much easier!"

"The thing is, I don't know. Book Zero *is* full of cyphers. Moxley worked in *Crypto-linguistics* at the Foreign Office in the 70s before he became an academic. He loved puzzles and games. I haven't yet identified what type of cypher it is. I guess that it will take days, even weeks to decrypt, if ever!"

Declan took the final three photographs of the wall and then checked the shots to ensure he'd gotten what he wanted. Then he pulled the drawstring to close the red drapes.

"Are you done?"

"Aye, I think we've found more than we expected."

"Yes," Sam agreed, "And I need to get out of here—too many ghosts."

****

CHAPTER 16
ZERO INTEL

Their new found freedom soon came to an end. Two brand new work phones were delivered by a courier the next morning, preloaded with updated contact details for Mrs K and a host of A.L.L. staff. This reassured Sam a little. Declan was more pensive about the move. He'd enjoyed a modicum of freedom at not being at anyone's beck and call. It was fun investigating at their chosen speed, letting the cards fall where they would, and acting without needing permission to break wind.

Sam had worked overnight on the cyphers in Book Zero and was surprised how easy he'd found it to break the code. They now had a list of names but delving further would have to wait. An encrypted message was received on both phones at ten a.m. It was curious. Sam opened it to see it contained satellite navigation coordinates and nothing else.

Sam sent his husband a raised brow. This is what he'd been waiting for. "It's from Mrs K, I'm sure of it." Akiko Kimura had shut them out of all A.L.L. business since James' abduction, and now, she was letting them back in. Both men hurriedly grabbed their phones and go-bags, in case they'd need to overnight somewhere, and then headed for the SUV parked outside their Mayfair apartment.

In the car, Sam typed the coordinates into the Sat-Nav

before Declan moved off into the sluggish flow of central London traffic.

"Head west on Mount St and take the left turn onto Park Lane," The jaunty male Irish AI voice said.

"Ye changed the bloody voice again," Declan complained. The choice of voice for the inbuilt Satellite navigation was a constant battle between the couple.

Declan scowled, giving Sam a side glance and Sam snickered. "The Irishman's my favourite so far! He sounds happy to tell us where to go." Declan was not impressed.

"I'll be happy te tell ye where te go," he muttered morosely under his breath.

"Continue towards Constitution Hill. Take Birdcage Walk, A302 and Westminster Bridge Road to New Kent Road A201,"

Declan rubbed a despairing hand over his face and with a flat, unimpressed tone said "Samuel Aiken-Ramsay. If you love me, ye have got te change his voice back te Scots".

"Of course I love you. But I like the Irish voice!" Sam countered with amusement, "He's plucky and spunky. You gotta love a bit of pluck and spunk! And, no, I will not fall for your emotional blackmail."

"Ugggh, Saaam," Declan whined. "He's creepy. I nearly jump outa my skin every time he gives directions. I'd even prefer the laidback Aussie, now he's sexy!"

"Right-oh, lover, I'll keep that in mind for next time I go down...under!" Sam said in an Australian accent. Declan gave his husband a side glance and laughed to see Sam wiggling his brows. Declan couldn't help but smirk and shook his head. He loved this man so much!

"Untwist your panties, babe. Seamus is staying for the journey. You can choose the voice for the way back."

"Fine," Declan replied in a not-so-fine tone. "Anyways, it's nice te have a day trip in the same vehicle this time,".

"You know what; we should have bought some travel sweeties. It's not a proper road trip without snacks!"

"I'll stop at the next service station and we can stock up," Declan suggested keenly. Sam grinned, knowing full well that just the mention of sweets would get Declan's tummy rumbling.

"Where are we going anyways?"

Sam carried out a quick internet search on his phone. "Drakes Lodge Equestrian Center, a riding school outside Gillingham," Sam informed.

"Drakes Lodge was built without the appropriate planning permission. The local council forced it to close in 2017," Sam read, "It's scheduled to be demolished in two months."

"Why the hell are we on our way to an abandoned riding school?"

Sam didn't have an answer and kept his thoughts to himself. He had an inkling something big was happening. Was this the new location for the A.L.L. unit or something else? What would he do if they'd found his father?

Driving time was thinking time, and there was nothing like an impromptu road trip to get thoughts circling in the mind like a murder of crows at dusk. The radio was set at a low background hum of 80s pop music as Declan drove. The silence between the men was companionable and Sam rested his head on the back of the seat and closed his eyes for a few minutes… which turned into an hour. He was awoken when the radio cut off and the Irish Sat Nav chirped up,

"Take the next junction for the A2."

Declan took the junction and headed towards Gillingham, a coastal town in Kent.

Sam rubbed his face to wake himself up and fixed a dopey, sleepy smile on his boyish face as he turned to Declan.

"Do you want anything love?" he asked as he leaned down and rifled through the carrier bag of snacks and drinks they'd bought at the Marks & Spencer shop at the service station.

"Nah, I'm all good. We'll reach the destination soon."

Sam pulled a bag of Cola Colin Caterpillar jellies from the carrier bag. He opened the packet, picked one out, and then held the bag out for Declan.

"What do ye think this is about? Why do they want us te drive te the arse end of nowhere?" Declan grumbled then blindly put his hand into the bag and snagged a caterpillar gummi.

"It's not unusual for us to get zero Intel," Sam shrugged. "You know that. We're supposed to be prepared for anything!"

Declan chewed thoughtfully and then speculated, "I bet it's something to do wi yer da, that's why it's extra hush-hush," his index finger tapped his nose conspiratorially.

"Could be. We'll find out soon enough." Sam shrugged and sighed, and then plucked another caterpillar from the

183

bag. "God! These are addictive," he said threading another cola-flavoured gummi caterpillar into his mouth.

"Gimmie!" Declan took a hand from the wheel and Sam put a few sweets in his palm.

The late-May day was bright, the sky full of cotton bud clouds, and after an hour and a half of driving they were in deep countryside. It was single-lane roads from now on with the occasional farm turn-off, cottage, or village shop.

"Turn left at the next junction," Seamus the Sat Nav said. Declan sped past.

"Shite!" he cursed. He'd been lost in his thoughts and not paying attention. To his relief, there was no other traffic on the one-lane country road. Declan put his foot down sharply on the break, carried out a wicked reverse and spin manoeuvre that he'd learned on his Black Ops training course, and then retraced his tracks and took the correct road.

"Impressive," Sam spluttered at the sudden turnabout. "I've even managed to keep my food down."

The approach to the Drakes Lodge Equestrian Center was overgrown. The entrance sign had a demolition notice nailed to it, printed in a serious large red blocky font. Declan warily eased the car up the gravel drive.

They could see a group of large white buildings ahead. Over the horse fencing on either side of the weed-strewn driveway were overgrown paddocks. The paddocks were littered with rusting striped poles from the jumps, abandoned landscaping machinery, and there was evidence of decay and vandalism over many years. It was clear at first sight that the centre was a hangout for local kids and ne'er-do-wells. An old sofa and two armchairs had been moved into the centre of one of the paddocks to create a false domestic set-up. A black hole in the centre showed the blackened remains of a fire.

A high-roofed black van was parked outside one of the single-storey warehouse-style buildings. It appeared that attempts had been made to stop vandals from gaining access to the structure by bricking up the windows and main entrance, but the building was scarred with multicoloured graffiti tags and part of the roof had fallen in.

Seamus the Sat Nav spoke up, pulling Sam from his thoughts.

"Congratulations! You've reached your destination."

Declan brought the vehicle to a halt close to the black van outside what could now be identified as the Equestrian arena. The side door of the van slid open and a man in black stepped out wearing a tactical vest, and a holstered gun. He was stocky, had shaggy brown hair and a full dark beard flecked with ginger. He gave a wide puppyish smile on seeing Sam and Declan and sent them a cordial wave.

Declan stepped out of the vehicle, opened the back door and reached into the back seat for his jacket.

"Desert Fox, Lucky Boy. Yez made good time," the man called in a pleasant Irish accent as he strode towards their vehicle.

"See, another lovely Irish accent," Sam poked mischievously.

"What's yer name?" Declan hollered to the man as he

185

strode closer

"Agent Aiden Farrell, codename Lightsaber, sir." Sam had moved to Declan's side.

"A pleasure to meet yez both, big fan of yer work, big fan!" The agent added excitedly slapping Declan on the shoulder in a display of manly bravado as they shook hands. He appeared as giddy as a schoolboy meeting his idol. Declan saw the smirk on Sam's face at the Irish agent's enthusiastic attention and he wanted to swat him across the head. Sam took the agent's hand and shook it. The agent looked down at his palm as if he'd never wash that hand again.

"Have yez been briefed at all, lads?" Farrell asked as if they were long-time friends.

"Not a sausie! It would be nice to know what the hell is goin' on fer once!" Declan harrumphed.

"Between you an' me, this is fookin' huge," Farrell said, his hands miming a 'mind-blown' gesture.

"Who else is here? Who are you working with?" Sam asked.

"Agent Claudia Feurig, codename Storm Song," Aiden said and as if on cue the window of the driver's side of the van slid down and a manicured hand shot out and gave a nonchalant wave. They'd met Feurig briefly before when they interrogated Akiko.

"Agent Lena Weber, codename Deep Clean is our medic, she's with Running Bear. They're dealing with the guest." Aiden said, using air quotes as he said the word 'guest'.

"Running Bear?" Sam and Declan said in shocked

unison. Hearing Agent Devon Brody was at the location made the jigsaw pieces slip into place.

"Oh, my God! He did it! He found the devil and got him out of Afghanistan!" Sam exclaimed in shock. Now they knew exactly why they were at this abandoned Equestrian centre, and why there was zero Intel before their journey. Sam and Declan shared a look of understanding. Farrell was right. This *was* mind-blowing. This was a Black Site and they were about to interrogate the man Erik Madsson idolized, *Ali Amir Alzzalam* a.k.a Ali the Devil. Whatever happened here...never happened.

"Mrs K will be watching the interrogation remotely. If you'd like to follow me, we'll get yez kitted out before you go in." Farrell said.

****

CHAPTER 17
NEED TO KNOW

Sam and Declan followed Agent Farrell into the high-roofed black van. It was kitted out as a monitoring station, similar to the one that Strauss had manned in Munich. There was a mobile server, power bank, computers, monitors, and lots of flashing lights.

Farrell took a seat at the workstation with a bank of screens in front of him. The armoured door between the driver's area and the back of the van opened and a woman stepped through.

Agent Claudia Feurig was svelte in her early fifties, dressed in the same black combat gear as Farrell. She wore round, Lennon-style glasses, had long honey-blond hair tied into a braid and a zero fucks smile on her face. As Claudia came closer Sam noticed that she smelled of vanilla and cut grass, with a hint of wet dog. He wondered if she'd stowed a puppy somewhere in the van! She offered her hand to the newcomers who shook it.

"I've completed the set up of the high-resolution cameras and motion sensors around the perimeter of the complex," the German agent relayed. "If a fox farts near one of our sensors, we'll know!"

Farrell pushed himself backwards in his wheeled office chair and uttered an unselfconscious "Wheee!" The chair

188

came to a halt beside an inbuilt storage locker.

"Damn, I can't believe I said that out loud," he muttered and gave the three agents watching him a sheepish grin. He retrieved an aluminium case from one of the lockers and walked his wheeled chair back to the console table, then handed the case to his partner. She laid the case on the console counter and pressed her thumbs to the two print readers on the outside where keyholes would usually have been. The case lock clicked and Feurig opened it to reveal that it contained two thin ballistics and anti-stab vests, and beneath them in protective wrappings was a pair of chest cameras with mics and holsters.

"You'll need to undress," the agent informed, and so Sam and Declan hurriedly removed their suit jackets, and shirts. Claudia's once stern mouth hitched to a lecherous grin as the two well-toned men stripped in the van. Now they were bare-chested, she passed each of them a black vest.

"This is like a body condom!" Sam complained as he pulled his stab vest over his head and got stuck with his arms in the air. "A little assistance, love?" Sam called. Keen-eyed, Claudia stepped forward to assist.

"Its fine," Declan said, stopping her in her tracks.

"Turn around babe, it's bundled up at the back," Declan snickered. Sam did as he was told, and Declan tugged the vest down past Sam's hips, smoothing his hands further down, over Sam's warm arse to make him shiver. Sam let out a gasp, not because he was relieved to be able to breathe again, but because his husband's sinful touch in public had made his skin prickle.

189

"Christ, we should have lubed-up for this," Sam scoffed as he returned the favour and pulled Declan's vest down to hug his musculature, giving his firm arse a punishing squeeze in return as Agent Feurig looked on, her cheeks pinking to blush at the inappropriate handsy display.

"I hope you've got scissors handy cos ye might need te cut us out of these!"

"There is no need for that. The material will expand a little with your body heat. Give it a few minutes, you'll be more comfortable," Claudia explained. "And, you can put your shirts back on," she said with reluctance. "Now," she reaffirmed, seeming a little flustered.

"Come and get a look at the map," Agent Farrell invited. Sam and Declan moved to stand behind his chair. "We're here," he explained a pointer directing on the screen. "The location backs onto woodland, scrub, and then there's a beach. This here is the bank of the River Medway, the Medway leads to the North Sea."

A sharp knock on the van door startled them all. Declan pulled the door open to see Devon Brody standing there.

"Jeeze, am I glad te see you, buddy!" Declan brightened, jumping out of the van and pulling his friend into a bear hug. When Declan had let Brody go Sam did the same. Brody had gone dark nearly a year ago, but he appeared to have aged several years more. His once close-cropped black hair had grown wild and silvered at the temple, and he'd curated a long-ass beard to help with his disguise. He was dressed in a desert-issue *Olive drab* camouflage uniform. He looked exhausted, smelled over ripe, and needed a shower.

He'd been living in harsh conditions while tracking Ali the Devil and, as he was here it seemed his painstaking work had finally paid off.

"Sorry about the Intel blackout guys, we're being extra-vigilant with this one."

"Yeah, we get it," Sam said,

"If it was known that an *Ali Amir Alzzalam* escaped during the evacuation of Kabul and was in the U.K—" Brody made a cutting gesture across his throat. "We've got Afghani interpreters, drivers, and trackers on the allied payroll to think about. Anyone who aided the allies is in mortal danger. He had to disappear quietly, and completely."

The situation in Afghanistan was so confusing and millions of people had been displaced, so it was plausible that this one man could vanish. But this particular man was important. He was a vital link in the supply chain of goods and weaponry from the West into Afghanistan. The scarce Intel they had on the mysterious devil told of a man who played both sides—who controlled the borderlands between Pakistan and Afghanistan with backhanders to corrupt officials. He paid homage to the Taliban by supplying them with whatever they needed; all to ensure his supply chain remained unmolested. An asset this valuable came along once in a blue moon.

"What's the situation with the guest?" Declan asked.

"*Alzzalam* believes I'm CIA. He's been on the run for a couple of weeks and he's malnourished. Our medic doctored his water and sedated him for the plane journey.

191

He's on a vitamin drip now to give him some temporary respite. He doesn't know he's in the U.K. I told him that we would land at Ramstein U.S. airbase in Germany. He was adamant that landing in the U.K. was a deal breaker."

"What did ye promise him?"

"I said I'd extract him from Afghanistan if he'd talk. I got a list of his aliases as a down payment of sorts – the analysts are running them through the database. He's under the impression we'll exchange information and I'll let him go!"

"He'd better get used to disappointment," Sam said.

"Oh, and this is a curve ball," Brody added, "He's British."

"What?" Sam and Declan said in shocked unison.

"He's British military, knew how to play the game. The Intel I got while in Afghanistan proved he has contacts high up in the far-right of U.S. politics; they bankrolled some of his activities to speed up the U.S. withdrawal. He thinks they'll step in and help him now. The State Department hasn't been informed of his capture, but MI6 have. We've got him for twenty-four hours on British soil, and then he belongs to Six. That was the deal to get him on a UK-bound cargo plane."

"Sorry to interrupt but as you said, we have him for only twenty-two hours. I need to fit your chest cameras and test them immediately!" Agent Feurig reminded.

Sam stepped back into the van and Claudia unwrapped a body cam from the protective packaging. "This has enough battery charge for twelve hours. If the interrogation goes on longer we'll switch batteries," she said clipping the surprisingly lightweight camera into its holster and on to Sam's shirt at his sternum. "You record and stop recording by pressing this button here, one tap on, two taps off." Sam nodded.

Agent Feurig's face appeared on one of the monitors as she tested the camera.

"Lookin' good from here," Farrell called.

"The device has a micro SD and it's connected to our feed which goes directly to Mrs K and our analysts. They'll verify or refute any details he gives us." Claudia explained as she passed Sam his in-ear Comms device. Declan stepped into the van to have his camera and Comms device fitted.

"Your orders are to begin recording as soon as you step into the arena. Mrs K is watching. She wants to see everything," Agent Farrell explained.

Ready, Sam and Declan both jumped out of the van.

"How are you guys gonna play this?" Brody asked. "Weber's gonna stick around to keep an eye on the asset's vitals, I'll be there as backup but out of Ali's eye line. Dude is gonna be pissed."

"I think Declan should take lead on this," Sam said, "I'll stand behind the prisoner. He might recognize me as James' son." Declan nodded in agreement.

"I also speak both *Dari* and *Pashto*," Sam informed. "There are regional variations, but if he refuses to speak English then I'll step in."

****

CHAPTER 18
ALI AMIR ALZZALAM

Declan took a few deep centering breaths to calm his nerves and nodded to Sam before tapping his body cam button to begin recording. He stepped through the gap that had been smashed into the bricked-up entrance leading to what was once a horse show jumping arena. He crunched over shattered Thermalite bricks that crumbled underfoot like desiccated bread, releasing a moldering damp smell. The packed sand floor was strewn with detritus, old leaves, crumpled drinks cans, cigarette butts, empty crisp packets, chocolate bar wrappers, and cheap brand beer bottles. The scent of horses was long gone, replaced by cloying dampness, mould, decay, and piss. This interrogation was the most high-profile Declan had yet been involved in. He'd been trained to use the PEACE method of interrogation favoured in the UK. With this method, interrogators allowed a suspect to tell his or her story without interruption, before presenting the suspect with any inconsistencies or contradictions between the story and other evidence.

Declan had kept up-to-speed with the evolving situation in Afghanistan over the years. He was, after all, emotionally invested in it through thoughts of the Military life he could have had, of a lost friend, never forgotten. He'd honed in on news reports about the machinations of international leaders which led to troops pulling out and abandoning the country even though after twenty years they'd failed in their primary objective to leave only when the terrorist threat was gone and there was a stable government in place. It was clear to Declan, that with the international armed support system removed the country was bound to fall like a house of cards, and it did, with the Taliban taking Afghanistan back under strict Sharia Law in just ten days. This particular captive was a shadow, and had been in the middle of the conflict and politics. Declan wanted to bring him into the light and get as much actionable Intel as he could.

Sam entered the arena, walking behind Declan, and Brody followed. As Declan's eyes became accustomed to the low light he paused and took in the scene. The show jumping arena displayed yet more signs of vandalism inside. The plastic-tiered seating that wrapped around the arena had been set alight in sections and the melted remains of congealed orange plastic bucket seats looked ghoulish in the waning light. Unlit construction lamps were placed around the space. In the centre of the arena, *Alzzalam* was secured to a chair, hunched in on himself, a black cotton bag loosely over his head. Weights from the horse jumps had been threaded through the supports of the chair to hold it down. There was no way the captive could push himself forward, backwards, left, or right.

Declan's gut churned at the sight of the bound man. He'd been in the very same position several times and the helplessness he'd felt on waking to discover he was unable to escape had been horrifying. *This man's lucky*, Declan mused *he's no' being interrogated by the Taliban, or by Mrs K for that matter!*

A tall, wiry blonde woman in tactical gear stood beside the seated man, a wheeled hard plastic trolley bag beside her. There was a bag of liquid attached to an extended handle on the trolley bag. The prisoner's left sleeve was cut away and a tube was running from the bag to his arm.

Suddenly the construction lamps blazed to life lighting up the space. Declan closed his eyes for a second and blinked several times to dispel the glare. He proceeded across the arena. The medic, Agent Weber had finished checking the prisoner's vitals. She walked around the seated man, ensuring his bonds were secure.

A second chair sat two meters in front of the prisoner, and there was a chair behind. Sam moved behind, and Declan headed for the chair in front.

Agent Weber pulled a bottle of water from her medical bag. She turned to Declan and he nodded hello.

"Don't let the state of him deceive you. He's much healthier than he looks. The intravenous line is a vitamin drip to tide him over," the Austrian explained.

"Are we ready?" Declan asked. Brody positioned himself a few meters to the left of Sam, beside the arena barrier. He put two thumbs up. Then Declan looked at Sam, who nodded.

Declan stood in front of the chair opposite the captive, his hands on his hips. It was time for the cotton bag to be removed and to finally see the face of the mythic warlord

196

who had sent shockwaves of fear into the hearts of Afghan people and allies alike.

Agent Weber removed a syringe from her medical kit. "I'm going to administer a small shot of Ritalin to wake him up," she explained as she inserted the needle into the injection port on the drip line and depressed the plunger. She then stood in front of the prisoner and dragged the cotton bag from the man's head.

"Hey, sir, wake up, it's time to wake up," she said giving his bearded cheek a light slap. The agent opened a water bottle and poured a little over the man's head. He shuddered and jerked as the cold water ran down his neck, and his dry scratchy voice yelled,

"Wha' the fuck!"

Hearing him speak made Declan's blood run cold. His gunmetal grey eyes darted to meet Sam's brilliant green and they shared a quizzical look. *Ali Amir Alzzalam* had a...Scottish accent.

Weber gripped the back of the man's head, pulled his head back, and held the bottle to his lips. Without struggling, he drank the contents of the bottle. When the agent stepped aside and nodded for Declan to proceed. Declan set his gaze on *Ali Amir Alzzalam* for the first time and said,

"As-salaam alaikum".

The prisoner had russet ginger hair, wind-burned skin, and a thick beard that was a hundred different hues of ginger, orange, and red. Physically, he was well-built, bullish with broad shoulders, muscled biceps, and a thick

197

neck. The prisoner looked up and stared, glassy-eyed at Declan, who, on meeting his gaze inhaled a sharp breath. Declan knew those eyes...would know those eyes until his final breath...which, with the shock of this revelation could be very soon! The man's boyish charms were long gone, but even so, a lightning bolt of shock, horror, and grief shot through Declan's body. He exhaled a whispered, "No", and then folded in the middle as if he'd been punched; the chair behind him catching his fall as he sat heavily. Declan looked up in disbelief at the prisoner. *Ali Amir Alzzalam* was disguised, wearing the same desert-issue cammo uniform as Brody for his escape on a CIA cargo plane. He stared straight back at Declan, his opposite in every way, with his black-styled hair and well-trimmed beard, the sharply tailored suit jacket fitting his muscled frame like a glove.

An unearthly stillness fell between them, the prisoner staring at his interrogator with electrifying watchfulness. Uncomfortable moments passed before the prisoner said in a sand-worn voice,

"Wha' are ye doin' here Numpty? Where are we Dec? Is this hell?"

Declan's heart drummed a tattoo, this was most certainly hell. The prisoner had used his real name and his affectionate nickname, Numpty in front of the other agents. There could be no denying the prisoner knew him—that he knew this man. As the reality of his situation hit home the prisoner's furious eyes widened.

"BASTARD! Where is he, where is he? Where's that big American bastard? You fuckin' liar, you liar, you said we'd be landing at Ramstein. I told ye comin' to the UK was a deal breaker," he roared into the void, struggling in his seat, trying unsuccessfully to loosen the bonds. The weights placed on the chair legs prevented the chair from moving even an inch, let alone toppling and so his attempts to free himself were fruitless. Sam stepped up behind the roaring man and placed a hand on the prisoner's shoulder.

"Peace be with you. Calm down brother, take a few deep breaths," Sam said in Dari. The prisoner stilled and yet he glared at Declan, a look of confusion and betrayal.

Declan was sweating, his blood burning in his veins, he couldn't breathe, couldn't focus, gods, he couldn't deal with this. He stood abruptly,

"I...I need some air," he said, then bolted from his chair and ran toward the hole in the wall.

Sam turned his concerned gaze to Brody who returned one of alarm and confusion.

"Give us a sec," Sam said and then swiftly strode after his partner.

****

"Which way did he go?" Sam asked Agent Farrell sternly as he grabbed the bottle of water Agent Feurig offered.

"Take the left and go into the copse of trees," Farrell suggested, "He hasn't gone far," he added, pointing to where Declan's movement had set off one of the motion sensors.

Sam rushed away from the van, clambering over metal debris, timber supports and smashed brick to find the pathway of flattened weeds that led into the trees. When he caught up, Declan was sitting on a storm felled tree trunk. His face was ashen and the thousand-yard stare told Sam that Declan's mind was miles away. Sam pressed his body cam button to stop recording.

"Turn off your camera," Sam hollered in a commanding tone as he approached. Declan shuddered as if he hadn't heard Sam's footfall and then he absently pressed the button twice to turn the camera off.

"What's going on?" Sam asked tentatively as he sat on the log beside his partner. His voice took on a calm timber that masked his true confused feelings. "Who is he, because he seems to think he knows you, love."

"Ah, he knows me alright…" Declan said grimly, "but I don't have a fuckin' clue who that man is. The person I knew, the one that looks and sounds like him… is long dead," he sneered.

"*Ali Amir Alzzalam*…Ali the Devil…is Alasdair Frazer, isn't he? He's the friend you joined up with, the friend who was killed on patrol in Helmand, the friend you were secretly in love with."

Declan's bowed head nodded and his hands rose to cup his face. This revelation had cut Declan Ramsay to the core. Sam's heart shattered as his husband began to weep.

****

CHAPTER 19

INTERROGATE

Declan's childhood best friends Alasdair Frazer and Dominic Hennessey both joined the SCOT's Regiment with him when they'd turned eighteen. Sam had heard the story before, but he passed the open water bottle to his husband and gave Declan what he needed, a shoulder to cry on and time. Declan took a long swallow from the bottle before he said,

"You know how this went down. I was an eejit. I had te be in remission fer five years before joining up. I was only in remission fer four at the time. I lied on my application, I lied when I had mah medical. It was a stupid, stupid thing te do. I should have waited a year until I would have been all-clear, but I didnae want te get left behind, I wanted te be with mah boys." Declan paused for a gulp of water from the bottle.

"Anyways, somehow the Army found out I'd lied and even though I was doing well...the best in our unit, they gave me a medical discharge. I was so fuckin' gutted when Dominic and Alasdair got deployed... and even more so when Alasdair never came back."

"You were told he'd died during a patrol?"

"Aye, that was the story his family was given. I always knew in mah gut that somethin' wasnea right about it. The

201

MoD said he went out on night patrol and his fire team was attacked by rebels. They got split up. His team returned to the base, but Alasdair never did and a search later found a burned body with his tags. I'm guessing now that was all a set-up." Declan said morosely.

Sam knew that Alasdair had not only been Declan's best mate but his secret first love and Declan had carried the guilty belief that he'd let his friend down. He'd believed he should have been with Alasdair in Afghanistan to have his six. He'd blamed himself for the loss, and it had crippled him emotionally. It was only with Sam's understanding, love, and devotion that Declan began to heal, tear down his walls, and let go of all of the things he couldn't control about his past.

"When somebody dies ye always wish fer just ten more minutes wi' them just a chance to tell them how loved they are an' how much ye miss them," Declan said. Sam reached out and rubbed Declan's back.

"Fer years I wished I'd had more time wi' Alasdair and now I've got mah wish an' it turns out Alasdair not only faked his death, but he's the lying, murdering, conniving bastard we've been searching for." Declan roughly swiped the tears from his swollen eyes.

"Gods. Ye couldnae make this shite up, could ye." He huffed a humourless laugh as Sam pulled him in for an embrace.

"I'm so sorry love," Sam said as he held his husband. Sam was grateful that Declan trusted him and loved him so much that he could be vulnerable in Sam's arms. They

202

remained in the hug for a while, the muffled sounds of Declan's grief and the birdsong among the trees anchoring them.

Declan pulled away from Sam and said a self-conscious, "Thanks," as if ashamed of his outburst. He removed a cotton handkerchief from his pocket, wiped his face, and blew his nose.

"I know this is a huge shock, but, and I don't want you to think I'm being insensitive, but we're on the clock. If you want me to take the lead I'll do it." Sam offered.

"Oh no, no, no. This interrogation's mine," Declan insisted. "I need answers. I need a reckoning. We have te understand what the hell he was involved in an' what it has te do wi James. I can do this. Just give me a minute to get my head on straight. I can get answers fer both of us," Declan said fiercely. "I'm sure of it!"

"The Intel we have on him shows he's a master manipulator. Distance yourself. He is not your friend. He'll use your name but don't call him by his name because that makes it personal, makes him human. We'll leave him for an hour to have a nice long think before we go back in."

"Right, okay. You go back, I'll get myself together."

****

They'd left the prisoner alone to stew, and watched him on the monitors in the van. Now, sitting opposite the man he was to interrogate, Declan Ramsay set his slate grey eyes on Alasdair Frazer's dazzling blue gaze and held the stormy stare. It had been eighteen years since the childhood friends were parted because of Declan's little lie—a little lie that had

203

changed Declan's life path in immeasurable ways. Declan hadn't considered rejoining the army when he could have. His mates had moved on, they were at the infantry training centre at Catterick Garrison in Yorkshire and Declan had moved on to begin a degree at university in Edinburgh. There seemed to be no point in pursuing his army dream if he couldn't be with his boys. Declan had felt adrift, locked out of the life he believed he was supposed to have. Two years later it had hurt to see his friends board the aircraft carrier to Helmand, and for only one to return alive. The experience of losing his chosen career and then his best friend was a pivotal moment that moulded Declan's life and his choices. To discover it was all a lie broke something inside him. It was the newly released anger and energy that spurred Declan on.

"Security Services eh, Numpty!" Frazer huffed, "I guess congrats are in order. They got ye in the end," he said, falling into the familiar deep Scots brogue that he probably hadn't unpacked in years.

"You were always were the best of us, always ready to play the hero, weren't ye," Frazer goaded, a heavy hint of jealousy and resentment in the comment.

Declan took in the man's words and mulled them over. What did Frazer mean by saying *'They got you in the end'*? Apart from questioning by MI5 after he accidentally thwarted the bombing of the Icelandic ferry, Declan never knowingly been approached by the Security Services in his youth. His curiosity peeked. He needed to take this slowly, regain Frazer's trust, and make him open up. Sam suggested that Declan should distance himself, and not treat Frazer as a human, but his past connection with Alasdair was a weapon in his arsenal, and Declan was going to use it as long as it suited his aims.

"Do us a favour will ye bud?" the captive grinned. "Send a wee message to General William Jakes with the US State Department. Let him know I'm here. He'll sort everything out," Frazer winked. Declan gave Frazer the hairy eyeball but remained silent. Did he really believe a phone call was his get-out-of-jail-free card? That was either wishful thinking on Frazer's part, or he honestly believed it would work—that he had the power to circumnavigate scrutiny and justice by knowing the right people.

"Off ye go now, there's a good lad," Frazer urged with patronizing glee. Declan needed to do something with his hands, like ball them into fists and...no, instead he ran a hand over his mouth, his beard rasping against his palm. He'd forgotten what a dick Alasdair could be.

Declan recalled from their youth, Frazer always did like to puff his chest out and play the big man–fine when he was protecting young Declan from bullies in the school playground when, at thirteen, he began to weaken from what was later diagnosed as Leukaemia, but they weren't kids anymore and Declan could do without the attitude directed at him now.

"You were dead, Alasdair. We were all devastated by your loss. I couldnae look yer ma and da in the eye cos I was supposed te have yer back," Declan stated, his tone emotionless.

"Dom was a fuckin' mess, we both were... they told us there was nothing left of ye. No one should have te bury an empty fuckin' coffin," Declan ran a hand over his beard again and shook his head disdainfully. "How could ye do that to us... to yer family?"

That knife blade hit its mark because Frazer looked stricken for the blink of an eye as if his mask had slipped, but he closed his eyes, took a breath in through his nose, and slowly let it out through his mouth. He straightened in the seat, opened his eyes, and fixed Declan's storm-grey glare. In a measured drawl Alasdair said,

"Aye, you're right, no one should have te bury an empty coffin. It was a bad, bad thing te do. Unfortunate, but...*necessary*," he added with a sneer, his cornflower blue eyes taking on an arctic chill.

"Necessary?" Declan was appalled by the statement. "Why was it necessary? What the hell did you get tangled up in, cos this is nae looking good fer you, *bud*. I won't be your messenger. We've got ye fer just 24 hours, an' then the people who deal with traitors and terrorists are coming for ye. Your fate is out of my hands." Declan sat back and crossed his legs, the posture relaxed and confident as if he had all the time in the world.

"This is yer one chance, just one chance to air yer dirty laundry and te give yer folks and me some closure."

"Now, why would I want te do that?" Frazer exclaimed camply. Again Declan was stunned by the cruel response but he kept his features schooled. He'd always liked Mr and Mrs Frazer. They'd been good to him and didn't deserve to

206

be betrayed by their son. Declan waited and observed until the silence became awkward for Frazer. He sighed dramatically and conceded,

"Och, ye wouldnae understand, Dec."

"Try me."

Frazer eyed the wedding band on Declan's ring finger and then he met Declan's gaze.

"You married? Congrats," he said conversationally, trying to put Declan off his game.

"We're not here to talk about me. This is all about you, so tell me, what would I no' understand? Why were the betrayal and the lies necessary?"

"Fine, I did it fer love...for Allah. That's why it was necessary."

The reply was something Declan had not anticipated. Neither man was from a devoutly religious family. Religion wasn't a part of Declan's life. When had it become part of Alasdair's life? Declan's gaze drifted up and met Sam's, and Sam gave a nod of encouragement.

"Would ye care to elaborate?" Declan asked.

"No' really, but I suppose we've got some time te kill before ye hand me over to... who is it? The CIA, Interpol, MI6?" Frazer paused, watching Declan for a tell but Declan remained stony-faced. Declan seemed to have rattled Frazer for refusing the request to let his US contact know he was in the UK. It was good that the prisoner was unclear about who was running the show.

"Mebe, the FSB, or ISI in Pakistan?" Frazer hedged. "I know they'd be delighted te get their grubby mitts on me!"

"If you want, I'll listen te yer confession." The men stared at one another in a silent battle, before Frazer said,

"I am Muslim. Sins are to be kept to oneself until a believer seeks forgiveness from Allah. God forgives those who seek his forgiveness and commit themselves to not repeating the sin. The only power who can absolve me is Allah, not man, not you Ramsay!" Frazer spat derisively.

Declan backtracked. "Just think of me as yer old friend then. You spent half your life in Scotland with me, and from what I understand, the other half in Afghanistan. Tell me yer story. I'm here for ye Frazer, just like I promised I would be when we were bairns. You should know by now that I keep mah promises." A heated look shot between the men that told of deep friendship, love, pain, and betrayal.

"Hmmm," Frazer said thoughtfully. "I guess I could spin a yarn… but I've got conditions."

"And they are?"

"Cut the cuffs."

Declan's gaze shot to Brody who gave him a sharp shake of the head.

"Not happening. What else?"

"I stay dead. It's not as if I'm ever going home again, is it? I don't want anybody in our circle to know I'm not dead. I mean it. Dom, don't tell him, an' if my Ma's still around, don't say a word. Leave her be. D'ye understand? Alasdair Frazer died. I'm Alistair to you, but to the rest of the world I'm *Ali Amir Alzzalam*."

Declan didn't need to gauge Brody's response to that request. Declan couldn't break Alasdair's mother's heart again and Dom was happy, settled with Declan's sister, Freya, and they had a baby on the way. Declan couldn't throw them off course with the horrific reality of what Frazer had done. "Very well, is that it?"

"Nah," Frazer gave Declan a wan smile and said, "I'm no' getting out of this alive, am I Dec? I don't suppose ye could get me a box of *Tunnocks Teacakes*. Wi' the desert heat, they're the one thing I couldnae safely smuggle."

Declan's eyes met Sam's. It just so happened that there was a box of the Scottish treats in a carrier bag in the SUV. Sam nodded in wordless understanding, and then he swiftly left the arena. Declan was surprised that Frazer hadn't asked for more. As far as they were aware from their Intel, Ali the Devil had been a fearsome warlord who ruled the border provinces with Pakistan and ensured the supply chain of illicit goods, weapons, drugs, and people in and out of Afghanistan. He knew a lot of information that would be valuable to Pakistan and the western allies. Frazer could have asked for money, transport, and a way out in return for information. Maybe he truly did believe he had an ace and would be free when his contact found out he was being held captive. Declan observed him. Frazer didn't come across as the fearsome devil that the hype portrayed. He was the shell of a man, a man who'd lost everything. Why would Erik Madsson worship a man like this? Was the myth of Ali just that, a myth, smoke, and mirrors?

"I'm parched Dec. Can I get some water?"

Agent Weber sent her gaze to Declan and he nodded. She retrieved a new bottle of water from her medical bag, opened it, and stepped in front of the bound man. She held it to his wind-burned, peeling lips and let him drink. After a few thirsty gulps, Frazer sneered lecherously at the female agent and said,

"Cheers darlin'. Will ye be as handy later and hold my cock when I need te pish?" Weber returned a glacier look and twisted the cap back on the water bottle. Frazer's filthy laugh echoed in the derelict shell of the horse arena.

Sam returned then holding an iconic yellow and red box containing six *Tunnocks Teacakes* stopping Frazer's laughter in its tracks. He placed the box on the ground between Declan and Alasdair.

Frazer appeared stunned to see the box as if the crown jewels had been placed in front of him and not a box of cakes. "Wow. I'm, I'm impressed," he admitted. "Well played my friend. Well played," Frazer said thoughtfully. "Yer no such a Numpty anymore are ye?"

"Enough fuckin' about," Declan asserted. "You know as well as I that I can down that whole box of teacakes in six bites. If ye want to taste even one of them, talk te me!"

****

CHAPTER 20
THE REBEL CANDIDATE

"Where does this sorry tale begin?"

Alasdair stared at his interrogator, eyes stony, before jutting out his chin and admitting.

"It begins with *you*, my friend." That intimate announcement put Declan on the back foot. He shared a glance with Sam, and then his gaze flicked to Brody and Weber who had taken a seat beside the wrecked outer fence of the arena.

"You were what, fourteen when ye got so sick that they took you away from me?"

A lump formed in Declan's throat. It wouldn't do to show any emotion. He would not allow Alasdair to manipulate him and gain the upper hand. It was as Sam said; this man was not his friend. He was a liar and a traitor.

"I know it happened a long, long time ago, another lifetime, but we'd had such an uncomplicated childhood until then. It floored me when my da told me you were sick. I never knew anyone who was dyin' before. Everyone thought you didnae have a hope in hell of recovery," he paused and in a near childlike tone said, "I heard my ma and da talkin' about it all when they thought I was asleep on the couch. *That poor wee lad doesnae have a chance*, my ma said," Frazer's gaze swept up and down the man sitting

211

opposite while Declan returned a stern gunmetal stare.

"An' look at you now, big man. You're a fuckin' miracle. Nobody would know now that ye were ever sick." Alasdair shook his head and grimaced. "Back then I was so sure you were gonna die and there was nothin' I could do about it. I kinda withdrew into mesel'," he admitted.

Declan had never really considered how his friends coped while he was fighting for his life, but thinking about it now, it must have been a struggle for them too.

"I was so angry at God for doin' that to you. How can there be a just and merciful God if good people, if bairns get sick and die?"

The words hurt Declan's heart. Alasdair was stripping him to his core.

"They said I couldn't visit ye in case I gave you a cold or something. It was like you'd already died. I started fallin' behind at school, gettin' inte fights, acting out. Mah folks didn't know what to do with me. I was so angry, all the time and I just *couldn't* be around anyone. Da thought that buying me a new desktop computer would take my mind off things and help me with schoolwork. It did help, in a way," Frazer shrugged lost in reminiscence.

"I was gaming an' using chat rooms. They were supposed to be fer over eighteen's, but everyone lied about their age. You could get instant access to the chat room an' chat with people from all around the world. It was exciting and I got off on the anonymity of it. I didnae have te be fifteen-year-old Ally Frazer from Stirling. I could be anyone I wanted te to be." Frazer smiled at the memory.

"You got addicted?"

"I guess I was an addict from the get-go. The games were all war, first-person shooter. I got sucked in, made a few friends and we all competed te get into the Champion's chat room. Took me a while of playing obsessively and honing my skills to get in, and when I did I got chatting with some real soldiers and I understood my purpose." Alasdair said cryptically.

Declan was aware gaming platforms had been a recruiting ground since the dawn of the internet. And twenty years ago, when cyber security was arguably in its infancy, it was easier for bad actors to infiltrate chat rooms.

The interrogation was unearthing all kinds of memories and feelings that Declan had buried. He recalled how Alasdair was different when he returned home to Scotland from the Swiss clinic. Alasdair had shot up, grown into himself, and gained confidence and determination. His once wiry teenage frame sported newly packed muscle from working out, along with a smattering of ginger peach fuzz stubble lining his jaw and above his upper lip. It had been strange to return and see how Alasdair had grown, to admire his developing masculine physique, and feel...something else for his friend.

"You were radicalized?" Declan stated flatly.

"Radicalized!" Frazer chuffed a mirthless laugh.

"Well, ye could say that if you were being overdramatic, or ye could say I finally met my people and found the righteous path of Allah. When ye got better I knew it was a sign. I understood that Allah had listened to my prayers

213

and you were healed because of my faith. Dec, you helped me to find my God, my people, and my true path. Thank you." Frazer said with a respectful nod of his head.

Declan shuddered. What disturbed him the most was the adamant sincerity with which Frazer explained his conversion. Frazer had constructed a false narrative, connecting Declan's recovery with his religious calling.

Declan folded his arms. "Yer a Scotsman, Frazer, the fights in yer blood. But I never saw even a hint that ye gave a shite about freedom and independence for Scotland? Why was that? Why was betraying your family and country preferable to fighting for them?"

"Everything I did was Allah's will. You have no right to question it. Allah chose a path for me alone," he replied fiercely.

"Oh aye. And what was your particular path?" Declan said sarcastically. "I'm not judging, I'm honestly interested to know what happened to you when I was at the Swiss clinic."

"It's simple. I played hooky from school and attended Edinburgh Central Mosque for Friday prayers, to pray for you. I met a boy my age. He helped me understand the rituals to prepare for the congregational prayers, gave me an English translation of the Holy Qu'ran, and helped me to learn some Dari. We became friends, and I told him I wanted to learn how to fight. He introduced me to some elders, and one day, I was taken to a side room to meet a visiting cleric, *Mahmood Al Raami*."

Declan gulped and he and Sam shared a wide-eyed look

of surprise. Al Raami had been the head of a known Jihadist group. He'd travelled widely around the world in his role as a cleric and covertly connected those who wanted to join the armed struggle to his contacts in Al-Qaeda and ISIS, ensuring a supply of willing young men pumped up on rhetoric and ready to fight for the cause.

"He encouraged me to join up to the British Army, told me that real men fight for what they believe in. *'It takes one match to light a fire, the prophet wants you to be the match'*, he told me. And he was right. What was the point of playing fuckin' war games on computers when there was a real war that needed soldiers?"

Brody chipped in then, "Did you know Al Raami got the justice he deserved for sending thousands of young men to their deaths in the name of Jihad? The US government took out his compound in a drone attack in 2017. He's dead."

"I know. *Al Raami* was a martyr. *Inna lillahi wa inna ilayhi raji'un*" (Verily we belong to Allah, and truly to Him shall we return) Frazer recited.

"Al Raami was a groomer," Brody shot back. "He brainwashed vulnerable young men, took them from their families, and sent them to their deaths with explosives strapped to their chests," he countered fiercely.

"Much like US Military recruitment," Frazer shot back. Electric silence sizzled. After a drawn-out minute, he said, "Do ye think I don't know what Al Raami did? Ye have te understand. I was just sixteen when I met him. I suppose I was easy pickings, thought I knew everything, but I was green. I didnae understand the complex politics of

215

Afghanistan. I didnae know what I was gettin' into. You're right. I can see now, in hindsight, that I was just a naïve stupid wee boy." Frazer admitted regretfully. "But I paid the price for my involvement wi' Al Raami," he asserted, a pained expression on his face. "I have the scars to prove it."

"So, having been recruited into Al Raami's network you signed up to join the British Army and two years later got your first tour of duty."

"Aye. It was a long game. There were a few hiccups along the way but I eventually got where he needed me te be."

Declan was with Alasdair throughout this time, and yet, as the story unravelled Declan saw he'd never known the man at all. Nobody ever questioned that Frazer was born to be a Jock guard as he'd taken to the regimen of military life like a duck to water, and yet Frazer kept his true beliefs, his true nature hidden so well.

"Hiccups?"

"I had to make sacrifices. There was always gonna be casualties." Frazer sneered.

Hearing those words made Declan's blood run cold. "What did you do?" The words flew like arrows of ice.

"Don't fuckin' look at me like that Dec." Frazer snarled. "I saved your fuckin' life, that's what I did. You'd already endured so much to stay alive. I couldn't risk havin' you around when I carried out Al Raami's orders. You were my Achilles heel, Numpty. You were the only one who coulda stopped me."

Declan sent a sharp alarmed look to Sam, who gestured

216

with his hands for Declan to keep his calm. Declan knew what Alasdair was going to say before he said it. He wanted to wring the backstabbing bastard's neck.

"I was the one who scuppered your army career. I had to do it, especially after the suits came to the barracks."

"What?" Declan exhaled in shock, "Suits? What suits?"

The Scots Guards had forged a reputation of being one of the toughest infantry units in the British Army. The initial training was carried out at Catterick Barracks in Yorkshire, and then they went down to Mons Barracks in Aldershot.

"You came back from that clinic, not just well, but changed, improved. Dom an' I used te joke that they'd given you superpowers," Frazer scoffed. "At home, ye never sat down. You were either running in the hills or had yer head in a book just eatin' up information."

Declan remembered that. He'd felt so well, so happy to be alive, and he'd continued the routine when he'd shared a dorm with his mates at the barracks. Dr Schroeder's treatment had initially delayed his puberty but by the time he was eighteen hormones were like raging lava boiling in his blood. He'd tried everything to take his mind off his growing feelings for Frazer, but they were in the same fire team, they showered together, ate together, slept in the same bunk beds, Declan on top! And so during his downtime to relieve the sexual tension, Declan trained.

"Tell me about these suits," Declan demanded.

"I was on sentry duty, near the end of my shift when a group of men arrived in a black SUV. I viewed their IDs. They were MoD, SIS, and the like. I was a curious wee shite, and so when my shift was done I went past the meeting room and, wha-de-ye know, the door was ajar," he said theatrically.

"I waited and I listened. They were talking about the possibility of a future deployment in Afghanistan and the difficulties with getting trustworthy Intel. They were looking for a cadet to join military intelligence, a new guy with potential but no experience that they could train up. Your name was mentioned, and a posh guy said they'd been watching you fer a while."

"You're lying." Declan's head swam as he was again, sucker punched. Frazer had no reason to lie about this. Declan looked up searching for the anchor of Sam's fern green eyes and saw that Sam had his phone out and he was looking for something.

"I shit you not," Frazer insisted. "When I heard they wanted you for military Intel I knew it would put us at loggerheads. You're no' my enemy, Dec, ye never were. I had to get you out of the picture so I left an anonymous note for our CO telling him that you were a liability, and you'd lied on yer application."

"Ye backstabbing bastard!" Declan couldn't rein his anger in any longer. He lurched up from his chair, appalled by the betrayal but before he could lay a finger on Alasdair, Brody had his meaty grip around Declan's waist pulling him aside, pushing him against the arena barrier and then crowding Declan's body with his bulk. The American's dark coffee eyes fixed on Declan and in a low rumbly whisper, he said.

"I know it's hard. But you got to keep it together bro. Don't let him know he's getting to you."

"It's a bit fuckin' late fer that!" Declan ground out as he seethed.

"You've been doin' great, we've got some good Intel here but you've just scratched the surface. Now, take a breath, find your core, remember why the hell you're here, and then get back in the ring. You got this!" Declan was a fighter in a boxing match and Brody was his coach.

"Och, come on, Dec," Frazer pleaded, "It was a long time ago, another lifetime. And, the SIS got you in the end so everything worked out well for ye," he called in justification.

Declan breathed in through his nostrils and let the breath out slowly as he fought to keep his emotions in check. He remembered why he was here. Erik Madsson had tried to kill the man Declan loved, twice, and James had been abducted. Frazer knew something pertinent to these events and they had to find out what that was. Declan nodded to Brody,

"Comprendez. I got this. Thank you."

Brody then stepped back out of Declan's space and retook his sentry spot by the arena barrier to the right of the prisoner. Declan straightened his suit jacket and then returned to his seat.

"Who were the men from the MoD and the SIS? Do you remember any names?"

"Christ, are ye mad? It was what? Eighteen years ago." Frazer scoffed. "They flashed their ID cards at me fer a few seconds. I cannea remember when I last had a shite, let

219

alone the names of random suits from years ago!"

Sam stepped between the two men and wordlessly passed Declan his phone. Declan scanned the image on the screen. He'd never seen the photograph before but was sure it was from one of James's parties. The gorgeous turquoise blue tiled wall, ornate stained glass, and carved stone column in the background told Declan the location was one he'd attended a party at, Freemason's Hall in Covent Garden. James appeared younger, disturbingly attractive and he stood with a group of men, some in high-ranking Military uniforms, and others in suits. They all held champagne flutes and smiled cordially for the camera while a sea of the well-to-do milled in the background. Declan realised to his horror he recognized another one of the men— a man he didn't know had any connection to James from before Oliver and Belle's wedding. His doctor, Karl Schroeder. That was curious. Declan turned the phone screen and leaned forward so that Alasdair could see.

"Do you recognize anyone in this photo?"

Alasdair squinted a little and leaned in and perused the image. "Might do," he said speculatively "Fer a teacake."

"You're really pushin' yer luck!" This was a man who'd struck fear into tribesmen, Taliban, and international security agencies for at least ten years and here he was begging for a treat like a desperate puppy. What had happened before the withdrawal of allied forces to make Frazer so desperate, and why was he willing to sing like a caged bird for a fucking *Tunnocks Teacake*? Declan clenched his jaw, looked up and nodded to Sam who rounded the

220

chair, retrieved and unwrapped the foil from the sweet cake and held it to Alasdair's lips. The man lurched forward and in an animalistic gesture took the whole thing in his mouth, his eyes closed, and he moaned orgasmically as he chewed, chocolate, saliva, and Italian meringue covering his lips as it spilt out of his mouth. After half a minute he swallowed and licked his lips ensuring not a crumb escaped.

"Fuckin' hell," Alasdair sighed "that brings me back. D'ye remember sitting up on Arthur's Seat and each of us going through a ten-pack while watching the world go by?"

Declan refused to be thrown off course by reminiscence this time. "Who do you recognize in the photo?" Declan asked again, his voice stern as he held the phone up for Frazer to view.

"Fuuck," Frazer sighed resignedly. "The guy in the middle was some kind of scientist. Second on the left...that guy's MoD," he said picking out a man in Army uniform, "And the blond man, he was deffo a spook. We've crossed paths many times over the years."

So, he'd recognized James, Declan's physician Karl Schroeder, and a high-ranking member of the Army. What the ever-loving fuck was going on?

Sam spoke up. "There's another photo I want you to look at," he said, coming around to Declan's side and taking his phone back. He scrolled and turned the screen to face the prisoner. The reaction was immediate and priceless. Frazer's feet scraped on the sandy surface of the horse arena as he tried to push his chair back, away from the image. The weights on the chair ensured there was no escape.

"No, no, no! I'm not sayin' another word, I've said too much already," he spat unable to hide his terror. Sam turned the screen for Declan to see and Declan nodded in understanding. Sam had shown Frazer the photo of the Alphabet Club.

Brody spoke up, "We've been at this for two hours. Let's take a break, get some food, and start again."

****

CHAPTER 21
PHONE HOME

Declan was relieved to turn off his body cam, get out of the arena, and away from Alasdair Frazer. He'd never thought he'd want to run from Alasdair, but being in the same room as him, looking into his eyes and knowing the pain he'd caused made Declan feel things he wasn't proud of. He was crushed and confused by Frazer's sudden resurrection and his revelations had gotten the cogs whirring in Declan's brain. Agent Feurig stood with her arms crossed in the open side door of the surveillance van,

"We have sandwiches, protein bars, and drinks. I'll take some into the others and feed the prisoner."

Declan snagged sandwiches and drinks for himself and Sam and followed Sam to the privacy of their SUV.

Declan sat in the vehicle, distracted by the maelstrom of thoughts in his head. Sam chomped away on his sandwich.

"Are you going to eat that?" Sam prompted after he'd finished his first triangle. "Hey, Buttercup, where are you?" he waved a hand in front of Declan's face.

Declan shuddered out of his daze. "I'm here," he said and opened the sandwich box.

"Are you sure? You looked to be miles away."

Declan dry washed his face with his hands, "This has thrown me for a loop, is all."

"I can see," Sam sighed. "Look. You might not like it, but I think it would be best if I took over when we go back in. I understand the customs and traditions Frazer has been living with."

"But...I was getting somewhere..." Declan complained.

"Yes you were, but we don't have the time to get a blow-by-blow of how he faked his death, and how he survived as a Westerner in Taliban-controlled territory. I need to push him on the details of his smuggling network. Who were his contacts, and what's his connection to Madsson? Our missing links are between Frazer, Madsson, and whoever's employing him in his campaign of terror against A.L.L. MI6 has Frazer for longer and they can squeeze him for the whole story."

Declan appeared uncharacteristically pale and drawn, a half-eaten limp sandwich in his hand.

"I know you cared about him," Sam said softly, "But he's right in one respect. He's not the boy you once knew and loved. Frazer was radicalized as a teenager and, I know this sounds harsh, but it happened right under your nose." Declan turned and glared reproachfully at Sam, but Sam held his hand up in a calming gesture.

"That's not on you. But it shows how manipulative he can be. Frazer compartmentalized and kept that part of himself secret from you. He joined the army with the prime objective of betraying his comrades and country for holy war. He's clever and he's cunning. He faked his death and somehow survived and thrived amid a brutal regime that sees westerners as a danger to their values and way of life.

The Taliban accepted him as a brother...." Sam said with exasperation.

"Until they didnae."

"Yes. We don't know what happened to expedite his extraction from Afghanistan. But you bear no responsibility for how he turned out or the path he chose. He's using your shared past to manipulate you. He's stringing his story out to steer clear of the vital information we need. I have no emotional ties to him. I'll get the Intel we need."

"Fine," Declan conceded, the fight all but knocked out of him. "He's all yours." They both chomped on ham salad sandwiches for a few minutes before, with a worn-out sigh, Declan said

"I think I need to call my father."

"Okay, but you can't let him know our location, or that Frazer's alive."

Declan pinched the bridge of his nose in frustration. "I may not have been at this fer as long as you but I'm not stupid," he roared, uncharacteristically brusque with Sam. Declan rarely raised his voice to Sam and an alien fragile silence fell between them as they looked ahead through the windscreen and focused on Agent Farrell, jumping out of the van and stretching his weary bones.

"Look. I'm sorry fer roaring at ye. I'm just... untethered," Declan admitted. "This whole thing's floored me, and something's been niggling in the back of my mind. That photo of James and the men in suits. I'd never seen it before. Where did it come from?"

"I found it in a folder of images of Dad's events over the

years. That was one of the earliest."

"Well," Declan sighed, "It not only showed a member of the MoD with yer da but my doctor, Karl Schroeder."

"He was at Oliver and Belle's wedding," Sam recalled.

"My Da invited him. As far as I'm aware he and Karl have been golfing buddy's fer years, but I don't know how Karl is connected to James. I need to understand how my da met him because I've got the sneaking suspicion that the reason your father has had his eye on me for so long is that he's... invested in me somehow." Declan admitted.

"Are you serious?" Sam said, shocked as he glared at his husband's expression. "Gods, you are!"

"Aye. Think about it. I went into remission at fifteen, that's twenty-one years ago and still, Schroeder's research hasnae made it into the public realm. There are no research papers about it, no reports. Why not? The treatment I had could help millions of people. The immunotherapy top-ups keep me well and I've got no fucking clue what's actually in it. Schroeder said that it's genetically engineered cells that hunt down anything that could make me sick. I don't get sick...ever. And because I've been so fit fer so long I never questioned it, why would I? Now I find out that James has had an unnatural interest in me practically since I got out of the clinic," Declan said insistently. "I'm nothing special...but they seem to think I am."

Sam leaned across the centre console, gripped Declan's jaw and turned his head to ensure they locked eyes, "You're special to me, love." he said softly, "Do what you need to do to be at peace with your past. I believe in you and I'll do

226

what I can to help you get to the bottom of this," he purred, his eyes shining with love.

Declan appreciated Sam's support more than he could say. His Adam's apple bobbed as he tried to keep his emotions in check but a rebel tear escaped and rolled down his cheek. Sam laid a soft kiss on the tear and then moved to claim Declan's mouth. When they broke the salty kiss Sam shattered the tender moment,

"I'll give you some space to make the call, I need a piss," he grinned, then hopped out of the car, and headed for the trees.

Declan knew he should have called his father before now and he'd been dodging his calls. He took a few calming breaths to gird his loins for what would be a tricky conversation. He palmed his phone and using an encrypted app, made the call.

"Da..." he said tentatively when his father picked up.

"Son, Gods, I've been going frantic." Donal Ramsay sounded older and far more fragile than Declan remembered. "You've not been picking up my calls. I havenae heard a peep from Eileen and Oliver's phone goes straight te voicemail. What's goin' on?" I was wonderin' whether I should call the police." Declan didn't want to scare his dad, but he also couldn't leave him in the dark any longer.

"Mum's okay. She's with Oli and Belle, helping to look after baby Rosa."

"That must be it, I bet she's in her element an' doesnae have a minute fer little old me."

"That's… not it," Declan said hesitantly.

"Whadaya mean?"

"Dad, look. You cannot tell a soul what I tell you now… not even Freya and Dom. I'm serious, d'ye understand?"

"Aye, aye… just tell me what's going on son, yer scaring me,"

"Something happened down here last week. James was abducted by a home invasion gang. They're holding him fer ransom. The family was moved to a safe house while a specialist kidnap retrieval company gets James back."

"What? No? Can I speak to Eileen?" Donal asked sounding terrified. Declan had messed this up, and his plan to not scare his father had backfired spectacularly!

"I havenae even seen a photo of my granddaughter."

"Sorry Da. I know yer worried, but fer their safety even I don't know their location. But I trust the people who are keeping our family safe."

"How long will they be at this…this safe house?"

"I don't know, but please don't fret. I'll let you know when we get James back and I'll bring you down to meet wee Rosa."

"Okay,"

Declan paused for an instant before tentatively saying, "I need to ask you some questions Da, and they're not connected to this."

"Aye," Donal said, sounding dazed.

"Karl Schroeder. Tell me about him. How did you meet? When did you meet?"

"Karl?" Donal said, confused. "What de ye want to

228

know about Karl for?"

"Just answer the question, please Da." Declan was trying hard to keep his voice calm and conversational, but it was a struggle.

"Gods, I've known him fer so long...let me think fer a sec, my old noggin isn't as sharp as it used te be!"

A few tense moments passed before Donal said,

"He was at the Children's Hospital when you were having a session of Chemo. Your mother and I were so devastated by your illness an' I just hated seeing my wee boy with needles in yer arm. Karl sat at my table in the cafeteria. I told him how sick you were. We got talking about golf...he asked me if I'd like a round to take my mind off things. We got on so well and yer mother liked him too."

This wasn't the story he'd remembered as a child, but then again, he'd been on so much medication back then it was a blur.

"I know you paid him a lot of money to get me into that clinical trial. Do you have any idea what the treatment consisted of?"

"Karl said it was experimental immunotherapy. Neither of us is a doctor, son. We were desperate; we'd have done anything to save you. It was immunotherapy; they jolted yer immune cells to kill the cancer," Donal said determinedly. "And it worked. Why do ye want to know this now anyways? Are you sick?"

"No, no, I'm fine. I just heard something that made me wonder," Declan said cryptically.

"Why are you questioning your treatment now? You

survived… isn't that enough? I'll never be able to repay Karl for saving you, never. He's a good friend, and a good man," Donal said fiercely.

"Sorry to upset you… I didnae mean to…look, forget it…it was nothing." Declan backtracked feeling a wave of guilt at causing his placid father to raise his voice.

"I've got te get back to work…I'll call you later and we'll have a good chat. I'll send you some photos of wee Rosa, aye?"

"Aye, son, I'd like that. I hope Sam's okay, he must be in pieces. You look after that boy, ye hear."

"I will, don't ye worry. Bye Da."

****

CHAPTER 22
DESERT FOX

It was all change when Sam and Declan returned to the arena. Agent Brody stood behind the prisoner in an assertive military posture. His menacing bulk and intimidating presence made Frazer appear more than a little uncomfortable and twitchier than before.

Sam took the seat opposite the prisoner and Declan stood out of Frazer's eye-line, leaning on the arena barrier where Brody had stood before. Time was running out. MI6 would arrive to collect Frazer by lunchtime tomorrow. Sam's goal was to drill down now and get specifics. He needed to focus on Frazer's smuggling operation and his connection to James—a revelation that Sam was appalled to learn about after twelve months of James pleading ignorance. But, Sam's priority was to find out about Ali's relationship with mercenary Erik Madsson.

Madsson had, under the effects of strong Valerian and hypnosis, told of how he was captured and imprisoned in an Afghani sinkhole prison, and later rescued by Ali. The medical reports from his interrogation suggested that he'd undergone some kind of mental breakdown while imprisoned in the hole in the ground with the torturous sun baking him. He may have started having hallucinations due to dehydration, so when Ali found him and pulled him up

231

into the light it could have seemed like a religious experience. Ali had most definitely saved Madsson's life, and therefore Erik Madsson could have developed what he believed was an unbreakable bond with the rebel warlord.

"You've got quite the reputation Ali Amir Alzzalam; I've heard some eye-opening stories about you!" Sam said, deciding to speak in Dari. The prisoner grinned at hearing the language and replied in kind,

"I've learned a fair bit about controlling my brand, as it were. It's amazing what giving a few Afghani notes to gossipy women in market squares can do. Ali the devil was everywhere and nowhere. They did like to embroider stories as they passed them on," he grinned. "My exploits amaze even me. I'd have had to be in ten places at once to carry out all of the insurgent attacks and smuggling schemes attributed to me," he snickered.

Sam found this admission curious. Afghanistan was a multi-ethnic and mostly tribal society with at least seventeen different tribes making up the Afghani people. Word of mouth was an excellent way to spread rumours of a fearsome warlord, a redheaded devil who'd been sent as Allah's messenger. It made sense that this was why *Ali Amir Alzzalam* had been so difficult to pin down–because the word-of-mouth tales mutated and changed as they were passed throughout the villages and towns. Intel from tribes-people would have placed Ali in many different locations at the same time, and attributed all kinds of misdeeds to him; therefore, intelligence on Ali the Devil proved unreliable.

"It must have been hard for you...betraying your British

232

comrades out there in the desert. Did you ever have second thoughts…try to back out?" Sam said in English.

Frazer snort-laughed and shook his head as if Sam were an imbecile. "Why am I dealing wi a fuckin' child? Do you guys recruit straight outa pre-school these days?" he scoffed, but the grin was soon removed from his face and replaced by a grimace. Brody gripped his unruly red mane and tugged Frazer's head back. The man mountain leaned down until he was face-to-face with the prisoner.

"My colleague will ask the questions and you will damn well answer the questions, understand how this works?" he said in a low, menacing drawl as he pinned the prisoner with cold dark eyes. "Do. You. Understand?" he repeated, but this time he used a parade ground roar that seemed to make the ground beneath them shudder.

"Aye…aye, yes, I understand," Frazer winced. Brody let go.

Frazer's head hung down for a moment before he looked up, anger simmering in his fierce blue eyes.

"Do I need to repeat the question?" Sam asked.

"No…I remember," he snarled, pausing before he revealed, "I knew as soon as I met with my off-base contact, I couldnae back out. He was an Afghani police officer—had me by the balls from the get-go. If I didnae follow Al Raami's orders and pass on Intel about the layout of the base and the times of patrols, there was a bullet wi my name on it."

"But that didn't happen…you were useful to the rebels?"

"Aye. I was the perfect candidate, completely invested in

233

my mission, I had western military training, I'd converted to Islam, and I'd believed in their cause. If ye cannea give one hundred per cent, don't bother startin'...that's my motto fer life." Frazer sneered.

The bravado was fake Sam was sure of it. He noted that the man said he'd 'believed' instead of 'believe'. Sam deduced that Frazer's initial motivations were no longer relevant because he'd discovered the falsehoods in the rhetoric he'd been fed. Alasdair Frazer had begun on his journey as a disillusioned teenager, groomed to become a weapon. Sam could relate to that. But, now Frazer was a grown man of thirty-six, and whatever life he'd built in Afghanistan crumbled after the safety net of the allied forces pulled out. The Taliban took power quickly and they violently enforced their belief that foreigners were a threat to their families and values.

"You gave the rebels Intel and faked your death. What happened afterwards?"

"Things, eh... didnae go to plan."

"How come?"

"I was instructed to go to the compound of a guy named Mullah Ayesha. I was duped. When arrived I was taken at gunpoint and laughed at for falling for their rouse. Turns out my captors weren't the brothers I'd hoped they'd be. They imprisoned and tortured me fer six fuckin' months." Frazer scowled.

Sam wasn't surprised. The one thing that connects those who became indoctrinated by terrorists, whether by the far right in the US, the IRA in Ireland, or the Taliban in

Afghanistan—they all believe that they're helping free their country from tyranny and that their actions have a purpose. The purpose is always that those at the top of the ladder profit from the grunt work done by those at the bottom…and every soldier is expendable.

"They didn't kill you? Why was that? I'd say you were quite a liability after they'd received the information they wanted."

"It was touch and go. The fact I spoke Dari was what saved me. I probably should have hated those men, but, they were soldiers just like me…we were on the same side. Mullah Ayesha called me a foreign red devil. Took me a while, but I convinced Ayesha I was genuine. I asked to pray with the men, and he couldn't refuse me that. I convinced him I was willing to risk my life for the country and cause."

"Ah, the old Lie: *Dulce et decorum est Pro patria mori*—It is sweet and fitting to die for the homeland," Sam recited. "And they believed you would die for them?"

"I was a British soldier. Some of them hated me for that alone. But I talked to my guards, I told them I could be an asset and could help them organize attacks on convoys of supplies to the bases. All I needed te do was lie down in the middle of a road and a convoy would stop to help me thinking I was an injured soldier. One of the guards took the idea to Ayesha and he agreed to give me a chance to prove my loyalty. We successfully attacked the supply lines from Pakistan to Kabul fer a few weeks before the allied commanders put two and two together. But that was enough. We'd built solidarity. I'd ensured that the men trusted me. We'd gotten such a haul of supplies…food, weapons, Comms devices."

"So, now you're one of the boys?"

"Yeah. Fer the blink of an eye. Ayesha was threatened by my success…believed I was a danger to his leadership. Fucker tried to kill me as we ate our meal together. I was ready for him. I slit his throat, the men watched. No one fought me, they were too scared. It was my brothers in the compound who named me *Ali Amir Alzzalam*."

"We have evidence of you running a smuggling business along a surprisingly large area of the borderlands with Pakistan. What kind of goods are we talking about? Drugs, weapons?"

Frazer laughed then and pinned Sam with a mischievous glare. "You know as well as I do, where there's war there's always men who'll profit from it. After what I'd been through, I had no problem being one of those men!" he revealed. "Ye could say I was the Amazon of Afghanistan fer a few years. You want it, I'd source it", he preened.

"What about your customer base?"

Frazer paused, thoughtful for a moment. "Ye know, if you'd have asked me that question a year ago I'd have had no option but to kill you." Frazer let his eyes run up and down his interrogator.

"You seem like an intelligent kid. What do you know about the war in Afghanistan?"

Sam held in a grimace at yet again being called a kid, "I know enough," he said calmly.

"Did you know that the Pakistan Secret Service, the ISI, created the Taliban in the 70s...gave them weapons, safe havens inside Pakistan, funded their campaigns?"

Sam nodded.

"Afghanistan is stuck in tit-for-tat tribal warfare. On and on it goes. After living there for sixteen years I can't see there ever being a final solution." Frazer explained, "War isnae about good versus evil, right and wrong, religion, it's about power and money. It may sound callous, but I was able to turn that fact to my advantage and play all sides. I made *a lot* of money—from Military contractors, the CIA, ISI, MI6, and the Russians, as well as private individuals who wanted to get product in and out. I smuggled agents, weapons, drugs, you name it, in and out fer years," the prisoner boasted.

"How did you evade capture?"

"No one was gonna share my true identity. I was far too valuable. They all needed me, needed my network, needed the myth of Ali the Devil as a cover to ensure their business operations ran smoothly."

"But someone did share your identity, if they hadn't you wouldn't be here. What happened?"

Frazer scowled and stared at his feet as if processing his fall from grace. He was quiet for a minute.

"When the US Military began its withdrawal at the end of February of 2020 security at the bases became... lax. I'm sure this isn't a secret anymore...but there was a security breach and the Taliban got hold of lists of Afghanis who had worked for the allied military. These were ordinary people who just needed to earn a living—the secretaries, the translators, drivers, right down to the cleaners. To the Taliban, this was a list of people who had betrayed them. These were kill lists. The lists were a rumour at first, but after the Taliban took Kabul they weren't a rumour anymore. This is why the evacuation became so frantic. I played both sides. I was on the list." Frazer's blue eyes glazed with tears as he said, "They murdered my wife, and...mah wee boys." Sam shot a look at Declan to see his face was stony with shock.

"I'd been on the run since March...friends sold me out. I was demoted from being a brother to a westerner in the blink of an eye," Frazer's head hung down as he sobbed, "My family's gone, my business is gone, I've nothin' left."

Was this true? Could Sam believe a word the man said? Frazer was a manipulative, duplicitous character. The interrogation needed to stop. They had a list of their own, a list of Frazer's aliases. Sam wanted to read the report from the analyst to sort out the truth from the lies. Frazer could be left to stew for a while.

Sam sent his gaze to the assembled agents and nodded. They said nothing and all began strolling towards the hole-in-the-wall leaving Frazer alone as the evening chill began to creep in.

****

An hour later, after a call with Mrs K, Sam was sent the results of the deep dive into Frazer's movements in

238

Afghanistan using his list of aliases. The report and Alasdair Frazer's military file made for interesting reading. Sam absorbed the information and passed it to Declan as they'd all enjoyed instant cocoa in the surveillance van. Agent Farrell piped up.

"Shite. Looks like our guest's had enough." Declan peered up from the report to the monitor screen. Frazer had pissed himself and he roared furiously in a language the others didn't understand, but Sam spoke up and translated the Dari phrases,

"Come on then, you sons of snakes, get back here and finish this!"

Sam had been called 'son of a snake' by Erik Madsson during the fateful interrogation and so it led quite nicely to the next subject to be pulled apart—Frazer's connection to the mercenary.

****

"Christ, ye bastards! This is against mah human rights. I should be allowed te take a fuckin' leak," Frazer complained in a rough roar when the agents strolled back into the arena.

"Well, it looks like you already did," Sam said airily as he resumed his seat opposite the prisoner. Sam ignored the acrid smell of fresh piss, mixed now with the cloying scent in the horse arena.

"We have your medical records and know you lied to us," Sam informed immediately. Frazer's face was an unreadable mask.

239

"When you were a baby you suffered from testicular torsion and one of your testes was removed. A follow-up exam when you hit puberty showed that you were infertile. There were no children, were there, Frazer, no children and no wife killed by the Taliban." Frazer's lips drew back and he growled showing his teeth.

"The family courts in Kabul are the central registry of all marriages. They have no evidence of any of your aliases listed on a marriage certificate. The name you gave of your wife does not exist. Your sob story didn't work. So, what was it that made the Taliban put a ticket out on you? Sometimes all it takes is pissing off the wrong person, but being a westerner when the allied forces were pulling out, that would do it too." Sam continued.

Frazer's head hung and his body slumped forward, his arms taut as the bonds cut into his wrists. He was on the ropes now, bound, exhausted, cold, and reeking of piss, his lies were uncovered and he was out of options.

"You met a Swedish mercenary, named Erik Madsson. By all accounts, he was rather infatuated with you. Tell me how you met."

Frazer's head shot up and he anxiously asked, "He's alive?"

"I'll answer your question after you answer mine."

Another impasse, more malevolent glaring as Frazer worked out his next move. Sam was tired now but he couldn't let the captive see just how much he wanted this to be over. Sam needed to get these last puzzle pieces into place and then Frazer could go to hell.

"He was Swedish Special Forces, honourably discharged...wasn't a day out of the military before he was contacted and offered a job as a mercenary,"

"Who offered him the job? Who was his target?"

"I don't know who his boss was, or the mark. The job went sideways. His hummer hit a landmine on the road to Kandahar. He was dragged out of the vehicle, taken by tribesmen, interrogated, and thrown down a hell hole to die." Frazer paused pensively before he said, "They shouldnae have done that to him. I've experienced all kinds of torture over the years, but a hell hole...I wouldnae put my worst enemy down one of those."

"So you found him?"

"Aye. He was off his rocker when I got my men to pull him out. That hole messed wi' his head, scrambled his brains. He was delusional."

"And what did you do with him?"

"What kinda man do you think I am? I'm no' a heartless bastard. I couldnae leave him out in the desert. We brought him to the nearest village. I paid a woman to tend to him, feed him up. I stuck close and checked in on him. When he was well he said he wanted to repay my kindness. He joined my team for a job." He paused. "Now tell me, Is Erik alive?"

"Yes, he's alive."

This news seemed to spark something inside Frazer.

"Tell me about Operation Paragon." The suddenness of the question caught Frazer unawares. He couldn't disguise his shudder and wide eyes, even though he kept his mouth

241

in an inexpressive line. Paragon was the code name that Sam used during his interrogation of Erik Madsson. It was the name that had acted like a key to infiltrate Madsson's mind and get him to spill that his employer was Alphabet. They had no idea what the operation entailed or why the name had been used as a key.

"That's got nothin' to do wi me," Frazer insisted, unable to hide his alarm.

"Answer the question…there's another teacake in it for you," Sam hedged.

"Really? D'ye think that'll work a second time? I'm no that desperate te spill mah guts."

Frazer's glare shot down to the box and he unconsciously licked his cracked lips. The man was exhausted, sore, and hungry, and he smelled like a toilet. Declan strode over and picked up the box, removed a foil-covered cake, unwrapped it and stuffed it whole into his mouth, then grinned.

"Fucker," Frazer muttered. Seconds of tense silence followed.

"Fine," he eventually relented. "Around ten years ago I was contacted by a tribal leader; he had this wild story, reports of a team of around six soldiers in the Panjshir Valley, could have been British or American or Russian, he wasnae sure. One thing he was sure of was that they were searching for a cell of jihadists and they paid well for Intel. I later heard that a load of bodies were found in caves in the Hindu Kush Mountains. One woman survived. I tracked her down. She said they didn't even have the chance to reach for their weapons. She told me that she hid in a hole in the rock, she saw only shadows on the walls of the caves, the soldiers were big, silent, and they were fast." Frazer relayed dramatically. "I asked around and chatted to several military contractors I was on good terms with. I mentioned the name Operation Paragon and saw only terror in their eyes. No one would say a word about it and I couldn't get any specifics...not at any price. Over the years the Black Ops soldiers became a kind of fireside ghost story. It was said that they could appear out of the air and were so fast you wouldn't see the killing blow coming. I heard stories from Kandahar province, Helmand, and the Nuristan forest. I don't know what was true, but it wouldn't be the first time a conflict was used as the backdrop for some kind of sketchy military experiment."

Sam's gaze moved to Declan who stared into the distance, seeming miles away. But before Sam could ask any further questions Agent Feurig thrust her head through the hole in the wall and advised, "The perimeter was just breached. Three black SUV's are coming. We've got five minutes tops until they arrive. Looks like our time's up."

Sam's blood bubbled with fury. This wasn't the agreement. Mrs K had agreed they'd hand the captive over to MI6 after 24 hours. With one last chance to get something actionable, Sam spat,

"What do you know about Alphabet?" He expected Frazer to make some kind of joke, but the remaining colour fled from the prisoner's face.

"Why are you so afraid of Alphabet?"

Frazer looked stricken.

"Why are you afraid of Alphabet?" Sam demanded again.

"Why are you not?" Frazer exclaimed in horror.

"Untie me fer fucks sake! Dec, please, please, untie me," Frazer pleaded.

"Give me one reason why I should?" Declan asked.

"If they've sent a strike team here we're all fuckin' dead. Don't yez know? Alphabet doesnae leave witnesses."

****

CHAPTER 23

STRIKE

Sam traded swift gazes with the other agents. Automatically, they all clicked to turn their body cam's off. Sam left the arena and sprinted to the SUV.

Agent Weber passed Brody a knife from her medical box. He sliced the cable tie bindings on Frazer's ankles and arms, as Lena removed the drip line. They didn't remove the cable ties keeping his wrists secured behind his back. Frazer was unceremoniously dragged up from the chair by the two agents. His legs wouldn't hold his weight, and he cried out as cramps shot up his calf muscles.

"I'll take him, he needs to walk it off," Declan insisted, thrusting his arm around Frazer's back, taking his weight from Brody and Weber. He walked Frazer toward the exit. Declan then saw Sam just finishing a phone call.

"They're not MI6. Evacuation protocols," Sam shouted.

"Sam, we need to split up, I'll take Frazer on foot. We'll cut through the woods and meet ye on the main road by the riding school sign."

Sam gave Declan an enquiring look as he supported his former best friend. As if Sam could read Declan's mind, he didn't need to say another word.

"Great stuff, I could do wi' a wee walk, stretch the auld legs," Frazer said, his raspy voice dripping with sarcasm.

Sam gave the prisoner a withering glare.

"I'll get you a weapon," Sam said to Declan, then turned and hurried to the surveillance van. Weber and Brody returned from stowing Brody's kit bag and Weber's medical kit in the SUV. They were now arming themselves from the supply of weapons in the van. A quick discussion was had with the other four agents out of Declan's and Frazer's earshot. Sam returned with the loaded Glock and a torch. Declan stowed the gun and threaded his hand through the torch strap loop. It was close to 10 p.m. and the temperature had dropped with the encroaching darkness.

"The van will go first, it's reinforced and bulletproof. Farrell said he can try and run them off the road. I'll go next. I hope they take the bait and think he's in the van. Be at the riding school sign on Lower Rainham Road by twenty-three hundred hours." Sam leaned in and kissed Declan, preening at the look of shock on Frazer's face.

"Be safe Buttercup, do what you have to do,"

"I will Westley." Declan saw the headlight beams of three vehicles turning onto the long road that led to the driveway. He didn't think, not for one more second, just turned, and dragged the weak prisoner with him into the trees.

The darkness, when they got into the woods, was absolute. Frazer tripped and needed to be dragged to his feet twice before Declan thought they were far enough away to put the torch on. He'd seen the map earlier. If they went east they'd arrive at the beach, north would take them down to the main road. It was a couple of miles either way.

Declan knew what he had to do. He had a head start and a loaded gun. Declan had carried guilt for so long, this was a second chance, and this time he could make the choice and do things differently.

"I know you don't owe me any favours Dec…" Frazer said in a rough whisper as he staggered by Declan's side.

"Shut the fuck up, just keep movin'," Declan groused impatiently as he trampled through the tangle of bushes and trees.

The riding school was open ground so the sounds of what was happening there carried. Declan heard vehicles on gravel and gunfire. Voices shouting, rough deep voices.

"Russian," Declan exclaimed dragging Frazer and pushing him against the thick trunk of an Oak, his cuffed hands behind his back pressing into the bark. Declan pointed the torch directly in Alasdair's face. "What the fuck do Russians want wi you?"

Frazer shied away from the light, he looked exhausted and drained, and he stank of sweat and piss. He started sobbing, and then recited a Muslim prayer chant, over and over.

"*Allaho Akbar wa lillahil hamd.*" (Allah is the Greatest and all praise belongs to Allah.)

Declan shook him, dragged him forward and then slammed him against the tree. This pulled Alasdair from his mental spiral.

"Please Dec, please, just let me go. I've dealt wi' worse than the Russians but I cannae help meself if my hands are cuffed. These are bad, bad people. You'll never see me

247

again. Ye don't need te get involved."

"Do ye really think I'm a fuckin' novice? This is mah job! I don't need your protection, and I never asked fer it in the first place," Declan said fiercely as he stared at the living ghost in front of him.

"Do you have any idea what you did back then? You stole part of my life from me, Alasdair. I grieved fer you...I...loved you," he choked out. Finally, Declan had said the words he never thought he'd get to say to Alasdair Frazer. No matter the man's response, Declan could sense a weight in his heart lift when the words were out.

"I know. I saw the way you'd look at me," Alasdair admitted. "I loved ye like a brother. You were always my best bud, but that was all it could ever be." Declan knew this, had always known, but the words still stung.

A familiar voice at Declan's left side. He turned to see Young Declan. The hallucination of his younger self in a SCOTs regiment uniform appeared at times of extreme stress to help Declan find his way forward. This time the younger version was furious.

"The bastard's no dead. Are ye fuckin' shittin' me? We idolized him, built him up in our head to be the ideal man, a tragic military hero, a lost unrequited love."

"It was all lies. None of it was real," Declan said out loud in reply to Young Declan.

"Our friendship wasnae a lie. I always cared for ye, loved ye like a brother, that wasnae a lie," Frazer insisted.

"He betrayed us, betrayed his family an' comrades, he faked his death for what... a fuckin' holy war." Young Declan scoffed,

"Give me a fuckin' break."

Declan and Alasdair stared at one another. "Dec. If you loved me, you'd let me go. Maybe you think I'm a selfish bastard, and maybe you're right, but if these guys get me I'll never see daylight again. Is that what you want? Give me a chance to go out my way."

"We've grieved for this undeserving fucker fer too long. He's always underestimated us, this bullshit has te end," Young Declan insisted. Declan knew his younger self was right.

He parroted the words, "Ye've always fuckin' underestimated me, Frazer, always seen me as a weak and fragile wee thing. Well, no more." Declan pulled the gun from his jacket pocket and held it to Frazer's temple.

Could he do it?

Could he put down this wolf?

It would take a second, easy pressure on the trigger and then Alasdair Frazer would be a ghost again, just like he'd been for the past eighteen years. But this time, Declan wasn't like his younger self, desperate for comradeship and love, he was a grown man and now *he* was in control of Frazer's destiny.

Silence fell between them, Declan's bulk crowding the cuffed prisoner to the tree trunk. Both men fixed one another with raw direct eye contact. All of Declan's love, fear, disappointment, and loss reflected in his silver-grey eyes. Frazer's ice-blue gaze determinedly looked back in a challenge. If Declan was going to pull the trigger Frazer wasn't going to shy away from his fate.

The rough calls of the Russians at the derelict riding

249

school still echoed, so Declan figured at least one vehicle had remained while the other two gave chase.

Time was ticking. Declan had a gun to the man's head and a choice to make. This time, Young Declan didn't offer an opinion.

****

CHAPTER 24
AMBER HEADLIGHTS

The bright amber beam of headlights blinded Declan for a second as the black SUV pulled over. There were a few bullet dings to the chassis but the vehicle was intact. A heavenly vision of a man was sitting in the driver's seat.

Declan had run hard after it was done, so hard his lungs burned and his eyes watered. His heart thrummed with grief and anxiety at every step, and now with the joy of seeing Sam, knowing he was safe, Declan was cleansed. Declan stepped out from behind the vandalized riding school sign with a bloody trail running down his face from a cut on the head. He hurried to the car and got in.

Devon Brody grabbed his shoulder, "You're alone. What the hell happened?"

Declan pulled away from his colleague's meaty grip. "I don't wanna talk about it,"

"I don't fucking care what you want. Where's Ali?" Brody spat.

"I don't know… he's gone."

"Muthafucker!" Brody roared furiously.

"My torch was a piece of shite. Couldnae get the thing working. It was dark, Frazer tripped over a tree root, and when he fell, the cable tie cuffs musta snapped. I didnae know he was uncuffed until the bastard whacked me over the head with a tree branch and legged it. I'm no' proud of mahself. I know I fucked up," Declan justified.

"Gaddamn it!" Brody raged. He sat behind Declan's seat breathing through his nose, snorting like a rutting stag. Declan would be lying if he said he wasn't a little scared of what Brody would do next.

"Well, Fuhhk," Brody exclaimed thumping the back of Declan's seat. "I found that slippery bastard before, and I'll find him again."

He'd been trailing Ali the Devil for a year and no one would dare argue with Running Bear when he had a mission to complete.

"Open the trunk, I'll get my kit bag," he ordered.

"You want company? When we find him he'll need medical attention," Agent Weber said. Brody nodded.

When they'd retrieved their bags and said frosty goodbyes Sam drove off towards Gillingham town, heading for the motorway to London.

"There's a packet of wet wipes in the glove box," Sam offered after a few minutes of seething silence. "And water in the carrier bag behind your seat."

Declan retrieved the wet wipes and pulled the shade down. He opened the mirror flap to see himself.

"Jesus, I look like shite," he said, pulling out a couple of wipes and beginning the chore of cleaning the blood from his face.

"You let him go, didn't you?"

"Why d'ye say that?" Declan replied conversationally as he rubbed the dried blood from his beard.

"Because I know you, Declan Ramsay-Aiken. Your love isn't given lightly. No matter how much someone hurts you, there's always a spark of kindness left in your heart that gives a second chance."

"Is that right!"

"Yes. You once loved Alasdair, even though he never loved you back the way you wanted. The way your mind works, you're thinking, he made some terrible choices and even though he hurt you he deserves a chance."

Declan paused in his cleaning and turned to Sam.

"You must think I'm a right numpty!"

"Not at all. You didn't just set him free, you set yourself free from any obligation you believe you owed him. He's on his own. I don't envy Frazer if he's got Taliban *and* a Russian strike team on his arse. Just understand that no matter Alasdair's fate, you're not responsible."

Declan turned and stared out of the window at the sleepy suburban houses. Brittle moments passed as he computed what it meant to be *known*.

"I love you, Sam Aiken-Ramsay."

Sam slowed the vehicle and stepped on the break at traffic lights on a road just outside Gillingham. There was no other traffic. He turned to face his husband and reached out to take Declan's right hand.

"I know you love me. How do you feel?"

Another pause for consideration, "I guess my heart's a wee bit lighter."

"Good. That leaves more space for me to fill." Sam leaned in and pressed his lips to Declan's. The traffic lights on the empty road cycled twice through red, amber, and then green before they emerged, panting from the kiss.

****

CHAPTER 25

PERFECT CIRCLE

"Ah, Declan, come in, come in." Dr Karl Schroeder was upbeat, "This is quite unexpected, but I'll always find time for you. Are you well?" He beckoned Declan to take a seat in front of the large oak desk he sat behind.

Declan was impeccably dressed in a charcoal and blue tartan business suit, pastel blue shirt, and navy tie. He hitched the legs of his trousers a little and eased down into the chair, but said nothing for a second as he perused the office. Apart from the occasional repaint and tech upgrades, this was the same office Declan had been visiting for years to be given his Immunotherapy top-ups. He bit his bottom lip as if considering how to proceed and then fixed Dr Schroeder's gaze.

"Karl, you've been mah doctor fer a long time now",

"Yes, let me think...twenty-one years I believe, how time flies," Schroeder smiled. "What's this all about, are you unwell, having any unusual symptoms?"

"No, no, nothin' like that, it's been a stressful few days," Declan said softly then paused, the silence tentative.

"I'd like te ask a few questions about the ins and outs of my treatment." Dr. Schroeder pursed his lips and his brows knitted in confusion.

"I want you to be straight with me, Karl. I need to

255

understand what you did to mah body."

"What I did to your body? Your tone is somewhat accusatory Declan! What exactly do you think my treatment has done?" the Dr said a smiling chuckle failing to hide his discomfort. Elbows on the desk, and steepled fingers, Dr Schroeder took on the pretence of a man of power listening intently, waiting for a response.

"How did ye meet mah father?"

"I beg your pardon?" Dr Schroeder let out another nervous chuckle as if amused by the change in direction. He relaxed his posture and sat back in his Captain's chair.

"Donal and I have been golf buddies for years," he said a smile in his voice.

"As for meeting him, I think it was... Stirling Golf Club, yes..." he said thoughtfully, "I'd booked a game but my partner didn't arrive and Donal was playing alone. We decided to pall-up and play nineteen holes."

"Funny," Declan said dryly, "My Da tells a different story. One with me desperately ill in Edinburgh Children's Hospital, and you, befriending him at his lowest ebb. Ye told him you were looking for Cancer patients to volunteer for your clinical trial. It's almost as if you were trawling the ward and manipulated a desperate father into volunteering his son to be used as a medical experiment!" Declan's tone was as sharp as broken glass.

"Declan!" Dr Schroeder barked indignantly as he sat erect in his chair, "How can you think that? I am the reason you're still alive. My treatment cured you of Leukaemia; you're a strong, vital, healthy man, and you no longer get sick. In fact, your immune system is more robust than any patient I've ever treated," he exclaimed. "Forgive me, but your tone is deeply hurtful and ungrateful. What is going on here, Declan? Why are you asking these ridiculous questions?"

The men both shot mistrustful dagger glares at one another before Declan stated,

"At my last appointment, I told you I'd wed Samuel Aiken. You replied in an off-the-cuff manner, saying that the name Aiken sounded familiar. Of course, it sounded familiar. You know Sam's father, Sir James Aiken; and you know him because he's invested millions of pounds into your clinical research. So why did you lie to me? You were both at Oliver and Belle's wedding fer god sake, so your behaviour is more than a wee bit suspect, don't ye think?"

Dr Schroeder's face took on a ghostly pallor. Declan removed a phone from his inner breast pocket, swiped to the group photo of James with Dr Schroeder and members of the military and turned the screen so Dr Schroeder could see. Declan noticed the way the old man's Adam's apple bobbed in his throat on observing the image.

"Cards on the table. We both know that James runs a covert intelligence agency for which I work. And here you are with members of the Ministry of Defence and Secret Service. Just what kind of research are you involved in?"

Schroeder held his hands up, "I can explain," he insisted.

"I hope ye can because I've been doing some in-depth research myself and Sir James Aiken has been my shadow since I left your clinic. The deeper I dig, the more I find he's

257

always been there, observing me. And, I cannae think of a reason he'd do that unless he was keeping an eye on his investment in the wild." Declan sat back in the chair, crossed his legs and set his elbows on the chair arms. Schroeder glared at him and Declan noted the man was trembling. He remained silent; Declan had all the time in the world. Dr Schroeder, it appeared, didn't.

"You need to understand—" Dr Schroeder began urgently, "—the nature of funding medical progress. Cellular engineering was a contentious field not so long ago, and what I proposed with my research—to edit immune cells and give them a payload to attract and destroy Cancer cells was revolutionary—" Schroeder paused for a beat, "—and revolutionary progress always involves great risk." The doctor wrung his hands nervously as he spoke.

"And money," Declan observed, "I expect this kind of progress costs a lot of money."

Dr. Schroeder winced. "My initial trials in the mid-nineties had not gone as well as I'd hoped. I'd gained a reputation within the medical community—an unfair reputation I might add—of recklessness and giving false hope. The pharmaceutical companies saw me as a failure...closed their doors to me. I had no luck when applying for funding. I knew *knew* I had the beginnings of a biomedical miracle that would change the way we treat blood-borne cancers. I believed that, if I could master the technique of cellular engineering it could be applied to all manner of treatments to boost immune cells and make the body heal itself in circumstances where the immune

258

response was compromised," Dr Schroeder passionately explained.

"So you turned to private investors to fund the research?"

"Yes. Sir James' late wife Rosalind was my patient. She volunteered for the later immunotherapy trial. I'd ironed out the issues and she benefited greatly from the treatment... as did you. Rosalind Aiken was in remission for six years before the Cancer came back. We fought for two years to eradicate the disease but sadly, the treatment didn't work a second time."

Declan was stunned to learn this.

"After Rosalind passed, James said he wanted to continue funding the research for his wife's legacy."

So, this meant that since the year 2000 James and his aristocratic wife had been funding Schroeder's cell engineering research. Declan stood and paced to the window considering what he'd learned. He watched the comings and goings on Harley Street. A black cab dropped off a fare, and a woman rushed to catch the cab before it pulled away from the curb.

"You are my life's work, Declan; you are the miracle, the purest outcome for my vision, my Paragon. Do you not know how special you are?"

Declan shivered at being labelled the *Paragon*. He turned from the window and stood with his hands on his hips. He recalled that the word *Paragon* was the trigger to access Erik Madsson's deepest thoughts during his interrogation with Sam—and was the name of the Black Ops military operation that Alasdair Frazer had stumbled upon in the Afghan mountains.

"I'm your Paragon?" Declan spat with confusion and rising anger. "What does that even mean? Ye keep sayin' I'm special but I don't understand why. Are ye waitin' for me to sprout antlers or hulk out? I'm just a regular bloke, I'm nothin' special," he insisted.

"But you are special. Don't you understand? This is not the stuff of Hollywood superhero movies. This is real, *pure science*. The treatment was named Project Paragon. Out of all of the patients who were administered my immunotherapy, you are the strongest. Declan, you are the only one who is still alive twenty years after the treatment. You are patient zero. I've tried out all of my... shall we say *adjustments* on you first and you continue to thrive. You're impenetrable."

"Adjustments?" A macabre sense of dread made Declan's blood run cold.

"Yes. I've refined the treatment over the past twenty years and administered them in the immunotherapy top-ups."

Declan felt like he'd been punched in the gut. He was such a fool. He'd trusted Karl with his life and the man had filled his body with, what?

"So I'm living proof that your cell engineering process works? Why is there nothing in medical journals about the success of your techniques?"

"The answer to your question is quite simple. I do not own my life's work." Schroeder paused for an instant before regretfully admitting,

"I sold my soul." The doctor worried a hand over his short grey beard and his shoulders slumped in resignation at the revelation.

"What de ye mean, you don't own your work? Who the hell owns it?"

"Sir James, initially. He financed the Paragon Project; he owns the patents for my research, and that photograph on your phone...that was where he brokered a deal with the Ministry of Defence for Paragon. This is *God technology*, Declan. I could have played God, changed the world, and brought an end to blood-borne Cancer, but I had no choice. The research does not belong to me, never has. My life-changing work is yet another secret project at Porton Down."

"Your research is owned by the military? What de they want with it?"

"I've signed the Official Secrets Act. You of all men should understand I cannot possibly comment. Even discussing this with you in the broadest sense is dangerous."

"What is Operation Paragon?" Declan asserted.

Dr Schroeder remained silent, but his fingers began tapping nervously on his desk.

"Could I hazard a guess? There have been whispers about a covert super soldier program." Declan hedged. Dr Schroeder's left eye twitched and he replied,

"Paragon has been, how to put this... Frankensteined for military use. Test subjects are not given engineered cells with cancer-killing therapies. That is all I can say. The evolution of Project Paragon is beyond my control."

Declan turned from the window and paced again. A sharp cracking sound stole his awareness. He flinched, and then pivoted to look at where the sound originated... at the sash window he'd just stepped away from. He swiftly strode closer to inspect one of the panes where a small perfect circle of glass was missing. Alarmed he exclaimed, "What the hell?" as he turned back to Dr Schroeder to see that the older man's eyes were glazed, fixed, and unmoving. The mirror image of that perfect circle was now tattooed in the centre of his brow.

****

CHAPTER 26
ONE STEP

Declan Ramsay had witnessed a professional hit, and he was internally paralysed with fear. The death of Dr Karl Schroeder was not something that could be swept under the rug by calling Mrs K to clean up the scene. He stood in the hallway at home staring into space. He knew on some level it was shock, but his mental faculties were fixed on the realization that if he hadn't stepped from the window, that one single bullet would have passed through his head before hitting Schroeder—two birds, one stone in action.

At the scene, the Police were suspicious of Declan's involvement. He was swabbed for gunshot residue, questioned, fingerprinted, and then ruled out as a suspect. They decided he was just an unlucky patient, a witness and a victim.

Declan had struggled to rein himself in when dealing with the stroppy DI who'd questioned him, but with the bullish way the detective had carried out the initial interview Declan couldn't help but state the bleedin' obvious—that there was a hole in the window pane that displayed the trajectory of the bullet, and therefore the sniper had been positioned in the attic window of a house on the opposite side of Harley Street.

Schroeder's secrets had died with him and Declan

wondered what would happen now. Was he a target or just in the wrong place at the wrong time again? Was Dr Schroeder's office bugged? The timing of his assassination seemed too perfect to not be connected to what the doctor revealed during their final conversation.

And, what about the Immunotherapy? Had Declan needed it at all after he went into remission? How would his body cope without those special little cells fighting off everyday infections? What payload had his engineered cells contained?

"Buttercup?"

Declan shivered back to awareness. His keys were gripped in his hand, the impression of cold metal imprinted onto his palm. He hadn't moved a step from the closed front door. He felt numb to his bones.

"Buttercup?" Sam prompted again as he strode from the kitchen to stand in front of his husband. Declan inhaled then and the fresh scents of coconut and vanilla tickled his senses. Sam was wearing his new *Bum Chums,* and a smile, but the smile soon faded. His concerned gaze eviscerated Declan. This was his safe place. It was okay to fall. Sam opened his arms and Declan stepped into them and began to tremble uncontrollably.

"Hey, what the hell happened?"

Declan couldn't speak, not yet, not until he processed the enormity of what he'd witnessed, not until his body stopped fucking shaking. Declan had never seen a person get shot in the head before, and the immediacy of it, the swiftness of it was overwhelming. Dr Schroeder had saved his life, used him, lied to him…and yet Declan still felt fondly towards the old man, had liked him, and considered him a friend of sorts. One bullet in the head and that life was extinct. The tangle of thoughts and feelings wouldn't unravel. Declan just needed to stop thinking.

"Fuck me…I need you to fuck me. Please," he begged. Sam drew back from their embrace, unable to hide his concern.

"Of course, I'll give you anything you need."

Without question, Sam led Declan by the hand into their bedroom. Declan stood, his body still shaking, and allowed Sam to undress him. Sam then drew back the duvet, led Declan to their bed, and sat him down.

"Lay back love," Sam instructed softly, and Declan did so. Sam dragged the cover back over him and rubbed the soft comforting feather duvet all over Declan's body to warm him up. Declan watched Sam's every move as if he was scared Sam would vanish in a puff of smoke. Sam hurriedly removed the underwear, rounded the bed, and slid in beside his husband. He scooted over pressing his lithe warmth to Declan's side and placed a stilling hand on Declan's fury chest, over his heart.

The feeling of Sam's anchoring touch and his breath on Declan's skin began the thaw, and the full-body tremors settled. Declan lay in the silent embrace for several minutes before he started to come back to himself.

"Schroeder's dead," he revealed finally. He felt Sam stiffen beside him.

"Christ, I'm so sorry. What happened?"

"Sniper, one shot."

"A sniper...what? In Harley Street?" Sam asked, confused before he understood the reason for Declan's odd behaviour since arriving home.

"You were there," Sam exclaimed in a whisper.

"Aye, I was there," Declan admitted, then near-vomited the information. He'd needed to get it out of his head and so explained how he'd gone to Dr Schroeder's office without an appointment to confront the doctor about the nature of the medical treatment. Dr Schroeder spoke of Paragon; the word both he and Sam had noticed kept cropping up. Then he told how Schroeder admitted what and *who* Paragon was. Hearing himself say the words felt like a kind of madness, like he was reciting an outlandish movie script. But this was real, and he'd nearly died.

During the monologue, Sam hadn't asked any questions. He'd stroked Declan's chest, swirling a finger in his chest hair and listened as Declan unburdened himself. Having a lover with whom there were no secrets, who accepted Declan and his emotional storms was a blessing. His mother, Eileen had once told him, "Just you find the person who connects ye to the world," and this was what loving Sam did. Having Sam by his side, Declan could almost believe in the divine.

Sam cupped Declan's cheek and turned his face so their eyes met. "It seems I nearly lost you today," Sam said matter-of-factly. "I'm so grateful you're okay...that I get the time to love you more. What do you need?"

"Fuck me. Make me remember what it feels like to be

alive, to be claimed." Declan said.

"I can do that." Sam leaned in and kissed Declan, softly at first, then Declan threaded his arms around Sam, gripping his arse, and dragging him to lie on top. Sam levered up and adjusted their cocks before sinking into Declan's embrace. He clasped Declan's bearded face, ensuring unnervingly intimate eye contact and then Sam circled his hips in a delicious slow tease. Declan groaned, the sensual movements making his cock fill up quickly and slide in tandem beside Sam's silken erection. Declan couldn't look away, so he lost himself in the pools of Sam's green eyes. This was where life made sense, with gentle rocking friction, bodies sandwiched together, lovers adrift on a tiny boat.

The kisses went on for what felt like hours as Sam took control of the bump and grind of their lovemaking. Declan took every claiming, pounding thrust as a gift he might never have known…if he hadn't taken that one step away from the window.

****

CHAPTER 27
PROOF

The incessant buzzing of a vibrating phone dragged them from the arms of sleep; first Sam's phone and when it was ignored; Declan's phone began to vibrate in the pocket of his trousers draped over a chair. Both men were so exhausted from fucking all evening that they'd let the calls go to voicemail.

Sam's sleepy rasp broke the silence. "You awake, babe?"

Declan let out a sigh, "Aye, are we ever gonna get a fuckin' break? Whoever's calling, it cannae be good." Declan yawned, stretched, and turned his head to glance at the alarm clock, "Fuck, it's five past two...." he groaned.

Sam reached for his phone, pressed his thumb to the screen to open it, and then clicked on the voicemail he found there. The couple lay in the darkness, the scents of their sex and sleep sweat pungent in the air, a distant siren tore through the slumbering city. With trepidation, they listened to the message.

"Samuel, its Dominic Soames. I'm awfully sorry to call you so early." The upper-crust voice sounded as exhausted as they both felt, *"I'm heading into the office. We've received a proof of life video. Can you both please come in a.s.a.p? I'm trying to get hold of Mrs Kimura too. I'll see you soon."* The voicemail from Dominic Soames hit Sam like a kick in the gut.

268

"The fuckers cut it fine," Declan growled. "It's been thirteen days. They had just one day before James unleashed hell by proxy." He expelled an exhausted groan and rubbed his bristly beard, the scritch-scratch sounding loud in the silence. Declan lay there for a few seconds listening to Sam's breathing. It was not the shallow rise and fall of sleep, but rapid and anxious. Declan tossed the duvet back, shuddering as the cold air hit his heated skin. He rolled to Sam's side, placed his hand on Sam's bare abdomen, and gave a comforting rub.

"C'mon Westley," he said softly. "This is what we've been waiting for. You jump into the shower, an' I'll make coffee-to-go."

Sam remained prone in bed and chewed his bottom lip.

"Ah, love—" Declan gentled.

"We've both seen ransom videos." Sam began, "My mind's been going in circles ever since dad was taken wondering what they're doing to him, are they beating him, starving him, does he even have water, or a mattress to sleep on? And, what about his injuries? What did Madsson do to him before he was taken?"

"Hey, easy there, easy," Declan said in a low comforting purr. He wrapped his arms around Sam and rolled him back over. Warm tears fell and settled in Declan's chest hair.

"Going back to the house made it worse fer ye didn't it?"

"It made me remember him—remember what he was like when he was... *my dad*...a proper dad... and not my boss. I feel guilty for not seeing how much he loved mum and the pain he was in all these years. I never thought to question

269

why he'd never remarried, why the girlfriends were transient."

"I get it, Sam, I do. But none of this is your fault. You were a child, you'd lost yer mother. James threw you into the adult world with no support. None of yer father's pain justifies his treatment of you…his homophobia. He's a parent. He had one fuckin' job—to protect his children. Nothing justifies putting you in the hands of a mercenary, *twice*. James is not God, and he doesn't get te to sacrifice his only son… not while there's breath in my body! James is alive. If the kidnappers want money, they'll get a shit-tonne of it to let yer father go. It's all been arranged, a simple transaction, you'll see." Declan embraced Sam until Sam pulled away.

"Now g'wan, hop in the shower and I'll make coffee," Declan pulled Sam with him as he got out of bed, and then patted Sam on the bottom to encourage him toward the bathroom. Sam nodded meekly and then did as instructed.

When Declan was satisfied that Sam wasn't going to backtrack and curl up under the duvet to hide, he strode out of the bedroom toward the kitchen privately kicking himself for the rare occurrence of lying to Sam. Declan didn't believe for one second that whatever was to come would be an easy transaction. Nothing about this was easy and his gut knotted with dread wondering what the kidnappers wanted in exchange for James' safe return.

****

270

CHAPTER 28
LIES & VIDEOTAPE

By three a.m. they were outside the glass monolith building that housed the offices of the Chance Bailey law firm. The night was clear, crisp, and cold, and the Canary Wharf financial district was deserted. Sam cupped his hands and looked through the glass doors into the darkened foyer. He could see the form of a security guard sitting behind the reception desk, the light of his laptop and a desk lamp the only illumination.

"Yeah, there's a guard, knock," Sam instructed. Declan rapped a knuckle on the glass door, the sharp high sound making the security guard jump in his seat. He looked up from the laptop, focused on the two men at the door then pointed to the right. Declan pivoted and saw an intercom hidden in a shadowed niche.

"Can I help you?" the night guard said warily, his accent Eastern European.

"Sam Aiken and Declan Ramsay to see Dominic Soames. We got a call to come down immediately."

"Do you have ID, driving license, passport? Please hold it to the camera."

Declan slid his wallet from his inner breast pocket and drew out his driving license. Sam did the same and passed the license to Declan who held the two cards up to the tiny

271

fish eye lens.

"Thank you. One moment please."

Sam watched through cupped hands as the security guard made a phone call, then clicked a few keys on the laptop and after a couple of minutes rose and strode from behind the reception desk, a master key card dangling at his hip on a metal rope. At the door, with a thick finger, he punched his access code into a keypad and then inserted the master key card into a slot beneath. The doors silently slid open.

"Come in gentlemen, quick as you can," he said warily. Sam and Declan stepped in and the guard closed the door and locked up again.

"The elevator is functional with this key card," he informed passing a black plastic card to Sam. "Mr Soames is expecting you. Please go to floor six."

"Got it, thanks bud," Declan nodded.

They rode the elevator up to the sixth floor Sam gripping onto Declan's hand as if the glass box elevator was about to shatter and drop them at any second.

"You can do this, love. We'll just get it over an' done with, like ripping off a Band-Aid, and then we'll know where we stand. I'll be with ye every step, ye hear?" Sam said nothing his eyes distant.

"Hey!" Declan prompted shaking their joined hands, Sam's worried gaze darted right to meet Declan's then and he gave a weak smile.

"Thank you, I'm a bit out of it. I'm so fucking glad you're here," he said pulling their joined hands up to his mouth and kissing the back of Declan's hand.

There was no one to greet them when they reached the sixth floor. They stepped out of the elevator and walked the same halls that had bustled with life and business the last time they'd met with Soames.

Dominic Soames' office door was wide open when they reached it. Sam knocked on the polished timber surface before stepping into the room. He stopped abruptly and Declan bumped into his back. Soames wasn't seated behind his vast desk but instead was in the other half of the room where there was a lounge area with two nubuck leather couches opposite one another and a small glass coffee table between. An oversized smart TV was housed on the wall; the word *paused* was visible in the centre of the black screen. Dominic Soames was dressed in a Fair Isle pullover and navy lounge pants, not his usual sharp suit, and he was seated with Mrs K on one of the leather couches. Declan edged to the left of his husband and entered the room. Sam closed the door, the sound of the lock clicking echoing in the fragile silence.

Even though they'd messaged and spoken to Akiko during Frazer's interrogation, this was the first time they'd seen Akiko since the initial meeting with Soames. The fierce eye contact shared between Sam and Akiko was explosive. Akiko was wearing her biker gear, having been called at 2 a.m. and rushing across London on her Kawasaki Vulcan motorbike to attend the impromptu meeting. In his mind's eye, Sam saw the woman that he now knew to be Amanda Jamison disguised as Akiko striding to the HQ front door

273

and putting a bullet through the head of dear old Mr Steele. He shuddered.

Dominic Soames forced his lumbering bulk up from the couch and extended his hand to be shaken by each man. "Samuel, Declan, thank you for coming in at such short notice. Please, please, take a seat", he gestured to the couch opposite before slumping down again. Soames appeared exhausted and stressed. The atmosphere was palpable as Mrs K met the gaze of each man and nodded in greeting.

"Righty-oh. Now we're all here let's get down to business," Soames began. "I received an email at one a.m from a website called *Message in a Bottle*. I contacted a staff member in the IT department to see what was what. She informed me that the site is an encrypted direct transfer portal and in fact, the definitive way to move data anonymously and securely. The data is never stored anywhere. The *Message in a Bottle* server just acts as a go-between, immediately deleting data as it reaches the destination." Soames paused and leaned to the coffee table where he picked up the remote control for the television.

"The email contained a six-digit code. I opened the site browser, added the code and this video file was shared with me. I haven't watched the whole video, just the start to see what it was. I thought it best to wait for you all," the portly lawyer explained.

"What you saw is it bad?" Sam enquired reluctantly. Dominic gave Sam a pitying look and his shoulders slumped. "Samuel," he said softly, "James is a highly-skilled and well respected, if not feared operative. I can

274

guarantee he's gotten himself out worse scrapes than this. We'll get him back. This video is just a formality", Soames rationalized as if he was speaking to a child. Sam resented the pandering.

"Play it," Sam instructed determinedly. He was ready now, and as Declan had said earlier, Sam just wanted to rip off the Band-Aid and be done with it. Images of horror still swarmed in his mind, of his father in a filthy, cold concrete windowless room, a bucket to piss in if he was lucky, and a soiled mattress. His injuries would have become infected after being dragged through the filth of the underground river. James would be bound, he would be forced at gunpoint to look up at the camera, his eyes hollow from lack of food and sleep, and he would be made to read out the ransom demand.

"Play it!" Sam said again, his voice taking on a cold, emotionless tone. And so Dominic aimed the remote control at the TV and pressed play. The screen jumped to life as the four viewers held their collective breaths.

The first image to appear was the cover of the New York Times dated for the day before; the headline in thick bold type crowed about catastrophic flooding and apportioned blame for the slow disaster response. A hand came into view; it was big, veiny, and definitely male. Fine blond hairs were visible on the back of the hand and a straight scar could be seen in the centre. The fingers on the hand were a little crooked. The disembodied hand moved the newspaper out of the way to show a second newspaper, a copy of The Times with its headlines about the slow, inevitable fall of the Tory government, fraud, corruption, and their mishandling of the world energy crisis.

Those who needed to know recognized the hand belonged to Erik Madsson.

The camera, which, from its jerky movements was in Madsson's good hand, rose then and focused on a long oak and resin river table, panning up to show a view made up of a wide curving wall of glass, a dart of sunlight illuminating the timber floor. Behind the glass were chrome balcony railings, and then on the horizon, crystal clear turquoise sea met the cerulean blue sky. There was no land mass in sight, no boats, and nothing to assist in identifying the location. Sam and Declan shared a quizzical side glance, then fixed on the screen as James strode unaided to the table, pulled out a chair and seated himself. He was not handcuffed nor restrained in any way. James appeared…healthy, there was a healing scar across the bridge of his nose and a dressing covering a wound on the left side of his forehead, but apart from those two minor injuries, James looked well. From the manner of his entrance, he was free to walk around wherever he was being held captive.

Outrage bubbled up. "There's nae fuckin' guards? Ye've got to be kidding me!" Declan said roughly before he turned and his eyes darted to check on Sam's reaction. Sam's brows were knitted; his head tilted a little sharing Declan's confusion.

Sam had spent the past thirteen days fearing the worst and here was his father, in what appeared to be a sun-drenched paradise.

"This has got to be a joke, right?" Sam shot the accusation at Soames, whose piggy eyes widened in

276

response. On the video James was wearing a white linen shirt with a designer collar around his neck, his blond hair, silvering at the temples was clean and styled, and his face as closely shaven as if he'd visited Dunhill's barbers. James displayed no evidence of abuse or life-threatening injuries and no one was holding a gun to his head. Soames pointed the remote at the TV and halted the video. It looked, in that moment of stillness like the image could have been a photograph of James on vacation.

"What...the...hell...is...going...on!"

"Honestly, Samuel. I don't know. I don't understand this," Soames blustered. Like Sam and Declan, Dominic Soames appeared to be unsettled and confused by how well James looked. This was, after all, a man who had survived a violent, bloody abduction where thirteen of his employees were slaughtered in cold blood. But James was alive and still wore the same haughty, nonchalant mask of superiority. Was somebody fucking with them all?

"Play the rest of the message Mr Soames. We need to hear what he has to say." Mrs K's voice was icy and detached. Soames pointed the device at the screen and pressed the play button.

Madsson moved forward until he reached, then sat down on a chair closer to James. Then the camera, already attached to a desk tripod, was placed in the centre of the table facing James. Madsson then put a sheet of A4 paper in front of him. James's fingers tapped nervously on the tabletop. After a second his gaze flicked in Madsson's direction and then James picked the page up, blinked several times, and bit his bottom lip. This was the first tell that all was not as it seemed. The paper shook a little and Sam noticed that his father's hand was trembling, the digits of his free hand still tapping nervously. James looked warily to the left again, nodded, and then cleared his throat with an 'uh hmm' sound. Sitting up straight he began to read in an emotionless voice.

"My name is James Aiken; the date is May the twenty-ninth. This message is proof of life for my family and my lawyer, Dominic Soames of Chance Bailey Law firm in London." James paused and took a steadying breath. "My captors have attached a needle collar around my throat. The collar is remotely activated. It will be activated if I leave this location. The needle will inject Tetrodotoxin into my throat."

Declan held up a hand and Soames paused the video.

"Quick question. What's Tetro-do-toxin?" Declan asked Mrs K. She gave a sullen smile, appreciating that he knew she was the fountain of all knowledge when it came to drugs and toxins.

"TTX is one of the most powerful neurotoxins known to humans. You'd probably recognize it better as the poison from a Puffer fish…Fugu. It is twelve thousand times more toxic than cyanide."

"What does it do to a human?" Soames asked.

"It kills, quickly and painfully, attacking the central nervous system. The symptoms begin with a tingling at the sight of ingestion or injection, then paralysis and death due to respiratory or heart failure."

"Jesus! James has that millimetres from his jugular? Fuck me!" Declan ran a hand over his beard, astounded by the cruelty and malevolence of the deterrent.

"Please, continue", Sam addressed Soames. And as if James was in on their conversation, when the video continued he said,

"It will kill me, so please, no heroics. Follow all instructions to the letter." The paper James held shook violently for a moment and he looked from the page up into the camera. He blinked repeatedly as if trying to clear tears from his eyes and focus.

"Do not release the kompromat. Do not try to find me. My captors will send their demands within fourteen days and give full instructions as to the exchange."

The video then ended abruptly. The sudden silence in the room was too loud and a heavy atmosphere weighed in for a second before, appalled, Mrs K exclaimed,

"What? Is that it?"

Ashen-faced, Soames tossed the remote control onto the coffee table and slumped back on the couch as he ran a hand over his mouth.

"Well. One thing's fer sure, we know he's alive, so at least the scandalous info dump is on pause, aye." Declan stated.

"Agreed," Soames said but he didn't appear at all happy with the news. His gaze flicked to Sam who sat pensively, biting his plump bottom lip. "Sam," Dominic said softly as he leaned forward. Sam looked up to meet the lawyer's concerned gaze.

"I'm so terribly sorry, this is just awful...awful," he said his whole countenance deflating like a slow puncture. "While it's a relief to know James is still alive, I'd hoped for a ransom demand so we could get this nasty business dealt

279

with swiftly and with as little fuss as possible, but I'm afraid this isn't playing out the way I'd hoped." Soames then turned to Akiko.

"Mrs Kimura. You've had your chance to locate James and bring him home safely and you failed," he said coldly. "My responsibility is to my client and as per his instruction I believe it's time to call in Hawker."

"No. Please Mr Soames, please, give me these fourteen days."

Sam and Declan's eyes met with concern. Neither had heard Mrs K ever be accused of failure or beg for permission to do *anything*. Soames had bigger balls than they expected, and he was lucky he didn't have a steel-tipped chopstick in his eye.

Soames pursed his lips, "Do you have any leads to offer me to give at least a little confidence that you can locate my client in fourteen days?" he asked haughtily.

"I have leads and covert tracking technologies at play but the details are *need to know*."

"And you don't think I need to know?" Soames barked waspishly.

"I can bring James home. I *will* bring James home. This is a matter of honour. That is all *you* need to know," Mrs K stated with the same waspish tone, her back ramrod straight and her countenance demanding submission. Dominic and Akiko locked dagger eyes in a jousting competition, Akiko's deadly stare nailing Soames to the couch. The rotund lawyer lost his nerve swiftly and looked away.

"Very well," he conceded his voice a little shaky now,

"You have fourteen days. But that's all. If you don't locate and bring James home by the time we get the ransom message I'll contact Hawker and get the kidnap retrieval experts on this case."

"I need a copy of that video immediately, I'll pass it to my team," Mrs K instructed.

"I've had copies made for both of you." Soames eased up from the couch and lumbered to his desk where he extracted two memory keys from the desk drawer. He returned to the lounge area and passed a USB stick to Sam and one to Akiko.

"I'm as keen as you all to see James home as soon as possible. If there is anything I can do to grease the wheels of the investigation and retrieval, let me know. Now," Soames looked at his gold Rolex wristwatch, "It's 3:30, I think we should all try and recover what little we have left of our sleep, don't you?" he said dourly.

As Sam, Declan, and Akiko strode down the eerie, silent hallway towards the elevator the atmosphere between them was frigid. Sam seemed distracted by his thoughts and so Declan was the first to speak.

"We've some Intel that you'll find very interesting."

"Concerning?"

"The Alphabet Club."

Mrs K stopped in her tracks and then turned to face the agents. Her features remained stony and unreadable, but her eyes blazed, "You were both supposed to be enjoying rest and recuperation?" she asserted, even though she'd brought them both in to interrogate Frazer.

281

"There's no rest until my father is found," Sam replied. Akiko gave him a tight-lipped glare before saying,

"Report, tell me everything." Then she turned and strode down the hall toward the elevator.

In the glass elevator, Sam retrieved his phone and swiped to the photographs taken of the murder wall in his old family home. He nodded to Declan who slid their elevator key card in, allowed the doors to close and the descent to begin before pressing the hold button, leaving the glass box suspended between floors with a view of London's lights spread out before them like a vibrant twinkling Christmas display.

"I'm sure you're aware by now that my father was part of a cabal of Oxford elites who were led by an MI5 recruiter named Alfred Moxley," Sam began.

"I am."

"The Alphabet Club was formed by Moxley in 1981. He was obsessed with power plays on the world stage. His beliefs seem to be rooted in the philosophy of Neoliberalism and he planned to use these ideas to ennoble a group of young students. He groomed these men to believe they were future leaders, and they vowed to work together to bend the political and economic narrative, ensuring the moneyed class retained power and thrived through free markets, and low taxes while working against the distribution of wealth," Sam paused for a breath. "Considering the political climate of the past thirty years you'll see they appear to have been rather successful."

Mrs K pursed her lips in consideration. "How do you

282

know all of this? Your father is very talented at remaining tight-lipped when he wants to. I've had my analysts searching for traces of this club for the past year and they found nothing."

"Dad left me, let's call them...breadcrumbs. They led to information about Moxley's past, and this photograph—" Sam turned his phone to display the Alphabet Club image. "I also discovered a small address book that belonged to Moxley. The book contained the details of the twenty-six members of his boys' club, listed as cyphers of course, which I've recently decrypted. We have their names now."

"You have their names? I'll need that list," there was a hungry edge to Akiko's voice.

"My father has been intertwined with these men since his university days, but it appears his loyalty to the club wavered over the intervening years."

"With good reason," Declan interjected. "As ye can see on this murder wall image, members of this cabal are... being removed from the picture... turning up dead," Declan said gesturing to the image on Sam's phone screen,

"It looks like either James has taken to bumping off his old buddies, or was investigating their murders."

Mrs K took the phone from Sam and pinched the screen to enlarge the photo of the young men in tails, some with a red X across their face.

"This was the photo you showed Alasdair Frazer?"

"Yes. This is where it all begins, with the Alphabet Club," Declan asserted gesturing to the photograph. "It's all connected to why Sam's life was put in danger and to

283

James's abduction. James is being punished for stepping out of line, for betrayal. We can hazard a guess that the kompromat James holds is about these guys. They run Erik Madsson. They were behind the atrocity at HQ," Declan said, stabbing a finger at the image on Sam's phone.

"Send me this photograph and the list of names. I'll run the photo through our facial recognition software and get some analysts to dig into their identities," Mrs K said decisively. Then she nodded to Declan who released the hold button and set the elevator in motion. As the glass box slowly descended Mrs K admitted,

"This is excellent work gentlemen."

Sam and Declan shared a surprised look. Rare praise indeed.

"A team has been trawling through the list Viper left us and we'd drawn a blank," Akiko reluctantly admitted. "This Intel is the first solid lead. Let me know if you discover anything else—while on rest and recuperation!" She allowed a rare smile to grace her lips, but only for a second. The elevator doors slid open. Mrs K stepped out.

****

CHAPTER 29

CLUES

Declan drove back toward Mayfair through silent early morning London streets. He switched the radio on to hear if the assassination of a top Harley Street Cancer specialist had made it to the national headlines. The newsreader drawled telling of flooding, a car pile-up, yet more government sleaze allegations, and a stabbing in the West End, but nothing about the shooting of a prominent scientist. Declan paused at the traffic lights and turned to Sam.

"It's a cover-up," Sam said before Declan could speak, as if once again he'd read his husband's mind. "What did you expect? Schroeder was part of a secret military project, of course, the MoD covered up his death."

"It's a travesty!"

"It is. But, there's nothing we can do. I know you want to investigate but please, leave it in the hands of the Met," Sam implored.

Sam was right, Declan knew it. He'd wanted to find out who had assassinated his physician, but with this issue, Declan was too close to the action and out of his depth.

The traffic lights changed to green and the SUV moved off. "You headin' back te bed when we get in?" Declan asked when he parked up on Mount Street.

"No rest for the wicked. You'd better put the kettle on

285

love; we've got work to do. I need coffee, paper, and a pen."

Declan did as he was told, made coffee for them both and scrounged around in the cupboards for a packet of biscuits. He still wasn't sure why Sam was so determined to re-watch the video message now, but, Sam's reaction to the footage wasn't what Declan had expected.

The memory key that Dominic Soames had given them slotted into the USB port in the back of the TV and when turned on the static opening image of the newsprint front page appeared on the screen. They settled on the couch, Sam held a legal pad and pen, and Declan was in charge of the remote control.

"Play the part with my father's speech again, and this time reduce the speed to thirty frames per second," Sam instructed. Declan pressed play. Sam fixed his gaze on the screen and started scrawling on the page. Declan watched Sam's gaze flitting from the screen to the page. It was mesmerizing. He waited until Sam had finished and then asked,

"What can ye see?"

"Code,"

"Yer shittin' me!"

"I shit you not, my love. Rewind and play it again."

"You're reading code! Where? Explain to me what you're seeing," Declan pleaded confused. Declan enjoyed wordplay, patterns, and games. He's always believed he was pretty astute when it came to noticing the rhythms of speech and reading between the lines. He'd watched the same damn clip as many times as Sam and hadn't seen anything out of the ordinary.

"It came to me the first time we watched the message. He started tapping on the table. There was a game we used to play when I was a kid. We would communicate using blinking and tapping."

"Of course ye did!" Declan wasn't surprised to hear this.

"It was our secret, just a silly game." Sam smiled at the memory.

The video restarted and with the speed slowed James spoke in a distracting drawn-out drawl. Declan now knew it was movements, not speech that held the code. He muted the sound so that Sam could focus on James' micro-movements.

"The code is based on a *Polybius square*, that's a five times five grid of letters representing all the letters of the Alphabet. A new word is begun with a blink. There!" Sam said noting how James had blinked then began tapping on the table.

"Each letter is communicated by tapping two numbers, first the row and after a pause, the column."

Declan ran a hand over his beard, astonished as he found the rhythm of the blinking, tapping code. He was very impressed. "How old were you when he taught ye this?"

"Four or five, I think. I didn't know back then that dad was training me in basic code and there would be a use for it. I loved this game, it was the kind of mental challenge I revelled in."

When Declan was five, his favourite game was arranging all of his cars and toys in orderly lines, as if he'd amassed an army on his side of the bedroom floor facing Oliver's latest Lego build. He would then send the cars to smash whatever Oliver had built. He grinned at the memory of Oli's tantrums and the wrestling fights they used to get into.

"So you're the only one who knows the message he's trying to communicate?"

"Yeah, I guess, over time a code breaker could work it out, but this is between me and Dad. We haven't communicated like this in..." Sam paused, "It must be seventeen years."

Declan couldn't miss the note of melancholy in Sam's reminiscence, and considering Sam's upbringing, it made him feel unsettled.

"Replay the video again," Sam said. "I want to make sure I've got this right."

They both focused on James' micro-expressions and Declan squinted to see the tap and blink sequences. Sam smiled wistfully as he noted his fathers tells, and when the video ended Declan prompted,

"Well c'mon, don't keep me in suspense. What's the message?"

"It's a riddle."

Declan was non-plussed for a moment. Did everything to do with James Aiken have to be a fucking game? Sam then recited the message,

"I am the space between during war.
A castle not built on land or sky,
Approach from above and below

288

Nine shall assemble and all must die.
15-6-22"

Declan stood and began his familiar anxious pacing in front of the mantle. "Does yer da have a death wish or something? He's got a collar wi' a needle containing a deadly neurotoxin just millimetres from his fuckin' jugular an' he sends ye *a riddle*?"

He paused with his hands on his hips and faced Sam. "He could have given you the geo-location, but noooo, that would be far too easy," he added, the comment thick with sarcasm.

"It's not just a riddle, I understand it. This *is* his location and orders."

Declan glared at Sam with incredulity.

"See if you can work it out," Sam said an air of smug mischief in his voice as he offered the legal pad to his husband who snatched it from his hand.

"Okay *wunderkind*. I've got this!" Declan continued to pace as he read out, "I'm the space between during war." Then he vocalized his thoughts.

"What could that be? The frontline? A de-militarized zone? No Man's Land?" Declan suggested as he turned to pace away from the bay window.

"Correct", Sam praised.

"There are two places I can think of off the top o' mah head that currently have an official no man's land. The de-militarized zone between North and South Korea, and then there's the UN buffer zone between the Greek and Turkish-controlled territories in Cyprus." Declan relayed sagely.

"Go on...try the next line." Sam encouraged.

"A castle not built on land or sky. If not land or sky, then it's on water? A boat mebe? If it's a castle that's got te mean one of those massive cruise ships, ye know the kind, they're like cities on the sea. You could deffo smuggle someone aboard one of those ships and keep them under wraps fer a long while." Declan paused and turned to check Sam's reaction. "I'm I warm?"

"Nah. Arctic! Think of something a bit closer to home."

Declan began to pace again, moving to the window and prizing the blinds apart to view the painterly breaking dawn. It was still so early, and even though the coffee kept his eyes open, Declan felt like they'd done a day's work already.

"A castle not built on land or sky leaves only a castle built on the sea." Declan insisted. "Could it be a ship in dock?" He paused thoughtfully, then said, "Hang on a sec," and retrieved his phone and typed on the search engine.

"Well, fuck me sideways! There are four Napoleonic sea forts in The Solent just off the coast at Portsmouth. Spit Bank fort, St Helen's fort, Horse Sand fort, and No Man's Land fort."

Sam slow-clapped "Well done. Three points to Gryffindor!"

Declan tossed the notepad onto the coffee table then his attention was back on his website search.

"The forts were refurbished into luxury hotels a few years back, but two are up fer sale. One of them is No Man's

290

Land." Declan ran a hand over his beard, impressed by the breakthrough.

"Dad took me out to Spit Bank fort for my birthday when I was a kid. This was before the forts were sold off and refurbished. It was a desolate, cold place, derelict and damp. We brought sleeping bags and a picnic. Dad sent the boat away and said we were spending the night there as a survival exercise. We cooked sausages under the stars on a little disposable barbeque and Dad told me stories explaining the history of the Napoleonic war. He told me how the forts were built to defend the harbours at Portsmouth and Southampton from a French sea invasion but they were never actually used in battle. They were manned during the First and Second World Wars, and the Army specifically chose soldiers who didn't swim so they couldn't escape."

"Aww man, that's brutal...you were a child. Did ye have nightmares?"

"Did I ever! That story totally gave me the willies. I lay there imagining what it would be like to be stranded in the fort for months on end, unable to escape. Happy Birthday to me, eh!" Sam deadpanned.

"Jesus Sam, it's a miracle ye survived to adulthood." Sam gave a weak smile and shrugged his shoulders in an 'it is what it is' gesture.

Declan pulled up images of No Man's Land Fort on his phone, sat down beside Sam, and head to head they viewed the photos.

"Wow, will ye look at this! It's pretty fuckin' swanky!

They catered for weddings and other big events until a food poisoning outbreak shut the place down temporarily. It seems owners couldn't get past the bad press so they put it up fer sale a year ago."

"Not surprising really, it's not as if they can get passing trade." Sam paused, "Stop... there, do you see? That's the room they did the video message in."

"So, this is deffo the location, but what does the rest of that message mean?" Declan leaned forward to look at the notepad again and recited, *"Approach from above and below. Nine shall assemble and all must die."*

"I know exactly what it means." Sam's tone became serious and wary. "The kidnappers were stalling. They were never going to send a ransom demand. The Alphabet Club is meeting at No Man's Land fort on 15th June, that's in ten days. My guess is that they're going to decide what to do with my father. His orders are that we infiltrate the fort and kill them all."

Declan ran a worried hand across his beard, "He's off his trolley. I'm no' killing anyone fer James! What are we gonna do?"

"I'll send this Intel to Akiko and we wait for a call."

****

CHAPTER 30

SNAKE SKIN

Contact finally came three hours later by way of an encrypted email. They joined the secure video meeting with Mrs K, Devon Brody and two other agents, Claudia Feurig and Aiden Farrell.

"Thank you all for attending. We're here to discuss the logistics for *Operation Snake Skin*, a mission based on the new Intel supplied by Agents Aiken and Ramsay. We have just ten days until the cabal that abducted Viper meets and his fate is decided. I'm sure you will all agree that a ransom demand was never on the table, it was a stalling tactic. I've instructed the analyst teams to make this mission a top priority. I'll have the deep-dive on the specific members of this cabal by tomorrow. We will meet at HQ at thirteen hundred hours, but until then we can discuss the location and begin to plan. Agent Lightsaber, if you'd like to begin," Mrs K invited.

On-screen, Farrell appeared washed-out and exhausted. Declan wondered if he was a workaholic, or if Mrs K hadn't let the poor bastard go home since the fuckery at the Riding School. The bearded man's hair was sweaty and stuck to his brow, his clothes were dishevelled, and a coffee stain was visible on the front of his shirt pale blue work shirt.

"Thanks, Mrs Kimura. Now. This is a fast-moving

enquiry and it's still early days. I'll show you what we've got so far about the location," he said as a colourful general reference map of the South Coast of England appeared on the screen.

"No Man's Land fort is situated in the Solent, a strait of water between mainland UK, and the Isle of Wight," Farrell explained using a mouse to point out the areas of interest on the map before zooming in.

"The Solent is notorious for tricky tidal currents. The wide stretch of sea between No Man's Land fort, here, and Spit Bank fort, here, is a busy shipping lane, primarily for ferry, cargo, and cruise ships from Portsmouth to Jersey, France, and Spain. So there is near-constant sea traffic. The fort is remote, a perfect location for a high-security event. Access is limited, so gaining entrance to the fort covertly will be challenging," the agent paused and Agent Feurig took over.

"The greatest risk for an assault is the approach. They have a 360-degree sea view, so can observe any boat approaching and enforce security. There are two helipads on the roof of the fort, but an air assault would ensure Viper's captors are alerted and, because of the device Viper was forced to wear around his throat, there is a risk that, should we go in all guns blazing, he would be dead in seconds!" Claudia explained in a dry, German drawl.

"Agreed," Mrs K said, "We cannot let them know we're coming for him. We need to be...circumspect."

Agent Farrell spoke up again. "One thing we have on our side is the element of surprise. The kidnappers don't

294

know that Viper was able to alert us about his location. They don't know we're watching them. I drove down to the South Coast last night and sent a drone over the fort," he revealed.

Sam and Declan gave one another a side glance as if they'd both been thinking, *that explains why the guy looks like he's been dragged through a hedge.*

"There are just three heat signatures in the fort complex; all of them are here, in the building that looks like a lighthouse on top of the fort," he said displaying the drone footage and the orange blobs where the occupants were. "It's called the Crows Nest apartment. You can see the interior of the Crows Nest on the Fort Hotels website. We believe the heat signatures belong to Viper, Erik Madsson, and Amanda Jamison. There are no signs of any other guards or security measures in the fort," Farrell revealed, "They appear to be confident that the location and the toxic collar are sufficient security."

"The remoteness of this location is a double-edged sword. Yes, the fort is difficult to access, but for those inside, it's also difficult to leave," Akiko said sagely. "We can expect several security sweeps before even one of the ABCs set foot on the fort. When we know the details of each mark we can gather Intel on their security team."

Declan spoke up then, "The ABCs are wealthy, they're used to a certain level of service. They're not slumming it wi' tea and sandwiches on a fort in the middle of the sea. We need to find out which company is dealing with the hospitality requirements for this high-security conference. We can replace their staff with ours, no?"

"Yes, that's a great idea." Sam joined in enthusiastically,

"We'll use the Domestics as our inside team," Mrs K agreed. The Domestics were a team of field agents trained in hospitality. The agents fulfilled several roles for A.L.L. from chambermaids, or waiting staff, butlers, chefs, or housekeepers within a target's home or at an event. Each agent was able to blend into the background and remain unnoticed–as all efficient servants should.

"Agent Farrell, did you find any other ways to access the fort?" Mrs K asked.

"Actually, I did!" he grinned self-satisfied. "The architectural blueprints for the fort were in the National Maritime Archive." Faded blueprints appeared on the screen and Farrell zoomed in.

"On looking closely at the blueprints I discovered a little-known fact. The fort isn't completely secure," he explained. "I found contemporary video evidence to back this up. A couple of *UrbEx* lads accessed the fort last year when it was abandoned."

"*UrbEx*?" Mrs K queried.

"Oh sorry, *UrbEx* - urban explorers, they trespass into derelict houses, factories, all kinds of abandoned buildings. It's a hobby," Farrell, explained.

"Anyways. These two lads put this video of No Man's Land on YouTube. It's an excellent resource to help us to understand the interior layout of the fort once we gain access. I'll add a link to the first Intel packet so you can all watch the full video in your own time, but this bit here's what I wanted to show you." He then pulled up a YouTube web page and made it full-screen. Farrell pressed play twenty-seven minutes and forty-one seconds into the footage.

Two dorky-looking men in their early twenties, one in a red Puffa jacket, the other in a navy blue waterproof coat swung their phone cameras around. They guffawed and traded insults, their voices echoing in the cavernous fort basement as they each pivoted, their phone cameras on selfie-sticks, and their torches arching, showing curved whitewashed Victorian brick walls, vaulted ceilings, a polished flagstone floor worn from use, and thick iron girders. The footage was edited to flick between the camera feeds of both men, giving alternate points of view.

"Oy, Derek, do you hear that?" the man in the blue jacket said, suddenly alarmed, all humour snuffed out.

"Fuckin' 'ell, what is that?" Derek paused for an instant before, more alarmed he exclaimed, "Steve, what IS that? It's creeping the fuck outa me, what is it?" he asked, sounding terrified as a violent repetitive ssshhh-plonk sound was caught in the footage audio.

"Can you hang on for a minute, I have to find out what that is," Steve said. Derek turned, pointing his high beam torch, filming as Steve strode on ahead down a narrow whitewashed hall that was strewn at every doorway with tape warning 'Do Not Cross' as if the whole basement was a crime scene.

Steve sent his own torch beam on further ahead and said to the YouTube audience, "I don't know if our phones are picking this up. Can you hear that guys?" he stood still and a ferocious crashing sound was audible.

"Oh man, that is horrible; we have to find out what that is."
He moved forward, "Careful, the floor's wet,' Steve warned as he
stepped gingerly down the corridor, and ducked under warning
tape all whilst being filmed by his friend. Steve came to a white
timber door which had the word RESTRICTED stencilled in black
letters front and centre. Steve turned back and gave Derek a
portentous look. "It's coming from in here!"

"I dunno about you, but fuckin' ell mate, I'm getting really
creeped out. Imagine being stuck here during a storm…anything
could happen," Derek said ominously.

Steve turned back again and gave him a scowling glance of
disdain and then opened the rusty-hinged door and vanished
through the doorway. After a moment's silence, his voice echoed
as he yelled, "Oh my god, what the fuck is this?"

Derek followed his friend, the high beam filling the space,
showing the view of a narrow arched tunnel, thick granite walls
with white paint peeling, and graffiti scratched into the walls with
dates from World War 1 and World War 2. The floor was slatted
timber with gaps between each slat. Following his friend, to the
end of the tunnel Derek discovered what the eerie sound was. A
half-meter opening in the wall led to a gap between the inner and
outer ring walls of the fort, Steve's camera phone on a stick was
pushed over the side to show water in space between the walls. The
sea's violent rhythmic ingress was intense. A barnacle-encrusted
rusty ladder was secured to the outer wall.

"Oh, my God! It's a secret diver's passage." Steve enthused.
"Fuck me, I don't know what it is about this place, a feeling…but
this is really creepy,"

298

"Yeah, I guess it's one way to secretly dispose of bodies," Derek snickered grimly as the roaring sea thrashed against the walls.

"I can't believe you just said that," Steve complained. "You can be a right fuckin' arsehole, you know that!"

Agent Farrell stopped the video.

Sam turned to Declan and they shared a significant look. "That's our way in," he whispered grimly.

****

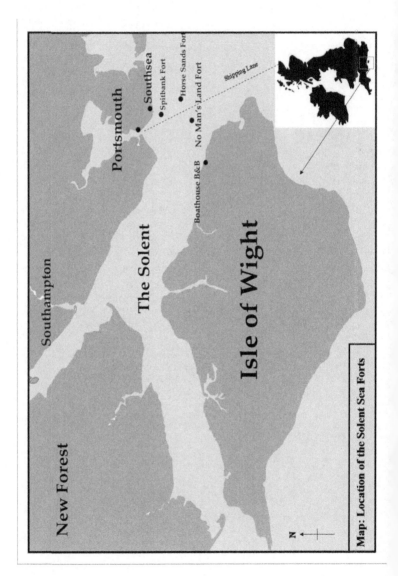

Map: Location of the Solent Sea Forts

CHAPTER 31

REVELATIONS

Sam did a slow drive-by of the HQ. "Keep your eyes peeled love."

"Christ, these roads have more tanks than a fuckin' military showroom," Declan scoffed as they passed Hummers, Jeeps, a Porsche Cayenne, several Range Rovers, and a big black armour-plated Karlmann King.

"There," Declan pointed at a red Bentley that was indicating to pull out and onto the road. Sam paused, waited for the vehicle to leave, and then hurriedly manoeuvred into the space at the far end of Abbotsbury Road. He and Declan walked back up to the house enjoying the clement June weather, loosening ties and the top buttons on their work shirts.

The house loomed, ominous and ordinary at the same time. As they strolled up the pathway towards the front door it opened and Devon Brody filled the doorway. The last time they'd seen Devon he'd just returned from Afghanistan and was still in his cammo gear, smelling like a ripe kebab left out in the sun. His beard had grown out to an unruly salt and pepper fuzz, and he'd gone from a close military crop to tight silver-flecked curls. They'd parted on bad terms after Declan 'lost' Brody's prize prisoner, the feared rebel warlord Ali Amir Alzzalam, who was, in reality,

301

Declan's old friend Alasdair Frazer, back from the dead. They'd not heard a peep from Brody in the days since the Russian strike team attacked the Black Site they were using to interrogate Frazer. Frazer was in the wind and now Devon Brody was manscaped and moisturized to perfection. His dark-skinned face was hair free and his head polished like a bowling ball. He wore a sharp suit which he filled out like an American Football star at a charity gala. Brody nodded a welcome to Sam and Declan and then beckoned them inside.

"I'm sorry man. I feel really bad about—" Declan began, desperate to clear the air, but Devon raised his palm and stopped him in his tracks.

"Shit happens. It sucks we lost him, but I know the type of man he is and what he's done. He got lucky this time, but at least now we know his true identity, and what he looks like. The Taliban and Russians are still on his tail, and he can add MI6 and the CIA into the mix," Brody said, virtually parroting the same thing that Sam had told him at the time.

"I'm glad he didn't permanently damage that pretty face of yours," Brody joked, giving Declan's cheek a playful slap. The cut on his brow was healing well. Declan took the ribbing, just glad there were no hard feelings between him and Brody.

"Good to see you. Nice suit!" Sam commented.

"It's *Ralph Lauren*, a little gift to myself," Brody grinned, straightening his suit jacket with pride.

Sam noticed immediately that things at the house had changed. Where once there had been a lift to take them

302

down to the basement complex, there was nothing but a white wall. A painting of a ship in a storm that Sam knew previously hung in the dining room adorned the wall, and beneath it, a console table with a simple Japanese Ikebana floral display.

Sam turned back to Brody and gestured to the wall. "What gives?" he asked, confused.

"False wall. The basement is still a murder scene, and honestly, no one wants to work down there. Those poor bastards in Active Ops didn't have a fuckin' chance. With the millions spent on security they were still sitting ducks," he explained in his gravely drawl. "The meeting's in the dining room."

The tip-tap of their shoes echoed as Sam and Declan followed Brody along sparkling marble floors to the rarely used dining room.

On entering the room Sam paused to take in the scene and Declan stilled at his side. The temporary base for *Operation Snake Skin* had been rapidly thrown together. All paintings and antiques had been removed from the room. The drapes were closed and the chandelier above sparkled with refracted light. Workstations were set up along the right-hand wall; meters of cables fed through guttering half pipes that had been attached to the wall. A tall wheeled server in one corner blinked with lights, and six analysts sat at the workstations and trawled banks of screens that crawled with data. The long mahogany dining table that once sat in the middle of the room and was only used for starchy dinner parties and Christmas had been moved to the left. A huge flat screen was installed where the ship in a storm painting once hung.

Four new agents were sitting quietly at the dining table all typing on their phones. The German agent Claudia Feurig sat beside Akiko Kimura, having been shoed-in to the position of her right hand after the death of Agent Strauss. The jovial Aiden Farrell was joined by Brody. Two seats remained at the table for Sam and Declan.

Mrs K looked up from her laptop and met the agents with a steely glare, then nodded. She stood and clapped her hands like a schoolmistress.

"Clear the room. Return in one hour," she ordered to the analysts, who, without a grumbling word collected their phones and were then escorted to the front door by Brody. When he returned he closed and locked the dining room door. Mrs K addressed the room.

"Operation Snake Skin is an off-books mission to extract Viper from No Man's Land fort in the Solent. Our initial play will be to get our hospitality agents, Mara Svensson, Jimmy Ahmed, Kyle Williamson, and Kirt Black into the fort," she said gesturing to each agent as she introduced them.

"We'll begin with a brief preamble about what was behind the invasion of this HQ and Viper's abduction," Akiko nodded at Agent Farrell, and he clicked on his laptop. A photograph appeared on the wall screen. A professionally taken photograph of twenty-six young men dressed in tailcoat suits, and one older man wearing a professor's cap and gown. Most of the men were white, and a handful was

304

of African and Asian descent. All of them were in their late teens or early twenties, apart from a rotund, ruddy-faced man who stood proudly with his boys, Professor Alfred Moxley.

"Agent Aiken, as you are personally connected, would you care to tell us about this photograph?" Mrs K asked. Sam nodded.

"This is The Alphabet Club. A secret society formed at Oxford University in 1981 by Alfred Moxley, a Linguistics Don, and undercover recruiter for the Secret Intelligence Service. Veering away from his official remit for the SIS, Moxley became obsessed with how the world would change when the Cold War ended. He trawled through the student body for twenty-six young men he could groom. They were a mixture of specially selected British elites and international students whose fathers had money and connections. The only anomaly in this group was James Aiken, my father, who, it may surprise you to know, had neither money nor connections, but he had something else to add to the mix. He was initially selected by Moxley for security service recruitment and was fast-tracked into MI6 on graduation."

Mrs K nodded to Farrell, who clicked to begin the presentation. The group photo vanished and contemporary headshots of each member of the ABCs appeared, putting names to the grown-up faces.

Mrs K rose from her seat and began a slow, deliberate walk up and down the length of the dining room. She spoke, almost casually, having seemingly memorized the report on the Alphabet Club members that the analyst team had collated overnight.

"Of these twenty-six men, sixteen have died over the past thirty years, some from natural causes, and others in suspicious circumstances. For instance, the two most recent deaths were Jimmy Kim, a Chinese tech billionaire who owned the internationally popular app *ClokWrk*. He was stabbed in the throat in a hotel bathroom in his native city, Beijing. And British Journalist Jason Severin who had the reputation of being quite the tenacious bulldog, died of a severe reaction to seafood. His wife insists Severin was allergic to all fish and would never have ordered a fish dish at a restaurant." Akiko paused for effect before continuing,

"And Agents Aiken and Ramsay are intimately aware of the suspicious death of Sir Peter Maythorpe… and the aftermath."

Sam and Declan shared a glance.

"Including Viper, ten members of the Alphabet Club remain alive. They're involved in a volatile power struggle that appears to have been going on for some years. Our remit for this mission is the safe extraction of Viper *only*." Akiko returned to her seat, unscrewed the cap from her water bottle and took a long sip, then nodded to Farrell. A photo of the fort appeared on the screen.

"A high-security meeting will occur here, at No Man's Land Fort in nine days. The schematics show this area, here, is where Viper is being held captive. He is not restrained, but he cannot escape. He was fitted with a needle collar that will inject a lethal toxin into his throat if he attempts to leave," Akiko explained. A still image from the video

306

appeared showing James and the wicked needle collar for all agents to see. Agents Black and Svensson both hissed when they saw the device.

Photos of the individual marks then appeared one by one.

"This is a face you'll all recognize," Mrs K said with a sneer. "Jonathon Brudenell-Brice." She paused and her stare trained on the agents one by one as they looked at the photo of the suited man in his sixties, his dyed black hair oiled and combed to display a widow's peak that gave him a vampiric appearance. The agents all appeared uncomfortable with the naming of this particular man.

"BB is the Conservative MP for North Devon and our current Foreign Secretary. As you'd expect, BB's security detail is MI5 and so we'll need to tread lightly when trailing him. As this is a highly irregular meeting he may, of course, decide to attend without official government-sanctioned security. There is a delicate power play here. You'll understand when I explain exactly who the Foreign Secretary is friends with." Akiko nodded to Farrell and the next headshot appeared on the screen.

"Valentin Molokovic, oligarch, and deputy chairman of the Security Council of Russia." The photo was of a stern-looking, gaunt sixty-year-old man with close-set beady eyes, and a well-tended, dyed beard that didn't match his silver grey hair.

"In 1981 Molokovic was a cultural exchange student at Oxford, his diplomat father having greased the wheels, so to speak, to get him a place. He studied PPE at *Magdalen*

307

College, the same degree as James Aiken. After graduating in 1985 Molokovic returned to Russia and worked his way up the ranks of the KGB, and then the FSB to become the current Russian premiers' confidant. He has a reputation for being ruthless and cunning. I consider Molokovic the most dangerous of the ABCs, and I believe that he is the hand behind the abduction. Next slide please."

Sam exchanged a stunned wide-eyed look with Declan which his husband returned. Without words, Sam knew they were on the same page with '*What the fucking fuck*' as the chapter title! James had been classmates with a fucking KGB agent? They'd both heard of Molokovic, he was hard to avoid having been whispered about in security circles in connection with a scientist, a doctor and three Russian CEO's all of whom spoke out against the leader. These people met their end by falling from windows in high-rise buildings. Molokovic was a bad, powerful man.

"Chad Eisen, CEO of Parker-Sharp Arms manufacturer in the US." A photo of a round-faced man with piggy blue eyes and a thatch of unnatural-looking blond hair poking out from beneath a white Stetson hat. "Eisen studied Economics at Oxford. His oil baron-father set him up in business as a graduation gift. Eisen Holdings, then he bought up a slew of failing businesses and picked them apart for profit. In 2000 Eisen Holdings bought Parker-Sharp Arms, a small, family-run gun manufacturer. When the sale was complete, he received a huge order from the US government. He expanded the business and made billions from the Iraq war, and the subsequent Afghan War. In recent years Eisen has publicly sided with the Fascio-Christian Republican movement."

A photo of a tall willow thin man in a military uniform appeared next. "Simon Ingram-Jones is a military strategist; he studied International Relations at Oxford before joining the army and most recently helped form the British Army's newest regiment, 13 Signal Regiment, which focuses on cyber warfare. He's just taken the position of Technical Director at the National Cyber Security Center."

The list of ABCs continued. "Jorg Garcia was another international exchange student. He's now the executive chairman of the Brazilian conglomerate *Media Internacional* and has become a powerful political force in South America. Next slide," Farrell clicked.

"William Jakes, U.S. military General, served in Iraq and Afghanistan now at the US State Department."

Sam and Declan shared a glance with Devon. They all knew that name. Jakes was the contact Frazer had goaded Declan to call as his 'get out of jail' card. This was yet more proof that Frazer was working with the Alphabet Club.

Mrs K continued, "Jin Xiao is the owner of China's most well-known pharmaceuticals manufacturer, Xiao Biologics, he has laboratories in mainland China, Europe, and the US. He's a favourite of the Communist Party. Next, Femi Zubari, billionaire, and CEO of *Africom*, Africa's largest telecommunications company. Along with his phone company, he's heavily invested in secure communications technology. Gregory Tisch, German billionaire, wind turbine manufacturer. He's an advocate of Green energy.

309

And of course, finally, we have Sir James Aiken."

****

The floor was passed to Agent Farrell.

"Let's get down to specifics. We'll have three teams, Team Alpha is me, agents Kimura, Brody, and Feurig. Team Bravo is agents Svensson, Williamson, Ahmed, and Black, and Team Charlie is agents Aiken, and Ramsay. Alpha will be situated in the control van on the seafront at Southsea," he said as an aerial shot of the fort was displayed.

Mrs K spoke up, "Feurig, you can fly a helicopter, yes?"

"Yes, I've had a pilot's license for six years."

"Good, Brody and Feurig will fly the two choppers we'll use for the extraction," Akiko decided.

Farrell continued, "Team Bravo your cover will be as staff from *Next Level Hospitality*. You'll deal with catering the event, as well as the initial prep work for the arrival of Team Charlie." The agents all shared glances.

"Team Bravo will arrive at the fort by boat the day before the event and will be expected to prepare the dining and meeting locations. As you already know, Erik Madsson and Amanda Jamison are Viper's guards and reside with him here in the Crows Nest apartment." Farrell directed them to the lighthouse apartment on the roof of the fort. "I'll put the full schematics and all links in the Intel packet."

Mrs K spoke up, "We expect there will be multiple security sweeps of the fort, and so we'll need to refrain from fitting cameras or listening devices until the last minute. Team Charlie, Viper's safe extraction is your responsibility. I'm sending you both to the Isle of Wight to reconnoitre.

310

Keep an eye on the comings and goings at the fort. The night before the meeting you'll both enter the fort covertly and prepare for the distraction, and extraction," Akiko ordered.

They both nodded. The next nine days were going to be intense. This was one final push before Sam and Declan claimed their freedom.

****

CHAPTER 32
RECONNOITRE

Sam stood at the bedroom window of the honeymoon suite in The Boathouse, an Isle of White beachside bed and breakfast pub. The early June sun blazed hotly and the sky was a cloudless wash of sapphire blue. Their suite was one of just six above the pub. The room had a sea view and was even more perfect because 1.4 nautical miles out to sea, directly opposite the bedroom window, was No Man's Land sea fort.

"They've got visitors", Sam singsonged as he peered through hi-tech binoculars scanning the traffic on the Solent.

"Can ye see who's in the boat?" Declan asked. He was seated at a small console desk, typing on a laptop.

"Hmmm...Four people, ah, good. These are ours. Team Bravo is starting event prep," Sam brightened. He was relieved to see the boat approach. The four agents, Svensson, Williamson, Ahmed, and Black were posing as the catering and hospitality staff. The preparations while on the fort today would make Sam and Declan's tasks later tonight so much easier.

"Oh, and just like buses we have another boat, two people, an IC1 female at the wheel, and an IC6 male passenger. Amanda's back," Sam said a bitchy sneer in his voice. He couldn't stand the manipulative murdering cow.

"The man with her fits the profile photo for Imran Fizel. He's working for Zubari, yes?"

The list of ABC's security teams was on Declan's laptop screen. "Aye. Fizel's an expert in executive protection and threat assessment. He's the last one on the list." Declan leaned back in the uncomfortable wooden chair and let out a sigh of relief. It had been a frustrating few days for them with James imprisoned mere minutes away, while their orders were to watch and wait. Both he and Sam just wanted to get this extraction over and done with.

During their eight days on the Isle of Wight, they'd completed a Scuba refresher course in the Solent, learned of the dangerous skittish tides, the busy shipping lanes, and that the area was a pupping ground for the likes of Ray and Thresher Shark.

From the beachside bed and breakfast facing the sea fort, they'd chomped through pub food while observing the comings and goings of boats and helicopters. Amanda was an early riser and would routinely leave each morning by speedboat, docking in Portsmouth harbour and returning with fresh grocery supplies and a stack of newspapers that Sam knew was to placate James. He did love his daily crosswords. During several of the trips, Amanda returned with a passenger aboard the boat. They never saw Erik Madsson leave the fort, but drone reports from Aiden Farrell showed that there were always two heat signatures in the fort when Amanda went shopping. Madsson was getting a lot of alone time with his captive.

Viper's rescue plan was agreed and the other players

knew their part. Act 1 was now in play, with Team Bravo unloading initial supplies onto the landing stage to be carried up three flights of weather-worn metal stairs and into the fort for the event set up to begin. Act 2 was up to Sam and Declan. They would breach the fort tonight.

Declan was more nervous about this job than any of the others he'd done for A.L.L. It was the last, no matter what happened in the fort, and this fact knotted his guts.

It was business as usual for Sam. Scuba diving at night to infiltrate the fort was a challenge to him, fun almost if he wasn't doing it to free his father from a horrific death. Declan wasn't as enthusiastic but knew the job needed to be done and they had one chance.

Declan turned from the laptop screen to observe Sam as he stood at the window gazing out to sea, the tips of his blond hair highlighted by the dancing sunbeams. He was awestruck by a Tsunami wave of love that came at him like an unexpected punch to his solar plexus. Sam turned to him at that moment. Their eyes met and widened in understanding. Sam's affectionate brilliant green gaze lit Declan up with a sizzle of adoration; he grinned helplessly and reached out a beckoning hand. Sam let the binoculars dangle on their strap around his neck and he stepped to Declan.

Sam straddled Declan's thighs and took his bearded face in his hands. He ran his thumbs through the wiry soft hair and then gave him a sweet peck on the tip of his nose.

"Boop," he said playfully.

Declan gave him a lopsided grin. "D'ye remember the

314

first time we kissed at the castle?" he asked as his hand moved to grip the nape of Sam's neck. He drew him in so they were brow to brow, eyes closed, letting their other senses do the work.

"Of course I do," Sam whispered.

Declan licked his lips. "You were such a cocky little shite, an' the more ye teased me the deeper I fell."

Sam let out a chuckle at the memory. "Yes, it's quite a skill. I was an insufferable pain in your arse, wasn't I?" he mused, and then let his lips ghost against his husband. Sam pulled back, opened his eyes, and whispered, "I knew I wanted you from the moment you bumped into me at the airport. You look positively sinful in a well-tailored suit. And—" Sam added in a low, sultry voice, "it's not every day that one gets bowled over by their soul mate."

Declan peppered light, sensual kisses up Sam's throat, to his ear, "I'm so glad you made the first move. That first kiss sealed my fate," and then he whispered huskily, "Your kisses tore mah world apart, an' then you re-made me. But you re-made me whole, Westley."

Sam sighed wistfully. "What did I do to deserve such a romantic soul?" He wrapped himself around Declan like a Koala. The kisses that followed were fevered and passionate as if it was their last day on earth.

Declan's broad veined hands gripped the globes of Sam's arse, he pulled him in tighter as they kissed, the wooden chair beneath creaking ominously with the weight of two grown men writhing. Declan pulled out of the kiss and buried his face in Sam's neck inhaling the scents of Sam's

315

sweat, his woodsy body spray, and home. He held on to Sam as if he was a buoy, his only point of reference in a rough sea.

*If I let go, if I lost Sam...*Declan needed to keep it together. There was so much riding on this job that fear might get the better of him. He loved Sam so goddamn much that if there was a repeat of what happened in the Highlands and Sam's life was in mortal danger, Declan might just lose his shit. If they were caught, or if either put a foot wrong they'd be fucked. Frazer had fearfully told them that the ABCs take no prisoners.

The passion waned as they sat in the warmth of one another's embrace soaking up comfort. Sam shifted a little and the chair made an alarming screeching sound. They both snickered.

Sam's feet found the floor and he eased himself backwards off Declan's lap, but kept hold of his hand and pulled him up from the death trap chair and into his arms.

"We've got hours before we need to go. Let's do something to ease the nerves, yes?" Sam suggested in a soft, sexy voice. Declan snickered into Sam's nape, then lifted and shook his head, he hadn't voiced one word to let on that he was feeling nervous. But Sam knew his moods. Sam got him like no other person Declan had ever known.

"What de ye have in mind? Cards mebe? Poker, or shall we play *I Spy*?" he grinned wolfishly.

"From this big bulge," Sam said, placing his hand over the erection concealed in Declan's jeans, "I have something more... adult in mind. A different type of poker, without

316

cards!" Sam wriggled his eyebrows suggestively.

"Really?" Declan bit his lower lip to stop from laughing and eased his hips forward seeking more pressure from Sam's wicked fingers. Sam brushed his lips against Declan's, pulling away swiftly to lure his lover to work for another. All the while Sam's efficient, nimble fingers got to work and unfastened both his and Declan's jeans.

Ten minutes later, Sam was bent over facing the window, his hands braced on the window sill. He was admiring a view of the sea and cerulean sky as Declan ate his ass. Sam gasped and pushed back, the rasp of Declan's beard and hot, wet tongue on his sensitive skin driving him out of his mind.

"You're so fucking good at that," Sam whimpered. Declan snickered and the vibrations of Declan's mouth against Sam's hole made his knees buckle. Declan held him up and pulled his mouth away.

"I think you're more than ready fer mah cock, don't you?"

"Fuck yeah!" Sam agreed as Declan's bare, lubed dick breached and was soon filling him. Sam was in heaven, he'd kept his eyes closed during the initial penetration so he could focus on the desire rushing through his nerves, bathing them in pleasure. Sam opened his eyes and glanced up, then exclaimed,

"Oh my god, it's so big!" a saucy lilt to his tone.

Declan chuckled, warmth and pride adding to arousal as he gave his boy all that he needed. Sam groped along the sill for the binoculars.

"Buttercup, I'm serious. Take a look at this big boy, it's a whopper." Declan thrust, seating himself deeply, making Sam cry out with pleasure. He leaned in and Sam placed the binoculars at his eye line. A massive super yacht had left Portsmouth harbour, but it wasn't heading for the shipping lane, it was heading towards No Man's Land fort.

"Who the fuck does tha' monster belong to?" Declan growled, "I guess we'll find out soon enough. But I cannae deal wi' anything else when I'm gunning to shoot mah load." Declan slapped Sam's backside, "Focus Westley!" he scolded.

"Fine," Sam laughed. He bent his knees, easing forward while his free hand reached behind and pulled Declan's slippery shaft from his body.

"Hey, I'm fuckin' close," Declan grumbled, but then Sam turned, leapt, and wrapped his thighs around Declan's hips. Drunk on love Declan gave a soppy grin as he staggered to get his balance, his hands automatically moving to cradle Sam's beautiful backside.

Sam reached behind and fed Declan's cock back inside his greedy hole. He wiggled and groaned as Declan gave a sharp thrust, seating himself deeply into his lover's heat.

Sam tossed the binoculars onto a hearth chair and then threaded his arms around his husband's neck. "Hard and fast, babe. Make me forget my name."

Declan did exactly that. He carried Sam to the closest bare wall, laid him against it, and fucked up with sharp, brutal precision, massaging Sam's P-spot with every thrust.

Sam was grateful that Declan held him so possessively. He was sure his arse cheeks would have fingerprint bruises and that was just fine by him. The desire flowing through his body made Sam's limbs feel like limp spaghetti, blood filling his cock to bursting. Sam didn't even have the energy to stroke himself. He focused only on the pleasure caused by the hard shaft impaling him over and over again, and the soulful silver eyes telling him how much he was loved.

****

Thirty minutes later they lay together in bed, satiated, Sam nesting between Declan's thighs. Sam had retrieved the binoculars. They were watching the glide of the super yacht as it effortlessly sliced through the grey-green water. Sam looked and then moved the binoculars to Declan's eyes so he could observe.

"It's a swift and elegant yacht, musta cost someone a packet!" Declan commented. Sam put the binoculars back to his eyes,

"Someone's hoisting a flag. They're flying a Jolly Roger."

"He's a cocky bastard alright!" Declan palmed his phone from the nightstand, put it on speaker and called Agent Farrell.

"Y'aright bud," Declan said when the man picked up. "Are you seeing this? A mega yacht's heading towards the fort. Do you know who owns it?"

"What? Shit! I was on a break." The agent said his voice distorted as if his mouth was full. The next sound was a slurp, then a loud burp.

"Sorry about that. Hang on. If memory serves, four of the ABCs have yachts, but none of the Intel said any of them are travelling here by boat. Their travel arrangements were all confirmed," Agent Farrell insisted. "Can you get the name of the yacht?"

Declan turned to Sam, "Yes, it's named *The Plot Twist*", Sam called.

"Did ye hear that?"

"Yeah, hang on a minute." The call went quiet except for the sound of rapidly clicking keys.

"Okay. The Plot Twist belongs to Valentin Molokovic. He has a mooring in St Tropez. The yacht was designed by *Espen Oino*, and it's worth…shit… 56 million dollars. And listen to these specs; it's got accommodation for up to 16 guests across eight staterooms including a master suite with a private deck. 3D cinema room, a fully equipped spa, a gym, and a helipad."

"Not too shabby eh!" Declan scoffed, "What the hell is Molokovic doing parking his yacht so close to the fort?"

This was a question that none of them yet had an answer to.

****

Sam watched as the A.L.L. agents left the fort at seven p.m. having completed their official preparations—and a few that were unofficial!

The Plot Twist finally dropped anchor a mile from No Mans Land, four men disembarked into a *Stingray* speedboat that had been tied up to the back of the super yacht. They visited the fort and spent an hour there, returning before sundown.

****

CHAPTER 33
INTO DARKNESS

It was a perfect night for a romantic stroll along the beach or even a little skinny dipping. The mid-June night was warm and still, the moon high, reflecting a pathway on the ever-moving sea. But romantic pursuits would have to wait.

Sam and Declan packed up their belongings and the security equipment they'd used during their stakeout. The metal flight cases were sealed, and ready for courier collection the following day. Unbeknown to the landlord of the Boathouse bed and breakfast, the men in the honeymoon suite would not be returning to spend the night.

Both men donned compression shorts, then their wet suits and added loose jogging pants and long-sleeved t-shirts over the top so that they could saunter through the pub without anyone noticing anything out of the ordinary.

Hopping in the SUV Sam drove a mile up the east coast to a small wetland area named Seaview. He parked up in the visitor's car park facing the sea where two other cars sat, both without drivers. They got out of the vehicle, stripped off their outdoor clothes and then, in their figure-hugging wetsuits, strode to the boot of the SUV where they'd stored the hired Scuba gear. They went through the routine of attaching tanks and regulators to the buoyancy vests, and then the valve of the regulator was screwed into to the tank valve.

When everything was attached, checked, and double-checked by their partner, the pair helped one another shrug into the buoyancy control vests. Phones were placed in dry bags and pushed into an easily accessible Velcro seal pocket on the vest, and then their high beam underwater torches were securely attached to vest karabiners.

They carried out the preparations in silence, following their Scuba refresher training to the letter. When all of the pre-dive preparations were complete, their eyes met and reflected with steely determination.

"How ye doin' love?" Declan asked softly.

"Good, I can't wait to get the show started." Sam smiled and the moonlight gave him an otherworldly mischievous cast, like a beautiful mythical trickster.

"You?"

"Same page. We've got this," Declan replied succinctly. He didn't want to let Sam know he was nervous. Night diving was always riskier, and they'd only dived at night together once. Declan leaned in and brushed his lips lightly upon Sam's, before pulling away.

"Oh, no you don't, Buttercup. That will never do." Sam then clasped Declan's face and pulled him in for a rough, passionate kiss.

"Aye, aye, ye've made yer point," Declan grinned when Sam broke the kiss.

"Ready?"

Declan nodded. Sam locked the car and hid the magnetized key fob in the front passenger side wheel well.

They then carried their flippers and goggles down to the shore.

The scent of the sea was salty fresh and calming, the distant bark of a dog and the eerie calls of seabirds night fishing echoed between the gentle lash of waves. Tonight's full moon meant higher tides than usual. This played to their advantage. They'd experienced the poor visibility in the silted green-grey water of the Solent during their refresher course, and with the amount of man-made disturbance to the seabed from the twisted wartime ironwork now camouflaged in barnacles and seaweed, they were aware to expect the unexpected beneath the waves. They'd carried out a preparatory dive two nights before and laid a line of Glo-rope, a luminescent rope that was generally used for underwater cave diving.

Sam and Declan pulled on their goggles, then flippers, then each inserted their regulator and took slow deep breaths. Then, hand in hand they flip-flopped into the waves, before letting go and easing beneath the black water.

****

The maximum depth to the seabed in this area of the Solent was ten meters, so this was classified as a shallow dive. Sam focused on slow deep breaths. As expected, the visibility was awful, the murky grey-green water turning inky black at night. Sam felt Declan swim up by his side, grip his forearm and squeeze once, meaning *all good*. Declan switched his torch on sending a beam of light to sever the darkness so they could orient themselves. The light beam waved around until another source of illumination was

323

visible. The torchlight had caught and activated the photo-luminescent Glo-rope.

Agent Farrell's research of the fort blueprints showed that during the Second World War, concrete blocks were sunk from No Man's Land fort to the coast of the Isle of Wight to act as a barrier against enemy submarines. The concrete blocks remained in situ, claimed by the sea, and camouflaged by sea life. This find proved to be very useful. During their preparatory dive, they'd tied the rope around each of the blocks giving them a secure pathway to swim directly to the fort.

The agents kicked off and glided towards the first block and the strand of glowing rope. Sam shone his torch on the rope ahead for just ten seconds and activated the next section of rope. They moved off swimming along the guideline. Within a few uneventful minutes of swimming with the fishes, their flashlights caught the massive cement foundation and curved solid granite wall of the fort ahead. They followed the rope around the vast body of the old foundations steering clear of the twisted rusty iron remnants of Victorian engineering technology that had been abandoned on the seabed. Apart from the occasional small fish hiding among the swathes of dancing seaweed nothing dangerous swam in their path.

Finally, after ten minutes they reached the pole of corroded rebar jutting out of the seabed where they'd tied off the rope. The fort wall was built as a double ring to protect from cannon fire. Directly above, there was a hole in the outer wall of the fort and inside this, a rusted, barnacled ladder would give them access.

They ascended slowly to help prevent decompression sickness. Poking his head above the water first, Declan removed his goggles and got his bearings. Sam popped up next, turned off his torch, spat out the regulator, and removed his goggles, threading the strap over his right wrist.

The calm, lapping summer waves and the distant calls of seabirds were the first things Sam heard, and then something else caught his attention. He nudged Declan, and they both turned to look at where the ostentatious mega-yacht had downed anchor. The thump of bass and peals of laughter sounded loud when compared to the sounds of nature.

Declan spat out his regulator and said, "Look's like Molokovic's havin' a party."

"I wonder who he's invited?" Sam mused.

"Not Jamesy, that's fer sure,"

Sam swam closer to the outer wall of the fort, "The dive was nice but uneventful, I'm a little disappointed."

"We're not out o' the water yet!" Declan snickered, cheered by his partner's love of a challenge. "Ladies first," he invited cheekily, shining his torch to show the arched underwater hole in the wall that led to the hidden ladder. Sam leaned in to kiss Declan, and then he dived under, reaching up for the rusty ladder, and dragged himself up to the first run. With the precarious scuba tank on his back, he began the climb.

****

CHAPTER 34
STORMIN' DA CASTLE

Sam switched his torch on again, clambered over the short concrete brick barrier wall and onto the slatted timber surface they'd seen the *Urbex* boys show in their YouTube exploration video, but what the video didn't tell them was the smell was fucking hideous. Years of decaying seaweed, fish and god knows what else had clung to the timber and stone in the narrow tunnel causing an oppressive funk. Sam stepped away from the opening to allow Declan to climb in.

"Jesus, wha' the ever-loving fuck?" Declan protested when the stench reached his nostrils.

"Did something crawl in here te die?" He planted his flippers on the timber slats and immediately moved forward, out of the tight entrance. He shrugged out of the cumbersome tanks and Scuba vest, closed the tank valve, and then took off the flippers.

Sam shone his torch down the tunnel, the light beam showing that a holdall, a couple of ropes and bath towels had been left for them. He shrugged his tanks and vest off and closed the tank valve, then passed them and his flippers to Declan who put them at the diver's opening beside his own. They set their torches down to light up the tunnel. Sam then retrieved the holdall and tossed Declan a towel. They helped one another out of the wetsuits, shivering a little as they dried off and dressed in the black tactical trousers with extra pockets and long-sleeved tops that had been left for them in the holdall. The stealth ensemble was finished off with socks and slip-on trainers. They dressed hurriedly and then retrieved their phones from the dry bags on their scuba vests. Declan was in charge of Comms. He sent a message.

We're in.

The response came as they were folding up the wetsuits and stuffing them into the holdall.

Two heat sigs in Crows Nest. Amanda at party on Plot Twist. Proceed as planned.

Declan relayed the reply to Sam.

"Maybe she *is* trying to bag a billionaire?" Sam sniped bitchily. Declan ran a hand over Sam's damp blond hair to flatten it.

"You know as well as I that it doesn't matter what she does. Amanda's gonna pay for every life she took!"

"Yes. Karma cannot come quick enough!"

Sam removed a lock pick kit from a pocket in the holdall. Then, to ensure their diving gear wasn't found they tied the ends of the two ropes onto the exterior ladder, attached their Scuba gear to the ropes and eased them over the side of the diver's hole. The tanks and holdall of gear were hidden from view by the outer ring wall and out of sight if anyone inspected the tunnel.

"Time check?"

Declan pressed his thumb to his phone screen "12:32 a.m" then he clicked and swiped to pull up the internal fort map. The fort structure was like three vast ring doughnuts made of iron and granite, one on top of the other, with an extra thick outer crust wall built to repel cannons. The hole in the middle of the fort was originally an open courtyard, but during renovations it had been fitted with floors and a glass dome to utilize the space. The fortification was a testament to the ingenuity of Victorian engineering but there wasn't a ninety-degree angle in the whole structure.

The first stone ring, the one they now stood in, was called the Sea Bunker. It was built on top of a vast concrete foundation and was closest to the sea bed. Therefore, it was the coldest level in the fort and the damp musty scent of briny water permeated the stone. The Sea Bunker was a warren of tunnels, larger workshop rooms, and storage for canned and bottled foodstuffs. It had escaped renovation, and the thick white layer of limewash paint on Victorian red bricks bubbled and peeled in place. This level contained the Royal Navy Maritime Museum exhibit of heavy iron engineering, wheeled canons, chains, ropes, and nautical salvage that told the bleak story of life on the fort.

The second level was five meters above the sea. The rooms here once house the Comms room, the armoury, and the soldier's quarters. During the refurbishment, these rooms were repurposed for the spa, salon, gym, an Old English pub called Lord Nelson, and the Mess Hall restaurant.

The third floor was named the Gun Floor and was where the forty-nine cannons were once housed giving the fort 360-degree firepower. The cannons were long gone and each cannon room was now guest accommodation, kitchens, crew lounges, a library nook, and offices. The 'doughnut hole' on this level was a raised atrium used for fine dining and special events, covered with a spectacular intricate dome of glass.

A red and white striped lighthouse known as the Crows Nest was built on the roof with two contemporary additions of helipads. The circular roof terrace gave spectacular views of the Solent, the Isle of Wight, and the mainland. On a good day when there was no sea mist, the coast of France was visible.

Sam opened the timber door at the end of the tunnel. He sent his torch beam down the dark corridor. "Clear," he said.

"Okay. We go straight ahead fer five meters, take the stairway on the left that leads up into the pub," Declan instructed.

"Ready?" Sam asked. Declan nodded.

Sam took the lead, keeping his torch low in case the place had been wired up to alert Madsson of intruders. The psycho had a history of using tripwires to his deadly advantage.

Declan followed behind, listening intently to the creaking and echoing groans of eerie sea swell against the stone walls. They found the staircase and Sam bolted up the stairs to find the cellar door of the pub open. He paused warily.

"Damn it," he complained in a whisper "I don't need to display my lock-picking skills." He sent his torch beam inside for a glancing pass, then stepping in, he followed the beam. There was an uncomfortable, ominous feeling in the Sea Bunker that followed when they stepped into the small pub too. Torchlight swept over the bar counter and the usual pub wall décor, crockery, brassware, and enamel signs for Guinness, and Bass. The torch then picked out the seating areas and illuminated the dust-covered glasses that remained on the tables, as though the customers had just popped out.

"You gettin' a *Marie-Celeste* vibe?"

"Yeah. It's creepy," Sam agreed.

Sam sent his torch in a wide arc until he located the front door. He headed through the lounge to the glass-pained door which, when pushed was again, unlocked and swung open on squeaky hinges. The ease of access inside the fort was disarming but not unexpected. It's not as if the owner needed to secure the place from passing thieves!

Sam stepped out with Declan at his back. They were now standing in a paved courtyard on the second storey. The place was airy, open plan and designed to look like a seaside village street. Then both men looked up to see the glass-covered roof of the atrium. Several wrought-iron spiral staircases lead up to the third-floor atrium sun terrace. Moonlight through the glass dome gave muted illumination. The air was much warmer here, cloying with glasshouse humidity, even at night.

"I don't know about you love, but this place totally gives me the willies."

"I know what you mean," Sam mused as he sent his torch to skirt their surroundings. "I feel like we're on a set for a dystopian disaster movie. Where to now?"

"Now we take a left until we find a sign for the blue stairs to the third level. We're in room six,"

They moved off again on light feet. The floor here was made to look like old cobblestones cast in concrete and resin. Display props were suspended above them, the wheel of a ship, a timber canoe, crossed oars, fishing nets full of plastic fish, harpoons, and fishing rods. At floor level in nooks and corners, old leather suitcases, piles of books, lanterns and other nautical items were also used for display. It didn't take long to find the doorway marked with blue tape around the porthole. They crept up the winding stairs to the accommodation level.

Moving swiftly, they hurried past the open doorway for a huge Billiards room, the table draped with a Holland cover. A loud bang from outside shocked them both. Declan backtracked and headed to the Billiards room window. Sam joined him to see The Plot Twist floating on the calm black sea lit up with strings of white bulbs. Someone was setting off fireworks from the helipad on the roof of the super yacht. The booming explosions were so loud, echoing in the vast emptiness of the Solent, colourful lights raining down like sparkling stars.

Sam hated every last person having fun on that yacht, what they stood for, and the damage their collective machinations had done to secure money and power. "They all seem suitably distracted. Come on, let's find our room," he said stonily.

Each of the twenty-two guest suites on the fort was

331

named after a British warship, HMS Dreadnought, HMS Nelson, HMS Belfast, HMS Victory etc. The room Sam and Declan would hide out in was labelled number 6 and perfectly titled HMS Revenge.

Opening the bedroom door Sam stepped in first with Declan close at his back. Declan turned and locked the door. Sam's torch displayed the hallway leading to the massive bedroom. To the right, was a high-spec bathroom with a big spa bath, double walk-in shower, and double basins. Moving further into the room to the left was a day bed couch and to the right a super king bed. Everything was pristine, laid out as if they were guests when in reality the fort hadn't taken customers in more than twelve months.

"Not bad", Declan praised, not even bothering to whisper. The granite block walls were half a meter thick between the rooms. No one would hear them, but they needed to be careful with lights because the squat square window that once housed a cannon barrel had no drapes.

Sam tossed the lit torch onto the bed facing away from the window to give them just enough light to help their eyesight adjust to the gloom. Declan moved directly to the built-in wardrobes where two small metal flight cases and a rucksack had been left for them. Declan handed the first flight case to Sam who laid it on the bed, and Declan took the second. Then Sam meticulously removed each of the items in his case, a tablet computer, two guns with clips of bullets, and three sealed packages. The third slender package was in a laboratory-sealed bag and something that Sam would be dealing with alone. Declan harrumphed when he pressed his thumb to the scanner and opened his case to see it contained two of the super-skin ballistics vests.

"I think I'll hedge mah bets tonight. There's no fuckin way I'm sweating mah tits off sleeping in that vest."

"Agreed!" Sam picked up a gun, checked, and loaded it. Declan did the same.

They placed their phones and weapons on the nightstand on either side of the bed and put the packages back in the case. They wouldn't be needed until later!

Declan then opened the rucksack. "Ah, you beauty!" As well as sandwiches, drinks, fruit, protein bars, and crisps, a six-pack box of Tunnocks Teacakes had been added.

"Ye hungry?" Declan asked as he ripped open the box and virtually inhaled one of the sweet cakes.

"Yeah, I could eat a horse."

"We're a wee bit low on horse, but there's a classy array of sandwiches. You could have the Cajun Chicken wrap, Ham and cheese baguette, or plain old egg salad," he said brightly, removing the boxed sandwiches from the rucksack and tossing them onto the bed.

"Oh, I'll eat anything," Sam replied distractedly. "First things first though. I'm gonna run the shower to see if we have hot water. I want to get the smell of the sea off my skin."

While Sam was in the shower Declan contacted Agent Farrell to give him an update. Then he joined his lover to rid himself of the salt and rotting seaweed scent. By the time they lay down on the massive bed, it was 1:34 a.m.

****

Neither man couldn't miss Amanda's triumphant return to the fort after attending the soirée on The Plot Twist. Their bedroom window was open a crack to let in a cool sea breeze and the sound of the speedboat engine set Sam to awareness in seconds. Alarmed by the sounds, Sam rolled off the bed and got up.

"I'll go check," he whispered to his dozing partner, then he left the bedroom and scurried across the dark hall into the glass-walled meeting room opposite that gave a lovely moonlit view of the atrium. Sam stayed low behind a couch and watched as Amanda sauntered up the entrance stairs like she was Cinderella and stepped into the atrium, her strappy-heeled sandals dangling from her fingers.

"Hi honey I'm hooome. Did yez miiiisss me boys?" she singsonged her Glaswegian accent slurring. Wearing a wig of long blonde tresses and lit only by the moonlight, she looked like a harmless older woman returning from a good night out. The reality was that Amanda was nothing of the sort. Amanda Jamison was a chameleon, a manipulator, a seducer, and a killer. She twirled on her tippy-toes, arms outstretched to bathe in the moonlight through the glass domed roof. Her slinky summer dress then caught between her thighs forcing her to topple to the floor. She lay there sprawled on the ground like a starfish for a few seconds and then let out a cackling joyful laugh.

"If yez could see me now, ye bastards," she roared venomously. "Yez said I'd amount te nothin'. But look at me now! I'm a whole, beautiful woman, an' I'm dining with fuckin' billionaires," Amanda bellowed drunkenly at her personal demons.

Sam *could* go out there now while she was three sheets to the wind and snap her neck. It was tempting after what she'd done, the clinical, cold-blooded way she'd assassinated two innocent men to access the HQ. But wouldn't that make him as bad as her? No matter the tug of temptation to end this woman, Sam knew he had to bide his time and hold on to his belief in Karma. And so, as Amanda rolled over and jumped to her feet with surprising grace then stumbled to the winding staircase that led up to the Crows Nest apartment, Sam retreated to the bedroom.

Declan lay on top of the coverlet, his chest bare. It was a warm night and the bright moonlight prevented the true darkness he needed to drift off.

"What was all tha' about?" he asked dozily when Sam slid onto the huge bed and rolled over to Declan's side.

"Cinders returned from the ball."

"Noisy bitch! Looks like nonea us 'll catch a wink tonight," he groused. Sam laid his head on Declan's chest and placed his hand over his husband's heart, relaxing as he listened to the gentle thrum of life coursing through his lover's veins. Minutes later he smiled at the sound of Declan's deep growly snore.

****

CHAPTER 35

STANDBY

They awoke with the sun baking them and a flock of seagulls making an unholy racket outside.

"Christ on a bike. I wish I could unload mah weapon inte those fucking birds," Declan rasped after trying to ignore the cacophonous squawking for ten minutes. He'd gone to sleep in a grouchy humour and woken up after too-few hours asleep in a worse mood. Sam rubbed his cheek into Declan's hairy chest, rolled his hips just an inch to complete full-body contact and ground his morning wood against his husband's firm thigh.

"Good morning darling. You can unload your weapon into me if it'll make you feel better. We've got plenty of time!" he said in a lazy purr. The silence that followed that saucy pronouncement made Sam come to full awareness and look up, worried. Declan was grinning.

"What?"

"You! I'm here growlin' like a bear an' you just say somethin' an' knock me fer six," Declan admitted rubbing a hand across his infectious smile.

"I guess that means you love me, Buttercup!"

Declan threaded his palm around the back of Sam's head and dragged him up to lie on top.

"I guess you're correct, Westley!" He pressed his sleep-swollen lips to Sam's, before slapping Sam's backside saying,

"Right-ho! Chop, chop! We've got no time fer smoochin'!"

"Cock tease!" Sam pouted as Declan rolled over, got up, and headed to the bathroom for a piss. Danger made Sam horny and he'd hoped for a little sweet lovin', but Declan was up and focused on the job.

"We need to get ready. I'd put money on the security team doing one more sweep before they allow the ABCs to come over," Declan called.

"Oh come on, surely a perk of working with one's spouse is sex on tap!" Sam complained. "I'll let it go this time, but you owe me a BJ," Sam replied as he butt-shuffled to the edge of the massive bed. A glance at his phone showed Sam a blinking green light. He picked it up and checked the message.

"Team Bravo ETA 9 a.m. set up the dining area and canapé prep. Restaurant delivery 6 p.m. Dinner 7p.m, Meeting 8 p.m. ABCs will begin to arrive anytime after 3 p.m."

Declan sauntered out of the bathroom. Sam read the message aloud. They had quite a day ahead.

****

After helping each other slide into the super-skin ballistics vests, and then packing up the remaining food and equipment, they hid the empty flight cases under the re-maid bed. Then taking the rucksack, they relocated back down to the Sea Bunker to wait out the security sweep.

They chose the wood workshop as their bolt-hole because

337

it had been left in a state of complete disarray with dozens of half-finished display boards for a new Navy exhibit abandoned with the fort. This disarray could be used to their advantage. There was a small tool storeroom cut into one of the oddly angled walls without a door. Declan shone his torch inside to see dusty tools and boxes of nails. In the main workshop, there were twelve large sheets of moisture-resistant MDF piled against one wall. Sam and Declan moved a couple of sheets in front of a tool store doorway ensuring that anyone who didn't know the fort wouldn't realize a doorway was covered up. Now they had a nice hiding place that made them invisible to anyone walking in to check the room. All they could do now was sit, and wait in the darkness for the all-clear from Agent Svensson.

A few minutes later Agent Farrell sent a message,

"What is it?"

"An update," Sam turned the screen to let Declan read it. Declan did so then reached into the rucksack for the computer tablet and booted it up to check if they could connect with the live feed for the camera on the landing stage.

Sam hated dark spaces, but he'd been pushing himself for the past eighteen months to fight the fear.

"What's wrong?" Declan asked, sensing all was not well with Sam.

"I'm just a little paranoid," Sam admitted. "We're so close to ending this, we can almost touch the other side," he sighed. "A niggling voice inside keeps telling me some other fuckery will push us off our path."

338

"Well, you can tell that wee voice te jog on. We're getting Viper safely to the chopper and then we're gone," Declan pressed his thumb to the touch screen to log into the computer, "In fact, we'd best start thinking about what breed of dog would suit us."

Sam brightened. "You'd let me have a dog?" He shuffled closer, took Declan's face in both hands, and gave him a big sloppy kiss.

Declan pulled away laughing. "Let ye? As if I could stop ye! But aye, if we're gonna be parents one day we'd best start by seeing if we can care for a pup!"

"Oh my God, I'm so excited!" Sam threw his arms around his husband and hugged him until the computer screen lit up.

"Hang on, we're in! Let's see if we can pick up the feed." Declan clicked on the encrypted video app and waited for the viewer to open. When it did, there were three live cameras listed, one on the landing stage, one on the roof terrace facing the helipads, and a third in the entrance hallway. It was great to have eyes on parts of the fort they couldn't access themselves. "Good goin' lads," Declan was impressed. This was all team Bravo could get away with until after the security sweep.

Declan clicked on the camera for the landing stage. It showed a white *Stingray* speedboat tied up to the two metal docking poles. The boat driver was buff, wearing a tight white uniform shirt and white shorts topped off with a white chauffeurs cap. He was passing boxes from the belly of the boat to the two assassins, who passed them to the hospitality staff who were doing the donkey work, carrying them up the three flights and into the fort. "Gods, Bravo picked the short straw. They're sweatin' their tits off!"

"Yeah, poor bastards." Everything from linens to glassware, crockery, and cutlery had been shipped over. The ABCs clearly expected the finest dining experience.

Erik Madsson was dressed casually in navy shorts, a white t-shirt, and boat shoes, his blond hair now cropped and his beard closely trimmed. He appeared healthy, well-rested and tanned, as if he'd been on vacation and caught the sun. The boat driver passed him a crate of wine, which he carried up the staircases into the fort entrance. Amanda and the disguised Agent Svensson took a crate between them labelled in large black font as 'crystal wine glasses'. Carefully they carried a box up the stairs.

"This is gonna go on for a while. Let's see if anything's happening on the roof," Sam suggested. Declan clicked on the roof camera feed. James was on the Astroturf lawn beside the helipad. He was wearing loose clothing and working through a routine of Taekwondo stretches. For a man who was nearing his sixtieth birthday, he was in excellent shape.

"Jamesy's getting limbered up fer a fight!" Declan observed, having had personal experience of hand-to-hand combat with Sam's father.

"It's a good sign. He's not giving up. He's waiting for us."

It made Sam feel twitchy watching his father moving through the different stretches when the evil needle collar

340

could kill him at any second.

Declan clicked on the entrance camera and saw how the boxes of supplies were piled in the hall, and then carried toward the kitchen.

On a whim, Declan clicked back to the landing stage camera and they saw that with the final four long boxes of fresh flowers waiting on the landing deck, the unloading was done. Madsson untied the first, then second boat line. He blocked the view of the camera for an instant and when he moved Sam and Declan saw the boat driver clearly. He'd removed his cap to wipe his sweaty brow. The clean-shaven man had a shock of ginger hair. Madsson tossed the line and the driver caught it in the air, then he threw it to the belly of the speedboat. He saluted Erik and then the boat moved off, turning in an impressive arc and causing water to spray up. The boat then sped back toward The Plot Twist. Both Sam and Dec were stunned to silence.

Sam was the first to break the silence.

"What did I just tell you? I fucking knew something else was going on. What the hell is Alasdair Frazer doing here?"

Declan didn't reply, he was on his phone, his fingers moving swiftly as he sent a message to Agent Svensson.

Where did the items you unloaded originate?

She responded seconds later. *The Plot Twist.*

"Fuck," Declan exclaimed. "Fuck, fuck, fuck!".

"Frazer's working for Molokovic," Sam stated before Declan could voice it.

"I'm such a numpty," he seethed. "But it all makes sense now. The men who came to the riding school weren't a

341

strike team. *He* told us they were a strike team and we believed the manipulative little shit. They didnae go there to kill Frazer…"

"It was an extraction, and Frazer didn't want you to get hurt."

"Aye", Declan rubbed a worried hand across his beard, not wanting to believe in the possibility that Alasdair had saved his life.

Sam considered this new information, "Apart from A.L.L. there were only two parties who knew that Frazer was in the UK—MI6 who would have then informed the Foreign Secretary, Jonathan Brudenell-Brice.

"Fuckin' Dracula leaked the Intel to Molokovic!" Declan stated furiously.

"And Molokovic extracted the ABCs asset," Sam said finishing Declan's thought.

Voicing his niggling concern Declan asked, "D'ye think Frazer knows were here?"

"I don't see how he could know. It appears he has his own agenda. During the interrogation, he was surprised to hear Madsson was alive. And seeing them together now, they looked to be on good terms. Maybe he's here for Erik?"

Sam relayed the new Intel directly to Mrs K. Her reply told, in uncharacteristic language, that she was furious that when it came to intelligence, the Foreign Secretary was as leaky as a sieve.

****

It was now just after 10 a.m. Declan's phone screen lit up. Team Bravo had begun setting up in the Mess Hall. The message was from Agent Svensson.

Imran Fizel just arrived with two men for the final security sweep. Bottom to top. Will text when gone.

Fizel was Femi Zubari's bodyguard. Declan angled the phone so Sam could read the message then pocketed the device. Silently, they sat in the pensive darkness. A scratching sound made Sam reach out and grip his husband's forearm.

"It's just a wee mouse," Declan whispered.

"Hmm...not a fan,"

Minutes later, footsteps and then muffled voices. The security team was in the Sea Bunker and as they got closer to the wood workshop, Declan noticed the men were all speaking in Russian. Sam squeezed his forearm again as if to say, *I've got this.*

They both tensed and held in their breaths as the strip light was turned on in the workshop and thin lines of bright white light were visible around the edges of their timber-covered doorway. Footsteps followed, a discussion was had, and orders were given. Then the light went out.

One man called to another, a minute passed and then another called back. Sam stiffened. He turned to Declan.

"They said that this level is a weak spot and they don't have the time to check every room. They're setting sensor wires across main doorways and the corridor," he whispered into his husband's ear. The thin, clear sensor wire could be fitted anywhere with just a drop of super glue and was undetectable until touched. When touched a signal was sent to a handheld receiver to alert of an intruder.

Sam slept, his head on Declan's shoulder. Declan closed his eyes and dozed until his phone vibrated in his pocket. He was shocked to see it was now nearly midday. Declan picked up the phone and placed his thumb on the sensor, the screen shone, blinding him for a moment.

All Clear, security left with Madsson onboard boat, Amanda went down to gym. Viper alone.

"Sam," Declan whispered and shrugged his shoulder. Sam startled awake.

"It's time. We've got a wee window of opportunity".

"Fuck, okay," Sam turned his torch on, then located the rucksack. He took out three packages passing one to Declan. He eased the thin package inside his skin-tight ballistics vest, the other one he held. They both opened their packages to see the contents. Declan's contained two rolls of what looked like transparent coins. They were micro speakers with self-adhesive backing. Declan's task was to place them securely and unobtrusively around the fort. The display props would come in handy as hiding places!

Sam's package held ten black tiny cameras. His task was to hide them in the Mess Hall, the main stairway, the Atrium sun room, and the winding stairs to the Crows Nest apartment. Camera placement was vital to ensure both they and Team Alpha on the mainland could watch the proceedings live.

Sam uncoiled, stood up, and stretched his limbs. Then gripping the edges of the sheet of marine timber he pushed it outward so they could squeeze out. The timber sheet was then eased back into place.

"We're no' gonna make the same mistake again," Declan said when his torch found the first sensor wire across the doorway to the workshop. The wire was set at knee height, probably to avoid false alarms caused by rodents. He stepped gingerly over it, and then Sam followed. Declan didn't want to take another step until Sam was safely beside him. Their torches showed the wires across each doorway off the corridor they were in, and six across the width of the corridor. They took it slow and cautiously stepped over the wires without touching them. They made their way to the stairway that led to the Lord Nelson pub. Reaching the top they discovered the door had been locked.

"Bastards," Sam grumbled. The agents had a very short window of time to plant their devices. Sam retrieved the lock-picking kit and Declan held a torch facing the lock as Sam worked his magic. They entered the pub and with bright daylight streaming in via the glazed front door, they turned off the torches and left them in a niche on the stairway. Again, Declan found the pub door had been locked and Sam got to work. When they were in the second-floor courtyard, Sam and Declan split up.

Declan began by removing the backing paper on each of the tiny speakers, then with a fingernail, he flicked a tiny switch on the back of each speaker so it would receive. He kept low and alert as he began planting the devices in inconspicuous places, on the back of the prop suitcases, then further on, he stuck one to a book, then a lantern, and under a flag displayed in a niche. He was excited to see this part of the plan come alive.

Sam crept down the stairway that led to the main entrance. To his left, the forlorn hotel reception and then the sad abandoned Cabaret Bar, and to the right the Mess Hall restaurant where the ABCs would be dining. A large circular table had been set up in front of a porthole window with a sea view. The table was set for nine diners, dressed with a fine white linen tablecloth, and laid for English-style Silver Service dining. James would not be permitted to join his old compatriots for one final meal.

The crockery was white with a blue band and Russian script around the rim of each plate in gold. Sam read 'Altýnnogo vóra véshayut, a poltínnogo chéstvuyut,' which translated as 'The thief who steals a little is hanged, the thief who steals a lot is honoured.' Molokovic had a dark sense of humour.

Large displays of tropical flowers in bloom were placed around the Mess Hall to detract from the vast emptiness of the restaurant. When the current owner abandoned the fort all food and alcohol were removed. Now the restaurant bar was fully stocked with wines, whiskey, and spirits that Molokovic had shipped over. *That's a lot of booze for such a short evening!* Sam observed. He worked out the best sightlines before setting up two cameras, one inside an old-fashioned steel and brass diving helmet, the camera looking out through the glass porthole, and the other in a floral display. When that was done he moved to the stiflingly hot atrium sunroom and set cameras there.

Staying low he saw Declan creep up the first spiral staircase, run a hand across his sweat-soaked brow, and begin planting more button speakers around the atrium. Their eyes met, and Sam gestured that he was going up to the Crows Nest lighthouse. Declan nodded and communicated using hand gestures to ensure that Sam knew had only twenty minutes to complete his task. Sam checked his phone; it was 12:15 p.m. He headed for the spiral staircase and darted up to the roof terrace.

Sam stepped through the door and onto the roof, relieved to breathe in the salty cool breeze coming in north from the English Channel. He remained low so that anyone watching the fort from The Plot Twist didn't see an unknown man in black skulking on the flat roof. He headed swiftly towards the French doors of the apartment which were open allowing a cool sea breeze into the sitting room. Sam took a quick wary look inside before straightening up and stepping in.

"Hello father."

****

CHAPTER 36
GHOSTS THAT HAUNT

Sir James Aiken sat in an armchair that faced the sea. He was reading a copy of The Telegraph, a cup of steaming Espresso on the small table beside the chair. He was clean-shaven, dressed in navy lounge pants, deck shoes, and a nautical striped t-shirt with the Fort Hotels logo that had been pilfered from the now-defunct gift shop in the fort below.

"You took your time," he sneered not lowering the newspaper to see who had stepped into the lounge through the French doors.

"I'm here aren't I?" Sam asserted his tone calm and cold.

"And I'm *so* terribly grateful that you took time out of your busy schedule, Samuel." James shot back a sarcastic bullet. It seemed to Sam that a month on the fort in the company of Madsson and Jamieson, *and* the possibility of instantaneous death had not put his father in an affable mood. Sam strode further into the sitting room and took a seat on the rather garish burgundy leather couch opposite his father's armchair. The sun was bright, almost too bright, sending swathes of sunlight through the white-walled room, reminding Sam not to get too comfortable. This was a room designed for the enjoyment of stunning sea views, not for privacy. He checked his phone, no messages, and there were just eighteen minutes left before he had to leave.

James lowered and folded the newspaper and then set it on the side table. He picked up the tiny Espresso cup, took a sip of thick, dark coffee, and then after placing the cup down, brought his hands together in his usual, dominant, steepled fingers gesture while staring out to sea. It was another rare cloudless day with the azure blue sky meeting the grey-green mirror of the Solent. In the distance, there was a cargo ship laden with containers sailing on calm seas towards Portsmouth harbour. James tracked it for a long moment.

"We don't have much time," Sam cautioned.

"Indeed. The Scottish harpy's just gone down to the gym. She usually does an hour, but I never know when she'll pop back up like a bad smell," James groused caustically.

"And the Swede," he continued in the same bored tone, "he's on that ostentatious eyesore of a yacht." James smiled thoughtfully before narrowing his blue-green eyes and pinning his son with an unreadable look.

"Now, exactly how are you planning to destroy this rat's nest, and how are you going to get this blasted collar off me? I can't say I care much for my new fashion accessory." He gestured to the moulded plastic abomination.

Sam considered James's list of demands. He wondered if sharing a virtual prison with Amanda had pushed James over the edge.

"Destroy? The Alphabet Club? You expect *me* to... kill them?" he asked confused.

349

"Yes, Samuel. You're here, therefore you deciphered my message. Your orders were clear."

Sam gave an airy chuckle. "I think you've got your wires crossed, father," he said sitting back and spreading his arms along the back of the couch in a display of confident machismo.

"Declan and I are not here to kill *anyone*. The only reason we came to assist with your extraction is for Annabelle. We're here to get you out and to say goodbye."

James opened his mouth to reprimand his son but before he could say a word Sam spoke up,

"No, I'm talking now," Sam said arrogantly, "You're not in a position to give orders. Do I need to remind you that you have a deadly collar around your throat and I have the means to prevent it from killing you? Take your revenge however you want, but, you're not the boss of me anymore, and I will not become a serial killer to appease you."

James did not react well to powerlessness. He glared at his son like a toddler ready to unleash a full-scale meltdown. Sam knew exactly how it felt to be powerless, to feel like you were out of options. James didn't realise how lucky he was, he at least had options. Sam remained quiet, observing his father as James processed his predicament. Sam knew so much more about James now. What a mask the man had constructed over the years to hide his pain, fear, and grief.

"How do you do it father?"

"Do what?" James snapped seemingly annoyed to realize he was out of moves and at his son's mercy.

"Keep so many plates spinning?"

James gave a wan smile. "I don't know what you mean."

"Come now, father. Your life is like an onion, when one layer is removed there's another, and another. Enough of the games," Sam asserted. "I took Declan to *the house*."

James paled at hearing that Sam had visited their family home...his secret place. He seemed to crumple in on himself like a deflated balloon, all dominance and bluster gone.

Sam sat forward and rested his elbows on his knees. "Why did you never sell it?"

James looked up and pinned his son with a glare of outrage, "It's your mother's house," he exclaimed.

"I know. But... mum's gone." The words hurt to say, had hurt from the first time he'd had to relay them.

"No!" James insisted. "My Rosa's still there," his tone was different, softer, more human.

"When I'm at that house it's almost as if Rosalind is in another room and we could meet again on the stairs," he added wistfully, his eyes glazing over with tears. "I keep it as it was, as she left it, to be close to her...to remember the man I was when she was alive."

"When you were my dad and not the heartless bastard you've become," Sam shot back. The comment was brittle and full of the pain of an abandoned child.

"Touché," James sighed. "I was deeply in love with you mother, you must know this," he asserted. "She can never be replaced. From the moment we met, I knew she would be my only love."

Sam did know this, had felt the love between his parents during his childhood. James, Rosalind, Annabelle and Sam

351

had been, for the blink of an eye, the epitome of happy families, even though the ever-present shadow of Cancer followed, waiting for the treatment to fail, waiting for his mother's body to grow too weak to fight back. They'd crammed so much into their days and so, as a grieving teen, the absence of simple affection burned in Sam's soul like the eye of Sauron.

"When Rosalind told me she'd won a place at Oxford and we could be together I knew it was fate. I could feel it; even then, after a few weeks as her boyfriend, I knew I would marry her."

Sam's skin prickled and his eyes burned, a tangled ball of emotion lodged in his windpipe as if the threads of loss and grief had twisted together over the years trapping all of the things he'd wanted to say to his father about how James had let him down. Sam couldn't allow the candid admission of his father's devotion to his mother to overwhelm him. It was James's actions toward his son, his manipulation, ill-use and disdain since Rosalind passed that James needed to atone for. But it would take more than the remaining sixteen minutes to work through everything that had gone wrong in their father-son relationship. Sam needed to remember why he was here. He had one opportunity to find out the truth. Sam gripped his phone in his hands to anchor himself, remaining on guard for a message from Declan.

"Tell me about the Alphabet Club."

"Hmmm, I suppose I owe you an explanation," James said dryly.

"I'm sure from the information my clues led you to,

you've filled in quite a few pieces of the puzzle."

"I suppose I did. I gained access to the MoD archive and retrieved the address book."

"Very well, if I tell you, you'll get this damnable collar off my neck?" he bargained.

Sam didn't respond, but James continued as if he'd heard Sam's agreement.

"You already know that my empire was built from your mother's inheritance. My father was a civil servant and my mother was a teacher, both gone long before you were born. We were ordinary, not moneyed, or privileged in any way. I was frustrated with the cards life had dealt me. I had...ambitions. I wanted to be *more*. I believed that if I remade myself and became like those born into privilege I would be...*good enough*. Oxford was the first step. I achieved my place on a scholarship. But, my god, looking back I was an imbecile, knew nothing of the world," James chuckled lightly to himself at the memory.

"I'd read that the only way to elevate and gain social acceptance was to pall up with boys who were born with connections and to do that I'd need to be in a society. I tried, and I failed miserably to join a drinking club. I didn't have the stomach for it. The boys humiliated me over and over again. I was never good enough; I wasn't their 'sort'." James paused for a breath. "Then I met Professor Alfred Moxley."

James reached blindly for the Espresso cup and knocked back the remaining contents like a shot of whisky before replacing the empty cup on the side table.

"Alfred saw something in me and said I was special. *Isn't that what every boy wants to hear?*" James supposed dreamily. Sam desperately wanted to speak up then, but he bit his lip to stop from interrupting while his father was unburdening.

"Alfred selected me for recruitment to the Secret Service and after the assessment, I was informed I was to be fast-tracked, a job was guaranteed as soon as I graduated. I thought that finally, this was my chance to excel. Alfred mentored me, became a father figure, he offered me everything I never thought I could have. Then he introduced me to the other boys and invited me to join his new secret society. It was intriguing, mysterious, and the natural next step to social acceptability. I had a group of friends who had my back, who opened doors for me, and I responded in kind."

"So, how did it come to this...to murder?" Sam gestured to the evil collar.

"When we agreed to join Moxley's club we all made a solemn vow to protect the club's interests. We recited an oath of secrecy and agreed that should any of us betray the club, another member would be selected at random, *names in a hat sort of thing*, to carry out our self-chosen *final punishment*," James explained conversationally.

"The benefits of the club would be vast, life-changing, and so the punishment for betrayal needed to match. We were full of testosterone, competing for Alfred's attention; we all wanted to appear to be the bravest, most loyal among the club members. The majority decided that their punishment for betrayal of the club's secrets would be death. Many even listed their preferred exit too. I chose a fate worse than my death."

"What punishment did you choose?" Sam asked, almost afraid to hear the answer.

James watched the slow passage of the container ship sailing on the Solent. He seemed to be miles away, and when he came back to himself he pleaded,

"You have to understand how it was. It was 1981. Most of us were just eighteen, newly free of our parents and learning what it meant to be men. Alfred offered us a group of like-minded peers, compatriots with the same goals. Men, who's shared priority was in becoming future leaders, in industry, politics, and finance—our influence would enable mutual enrichment. Alfred taught us how the world works, and offered us mentorship and advice," James insisted.

Sam was hyperaware of the anxious drumming of his heart and knew his father was stalling. "What punishment did you choose?" he asked again his tone hard and insistent.

James hesitated for an instant, then looked up from his steepled fingers and winced as he stuttered,

"*You*. I...I...I offered them you!"

"But I wasn't even born?" Sam exclaimed at comprehending his father's admission.

"It was a trick, of sorts. I promised that if I betrayed the secrets of the Alphabet Club they could kill my first son. I never expected to be a father. I was just a boy, cocky, full of himself. I thought it was a cunning way of ensuring the cabal had no actionable punishment for me should I slip

355

up."

There was childish logic to James's choice; a kind of fantasy scenario that might never have come to pass. Sam's gut lurched with nausea at finally understanding. This was why he had become the cabal's target.

"Fatherhood was not high on my list of priorities at eighteen. I wanted to have fun, make money, see the world, and fall in love."

"So, you sacrificed me to your psychopath's club and later betrayed them knowing the price was my life," Sam was appalled.

"No, it didn't happen like that." James asserted. "I never betrayed them, never. I would never want to put your life at risk."

Sam narrowed his eyes skeptically. This was pure gaslighting. Sam had lost count of the number of times James had put his life in danger.

"It may have escaped your memory old-man but Erik Madsson has been my deathly shadow for years. I was targeted for assassination twice. If you cared about my safety at all why didn't you ONCE fucking warn me?" Sam was angry now.

"It was *my* problem to deal with, *my* schoolboy error. I saw no reason anyone else needed to know—"

"What? That you're imperfect, flawed, that you're selfish and heartless and you made a fucking appalling choice when you were eighteen." The air was stifling and Sam's chest felt too tight. He was revolted and couldn't look at his father anymore. Sam found his feet and stalked away to the

356

French doors desperate for some fresh air.

"Look," James spat sharply. "I've had a great deal of time over the past month to reconsider my actions and behaviour," he admitted. "I'm loathed to say...I was wrong Sam, wrong to believe that joining the cabal would make me a better man, wrong to enable them, wrong to put you in their cross-hairs. I'm sorry."

Sam shook his head. Sam had dealt with his father's disdain for fourteen years. The apology was too little too late.

James's voice cracked with emotion as he revealed, "I stopped believing in their common goals a long time ago...*when you were born*." He pushed up from the armchair and strode over to stand at Sam's back.

"When Rosalind and I graduated, we married. We both wanted children by then, a perfect little family. It took such a long time for us to get pregnant. We were overjoyed when Annabelle arrived, she was our little miracle. But then you came along unexpectedly. When you were born, my first son...I realized what I'd done. The Alphabet Club had changed from boys playing at being men to men making decisions and enabling actions on the world stage. We had become too influential, too dangerous. What I'd promised the cabal came back to haunt me. I was so ashamed about the promise I made them. *And I was terrified to love you...*"

Sam's heart was in his throat. "You were all I had, but when mum died you abandoned me. In a way it felt like you died too," Sam whispered. "The only way to get your attention was to give in to your demands. You stopped seeing me as a child and trained me to be your weapon."

"I trained you so you could protect yourself from the dangers I knew the world would throw at you—" James insisted "—for being my son."

Sam turned and faced his father. It was like looking in a mirror, seeing himself in thirty years. Still rakishly handsome, with silver-grey threads ghosting through blond strands.

"I just wanted you to be my dad, to love me, be proud of me, and accept me for who I am."

"Your star has always shone too brightly Samuel. How could I accept you living *that* kind of lifestyle? It attracts far too much attention."

"Bullshit,"

"I was trying to protect you," James insisted his cheeks pinkening with rage.

Sam pinned his father with a fierce look.

"I'm gay, dad. I'm married to a man who loves me just as much as you loved mum. Our love is valid. I'm loved. Some parents would be satisfied with that. But no, not you. No matter what, I'll never be good enough because deep down you don't believe you'll ever be good enough. Your prejudice against me, against us, is senseless," Sam retorted. "It's always been about *your* insecurities, about what *you* want. You've always protected yourself."

The pair broke apart, the tension between them palpable. Seething, Sam turned away and walked further into the sitting room. James remained stoically in front of the open French doors, exasperated; he pinched the bridge of his nose.

Sam retrieved the thin package from inside his bulletproof vest and tossed it uncaring onto the coffee table, and then checked the time on his phone. James's comments had infuriated him. He had to get his head back in the game and remember who held the cards. There were just ten minutes left before he and Declan had to get back to their bolthole.

"Tell me what went wrong with the cabal?"

James hesitated, staring out to sea again before he said matter-of-factly, "I changed...grew up. I became a father... and I lost your mother."

The loss of Sam's mother was the turning point for his father. James was anchorless and his heart had turned to stone.

"Power plays within the cabal became a problem. Money, politics, and power inextricably linked us all with Alfred as the scheming puppet master. As we spread our web of influence corruption began to play a larger part in our activities. I didn't like it. I didn't agree with it, but I was trapped. I played along trying to find a way out. I saw that I'd been naïve and had allowed myself to become ensnared in a vicious cycle," James confessed.

"The club should have cut all ties with Valentin Molokovic when he was accepted into the fold of the Russian Security Council. He was always walking a fine line with his loyalty to us, but he became too influential, a liability. During one of our gatherings, I made my displeasure about the direction of our activities known and Valentin resented my outburst."

Sam recalled Mrs K had told of several people who'd

disagreed with Molokovic learning to fly without wings—out of the window of a high-rise building.

"Valentin came alive by fostering resentment and enabling division. He made his move and began his insidious work of pouring poison into their ears, turning the cabal against me. Until then, we'd all known one another's secrets. But men whom I'd believed were my friends, who had trusted me for most of my adult life, withdrew and took their lead from Valentin. They tried to dissuade contacts from continuing to do business with me. Those who disagreed with Valentin were removed from the game board." James let out a frustrated sigh, and then returned to sag bonelessly into the armchair.

"You saw the murder wall?" James asked.

"I did. And now I understand it. You and Molokovic began a tit-for-tat game, you collating evidence of the cabal's activity connected to a web of world leaders, financial institutions, and corrupt officials, and in retaliation, he started killing your compatriots to remove your support network. You used the Intel to leverage your safety…if they came for you it would be released and the whole house of cards would fall. Their response was to call in your debt…and target me."

"I simply could not allow Valentin to win!" James stamped a fist on the arm of his chair.

"Win? How fucking dare you! My life is not a gaming piece." Sam exclaimed with fury.

"I don't give a damn about the machinations, the money, and the power plays. Do you have *any* idea what you've

360

done?" Sam couldn't remember feeling angrier in his life. It burned like lava rushing through his veins and exploded in a fevered outburst.

"Do you understand what the fuck you put in motion *father*? Did they tell you what they did when they abducted you from the HQ?" he demanded.

"I was punched in the face, drugged and unconscious. Of course I don't know exactly what happened." James sneered, his voice stiff with anger and disdain at his son talking to him in such a way. "But I'm sure Akiko had everything in hand."

Sam stalked back to stand in front of his father. He wanted to strike him, to scream into the man's face and let out all of the anger and grief he'd been holding in. But instead, Sam eased down to sit on the coffee table and looked directly into his father's eyes, eyes he'd once looked into as a child believing this man to be his knight and protector. He spoke softly,

"Mr Steele opened the front door to Amanda Jamison. She shot him in the head. Point—blank—range."

The colour drained from James' complexion.

"She then murdered your gardener...your harmless, unarmed gardener for fucks sake! She left Piotr floating in the lap lane."

"No...I had no... idea..."James appeared to be having trouble catching a breath.

"After that, she accessed the basement and freed Erik Madsson, who came for you and knocked you out. But he didn't stop there. Oh no. He went on to execute the whole of your *Active Ops team* and plant a virus to try and destroy your kompromat and in the process crippling the agency's intranet."

James's face was ashen. He stared down at his hands as if they were on fire. "Th...there was no need... they can't all be dead!"

Sam inhaled the salty sea breeze through his nose and let the out slowly before saying, "And then there's Agent Ranier Strauss, who died trying to stop Madsson from dragging you into the underground tunnels." Sam paused.

"Are you happy now? To get your attention the Alphabet Club turned your home into a fucking charnel house!" Sam would never get the sight of the Active Ops team massacre out of his head. "I guess it worked."

"How many..." James whispered.

Sam pretended not to hear. "How many what?"

"How many...died?"

"Thirteen."

James's breath hitched with a sob. "It wasn't supposed to happen like this," he insisted, "I kept my secrets to avoid...unnecessary collateral damage. BrightNail was bait. I was baiting them to come for me...just me. I thought that if I could stage-manage a showdown I could end it all." James covered his face with his hands.

Sam wasn't sure if he wanted to laugh or cry at the absurdity of James's admission. For a smart man, James could be incredibly dumb. There had been *so much* unnecessary collateral damage here. Sam was burning with anger, zoning out as he watched the man in front of him weep. Was he weeping for those who were murdered because of him, or because of the dawning of his own fragile mortality? Sam didn't know, but James's tears were not enough. There was an incessant buzzing sound in his head...no, not buzzing...rotors. Sam stood and hurried to the door to the patio and looked out to sea. He rushed back to his father.

"Shit, we don't have much time left, a helicopter's coming, and it's definitely not ours!"

James was silent, stricken, and the hands covering his face shook.

"Father," Sam prompted sharply, dragging the man's hands from his face. James looked up pitifully at his son, his eyes red, puffy, and wet with tears.

"I've made so many terrible mistakes. I...I don't know what to do." James sounded old, worn out and vulnerable in a way that Sam had never heard before. James had lost himself to the game. Sam despised everything his father had done to get himself into such a perilous position. He was now a lamb to the slaughter among wolves he'd once believed were his compatriots. And so what could he do? He was entirely at the mercy of the son he'd treated like shit.

"Please, help me, Samuel. Maybe you think I don't deserve it... but this collar... death by *tetrodotoxin* is horrific...please."

Sam gritted his teeth, and even though he wanted to let his father fall on his sword, he had a heart and he couldn't. Annabelle would never forgive him if she found out Sam had a chance to save their father and had walked away.

363

"Make a promise to me now."

"Anything, anything,"

"End this poisonous cabal. Do whatever it takes, release the Kompromat and to hell with the fallout," Sam demanded. "Molokovic despises you and he won't stop until our whole family is wiped out. Do you want the next target to be your grandchild?"

This made James sit up straighter.

"Annabelle...and the baby... they're okay? Did she have a boy or a girl?" he asked tentatively.

"A girl. You have a granddaughter." Sam hesitated before he revealed, "They named her Rosalind."

James' eyes became glassy and welled up with tears again.

"Do you promise to end this?" Sam prompted.

"Yes...yes, I'll do it."

Sam pressed a thumb to his phone screen and swiped to the photos of Belle, Oliver, and baby Rosa. He passed the phone to his father.

"Oh, my..." James stared at the photograph mesmerized before asking, "Where are they?"

"They were sent to a safe house as per your instructions."

"Good, good," James said thoughtfully. "How do I get this vile contraption off my throat?"

Sam took his phone back. "I have a video message from Dr Goldblume, he'll explain." Sam clicked the video and passed it to James who watched the South African forensics expert speak as Sam retrieved the thin box.

"James. I've been looking into ways to get the collar off, but

cutting the damn thing it's too dangerous to leave in the hands of non-medical personnel. But I do have an alternative temporary solution. Graphene. Graphene is the strongest, thinnest material known to exist. It's transparent, conductive, and flexible—all at the same time, and two hundred times stronger than steel. I've supplied Sam with a thin sheet of Graphene to act as a protective collar. It was flown in from a Chinese nano-materials lab and cost you one point two million dollars. I got your neck size from your tailor. The sheet of Graphene needs to be placed around your throat and eased down between your skin and the needle collar. After a moment's contact with your skin, the Graphene will soften and adhere becoming a protective barrier. If the needle collar is activated the needle cannot penetrate your skin. This is the best I can do until I get you to the lab. Good luck my friend."

"Pssht!"

Sam turned to see Declan on his hands and knees in the open doorway to the patio. He rose to stand. "We're fucked from both ends babe. Amanda's done in the gym and she's comin' up, and a helicopter's on its way."

"Yes, I saw," Sam took his phone back, pushed it into his trouser pocket, and then opened the lab-sealed box. He removed the contents and passed the empty box to Declan who pocketed it. The Graphene was an inch in width and the length of a shirt collar. Sam curled the transparent strip into a circle. Without a word, James lifted his chin. Sweat beaded on the older man's throat. Sam placed the clear strip around his father's neck and eased it down between his skin and the murder collar. James pushed a finger around the edge of the Graphene to ensure it adhered to his skin. He gulped and sat back.

Sam observed him for a second. "Great. I can't see a thing," he said. "Now, down to business. The hospitality team is ours, the meal will be served at 7 in the Mess Hall, and they'll be up on the roof terrace for after-dinner drinks by 8. We've got a distraction planned. You control when the distraction begins. Here's a button mic," Sam said giving his father the tiny device. "The trigger phrase you'll say is 'With a bang'. You'll leave by helicopter."

"Coo-eee. Jamesy, get yer knickers on, looks like we have visitors!" Amanda singsonged as she began to climb the spiral staircase.

"Go", James ordered in a sharp whisper.

He stood, passed by his agents, and strolled out onto the patio, giving Sam and Declan time to duck out of the sitting room and exit the apartment through the front door.

****

CHAPTER 37

DEVILS

Safely back in the Sea Bunker, Declan turned on the tablet. Sam snuggled by his side, his head swimming with all he'd learned from his father.

"You alright love? That was pretty intense in there," Declan asked as clicked on the avatar for the roof camera.

"How alright can I be after finding out my father marked me for death before I was born?"

"Fuck! That is somethin' else. I heard some of what yez said. You were brave and strong, and ye stood up to the fucker. I'm proud of ye, love," he pulled Sam into a side hug and kissed his brow.

Sam gave himself to the comfort but remained silent, watching the tablet. The signal buffered for a second and then the view of the helicopter making its final approach to the fort filled the tablet screen. The black *Agusta Westland* helicopter was RAF. This make of aircraft was always used by government ministers and the Royal Family.

James was in the shot watching the helicopter as it came in to land. He'd just found out that thirteen of his employees had been massacred and yet, proving how easy he found it to put on a mask of nonchalant disdain, his face gave nothing of his inner turmoil away. Amanda, the monster in kitten heels who had assassinated his faithful

367

friend and butler, walked beside James to a decking area to the right of the Crows Nest lighthouse. The helicopter circled the fort once before coming into land, easing sideways and onto the helipad. The backdraft caused by the rotors made them both cover their eyes and turn away for a minute. When the chopper was safely on the helipad, a rear door opened and a tall thin man in a black suit with cropped mousey hair and mirror shades stepped out. He held the door open and beckoned another man to exit.

"It's fuckin' Dracula!" Declan grumbled.

"So, the Foreign Secretary and a Secret Service agent are the first to arrive at the party. I wonder why?"

James stood with his hands behind his back waiting for Jonathan Brudenell-Brice to make his way down the steps from the elevated helipad and walk to the timber deck. The helicopter didn't linger, taking off as soon as the men were down the stairs. It headed north towards Portsmouth harbour.

BB approached James and affably held his hand out. James did not take it. Amanda was still in her figure-hugging gym gear, a blue floral leotard, and half leggings, looking like an extra from a sketchy music video. She offered her hand to BB and said,

"Hello, it's a pleasure te meet you again," but the bodyguard stepped in.

"Mr Brudenell-Brice is here for a private meeting. If you don't mind," he gestured for her to leave.

Amanda wrinkled her nose in distaste and pursed her lips in annoyance at being sidelined. She held a false nailed index finger up and wagged it at BB.

"Just you remember who brought Viper in," she spat, her accent becoming acerbically Glaswegian. "We've done the job, babysat the miserable fucker fer a month now. All we want's our payment an' then we'll be out of yer... hair." She gave a sneering smirk while looking at the over-pomaded dyed black hair that had gotten BB the 'Dracula' moniker.

"Enough. I'll deal with you later," Brudenell-Brice snapped back, unhappy with being addressed in such a coarse way. Amanda gave him the hairy eyeball for an instant then turned and flounced back to the Crows Nest.

"She's pushin' it," Declan said.

"Don't tempt me. I've had fantasies about creeping up behind her and pushing her off the roof terrace."

Declan held his hands up. "I'm not stoppin' ye, babe. A good dunkin' might wipe the self-satisfied smile off the murderous bitch's face." They both chuckled.

****

James and BB strolled around the roof terrace talking for thirty minutes before James returned to the Crows Nest, and BB took a lot of lengthy phone calls.

The other guests began arriving just after 3 p.m. Finally, Sam and Declan could see which of the ABCs had stayed overnight on Molokovic's yacht. The first speedboat from The Plot Twist to the fort had nine occupants. Alasdair Frazer was at the wheel.

Sam and Declan watched the security cam view as Frazer reduced the power and eased the *Stingray Cruiser* speedboat sideways to the mooring. Erik Madsson disembarked onto

369

the landing stage first and tied the boat to the mooring posts. Then arms dealer Chad Eisen, Brazilian media mogul Jorg Garcia, Tech bro Femi Zubari and Eco wunderkind Gregory Tisch, along with one bodyguard each, stepped off the boat and began the long walk up the ramp to the three flights of metal stairs and into the fort.

Declan clicked to the entrance hall camera. The fort mood lighting system was on, showing the displays of naval artefacts and artwork under shades of red, white, and blue. Classical music played in the background, and two agents in traditional Silver Service uniforms of black slacks, white shirts, black waistcoats, and bow ties were inside the entranceway. Agents Ahmed and Williamson were holding trays, one with champagne flutes, and the other with non-alcoholic alternatives.

"Welcome aboard sirs. Please take the stairs ahead to the atrium sunroom where you can relax until your full party has arrived," Ahmed said.

Each man took his preferred drink and sauntered up the stairs where both Agents Svensson and Black were stationed to serve canapés.

The speedboat returned to The Plot Twist, and an hour later, another helicopter approached from the west. When it landed the bullish US Military General William Jakes exited the copter with his bodyguard. Another private boat left Portsmouth Harbour for the thirty-minute journey to the fort. When it docked Pharmaceuticals mogul Jin Xiao and his man-mountain of a Korean bodyguard stepped onto the pontoon and up the narrow staircases to join the rest of the party in the fort.

The final two members of the cabal arrived on Molokovic's Stingray at 5 p.m. Erik Madsson went down to the landing stage to meet them. Valentin Molokovic was in his sixties with a middle-aged spread that his sharp suit could not disguise. Simon Ingram-Jones, technical director at the National Cyber Security Center, was a tall, gangly man with thinning mousey hair. He was dressed in a tuxedo and naturally held himself in an erect military stance. They stepped off the boat and onto the landing stage with their respective bodyguards. Ingram-Jones's face lit up like a schoolboy as he surveyed the vast engineering marvel of the fort from sea level.

"Wow, what an exceptional choice of location, Val," he praised, "This is a boyhood dream come true. I've always wanted to visit here."

"Indeed. It has proved to be a successful cage for the snake." Molokovic chuckled, "It's for sale, you know. I think we should buy it."

Molokovic's bodyguard reached for a rucksack handed to him by Frazer. "Thank you, my friend," Molokovic said to Alasdair, "Ansel will send a message when we want to be picked up. I expect everything will be over by 9. Do not forget the body bag."

Alasdair nodded and then sent a curious look to Erik Madsson as he untied the ropes and tossed them onto the speedboat. Frazer saluted and turned the *Stingray* around, heading back to The Plot Twist.

"Shite!" Sam was stunned to hear the proof of intention.

"Shite indeed. That sounds ominous,"

"There can be no doubt. There's no fucking way they're letting dad go. They're all here to watch his execution."

****

Over the next few hours in their bolthole, they watched the ABCs touring the fort in twos and threes. The men were all in their late fifties and early sixties, but together the laughter and excitement at viewing the fort were almost boyish. The bodyguards trailed behind watchfully with faces fixed and stances rigid. The cabal drank copious amounts of alcohol, nibbled on canapés, and appeared to enjoy one another's company.

Molokovic's bodyguard Ansel was a problem though. The other bodyguards remained behind their bosses but Ansel was paranoid and roamed the fort...looking for what? With stocky shoulders, a trim waist and hands like shovels, the man had a flat brutish look as if someone had slammed an iron repeatedly into his face. This was a man made to fight and neither of them wanted to bump into him when they moved from their bolt hole.

They watched as BB met up with Molokovic and they too took a stroll on the roof without security guards and away from their compatriots.

"Those two, in particular, seem very cosy."

"Aye. That's quite the worry, the British Foreign Secretary an' the deputy chairman of the Security Council of Russia. They should have flashing warning signs on their backs saying 'security risk'!"

"Makes you wonder if the PM knows about it and chose

372

to ignore it, or if she's profiting from the alliance in some way."

"She wouldnae be the first corrupt Conservative Prime Minister! Russian money's been propping up the Conservative Party for decades."

A motorboat arrived just before 6 p.m. from Southsea promenade with freshly cooked food from the Michelin-starred restaurant beside the beach. Two of the agents retrieved the eight hot food bags and returned to the kitchen to begin plating up.

Declan was ready to eat his arm by then. He wished they'd had a bigger supply of food, but they were down to a just banana and a protein bar. "D'ye fancy going halfers?" he asked.

"I'm not hungry, you can have them," Sam replied. He still had that ball of tangled emotions lodged in his chest and was reeling from his father's revelations. Would it ever be over?

"You know he expected us to kill the whole lot of them for him, don't you," Sam said.

"He can expect what he wants, but he's fuckin' delusional. I'm no' gettin' blood on mah hands to cover up his mistakes."

"That's what I told him. We're here to extract him and then we're gone."

"Good." Declan reached for the banana and peeled it.

"But it feels like the world would be a better place if these men weren't in it. Their scheming, greed, and power games have done so much damage."

"I know," Declan took a bite, chomped and then swallowed before saying, "We cannae go around playing God. It's not up te us whether those fuckers live or die."

"True. They've got law enforcement, politicians, the secret service, and the military on the payroll. Money and influence have given them carte blanche to behave however they want. They believe they're untouchable."

"Aye, but they're no'. I believe in Karma. They'll get theirs. James has enough compromising material to bring them down. He promised you that he'd release the kompromat. It's only a matter of time before karma bites their hairy arses," Declan reassured.

****

The Alphabet Club was called to the Mess Hall for dinner and things went quiet around the fort for a while. The meal was served, and while the party was busy enjoying the fine five-course dinner Sam and Declan took the opportunity to move location and ready for the showdown.

The map of the fort showed that in the Lord Nelson Pub, there was a 'crew only' door which led to the corridors behind the scenes. It was just as well guests didn't see these corridors as they'd been abandoned in a less than salubrious state.

Sam and Declan hurried along the curved corridor until they found a 'crew only' staircase that would give them roof access. They scooted up the stairs, paused, and crouched beside the door. Declan pulled out the tablet, checked the camera view and then gave Sam the all-clear before Sam eased the door open.

It was a balmy night, the sun had set, and it was dark. The waning Gibbous moon was high and bright creating a pathway on the illuminated black waters of the Solent. Pinpoints of light on the mainland and the Isle of Wight reinforced the feeling of remoteness. No one would hear you scream here...except for the person inflicting the pain. The doorway led onto the roof terrace beside one of the red brick outbuildings that, from the sign on the door, was storage for deck chairs and outdoor games. Fairy lights and lanterns were strung up around the roof terrace, and the fire pit had been lit creating an intimate entertainment area on this summer night.

Sam scurried out and checked the storage building door. It didn't have a lock, and Sam supposed that no one would be stealing a deck chair from a fort in the middle of nowhere. He turned on his torch and entered the small building. Sam was wrong. Someone had stolen the Fort branded deckchairs because there were just two plastic boxes in the storage room and an umbrella that had turned inside out in a storm and been mangled and abandoned. One of the boxes contained a tangled tennis net, and the other rackets and balls. Sam returned to the door, stuck his head out, and gestured for Declan to come over.

"This is a pretty good hidey hole. We'll have a front-row seat," Declan brightened.

"On a box", Sam deadpanned.

"Beggars cannae be choosers. We won't be here long anyways. Svensson sent me a message. They're done with cheese and port. So, they'll be coming to the roof terrace for after-dinner drinks… and murder."

****

CHAPTER 38
ECDYSIS

The fort was as wide as a football pitch with a circumference of over sixty meters. The glass domed ceiling in the middle took up a radius of thirty meters and was surrounded by an Astroturf lawn, decked seating areas, a hot tub, and a host of outdoor entertainment possibilities.

Half of the bodyguards made their way up the spiral staircase first with Alphabet Club members next and the remainder of the guards at their backs. The security detail peeled off from the crowd of men and took stations around the vast ringed wall of the fort, standing tall with their hands behind their backs in a military stance. The ABCs appeared in good humour, well-fed and like all men's clubs seeded at university, they'd trained for a lifetime to imbibe a great deal of alcohol.

"Please, my brothers, get yourselves another drink, enjoy the sea air before tonight's entertainment," the Russian announced his arms outstretched like a ringmaster.

"This is a beautiful location yes? Such a view," he said directing to the far-off harbour at Portsmouth where fairy lights decorated the sail ropes of tall ships, and the massive steel and glass spiral of the contemporary Spinnaker building was lit up.

"And of course, feast your eyes on *moya krasivaya yakhta*" (*My beautiful yacht*)

"Val, I gotta say, I'm so gaddamn jealous of you for that yacht, she's a beauty," General Jakes admitted.

"Ah, Bill, you can take her for a spin later. I was planning to head back to Monaco tomorrow; you are welcome to join me." Molokovic invited.

"Generous as always Val. I might just take you up on that!" the American replied.

"This is the perfect place to give our former brother the send-off he deserves, yes!" Molokovic called to his compatriots. This comment got the response he was looking for with the peals of deep laughter echoing in the vast emptiness.

Molokovic strode towards the bar where Agent Williamson was the bartender.

"Did you know, my brothers," Molokovic called to the guests, "that the process of a snake shedding its skin is called *Ecdysis*? It would be fun to try this on the Viper, no? Peel off his skin, and hear him scream."

Watching on the tablet, Declan inhaled sharply at hearing Molokovic's evil suggestion. He sent a worried look towards Sam.

The reaction from the men was eerily similar. They sent one another sharp *'what the fuck'* looks and then laughed at the supposed joke. The sound was not convincing.

"Drinks, drinks for everyone," Molokovic hollered again.

Sam and Declan observed, flicking between camera feeds as arms dealer Chad Eisen strolled with fellow American

General Jakes puffing on a fat cigar. Jin Xiao moved to the bar, ordered a whisky on the rocks, and was joined by Simon Ingram-Jones, who ordered a rum and coke. Gregory Tisch walked the roof terrace alone, vaping and seemingly enjoying the natural location. Jorg Garcia and Femi Zubari had taken chilled bottles of beer from an ice bucket and were seated at the fire pit, the smoke of burning beech wood drifting lazily out to sea.

They lost sight of two of the men who moved out of range of the cameras. Then they heard deep masculine laughter not so far away from where they hid. The sweet sickly smoke of a cigar filtered under the door. The Americans were close.

"Did you see to it that Soames played his part?" One man asked.

"Yup. He agreed to destroy the Kompromat. Ten million pounds was sent to an offshore account...cheap at the price if you ask me."

"I hear ya General. Viper could still have a backup, but as long as the lawyer's destroyed his copy, Viper's got nothin'. He'll be dead soon enough and nobody will know where he's backed it up. I can't wait to see the muthafucker writhing, taking his last god-damn breath." That was the voice of arms manufacturer Chad Eisen. Sam shuddered. The Alphabet Club *were* all psychopaths. The Americans continued on their stroll.

Sam's gaze met Declan's who returned his look of shock. Dominic Soames was James' lawyer and had been a friend since university. He'd secretly been in contact with the kidnappers and sold James out for ten million pounds.

"Is there not one of James' contacts wi' a moral compass? They're all backstabbing, scheming bastards."

"You don't expect me to answer that, do you?"

Declan rubbed a hand over his beard and shook his head. Sam opened the door a crack and saw the club members had gathered together near the fire pit.

"You," Molokovic shouted at Agent Williamson. "Get your people and go, now!"

"But Sir, we'll need to clean up and then call for our boat to come from Portsmouth," Williamson simpered.

"I don't fucking care if you swim back, just get your people and fuck off." Molokovic was worse for wear with drink, and there was something in the tone of his voice that made him sound a little unhinged. Williamson bowed subserviently and strode, unhurried towards the stairway that led down into the fort. A second later Declan got a text message. "Stand by"

Molokovic moved on unsteady legs behind the bar counter. He drew a small bag of white powder from his jacket pocket and poured the powder onto the countertop. Then he pulled out his wallet and removed a platinum credit card and a one-hundred Dollar bill then divided the powder into lines, rolled up the bill, and used it to snort two lines. The Russian held his head back and pinched the bridge of his nose. After a minute he leaned on the bar and looked around blearily at his compatriots. "Please my friends help yourself, it's good!" he invited.

"Come now. I think we're a bit long in the tooth for such

things Val," Jin Xiao replied waspishly. "Leave the drugs for the youth."

"Not at all, we only live once, yes, so live large!" Valentin grabbed a bottle of champagne from an ice bucket on the bar, unwound the protective wire and thumbed off the cap, then with brute strength alone pulled the cork from the bottle sending a froth of bubbles into the air. He laughed, and his compatriots joined in. He put the bottle to his mouth, glugged down half the contents and then let out a macho roar that echoed in the silent night.

From the camera view Sam and Declan could see the other men looked uneasy. Molokovic was a loose cannon and had a habit of pushing people from high places. They were all on a fort in the middle of the sea and the Russian was on coke and booze, they had every right to feel uneasy.

Molokovic tossed the bottle aside and opened his arms as he addressed the eight other club members. "Come my friends, come. It is time for tonight's grand finale!" Several of the club members whooped and roared in celebration, their voices once again severing the fragile stillness of the marine location.

"Ansel, call for the boat, and then ask the other guests to join us,"

Sam and Declan's eyes locked. Declan nodded. He sent a text to Mrs K.

GO!

Sam reached out for Declan's hand, they threaded their fingers together and squeezed.

This was it.

CHAPTER 39
OVER THE TOP

Ansel made the call and then pocketed his phone. He lumbered towards the Crows Nest, entered the building and then several minutes later Amanda emerged wearing a flowery summer dress and dragging a large wheeled suitcase. Erik Madsson exited after her in combat trousers and a t-shirt, holding a military rucksack. Ansel returned alone and stood close to his boss.

The Alphabet Club was gathered in a circle on a large patch of the Astroturf by the boundary wall of the fort terrace overlooking the distant lights of the Isle of Wight. A gentle salty sea breeze made the fairy lights dance. Amanda left her suitcase near the stairway and then with Madsson on her heels, she strolled towards the circle of the powerful and connected. Erik removed what looked like a memory key on a lanyard from around his throat and passed it to Valentin Molokovic.

"Ah the trigger. Thank you for keeping this safe," Molokovic threaded it around his neck. "Where is he now?

"The slippery wee shite's locked in the bathroom," Amanda stated one hand on her hip and a smug, self-satisfied grin on her face.

"Good. Ansel," the Russian prompted.

The henchman collected a rucksack from behind the bar,

then stepped up and tossed the bulging bag to Erik who put it beside his own.

"I cut the fee by two hundred and fifty thousand because you failed to kill his little prince," Molokovic revealed.

In a blink, Amanda's face turned thunderous. She lurched forward.

"You thieving Russian bastard!" she screamed her claw-like nails raised as she moved, and was succinctly stopped in her tracks by Erik's arms gripping her around the waist to hold her back.

"Mr Molokovic, sir. My daughter, where is my daughter?" Madsson pleaded.

"Shit," Sam whispered, "Madsson does have a daughter kidnapped by the cabal. She was why he submitted to whatever Mind Fuck the Russian did to him."

Molokovic reached into his Tux breast pocket and drew out a cream envelope.

"Your daughter and her mother are here. The code for entry to the property is on the card."

Madsson snatched the envelope from his now ex-employer, ripped it open and read the details.

Seeming satisfied he met Molokovic's gaze, nodded, and without taking his eyes off the man, said to his partner. "Keep your mouth shut. Come. We wait for the boat downstairs."

"Fuck off Erik! Yer no' the boss of me. I'm stayin' te watch and then I want my cut."

Molokovic opened his arms again in a placating gesture. "Ladies, gentlemen, all are welcome to enjoy the entertainment. Ansel, bring out our special guest."

The bodyguard returned to the apartment. A minute later, James came out of the building, his face blank and unreadable, the horrific collar stark against his pale skin. Ansel was at his back, poking, poking, poking at every step to hurry him along to his death.

"Uh oh," Sam exhaled warily as they observed just meters away.

Ansel shoved James towards the centre of the circle. He tripped a step and then turned and through gritted teeth snarled,

"Don't touch me."

Valentin laughed and nodded at his henchman.

"You can play, but do not break him. That pleasure is for me."

Ansel licked his lips and grinned malevolently, like a wolf readying to toy with its food. He placed both hands on James's chest and pushed. James staggered back, but only a step. Ansel appeared confused. He had no idea that James was an exemplary fighter with solid core strength. He was about to find this fact out! James turned to move away then spun back at the bodyguard and delivered a kick to the chest. Caught off guard by the speed of the attack the man stumbled, reeling backwards, his arms flailing. Red-faced, wheezing, and unable to catch a breath, the stocky man gripped his thighs to get himself together. Everyone watched in fragile silence. The other bodyguards stationed around the roof terrace we're on high alert now. Molokovic held up his hand to halt them all from coming closer. Ansel

384

steadied himself, took in a couple of deep breaths then growled and set off towards James like a bull. James met him head-on. He spun on light feet and kicked again, his placement perfect, hitting the stocky man in the sternum again, and then again, and again. The concentrated power of the moves hurled the bodyguard backwards, his arms windmilling comically. He seemed to remain suspended in mid-air...before time moved on. The Russian brute screamed and toppled over the wall. Silence reigned for an instant before the splash.

Jin Xiao was the first to get to the boundary wall and look over. He shouted aggressively in Chinese and his burley bodyguard rushed to his side and removed a torch from his belt. He turned it on and sent the beam to search the surface of the black water.

"There!" BB called on spotting the body. "He's face down and his head's smashed in. He must have bounced off the wall on the way down."

"I'm a strong swimmer, I can pull him around to the landing stage," Gregory Tisch offered, scrambling hurriedly to take off his dinner jacket.

"No, leave him," Molokovic spat with knives in his words.

"But...but the boat is coming, yes. We cannot just leave him—"

Valentin Molokovic held his palm up to stop the German in his tracks. The Russian did not accept failure and his bodyguard had failed. Valentin strode to the wall, unhooked a lifebuoy ring, and tossed it into the sea in the

385

general direction of the dying man.

"There, we helped him."

Silence all around.

The unease among the ABCs was palpable, their bodyguards moving in to protect their employers.

"Did ye notice Madsson's lookin' te make a run for it?" Declan observed. It was true. During the fight, Erik Madsson had collected the two rucksacks and edged to the staircase leading down into the fort.

"Trouble in paradise?" Sam snarked.

"The fun is not yet over, gentlemen," Valentin growled, annoyed to have lost control of the proceedings. "I'll give you that one victory before you die, James. You cannot say I am not a fair man!"

"I don't think so," James drawled. "You killed thirteen innocent people in my employ. I'll need another twelve of yours," he sneered. "If I'm going out, it's *with a bang*!"

Declan immediately pressed an icon to wipe the tablet, he then shut it down and thrust it into the rucksack. He'd be leaving it behind. He withdrew his gun and clicked the safety off. Sam opened the door of the storage building a crack. Then on his phone, he clicked on a sound effects app and pressed play. From below, gunfire erupted and echoed, interspersed with the rough sounds of men shouting directions at one another. The effect was stunning, way better than they could have hoped for. It sounded like there was a whole battalion running riot in the fort.

"*Scheisse*! We are under attack!" the German billionaire shrieked, pulling his dinner jacket back on.

"Guards, go down and clear the way for us," Molokovic ordered roughly. The bodyguards all rushed to the stairs, and Erik Madsson with bags on his shoulders followed them down. Amanda struggled to squeeze her giant case down the spiral staircase.

Under the cover of the distraction, Sam and Declan crept out of their hiding place and moved stealthily into the shadows.

"My friends. The boat is on the way, two minutes, yes. We will all get on the boat and continue our party on The Plot Twist, apart from you, Viper," Molokovic announced.

Jonathan Brudenel-Brice strode to stand beside Valentin Molokovic. They were the model of the school bully and the sidekick, but the other members of the club appeared unsettled and they eyed one another shiftily. The Alphabet Club members were all in the autumn of their years and not match-fit. Only one of them was able for a physical fight, James.

"Gentlemen! It would be a shame to come all this way and not enjoy our victory…it will take but a moment," the Russian pleaded.

Zubari's bodyguard barreled up the stairs. "Sirs, sirs, someone is fucking with us. The gunfire was a sound effect," he reported.

"This location was supposed to be secure. How did you miss this?" The African billionaire roared indignantly.

"Sir…Mr Zubari, forgive me. We swept the fort many times. I don't know how this happened," the man stuttered.

Zubari turned his dark-eyed glare on his group of

friends. "Viper has been locked down, yes?"

"Of course, he's had no way of communicating with anyone," Molokovic reassured.

"Then somebody in our employ set this up." Zubari grimaced, showing bright white teeth as he glared at his fellow club members. They all remained twitchy and exchanged mistrustful glances.

"How many intruders?" Zubari barked.

"We are unsure...the team are searching," the bodyguard replied sheepishly.

"Um Gottes Willen!" Gregory Tisch dramatically threw his arms in the air and let out an exasperated breath. "We are in the middle of the fucking sea with enemies hidden among us. I refuse to stay here a moment longer. I'm out!" he delivered angrily before stalking towards the stairs.

"Gregory, please, there is no need to worry, our security will find them. Calm down my brother, have another drink," Valentin placated feebly.

Stormy eye contact was exchanged before General Jakes roared "Gaddamnit Val, this is bullcrap! We're under attack. Everyone to the boat!" Jakes shoved the bodyguard aside and lumbered down the spiral stairs after Gregory Tisch. One by one the Alphabet Club set their drinks down and hurried warily towards the staircase. Chad Eisen, Jorg Garcia, Femi Zubari, and Jin Xaoi followed anxiously on General Jakes' heels with the bodyguard at their back.

Remaining on the roof terrace were James, Jonathon Brudenell-Brice, Valentin Molokovic, and Simon Ingram-Jones. Unbeknownst to the cabal members, Sam and Declan were ready to pounce.

Sam pressed on his phone screen to turn off the sound effect and a sudden swathe of eerie silence washed over the fort. Then the sound of the speedboat engine, married with that of rotors in the distance alerted those remaining on the roof terrace that the boat was approaching and there were choppers just a few minutes out.

The two helipads were on the opposite side of the roof. Sam and Declan's objective was to get James away from the group and toward the helipad so he could be whisked away on the twenty-minute ride to London and to Dr Goldblume's lab.

Sam and Declan moved stealthily in the shadows as Molokovic tugged the lanyard with the button device from around his neck and held it in his hand. He stepped up to James and locked eyes. James stared back unyielding, refusing to show the man one fearful tremble of his lip.

"Your game is at an end, James. We all made a vow and chose our punishment for betrayal. You betrayed us, and did not give us your son. I must say, you trained him well. But, the failure to fulfill your promise means you now forfeit your life. I dreamed of this day for so many years, and now that we've secured the Kompromat hard drive from your lawyer, you have *nothing*," the Russian grinned full of malice. "I wanted this to last longer, play with you a little, hear you scream and beg me for death. But—" Molokovic shrugged in a 'such is life' gesture. He moved closer, right up to James' face as if he was planning on landing a farewell kiss. "I am going to take much pleasure in watching you

389

die."

Sam and Declan stepped out of the shadows together. Sam playfully hollered,

"Anybody want a peanut?" The Princess Bride quote stopped the men in their tracks and they all turned, shocked, to glare at the unexpected newcomers.

"Put the device down Mr Molokovic and step away," Sam roared his gun trained on the Russian while Declan's was aimed moving back and forth between BB and Ingram-Jones. Molokovic sent dagger looks at Sam, seemed to recognize him, then smiled widely and let out a laugh.

"This is priceless. The *'malen'kiy prints'* is here to rescue the duplicitous father who sentenced him to death before he was born. How...what is the English word... quaint?" He placed his thumb on the button.

"I am glad there is more of an audience to enjoy the finale, James. Your Little Prince has failed you. I'll see you in hell!" With that final barb, Molokovic pressed down on the button. Sam fired, his bullet missing Molokovic by millimetres. Declan weighed up his choices, shooting the Foreign Secretary was not an option so he fired and hit Ingram-Jones in the thigh. The world stopped. Ingram-Jones crumpled, writhing and wailing, a hand over the gushing hole in his leg. Molokovic's smile faded. James was not dead? Sir James Aiken stood with his hands behind his back, staring at the Russian with a shit-eating grin on his face. Molokovic's face twisted angrily and he pressed the button again.

"Why isn't this working?" he growled "Why won't you

390

fucking die?" he stabbed at the button.

"For God's sake, man!   Give that here," Jonathon Brudenell-Brice snatched the device from his compatriot's grip and elbowed him out of the way.

"Foreign Secretary, please, put the device down, I will shoot, and this time I will not miss." Sam warned.   BB turned, sneered haughtily at Sam, and then pressed firmly on the button.   He twitched and raised his hand automatically to his left eye.

"No!" Declan exclaimed in realization.   "The needle couldnae go forward—"

Sam completed his husband's sentence, "—so it went backwards."

They were right!   The Graphene had proved to be an impenetrable barrier and so the device had misfired sending the toxic needle to break through the plastic housing.   James smiled triumphantly at his ex-friend, whose uncovered eye had blown wide with the realization of what he'd done.   The British Foreign Secretary, Jonathan Brudenell- Brice turned to run from his fate as his MI5 bodyguard jogged up the stairs and shouted,

'The boat's here, we need to evacuate!"

BB's legs stopped working and he reached out toward his horrified bodyguard in a final desperate plea and then collapsed onto the fake grass, an unearthly gurgling yowl coming from his throat.

"Sir, sir? What's wrong? Fuck! Somebody help!" the bodyguard called in alarm rushing to his boss's side. Jonathan Brudenell-Brice was fully conscious as the toxin attacked his central nervous system and paralysis took hold of his body. He gasped for breath as all those around him watched helplessly, before his spine bowed up, his face twisted in a violent rictus and then his body relaxed for the final time.

The death was swift and horrifying. Stunned silence dragged on as they all comprehended what they'd witnessed. A Member of Parliament had just accidentally killed himself while trying to commit murder.

Then the world started again and in the same minute, several things happened at once.

In defeat Molokovic howled like a wounded dog as his long-held plans turned to shit. Sam was his first failure and he would not let this stand.

"I should have killed you myself!" he cried out as he rushed, uncoordinated, drunk and high but still bullishly fierce and driven.

"Stop, it's over Molokovic," Sam warned as the old man kept up his lumbering run across the Astroturf. Sam fired once to incapacitate, not kill. Molokovic fell to his knees, and his face buckled in pain from the bullet in his right foot. He sobbed as he crawled towards Sam, roaring in his native Russian,

"SUKIN TY SYN, GOVNYUK, UBLYUDOK, MOYA NOGA, TY PROSTRELIL MNE NOGU, YA UB'YU TEBYA... UB'YU TEBYA!"

("You son of a whore, shit-head, motherfucker, my foot, you've shot my foot, I'll kill you...kill you!")

His face ashen, Brudenell-Brice's bodyguard dropped to

his knees, "Sir?" he said in disbelief.

"Don't touch him," Declan called. The bodyguard looked up, then let out a rebel yell, and rushed at Declan.

Declan pushed his gun into the band of his trousers, held up a calming hand and locked eye contact on the man, "Mate, look, ye need te calm down. I'm not yer enemy. Yer boss did that to himself," Declan insisted as he and the MI5 bodyguard circled one another. The guard lunged and Declan tackled him head-on. He punched, kicked, and pulled the man's hair as they hit the deck, then they tumbled and wrestled on the ground.

While Declan was busy with his assailant James pivoted and began to stride towards the helipad. Simon Ingram Jones rolled over and viciously kicked out his good leg intercepting, and striking James on his bad kneecap. James screamed and his leg collapsed dropping him to the floor. Ingram Jones then attempted to kick James in the head. James caught his foot and rolled. Ingram-Jones let out an ear-splitting scream as his hip, knee and leg joints cracked.

Sam backed up, his gun still trained on the Russian as he crawled pitifully towards him like The Terminator's last gasp. Sam wasn't afraid of this unarmed, bitter old man. The helicopter was coming into land. Sam noticed his father had bested Ingram-Jones and was trying to get to his feet and make his way towards the helipad again. Declan was now sitting on the bodyguard's arse, pulling the man's hands behind, gripping both wrists with one hand, a position Sam had enjoyed many times. While checking on his loved ones Sam missed the approach of the Korean man-mountain who had come back upstairs on surprisingly light feet. The bodyguard barrelled into Sam's back sending him sprawling and his gun flying from his grip. Sam didn't get a chance to catch his breath. The guard picked him up in a fireman's carry and tossed him across the terrace like he was a pillow, sending him careening into Declan sitting on the back of the Foreign Secretary's bodyguard.

"Ga-ram, leave him, help me to the boat, NOW!" Molokovic ordered. The Korean guard turned from Sam, stalked over to Valentin, scooped him up into his arms, and then jogged towards the stairs.

Brudenell-Brice's man found his feet again and took on a fighting stance. He had a bloody nose and the imprint of Astroturf on his left cheek. Sam and Declan matched his stance.

"Who's side are you on?" he roared.

"We're here to prevent a murder. If you're MI5, your boss was the bad guy in this scenario and he did that to himself," Sam insisted directing to the Foreign Secretary's corpse. "You can't help him. Those bastards on that yacht don't give a shit if you live or die." The guard paused and looked between Sam and Declan, and then his gaze shot to Simon Ingram Jones, crippled, and crying. The bodyguard wiped a hand across his mouth where the blood flowed freely from the broken nose Declan had given him.

Team Bravo emerged on the roof, weapons drawn. "Stand down, they're right, we're not the enemy," Agent Black called. The MI5 man realized the game was up, he was outnumbered. Declan saw where the man was looking.

"We won't attack, just take him, and get the fuck outa here,"

The MI5 bodyguard hurried over, hefted Ingram Jones into a fireman's lift, and ran for the stairs.

"The ABCs are getting in the boat; they're going to get away!" Agent Williamson called as Team Bravo jogged over.

"Let them!" James ordered, "Help me up."

The agents assisted James, taking his weight under both arms and legs, and then carrying him to the stairs leading to the helipad. At last, it was over, the ABCs were gone. James was alive, safe, and ready for extraction.

The backdraft and noise from the helicopter distracted from the figure that appeared in the doorway of the crew-only staircase.

Erik Madsson said nothing as he raised his weapon and aimed at Sam, who was oblivious to the danger, watching the helicopter come in to land.

He fired.

"NO!" Declan ran and body-slammed Sam to the ground as the bullet hit. They crumpled together, Declan lying protectively over his lover. Sam was disorientated for an instant, then he eased his body from beneath Declan's weight and readied to fight, but Madsson was gone. The fucker had to have one last shot! Declan lay silently on his belly by Sam's side.

"Buttercup, shit, are you okay?" he whispered alarmed at seeing the singed bullet hole in the back of Declan's black tactical shirt.

Declan rolled over, opened his eyes a crack and coughed.

Sam was terrified; he ran a hand over Declan's brow pushing sweaty strands away. "Love, speak to me,"

Declan took a shuddering breath and said, "Shiiiiit! These fuckin' super skins are a nifty bit o' kit," he took another laboured breath, "I'm just a wee bit winded. Mebe a broken rib or two is all. Where's Madsson?"

"Gone."

"Damn. Help me up, babe."

Relieved to his bones that Declan was okay, Sam helped his husband to stand. The misshapen bullet fell to the ground. Sam hooked his arm around Declan's back and they moved off towards the helipad, leaving the corpse of Jonathan Brudenell-Brice to tell its own story.

James was being helped into the first helicopter, with Agent Feurig at the controls. Mrs K was seated in the back, ready to assist. Team Bravo climbed in too. When the four agents were onboard the helicopter took off and headed east towards London. Job done!

The second helicopter had been circling, its searchlight sending streams of light over the roof as Brody kept watch. It came in to land. Sam got Declan into the aircraft and they put on their headphones.

"Lucky boy, you injured?"

"Just a few scratches and a broken rib, I'll live,"

"Did you see? The stingray speedboat was full of ABCs, it headed for The Plot Twist," Brody informed.

"Devon, take us up," Sam said, "Alasdair Frazer's not just here as a driver, something else is going on."

Brody took off, the helicopter searchlight shining an

intense bright pathway onto the black water. The helicopter circled the fort once and then hovered, and on Sam's command Brody sent the searchlight from the fort to the yacht. They could see the bodyguards all standing on the landing stage, having been abandoned by their employers. The Stingray had reached The Plot Twist and the men hurriedly disembarked onto the mega yacht. Brody waited for a few minutes until the speedboat was in motion again and then aimed the spotlight to follow the path of the Stingray as it crested the waves with three figures remaining on board, Amanda Jamison, Erik Madsson, and Alasdair Frazer. The murderous blond Swede was at the wheel. Instead of going back to the fort to pick up the stranded bodyguards, the speedboat turned right and sped towards the shipping lane that led to France. When it was a few hundred meters away from the yacht, Sam saw Frazer stand behind Amanda and push her from the boat. The massive suitcase followed. Sam gasped in horror.

And then The Plot Twist exploded.

A fireball shot violently into the air in a mushroom cloud, the power of the explosion sending the helicopter careening. Warning alarms inside the helicopter screamed. Brody fought hard to regain control, and after a minute of squeaky bum time, he was in control again. He let out a sigh of relief. "Muthafucker, that was close," he growled. "What the ever-loving-fuck was that?"

Sam and Declan were glued to the window watching

with horrified fascination as the yacht burned with a red-orange glow.

"Fuh-ck! I'm getting out of here," Brody said "This place is gonna be crawling with harbour police,"

"But what about Madsson and Frazer?" Sam urged.

"Looks like they just assassinated eight of the richest men in the world. Those bastards won't ever sleep easy again."

****

EPILOGUE
ONE YEAR LATER

Declan padded from the bathroom, slipped back into bed and snuggled beside his warm, slumbering husband. The sun was beginning to rise over the Loch, the huge golden orb chasing the darkness away. The sight always took Declan's breath, especially when viewed through the vast triangular floor-to-ceiling window in the bedroom of their A-frame modular home.

They were living at the end of a valley among thirty-thousand acres of Scottish forest and rolling hills that included the Loch. There had been two tumbledown cottages on the land which made getting planning permission for replacement dwellings relatively simple. Their home was designed by Architect Campbell Bailey. It was Eco-friendly, made of glass, and timber. They were self-sufficient and off-grid.

The terrain was hilly with woodland flowing down to the water's edge and heather-strewn hills to the left and right. At the opposite end of the valley among Scot's pine trees, Sam's container apartment had been installed on a stilted platform and was now used as their office.

Declan had let his hair and beard grow, going for a lumberjack look. Nestled in bed with Sam watching the sunrise, life couldn't get any better. Declan leaned over and inhaled at Sam's nape. It was such a heady scent, musk, sleep sweat and the coconut and vanilla shampoo Sam liked. Declan's cock twitched. He rubbed his beard against Sam's skin and laid kisses from Sam's neck to his shoulder. Sam moaned appreciatively, his voice raspy with sleep, sexy as hell. Declan tugged lazily on his cock, and then massaged the hardening length against Sam's arse, continuing his wake-up assault. Sam lay pliant for a moment then let out a giggle as Declan walked his fingers over his ribs.

"I know you're awake, love!"

"You're insatiable," Sam turned his head and his mouth met Declan's lips.

"Good morning. You've brushed your teeth?" he queried as he pulled away.

"Aye, an' I'm prepped. It's a gorgeous sunrise an' I want that beautiful dick in me."

"Is that right!" Sam sat up, yawned, and stretched cat-like, "Such a thirsty boy!" he said playfully, "Gimme a minute."

Sam left the bed and went into the bathroom. Minutes later he returned. His naked form strutting around the bedroom was a source of so much pleasure for Declan; he could watch Sam all day and never get bored. Sam strode to the window and stood watching the dawn his pert arse giving a provocative wiggle. He turned to face Declan who marvelled at the sight of his lover, his body, pale and lithe with his cock jutting like a divining rod. Sam strode forward, paused at the foot of the bed, and grinned.

"C'mon, get back in," Declan said patting the warm

mattress beside him, "I wanna sit on yer lap an' ride ye into the sunrise."

"But we'll burn baby,"

"Aye, that's the plan!"

Sam's brows rose, and he smiled in mischief as he crawled over the duvet and teasingly kissed up his husband's muscular body, from his toes to his greedy mouth.

"Enough foreplay," Declan complained "We're racing the sun," he manhandled a giggling Sam into position sitting him with his back propped against the pillows and headboard. Declan straddled Sam, facing forward. Sam groaned at the view of Declan presenting himself for his pleasure. He rubbed his palms up Declan's back marvelling at how his muscles had hardened and defined while working at managing the woodland. Sam moved his hands to Declan's backside, massaged pale buttocks and leaned in. He bit Declan's left cheek and Declan cursed.

"What? I haven't had my breakfast yet!" Sam justified,

"But yer gonna be getting sausage!" Declan retorted.

"You first!" Sam laughed and slicked up his cock. Declan, urgent to be filled, pulled his cheeks apart, and Sam teased his entrance with his slippery cock head.

"Like that?"

Declan groaned, deep and wanton. "Oh aye, that's it. Stick it in. Fuck me, Westley."

Sam did as he was asked, pushing in and pistoning his hips up to meet the muscular backside coming down.

Declan bounced, a cock in his arse, his lover's arms

401

wrapped around his waist, Sam's hand fisting Declan's length in time to the impaling strokes he was giving. Perfect!

Declan let go and allowed himself to become engulfed in passion and peace. He wasn't the same man who'd met Sam Aiken at Dunloch Castle all those years ago. Declan's life had grown; love had made him evolve. This love they shared was simple and sacred. And each day he felt the primitive tug to make love with Sam and celebrate their devotion with the rising and setting of the sun.

****

"Come on girl," Declan called to Waverly. Their Siberian husky pup rushed over to him, her tongue lolling, and her startling indigo-blue eyes fixed as he completed his pre-run stretches. She danced excitedly, the pup loved this game. Apart from early morning sex, this was Declan's favourite part of the day. With so much untamed forest to run in, every day was an adventure. His four-legged and two-legged running companions made it so much fun.

Sam and Declan chose the husky breed because the personality of the dog matched them both. Huskies were well-known escape artists; intelligent, friendly, playful, athletic and a bit goofy. Waverly kept them both on their toes.

Wanting to put their many skills to good use they were both on the volunteer list for Scottish Mountain Rescue and helped the local mountain rescue team in an emergency. Declan was training Waverly in search and rescue skills too, and so each morning Sam would leave first, and Waverly would lead her Alpha to his mate.

Waverly was primarily Declan's pet project while Sam worked on the private translation of an ancient Arabic text, therefore, she was most definitely Buttercup's baby!

This summer morning, Sam had run off-trail through the forest on the way to the office, and he'd arrived there in time to boot up his desktop and check emails before he heard the joyful howl of the approaching dog…and then the warning beep of an alarm.

"Shit!" Sam clicked on the icon for the security camera feed. Someone had set off a sensor and breached onto their land. The only visitors they had were their friends from Mountain Rescue and the Ranger who helped manage the land. The camera showed a black SUV on the way up the long road that led to their new house. Sam rushed out of the office just as the excited barking and mesmerizing ice-chip eyes found him. Waverly pounced, pushing him to the ground and licking his face.

"You found me, who's a good girl, who's my best girl?" Sam baby talked, scrubbing at her ruff. Declan came bounding out of the trees a moment later.

Sam jumped to his feet. "Babe, someone's coming. The sensor was tripped, black SUV." The look they shared was a mixture of worry and anger. Who had dared to track them down?

"It's a long road an' will take them a while to get to the house. We can beat them."

"Come on girl. Let's go home," Declan called to the pup.

They all ran, darting through the dense forest, leaping

403

over fallen logs and tree roots, shifting between darts of sunlight breaking through the fir boughs. The run was exhilarating and Sam loved watching how Declan's body moved so naturally in this environment like he was born to it.

They made it to the house in record time. Sam rushed in and retrieved the hidden gun box, removed his loaded weapon, and shoved it behind into the waistband of his jeans. Then he hurried outside and met his husband and their dog. They stood stoically and waited. The last stretch of road was gravel and tense minutes later the crunch of wheels ensured they knew exactly where this vehicle was. It turned, finally making itself visible, but the tinted windows ensured they couldn't identify the driver. On seeing them the driver cut the engine. There was a silent stand-off for a minute as the engine ticked, cooling before the driver opened the door.

Alexander Deveraux stepped out of the vehicle and grinned. Sam leaned to Declan and quoted,

"He must be very desperate, or very frightened, or very stupid, or very brave."

"Very all four I should think," Declan replied completing the quote.

"Ah, there you are! My favourite ghosts. You both look well," Alexander said brightly.

"Deveraux! Fer fucks sake! How the hell did ye find us?" Declan roared in outrage. Waverly growled at the newcomer who'd upset her daddy.

"Easy there, girl," Sam said to the dog and scratched her

ruff to calm her. "This is, unexpected, Alex. How *did* you find us?" Sam parroted.

"It was certainly a test!" Deveraux said nonchalantly as he strolled up the drive to stand in front of them. "Initially I thought you'd choose to go off-grid in Canada or Germany but I hit a dead end. I trailed your sister and her baby for a while, but she only led me to the supermarket, the park, or mum and baby groups." Sam gritted his teeth at hearing this.

"Then I discovered your mother Sam, was a De Monfort. That was what led me here. Land Registry documents show the De Monforts own a huge swath of Scottish land that was put in trust for protection. I checked to see if any planning permission had been sought on De Monfort land, and here we are," Alex delivered with a theatrical sweeping hand gesture.

Sam and Declan shared a look. "Damn it. You might as well come in for tea," Sam pouted.

In the kitchen, Declan filled Waverly's water bowl with fresh water, as Sam prepared tea. Sitting at the old scrubbed oak table Alexander looked around, smug amusement on his face. He clutched his mug and took a sip.

"This place is nice. You've got a sweet set-up," he said conversationally.

"We have. What d'ye want?" Declan groused, neither of them joining Alex at the table.

"First of all, I must congratulate you both on pulling the biggest political coup this century,"

"What are you talking about?" Sam asked his brows

knitted in confusion.

"The Plot Twist!"

Sam stiffened at hearing the name of the Mega Yacht.

"That wasnea us," Declan insisted.

"Oh, come now, between friends? You must have been involved."

Calmly but firmly Declan said, "That was not us. We're not mass murderers."

"Shame, I was rather impressed by the spectacle. The fallout has been *epic*," Alexander said camply. "It *was* a fantastic plot twist, all of those rich, corrupt men finding karma at the same time, then all of that Kompromat leaked by Anonymous. The chaos it's caused," Alex continued cheerily. "But you were there, yes? I spoke to the landlord of The Boathouse pub on the Isle of Wight and he told me about a gay couple who stayed in his Honeymoon suite, which just so happens to overlook No Man's Land fort. The descriptions sounded like you both," he hedged. Neither man had left anything behind to identify that they'd been on or near No Man's Land fort during the event, so Alex was clutching at straws.

"The tabloids called it the *Billionaire Bonfire*," Alex scoffed. "Did you know about the connections between the late Foreign Secretary and head of the Security Council of Russia, Valentin Molokovic?" he mimed a head-exploding gesture, and then took another long sip of tea. Sam and Declan watched Alexander jabbering and drinking his tea, yet never said a word to confirm or deny anything.

"A.L.L. appears to have reduced operations in the past

year. James is no longer the party animal he once was, and you, my dears, both vanished so mysteriously," Alex waffled. "It would be remiss of me not to join the dots. What happened? Kai and I were starting to worry."

Declan stepped up behind Sam and wrapped his arms around his waist protectively. Sam sank back into the sturdy warmth.

"You're still with Kai? Give him my love. I do hope you're treating him well."

"Yes, we're very happy."

Declan was tired of the sound of the man's voice already. "Look, can we please cut the crap? What the fuck are ye doin' here, Deveraux?"

"Fine. C is very interested in you."

C was the head of MI6. This approach was not unexpected.

"He's aware that other parties are looking to headhunt you both...if they can find you! Six wants first dibs. Therefore, I'm in the market for a couple of gentlemen with particular skills for a job, off-books, big money." Alexander gave them a wide-eyed hopeful look.

Sam turned a little to meet Declan's gaze. A look of shared understanding passed between them.

"We're not interested," Sam said his voice flat and devoid of emotion.

"Oh come now, don't you even want to know the details?"

"Nope," Declan replied succinctly.

"But—"

Sam cut Alex off before he could say anymore.

"Open your eyes, Alex. Look around you. Why would we want to give up this...for a job?"

"But you must miss the game, the thrill, and the lifestyle?"

"We've been out of the game for just a year. So, no, not quite yet, but you never know," Sam retorted. He pinned Alex with his brilliant green-eyed gaze. Declan glared at the spook. Waverly whined, looked up from her water bowl, and pinned Alex, staring in accusation. All eyes were on him and Alex shifted uncomfortably on his seat.

"Now you're here we have a problem. You know where we live. We can't let you go, Alex," Sam frowned. "Sorry old bean,"

Alex blanched, "What?" he chucked nervously, "Are you going to keep me prisoner and put me to work whittling sticks into woodland creatures, or something equally Eco friendly?" he joked.

"Sadly not, you see, you turned up in our private place, uninvited, unwanted. That cannot go unpunished. I spiked your tea. Declan, love, get the spade," Sam said in an eerily placid tone.

Alex stood, alarmed, and tried to move but his legs couldn't hold him up. He crumpled to the floor.

"Oh dear. Did I put too much in?" Sam grinned full of mischief.

"Ah, mebe a smidge? The little shite'll sleep it off. Help me carry him back to his car."

With Alex soundly asleep in the passenger seat, Sam

disconnected the car's GPS tracking while Declan wiped his Sat Nav history. Declan found a phone in Alexander's pocket and then pressed the sleeping agent's thumb to the screen to open it. He scrolled through his emails, messages, and calls, finding all he needed to know, then passed the phone to Sam. Sam changed the biometrics to recognize his thumbprint, disabled the inbuilt tracker, and then turned the phone off and pocketed it.

Declan returned to the house, collected his wallet, phone, snacks, and bottles of water, then got into Alexander's car and drove it back the way it came.

****

Ten hours later Sam was in bed curled up with a book when he heard the sound of the front door opening and closing. Waverly let out a howl, and Sam could tell by the pitch of it that daddy was home. Sam released a relieved sigh, closed the book, turned off his night light, and feigned sleep.

Minutes later after settling the dog, Declan padded into the bedroom undressed, took a quick shower and then slid into bed.

"Busted! I know yer fakin' it," Declan laughed as he slid his cold hand over Sam's ribs and pulled him back to jigsaw their bodies together.

"So, where did you leave him?"

"I parked the car on the last ferry te Skye and did a runner. It was such a laugh. He was still sleepin' like a baby when I left him. I got a lift back."

"Oh Buttercup!" Sam snickered, "He'll be so fucking confused and pissed off. I hope it was a suitable deterrent."

"Aye. That'll teach him fer invading our privacy. He might be the first, but by the sound of it, won't be the last." Declan nestled his face into Sam's nape.

Sam was silent for a moment, enjoying the simple intimacy before he said,

"I can't say I'll never want to work in counter-intelligence again, but for now, I've had my fill. I love what we've done here, I love our life together."

"Aye. All I want is you. The rest of the world can go te hell. I love ye babe!"

Sam turned in Declan's arms to face him. He melted into his lover's adoring gaze,

"As you wish."

THE END

BOOKS BY ISOBEL STARLING

"The Christmas Bonus" Christmas Short story M/M

"Ball Play" Christmas novella

"Detective Fox" M/M Romantic Comedy Novella

AUDIOBOOKS

"As You Wish" (Shatterproof Bond #1

"Illuminate the Shadows" (Shatterproof Bond #2)

"Return to Zero" (Shatterproof Bond #3

"Counterblow" (Shatterproof Bond #4)

"Powder Burns" (Shatterproof Bond #5)

"The Rebel Candidate" (Shatterproof Bond #6)

"The Shatterproof Bond Box Set"

"Top Hat" (A Sam Aiken prequel)

"Sweet Thing"

"Detective Fox and the Christmas Caper"

"The M/M Romance Taste Me Box Set"

"The Shooting Season"

"The Gentleman's Thief"

"Apple Boy"

"Ball Play"

"Back Where He Belongs"

"MM Romance Christmas Box set"

"Fred and Ginger"

"Back Where He Belongs"

"MM Romance Taste-Me Box set

"Silken"

ABOUT THE AUTHOR

Isobel Starling has been a full-time writer since 2014. She writes thrillers, fantasy, historical, and romance books in the M/M genre. Including translations in German, French, Italian, and Spanish, Isobel has published 54 titles, 27 of them as audiobooks. "As You Wish", narrated by Gary Furlong won the Independent Audiobook Award for Romance in 2018, and was the first LGBTQ title to win a mainstream audiobook award.

In 2017 Isobel set up Decent Fellows Press. She publishes e-books, print, and audiobooks by John Wiltshire, and audiobooks by Harper Fox, LJ Hayward, and Anna Butler.

****

https://www.decentfellowspress.com

Please sign up for my newsletter at
https://isobelstarling.wix.com/books